A SMALL TOWN IN GERMANY

'For lovers of Mr Le Carré's work this is a classic of the genre ... every page carries the stamp of absolute authenticity. He has peopled it with characters who are as real as his scene, as unpredictable and as nice and nasty as one would suppose, and finally he has described a manhunt set against the looming backcloth of extreme fringe politics that provides a heart-stopping climax' —
London Illustrated News

'his best novel yet'—*Life Magazine*

'splendid and subtle'—*Sunday Express*

'something very special'—*Look*

'intricate ... engrossing ... fascinating'—
Sunday Telegraph

'The Sartre of diplomatic and espionage literature'—
Time

'everything a novel should be'—*Daily Mirror*

By the same author in Pan

THE SPY WHO CAME IN FROM THE COLD
THE LOOKING-GLASS WAR

First published 1968 by William Heinemann Ltd.
This edition published 1969 by Pan Books Ltd,
33 Tothill Street, London, S.W.1

330 02306 3

Printed and bound in England by
Hazell Watson & Viney Ltd,
Aylesbury, Bucks

JOHN LE CARRÉ

A SMALL TOWN
IN GERMANY

UNABRIDGED

PAN BOOKS LTD : LONDON

Prologue

Ten minutes to midnight: a pious Friday in May and a fine river mist lying in the market square. Bonn was a Balkan city, stained and secret, drawn over with tramwire. Bonn was a dark house where someone had died, a house draped in Catholic black and guarded by policemen. Their leather coats glistened in the lamplight, the black flags hung over them like birds. It was as if all but they had heard the alarm and fled. Now a car, now a pedestrian hurried past, and the silence followed like a wake. A tram sounded, but far away. In the grocer's shop, from a pyramid of tins, the handwritten notice advertised the emergency: 'Lay in your store now!' Among the crumbs, marzipan pigs like hairless mice proclaimed the forgotten Saint's Day.

Only the posters spoke. From trees and lanterns they fought their futile war, each at the same height as if that were the regulation; they were printed in radiant paint, mounted on hardboard, and draped in thin streamers of black bunting, and they rose at him vividly as he hastened past. 'Send the Foreign Workers Home!' 'Rid us of the Whore Bonn!' 'Unite Germany First, Europe Second!' And the largest was set above them, in a tall streamer right across the street: 'Open the road East, the road West has failed'. His dark eyes paid them no attention. A policeman stamped his boots and grimaced at him, making a hard joke of the weather; another challenged him but without conviction; and one called 'Guten Abend' but he offered no reply; for he had no mind for any but the plumper figure a hundred paces ahead of him who trotted hurriedly down the wide avenue, entering the shadow of a black flag, emerging as the tallow lamplight took him back.

The dark had made no ceremony of coming nor the grey day of leaving, but the night was crisp for once and smelt of winter. For most months, Bonn is not a place of seasons; the climate is all indoors, a climate of headaches, warm and flat like bottled water, a climate of waiting, of bitter tastes taken from the slow river, of fatigue and reluctant growth, and the air is an exhausted wind fallen on the plain, and the dusk when it comes is nothing but a darkening of the day's mist, a lighting of tube lamps in the howling streets. But on that spring night the winter had come back to visit, slipping up the Rhine valley under cover of the predatory darkness, and it quickened them as they went, hurt them with its unexpected chill. The eyes of the smaller man, straining ahead of him, shed tears of cold.

The avenue curved, taking them past the yellow walls of the University. 'Democrats! Hang the Press Baron!' 'The World belongs to the Young!' 'Let the English Lordlings beg!' 'Alex Springer to the gallows!' 'Long Live Axel Springer!' 'Protest is Freedom'. These posters were done in woodcut on a student press. Overhead the young foliage glittered in a fragmented canopy of green glass. The lights were brighter here, the police fewer. The men strode on, neither faster nor slower; the first busily, with a beadle's flurry. His stride though swift was stagy and awkward, as if he had stepped down from somewhere grander; a walk replete with a German burgher's dignity. His arms swung shortly at his sides and his back was straight. Did he know he was being followed? His head was held stiff in authority, but authority became him poorly. A man drawn forward by what he saw? Or driven by what lay behind? Was it fear that prevented him from turning? A man of substance does not move his head. The second man stepped lightly in his wake. A sprite, weightless as the dark, slipping through the shadows as if they were a net: a clown stalking a courtier.

They entered a narrow alley; the air was filled with the smells of sour food. Once more the walls cried to them, now in the tell-tale liturgy of German advertising: 'Strong Men Drink Beer!' 'Knowledge is Power, Read Molden Books!' Here for the first time the echo of their footsteps mingled in unmistakeable challenge; here for the first time the man of substance seemed to waken, sensing the danger behind. It was no more than a slur, a tiny imperfection in the determined rhythm of his portly march; but it took him to the edge of the pavement, away from the darkness of the walls, and he seemed to find

6

comfort in the brighter places, where the lamplight and the policemen could protect him. Yet his pursuer did not relent. 'Meet us in Hanover!' the poster cried. 'Karfield speaks in Hanover!' 'Meet us in Hanover on Sunday!'

An empty tram rolled past, its windows protected with adhesive mesh. A single church bell began its monotonous chime, a dirge for Christian virtue in an empty city. They were walking again, closer together, but still the man in front did not look back. They rounded another corner; ahead of them, the great spire of the Minster was cut like thin metal against the empty sky. Reluctantly the first chimes were answered by others, until all over the town there rose a slow cacophony of uncertain peals. An Angelus? An air raid? A young policeman, standing in the doorway of a sports shop, bared his head. In the Cathedral porch, a candle burned in a bowl of red glass; to one side stood a religious bookshop. The plump man paused, leaned forward as if to examine something in the window; glanced down the road; and in that moment the light from the window shone full upon his features. The smaller man ran forward: stopped; ran forward again; and was too late.

The limousine had drawn up, an Opel Rekord driven by a pale man hidden in the smoked glass. Its back door opened and closed; ponderously it gathered speed, indifferent to the one sharp cry, a cry of fury and of accusation, of total loss and total bitterness which, drawn as if by force from the breast of him who uttered it, rang abruptly down the empty street and, as abruptly, died. The policeman spun around, shone his torch. Held in its beam, the small man did not move; he was staring after the limousine. Shaking over the cobble, skidding on the wet tramlines, disregarding the traffic lights, it had vanished westward towards the illuminated hills.

'Who are you?'

The beam rested on the coat of English tweed, too hairy for such a little man, the fine, neat shoes grey with mud, the dark, unblinking eyes.

'Who are you?' the policeman repeated; for the bells were everywhere now, and their echoes persisted eerily.

One small hand disappeared into the folds of the coat and emerged with a leather holder. The policeman accepted it

7

gingerly, unfastened the catch while he juggled with his torch and the black pistol which he clutched inexpertly in his left hand.

'What was it?' the policeman asked, as he handed back the wallet. 'Why did you call out?'

The small man gave no answer. He had walked a few paces along the pavement.

'You never saw him before?' he asked, still looking after the car. 'You don't know who he was?' He spoke softly, as if there were children sleeping upstairs; a vulnerable voice, respectful of silence.

'No.'

The sharp, lined face broke into a conciliatory smile. 'Forgive me. I made a silly mistake. I thought I recognized him.' His accent was neither wholly English nor wholly German, but a privately elected no-man's land, picked and set between the two. And he would move it, he seemed to say, a little in either direction, if it chanced to inconvenience the listener.

'It's the season,' the small man said, determined to make conversation. 'The sudden cold, one looks at people more.' He had opened a tin of small Dutch cigars and was offering them to the policeman. The policeman declined so he lit one for himself.

'It's the riots,' the policeman answered slowly, 'The flags, the slogans. We're all nervous these days. This week Hanover, last week Frankfurt. It upsets the natural order.' He was a young man and had studied for his appointment. 'They should forbid them more,' he added, using the common dictum. 'Like the Communists.'

He saluted loosely; once more the stranger smiled, a last affecting smile, dependent, hinting at friendship, dwindling reluctantly. And was gone. Remaining where he was, the policeman listened attentively to the fading footfall. Now it stopped; to be resumed again, more quickly – was it his imagination? – with greater conviction then before. For a moment he pondered.

'In Bonn,' he said to himself with an inward sigh, recalling the stranger's weightless tread, 'even the flies are official.'

Taking out his notebook, he carefully wrote down the time and place and nature of the incident. He was not a fast-thinking man, but admired for his thoroughness. This done, he added the number of the motor-car, which for some reason had remained in his mind. Suddenly he stopped; and stared at what he had written; at the name and the car number; and he thought of the plump man and the long, marching stride, and his heart began beating very fast. He thought of the secret instruction he had read on the recreation-room noticeboard, and the little muffled photograph from long ago. The notebook still in his hand, he ran off for the telephone kiosk as fast as his boots would carry him.

Way over there in a
Small town in Germany
There lived a shoemaker
Schumann was his name
Ich bin ein Musikant
Ich bin für das Vaterland
I have a big bass drum
And this is how I play!

A drinking song sung in British military messes in Occupied
Germany, with obscene variations, to the tune of the *Marche
Militaire*

I

Mr Meadowes and Mr Cork

'WHY DON'T YOU get out and walk? I would if I was your age. Quicker than sitting with this scum.'

'I'll be all right,' said Cork, the albino cypher clerk, and looked anxiously at the older man in the driving seat beside him. 'We'll just have to hurry slowly,' he added in his most conciliatory tone. Cork was a cockney, bright as paint, and it worried him to see Meadowes all het up. 'We'll just have to let it happen to us, won't we, Arthur?'

'I'd like to throw the whole bloody lot of them in the Rhine.'

'You know you wouldn't really.'

It was Saturday morning, nine o'clock. The road from Friesdorf to the Embassy was packed tight with protesting cars, the pavements lined with photographs of the Movement's leader, and the banners were stretched across the road like advertisements at a rally: 'The West has deceived us; Germans can look East without shame.' 'End the Coca-Cola culture now!' At the very centre of the long column sat Cork and Meadowes, becalmed while the clamour of horns rose all round them in unceasing concert. Sometimes they sounded in series starting at the front and working slowly back, so that their roar passed overhead like an aeroplane sometimes in unison, dash dot dash, K for Karfeld our elected leader; and sometimes they just had a free for all, tuning for the symphony.

'What the hell do they want with it then? All the screaming? Bloody good haircut, that's what half of them need, a good hiding and back to school.'

'It's the farmers,' Cork said, 'I told you, they're picketing the Bundestag.'

'Farmers? This lot? They'd die if they got their feet wet, half of them. Kids. Look at that crowd there then. Disgusting, that's what I call it.'

To their right, in a red Volkswagen, sat three students, two boys and a girl. The driver wore a leather jacket and very long hair, and he was gazing intently through his windscreen at the car in front, his slim palm poised over the steering wheel, waiting for the signal to blow his horn. His two companions, intertwined, were kissing deeply.

'They're the supporting cast,' Cork said. 'It's a lark for them. You know the students' slogan: "Freedom's only real when you're fighting for it." It's not so different from what's going on at home, is it? Hear what they did in Grosvenor Square last night?' Cork asked, attempting once again to shift the ground. 'If that's education, I'll stick to ignorance.'

But Meadowes would not be distracted.

'They ought to bring in the National Service,' he declared, glaring at the Volkswagen. 'That would sort them out.'

'They've got it already. They've had it twenty years or more.' Sensing that Meadowes was preparing to relent, Cork chose the subject most likely to encourage him. 'Here, how did Myra's birthday party go, then? Good show was it? I'll bet she had a lovely time.'

But for some reason the question only cast Meadowes into even deeper gloom, and after that Cork chose silence as the wiser course. He had tried everything, and to no effect. Meadowes was a decent, churchy sort of bloke, the kind they didn't make any more, and worth a good deal of anybody's time; but there was a limit even to Cork's filial devotion. He'd tried the new Rover which Meadowes had bought for his retirement, tax free and at a ten per cent discount. He'd admired its build, its comfort and its fittings until he was blue in the face, and all he'd got for his trouble was a grunt. He'd tried the Exiles Motoring Club, of which Meadowes was a keen supporter; he'd tried the Commonwealth Children's Sports which they hoped to run that afternoon in the Embassy gardens. And now he had even tried last night's big party, which they hadn't liked to attend because of Janet's baby being so near; and as far as Cork was concerned, that was the whole menu and Meadowes could lump it. Short of a holiday, Cork decided, short of a long, sunny holiday away from Karfeld and the Brussels negotiations, and away from his daughter Myra, Arthur Meadowes was heading for the bend.

'Here,' said Cork trying one more throw, 'Dutch Shell's up another bob.'

'And Guest Keen are down three.'

Cork had resolutely invested in non-British stock, but Meadowes preferred to pay the price of patriotism.

'They'll go up again after Brussels, don't you worry.'

'Who are you kidding? The talks are as good as dead aren't they? I may not have your intelligence but I can read, you know.'

Meadowes, as Cork was the very first to concede, had every excuse for melancholy, quite apart from his investments in British steel. He'd come with hardly a break from four years in Warsaw which was enough to make anyone jumpy. He was on his last posting and facing retirement in the autumn, and in Cork's experience they got worse, not better, the nearer the day came. Not to mention having a nervous wreck for a daughter: Myra Meadowes was on the road to recovery, true enough, but if one half of what they said of her was to be believed, she'd got a long way to go yet.

Add to that the responsibilities of Chancery Registrar – of handling, that is, a political archive in the hottest crisis any of them could remember – and you had more than your work cut out. Even Cork, tucked away in Cyphers, had felt the draught a bit, what with the extra traffic, and the extra hours, and Janet's baby coming on, and the do-this-by-yesterday that you got from most of Chancery; and his own experience, as he well knew, was nothing beside what old Arthur had had to cope with. It was the coming from all directions, Cork decided, that threw you these days. You never knew where it would happen next. One minute you'd be getting off a Reply Immediate on the Bremen riots, or tomorrow's jamboree in Hanover, the next they'd be coming back at you with the gold rush, or Brussels, or raising another few hundred millions in Frankfurt and Zurich; and if it was tough in Cyphers, it was tougher still for those who had to track down the files, enter up the loose papers, mark in the new entries and get them back into circulation again . . . which reminded him, for some reason, that he must telephone his accountant. If the Krupp labour front was going on like this, he might take a little look at Swedish steel, just an in-and-outer for the baby's bank account . . .

'Hullo,' said Cork brightening. 'Going to have a scrap, are we?'

Two policemen had stepped off the kerb to remonstrate with a large agricultural man in a Mercedes Diesel. First he lowered the window and shouted at them; now he opened the door and shouted at them again. Quite suddenly, the police withdrew. Cork yawned in disappointment.

Once upon a time, Cork remembered wistfully, panics came singly. You had a scream on the Berlin corridor, Russian helicopters teasing up the border, an up-and-downer with the Four Power Steering Committee in Washington. Or there was intrigue: suspected German diplomatic initiative in Moscow that had to be nipped in the bud, a suspected fiddle on the Rhodesian embargo, hushing up a Rhine Army riot in Minden. And that was that. You bolted your food, opened shop, and stayed till the job was done; and you went home a free man. That was that; that was what life was made of; that was Bonn. Whether you were a dip like de Lisle, or a non-dip behind the green baize door, the scene was the same; a bit of drama, a lot of hot air, then tickle up the stocks and shares a bit, back to boredom and roll on your next posting.

Until Karfeld. Cork gazed disconsolately at the posters. Until Karfeld came along. Nine months, he reflected – the vast features were plump and lifeless, the expression one of flatulent sincerity – nine months since Arthur Meadowes had come bustling through the connecting door from Registry with the news of the Kiel demonstrations, the surprise nomination, the student sit-in, and the little bit of violence they had gradually learnt to expect. Who caught it that time? Some Socialist counter-demonstrators. One beaten to death, one stoned . . . it used to shock them in the old days. They were green then. Christ, he thought, it might have been ten years ago; but Cork could date it almost to the hour.

Kiel was the morning the Embassy doctor announced that Janet was expecting. From that day on, nothing had ever been the same.

16

The horns broke wildly into song again; the convoy jerked forward and stopped abruptly, clanging and screeching all different notes.

'Any luck with those files then?' Cork enquired, his mind lighting upon the suspected cause of Meadowes' anxiety.

'No.'

'Trolley hasn't turned up?'

'No, the trolley has *not* turned up.'

Ball-bearings, Cork thought suddenly: some nice little Swedish outfit with a get-up-and-go approach, a firm capable of moving in fast . . . two hundred quid's worth and away we all go . . .

'Come on Arthur, don't let it get you down. It's not Warsaw you know: you're in Bonn now. Look: know how many cups they're shy of in the canteen, just on the last six weeks alone? Not broken, mind, just lost: twenty-four.'

Meadowes was unimpressed.

'Now who wants to pinch an Embassy cup? No one. People are absent-minded. They're *involved*. It's the crisis, see. It's happening everywhere. It's the same with files.'

'Cups aren't secret, that's the difference.'

'Nor's file trolleys,' Cork pleaded, 'If it comes to that. Nor's the two-bar electric fire from the conference room which Admin are doing their nut about. Nor's the long-carriage typewriter from the Pool, nor – listen Arthur, *you* can't be blamed, not with so much going on; how can you? You know what dips are when they get to drafting telegrams. Look at de Lisle, look at Gaveston: dreamers. I'm not saying they aren't geniuses but they don't know where they are half the time, their heads are in the clouds. You can't be blamed for that.'

'I *can* be blamed. I'm responsible.'

'All right, torture yourself,' Cork snapped, his last patience gone. 'Anyway it's Bradfield's responsibility, not yours. He's Head of Chancery; he's responsible for security.'

With this parting comment, Cork once more fell to surveying the unprepossessing scene about him. In more ways than one, he decided, Karfeld had a lot to answer for.

The prospect which presented itself to Cork would have offered little comfort to any man, whatever his preoccupation. The weather was wretched. A blank Rhineland mist, like breath upon a mirror, lay over the whole developed wilderness of bureaucratic Bonn. Giant buildings, still unfinished, rose glumly out of the untilled fields. Ahead of him the British Embassy, all its windows lit, stood on its brown heathland like a makeshift hospital in the twilight of the battle. At the front gate, the Union Jack, mysteriously at half mast, drooped sadly over a cluster of German policemen.

The very choice of Bonn as the waiting house for Berlin has long been an anomaly; it is now an abuse. Perhaps only the Germans, having elected a Chancellor, would have brought their capital city to his door. To accommodate the immigration of diplomats, politicians and government servants which attended this unlooked for honour – and also to keep them at a distance – the townspeople have built a complete suburb outside their city walls. It was through the southern end of this that the traffic was now attempting to pass: a jumble of stodgy towers and lowflung contemporary hutments which stretched along the dual carriageway almost as far as the amiable sanatorium settlement of Bad Godesberg, whose principal industry, having once been bottled water, is now diplomacy. True, some Ministries have been admitted to Bonn itself, and have added their fake masonry to the cobble courtyards; true, some Embassies are in Bad Godesberg; but the seat of Federal Government and the great majority of the ninety odd Foreign Missions accredited to it, not to mention the lobbyists, the press, the political parties, the refugee organizations, the official residences of Federal Dignitaries, the Kuratorium for Indivisible Germany, and the whole bureaucratic superstructure of West Germany's provisional capital, are to be found to either side of this one arterial carriageway between the former seat of the Bishop of Cologne and the Victorian villas of a Rhineland spa.

Of this unnatural capital village, of this island state, which lacks both political identity and social hinterland, and is permanently committed to the condition of impermanence, the British Embassy is an inseparable part. Imagine a sprawling factory block of no merit, the kind of building you see in dozens on the Western by-pass, usually with a symbol of its product

18

set out on the roof; paint about it a sullen Rhenish sky, add an indefinable hint of Nazi architecture, just a breath, no more, and erect in the rough ground behind it two fading goalposts for the recreation of the unwashed, and you have portrayed with fair accuracy the mind and force of England in the Federal Republic. With one sprawling limb it holds down the past, with another it smoothes the present; while a third searches anxiously in the wet Rhenish earth to find what is buried for the future. Built as the Occupation drew to its premature end, it catches precisely that mood of graceless renunciation; a stone face turned towards a former foe, a grey smile offered to the present ally. To Cork's left, as they finally entered its gates, lay the headquarters of the Red Cross, to his right a Mercedes factory; behind him, across the road, the Social Democrats and a Coca-Cola depot. The Embassy is cut off from these improbable neighbours by a strip of waste land which, strewn with sorrel and bare clay, runs flatly to the neglected Rhine. This field is known as Bonn's green belt and is an object of great pride to the city's planners.

One day, perhaps, they will move to Berlin; the contingency, even in Bonn, is occasionally spoken of. One day, perhaps, the whole grey mountain will slip down the autobahn and silently take its place in the wet car parks of the gutted Reichstag; until that happens, these concrete tents will remain, discreetly temporary in deference to the dream, discreetly permanent in deference to reality; they will remain, multiply, and grow; for in Bonn, movement has replaced progress, and whatever will not grow must die.

Parking the car in his customary place behind the canteen, Meadowes walked slowly round it, as he always did after a journey, testing the handles and checking the coachwork for the marks of an errant pebble. Still deep in thought he crossed the forecourt to the front porch where two British military policemen, a sergeant and a corporal, were examining passes. Cork, still offended, followed at a distance, so that by the time he reached the front door Meadowes was already deep in conversation with the sentries.

'Who are *you* then?' the sergeant was wanting to know.

'Meadowes of Registry. He works for me.' Meadowes tried to look over the sergeant's shoulder, but the sergeant drew back the list against his tunic. 'He's been off sick you see. I wanted to enquire.'

'Then why's he under Ground Floor?'

'He has a room there. He has two functions. Two different jobs. One with me, one on the ground floor.'

'Zero,' said the sergeant, looking at the list again. A bunch of typists, their skirts as short as the Ambassadress permitted, came fluttering up the steps behind them.

Meadowes lingered, still unconvinced. 'You mean he's not come in?' he asked with the tenderness which longs for contradiction.

'That's what I do mean. Zero. He's not come in. He's not here. Right?'

They followed the girls into the lobby. Cork took his arm and drew him back into the shadow of the basement grille.

'What's going on, Arthur? What's your problem? It's not just the missing files, is it? What's eating you up?'

'Nothing's eating me.'

'Then what's all that about Leo being ill? He hasn't had a day's illness in his life.'

Meadowes did not reply.

'What's Leo been up to?' Cork demanded with deep suspicion.

'Nothing.'

'They why did you ask about him? You can't have lost him as well! Blimey, they've been trying to lose Leo for twenty years.'

Cork felt the decent hesitation in Meadowes, the proximity of revelation and the reluctant drawing back.

'You can't be responsible for Leo. Nobody can. You can't be everyone's father, Arthur. He's probably out flogging a few petrol coupons.'

The words were barely spoken before Meadowes rounded on him, very angry indeed.

'Don't you talk like that, d'you hear? Don't you dare! Leo's not like that; it's a shocking thing to say of anyone; flogging petrol coupons. Just because he's – a temporary.'

Cork's expression, as he followed Meadowes at a safe distance up the open-tread staircase to the first floor, spoke for itself. If that was what age did for you, retirement at sixty didn't come a day too early. Cork's own retirement would be from it to a Greek island. Crete, he thought; Spetsai. I could swing it at forty if those ball-bearings come home. Well, forty-five anyway.

A step along the corridor from Registry lay the cypher room and a step beyond that, the small, bright office occupied by Peter de Lisle. Chancery means no more than political section; its young men are the elite. It is here, if anywhere, that the popular dream of the brilliant English diplomat may be realized; and in no one more nearly than Peter de Lisle. He was an elegant, willowy, almost beautiful person, whose youth had persisted obstinately into his early forties, and his manner was languid to the point of lethargy. This lethargy was not affected, but simply deceptive. De Lisle's family tree had been disastrously pruned by two wars, and further depleted by a succession of small but violent catastrophes. A brother had died in a car accident; an uncle had committed suicide; a second brother was drowned on holiday in Penzance. Thus by degrees de Lisle himself had acquired both the energies and the duties of an improbable survivor. He had much rather not been called at all, his manner implied; but since that was the way of things, he had no alternative but to wear the mantle.

As Meadowes and Cork entered their separate estates, de Lisle was on the point of gathering together the sheets of blue draft paper which lay scattered in artistic confusion on his desk. Having shuffled them casually into order, he buttoned his waistcoat, stretched, cast a wistful look at the picture of Lake Windermere, issued by the Ministry of Works with the kind permission of the London, Midland and Scottish Railway, and drifted contentedly on to the landing to greet the new day. Lingering at the long window, he peered downward for a moment at the spines of the farmers' black cars and the small islands of blue where the police lights flashed.

'They have this *passion* for steel,' he observed to Mickie Crabbe, a ragged, leaky-eyed man permanently crippled by a hangover. Crabbe was slowly ascending the stairs, one hand reassuringly upon the banister, his thin shoulders hunched protectively. 'I'd quite forgotten. I'd remembered the blood, but forgotten the steel.'

'Rather,' Crabbe muttered, 'Rather,' and his voice trailed after him like the shreds of his own life. Only his hair had not aged; it grew dark and luxuriant on his little head, as if fertilized by alcohol.

'Sports,' Crabbe cried, making an unscheduled halt. 'Bloody marquee isn't up.'

'It'll come,' de Lisle assured him kindly. 'It's been held up by the Peasants' Revolt.'

'Back way empty as a church on the other road; bloody Huns,' Crabbe added vaguely as if it were a greeting, and continued painfully down his appointed track.

Slowly following him along the passage, de Lisle pushed open door after door, peering inside to call a name or a greeting, until he arrived by degrees at the Head of Chancery's room; and here he knocked hard, and leaned in.

'All present, Rawley,' he said. 'Ready when you are.'

'I'm ready now.'

'I say, you haven't pinched my electric fan by any chance, have you? It's absolutely vanished.'

'Fortunately I am not a kleptomaniac.'

'Ludwig Siebkron's asking for a meeting at four o'clock,' de Lisle added quietly, 'At the Ministry of the Interior. He won't say why. I pressed him and he got shirty. He just said he wanted to discuss our security arrangements.'

'Our arrangements are perfectly adequate as they stand. We discussed them with him last week; he is dining with me on Tuesday. I cannot imagine we need to do any more. The place is crawling with police as it is. I refuse to let him make a fortress of us.'

The voice was austere and self sufficient, an academic voice, yet military; a voice which held much in reserve; a voice which guarded its secrets and its sovereignty, drawled out but bitten short.

Taking a step into the room, de Lisle closed the door and dropped the latch.

'How did it go last night?'

'Adequately. You may read the minute if you wish. Meadowes is taking it to the Ambassador.'

'I imagined that was what Siebkron was ringing about.'

'I am not obliged to report to Siebkron; nor do I intend to. And I have no idea why he telephoned at this hour, nor why he should call a meeting. Your imagination is ahead of my own.'

'All the same, I accepted for you. It seemed wise.'

'At what time are we bidden?'

'Four o'clock. He's sending transport.'

Bradfield frowned in disapproval.

'He's worried about the traffic. He thinks an escort would make things easier,' de Lisle explained.

'I see. I thought for a moment he was saving us the expense.'

It was a joke they shared in silence.

2

'I could hear their screaming on the telephone . . .'

THE DAILY CHANCERY meeting in Bonn takes place in the ordinary way at ten o'clock, a time which allows everyone to open his mail, glance at his telegrams and his German newspapers and perhaps recover from the wearisome social round of the night before. As a ritual, de Lisle often likened it to morning prayers in an agnostic community: though contributing little in the way of inspiration or instruction, it set a tone for the day, served as a roll-call and imparted a sense of corporate activity. Once upon a time, Saturdays had been tweedy, voluntary, semi-retired affairs which restored one's lost detachment and one's sense of leisure. All that was gone now. Saturdays had been assumed into the general condition of alarm, and subjected to the discipline of weekdays.

They entered singly, de Lisle at their head. Those whose habit was to greet one another did so; the rest took their places silently in the half circle of chairs, either glancing through their bundles of coloured telegrams or staring blankly out of the big window at the remnants of their weekend. The morning fog was dispersing; black clouds had collected over the concrete rear wing of the Embassy; the aerials on the flat roof hung like surrealist trees against the new dark.

'Pretty ominous for the sports, I must say,' Mickie Crabbe called out, but Crabbe had no standing in Chancery and no one bothered to reply.

Facing them, alone at his steel desk, Bradfield ignored their arrival. He belonged to that school of civil servants who read with a pen; for it ran swiftly with his eye from line to line, poised at any time to correct or annotate.

'Can anyone tell me,' he enquired without lifting his head, 'How I translate *Geltungsbedürfnis*?'

'A need to assert oneself,' de Lisle suggested, and watched the pen pounce, and kill, and rise again.

'How very good. Shall we begin?'

Jenny Pargiter was the Information Officer and the only woman present. She read querulously as if she were contradicting a popular view; and she read without hope, secretly knowing that it was the lot of any woman, when imparting news, not to be believed.

'Apart from the farmers, Rawley, the main news item is yesterday's incident in Cologne, when student demonstrators, assisted by steel workers from Krupps, overturned the American Ambassador's car.'

'The American Ambassador's *empty* car. There is a difference you know.' He scribbled something in the margin of a telegram. Mickie Crabbe from his place at the door, mistakenly assuming this interruption to be humorous, laughed nervously.

'They also attacked an old man and chained him to the railings in the station square with his head shaved and a label round his neck saying "I tore down the Movement's posters". He's not supposed to be seriously hurt.'

'Supposed?'

'Considered.'

'Peter, you made a telegram during the night. We shall see a copy no doubt?'

'It sets out the principal implications.'

'Which are?'

De Lisle was equal to this. 'That the alliance between the dissident students and Karfeld's Movement is progressing fast. That the vicious circle continues: unrest creates unemployment, unemployment creates unrest. Halbach, the student leader, spent most of yesterday closeted with Karfeld in Cologne. They cooked the thing up together.'

'It was Halbach, was it not, who also led the anti-British student delegation to Brussels in January? The one that pelted Haliday-Pride with mud?'

'I have made that point in the telegram.'

'Go on, Jenny, please.'

'Most major papers carry comment.'

'Samples only.'

'*Neue Ruhrzeitung* and allied papers put their main emphasis on the youth of the demonstrators. They insist that they are not brownshirts and hooligans, but young Germans wholly disenchanted with the institutions of Bonn.'

'Who isn't?' de Lisle murmured.

'Thank you, Peter,' Bradfield said, without a trace of gratitude, and Jenny Pargiter blushed quite needlessly.

'Both *Welt* and *Frankfurter Allgemeine* draw parallels with recent events in England; they refer specifically to the anti-Vietnam protests in London, the race riots in Birmingham and the Owner Tenants Association protests on coloured housing. Both speak of the widespread alienation of voters from their elected Governments whether in England or Germany. The trouble begins with taxation, according to the *Frankfurter*; if the taxpayer doesn't think his money is being sensibly used, he argues that his vote is being wasted as well. They call it the new inertia.'

'Ah. Another slogan has been forged.'

Weary from his long vigil and the sheer familiarity of the topics, de Lisle listened at a distance, hearing the old phrases like an off-station broadcast: *increasingly worried by the anti-democratic sentiments of both left and right . . . the Federal Coalition Government should understand that only a really strong leadership, even at the expense of certain extravagant minorities, can contribute to European unity. . . . Germans must recover confidence, must think of politics as the solvent between thought and action . . .*

What was it, he wondered idly, about the jargon of German politics which, even in translation, rendered them totally unreal? Metaphysical fluff, that was the term he had introduced into his telegram last night, and he was rather pleased with it. A German had only to embark upon a political topic to be swept away in a current of ludicrous abstracts. . . . Yet was it only the abstracts that were so elusive? Even the most obvious fact was curiously implausible; even the most gruesome event, by the time it had travelled to Bonn, seemed to have lost its flavour. He tried to imagine what it would be like to be beaten up by Halbach's students; to be slapped until your cheeks bled; to be shaved and chained and kicked . . . it all seemed so far away. Yet where *was* Cologne? Seventeen miles? Seventeen thousand? He should get about more, he told himself, he should attend the meetings and see it happen on the ground. Yet how could he, when he and Bradfield between them drafted every major policy despatch? And when so many delicate and potentially embarrassing matters had to be taken care of here . . .

Jenny Pargiter was warming to her task. The *Neue Zürcher* had a speculative piece on our chances in Brussels, she was saying; she considered it vital that everyone in Chancery read it *most* closely. De Lisle sighed audibly. Would Bradfield never turn her off?

'The writer says we have *absolutely* no negotiating points left, Rawley. None. HMG is as played out as Bonn; no support with the electorate and very little with the parliamentary party. HMG sees Brussels as the magic cure for all the British ills; but ironically can only succeed by the goodwill of another failing Government.'

'Quite.'

'And even more ironically, the Common Market has virtually ceased to exist.'

'Quite.'

'The piece is called *The Beggar's Opera*. They also make the point that Karfeld is undermining our chances of effective German support for our application.'

'It all sounds very predictable to me.'

'And that Karfeld's plea for a Bonn–Moscow trade axis to exclude the French *and* the Anglo-Saxons is receiving serious attention in some circles.'

'What circles I wonder?' Bradfield murmured and the pen descended once more. 'The term Anglo-Saxon is out of court,' he added. 'I refuse to have my provenance dictated by de Gaulle.' This was a cue for the older graduates to raise a judicious intellectual laugh.

'What do the *Russians* think about the Bonn–Moscow axis?' someone ventured from the centre. It might have been Jackson, an ex-Colonial man who liked to offer commonsense as an anti-dote to intellectual hot air. 'I mean surely that's half the point, isn't it? Has anyone put it to them as a proposition?'

'See our last despatch,' de Lisle said.

Through the open window he fancied he could still hear the plaintive chorus of the farmers' horns. That's Bonn he thought suddenly: that road is our world: how many names did it have on those five miles between Mehlem and Bonn? Six? Seven? That's us: a verbal battle for something nobody wants. A constant, sterile cacophony of claim and protest. However new the models, however fast the traffic, however violent the collision, however high the buildings, the route is unchanged and the destination irrelevant.

'We'll keep the rest very short, shall we? Mickie?'

'I say my God yes.'

Crabbe, jerking into life, embarked upon a long and unintelligible story he had picked up from the *New York Times* correspondent at the American Club, who in turn had heard it from Karl-Heinz Saab, who in turn had heard it from someone in Siebkron's office. It was said that Karfeld was actually in Bonn last night; that after appearing with the students in Cologne yesterday, he had not, as was popularly believed, returned to Hanover to prepare for tomorrow's rally, but had driven himself by a back route to Bonn and attended a secret meeting in the town.

'They say he spoke to Ludwig Siebkron, you see, Rawley,' said Crabbe, but whatever conviction his voice might once have carried was strained thin by innumerable cocktails.

Bradfield, however, was irritated by this report, and struck back quite hard.

'They *always* say he spoke to Ludwig Siebkron. Why the devil shouldn't the two of them talk to one another? Siebkron's in charge of public order; Karfeld has a lot of enemies. Tell London,' he added wearily, making another note. 'Send them a telegram reporting the rumour. It can do no harm.' A gust of rain struck suddenly upward at the steel-framed window, and the angry rattle startled them all.

'Poor old Commonwealth Sports,' Crabbe whispered, but once again his concern received no recognition.

'Discipline,' Bradfield continued. 'Tomorrow's rally in Hanover begins at ten-thirty. It seems an extraordinary time to demonstrate but I understand they have a football match in

28

the afternoon. They play on Sundays here. I cannot imagine it will have any effect on us, but the Ambassador is asking all staff to remain at home after Matins unless they have business in the Embassy. At Siebkron's request there will be additional German police at the front and rear gates throughout Sunday, and for some extraordinary reasons of his own, plain clothes men will be in attendance at the sports this afternoon.'

'And plainer clothes,' de Lisle breathed, recalling a private joke, 'I have *never* seen.'

'Be quiet. Security. We have received the printed Embassy passes from London and these will be distributed on Monday and shown at all times thereafter. Fire Drill. For your information there will be a practice muster at midday on Monday. Perhaps you should all make a point of being available, it sets an example for the Junior Staff. Welfare. Commonwealth Sports this afternoon in the rear gardens of the Embassy; eliminating races. Once again I suggest you all put in an appearance. With your wives of course,' he added, as if that placed an even heavier burden on them. 'Mickie, the Ghanaian Chargé will need looking after. Keep him away from the Ambassadress.'

'Can I just make a point here, Rawley?' Crabbe writhed nervously; the cords of his neck were like chicken legs, stiffeners in the declining flesh. 'The Ambassadress is presenting the prizes at four, you see. Four. Could everyone sort of gravitate to the main marquee at quarter to? Sorry,' he added. 'Quarter to four, Rawley. Sorry.' It was said that he had been one of Montgomery's aides in the war and this was all that was left.

'Noted. Jenny?'

Nothing that *they* would listen to, her shrug declared.

De Lisle addressed them all, using as his focal point that middle air which is the special territory of the British ruling class.

'May I ask whether anyone is working on the Personalities Survey? Meadowes is pestering me for it and I swear I haven't touched it for months.'

'Who's it marked out to?'

'Well me apparently.'

'In that case,' Bradfield said shortly, 'Presumably you drew it.'

'I don't think I did, that's the point. I'm perfectly happy to take the rap, but I can't imagine what I would have wanted with it.'

'Well *has* anyone got it?'

All Crabbe's statements were confessions.

'It's marked out to me, too.' he whispered, from his dark place by the door, 'You see, Rawley.'

They waited.

'Before Peter, I'm supposed to have had it, and put it back. According to Meadowes, Rawley.'

Still no one helped him.

'Two weeks, Rawley. Only I never touched it. Sorry. Arthur Meadowes went for me like a maniac. No good, you see. Didn't have it. Lot of dirt about German industrialists. Not my form. I told Meadowes: best thing is ask Leo. He does Personalities. They're Leo's pigeon.'

He grinned weakly along the line of his colleagues until he came to the window where the empty chair was. Suddenly they were all peering in the same direction, at the empty chair; not with alarm or revelation, but curiously, noticing an absence for the first time. It was a plain chair of varnished pine, different from the others and slightly pink in colour, hinting remotely at the boudoir; and it had a small, embroidered cushion on the seat.

'Where is he?' Bradfield asked shortly. He alone had not followed Crabbe's gaze. 'Where's Harting?'

No one answered. No one looked at Bradfield. Jenny Pargiter, scarlet in the face, stared at her mannish, practical hands which rested on her broad lap.

'Stuck on that dreary ferry, I should think,' said de Lisle, coming too quickly to the rescue. 'God knows what the farmers are doing *that* side of the river.'

'Someone find out, will they?' Bradfield asked, in the most disinterested tone. 'Ring his house or something will you?'

It is a matter of record that no one who was present took this instruction as his own; and that they left the room in curious disarray, looking neither at Bradfield nor at one another, nor at Jenny Pargiter, whose confusion seemed beyond all bearing.

The last sack race was over. The strong wind, whipping over the waste land, dashed pebbles of rain against the flapping canvas. The wet rigging creaked painfully. Inside the marquee, the surviving children, mostly coloured, had rallied to the mast. The small flags of the Commonwealth, creased by storage and diminished by secession, swung unhappy in disarray. Beneath them, Mickie Crabbe, assisted by Cork the cypher clerk, was mustering the winners for the prize-giving.

'M'butu, Alistair,' Cork whispered. 'Where the hell's he got to?'

Crabbe put the megaphone to his mouth:

'Will Master Alistair M'butu please come forward. Alistair M'butu . . . Jesus,' he muttered, 'I can't even tell them apart.'

'And Kitty Delassus. She's white.'

'And Miss Kitty Delassus, please,' Crabbe added, nervously slurring the final 's'; for names, he had found by bitter experience, were a source of unholy offence.

The Ambassadress, in ragged mink, waited benignly at her trestle table behind a motley of gift-wrapped parcels from the Naafi. The wind struck again, venomously; the Ghanaian Chargé, despondent at Crabbe's side, shuddered and pulled up the fur collar of his overcoat.

'Disqualify them,' Cork urged. 'Give the prizes to the runners up.'

'I'll ring his neck,' Crabbe declared, blinking violently. 'I'll ring his bloody neck. Skulking the other side of the river. Whoopsadaisy.'

Janet Cork, heavily pregnant, had located the missing children and added them to the winners' enclosure.

'Wait till Monday,' Crabbe whispered, raising the megaphone to his lips, 'I'll tell him a thing or two.'

He wouldn't though, come to think of it. He wouldn't tell Leo anything. He'd keep bloody clear of Leo as a matter of fact; keep his head down and wait till it blew over.

'Ladies and Gentlemen, the Ambassadress will now present the prizes!'

They clapped, but not for Crabbe. The end was in sight. With a perfect *insouciance* that was as well suited to the launching of a ship as to the acceptance of a hand in marriage, the Ambassadress stepped forward to read her speech. Crabbe listened mindlessly: a family event . . . equal nations of the Commonwealth . . . if only the greater rivalries of the world could be resolved in so friendly a fashion . . . a heartfelt word of thanks to the Sports Committee, Messrs Jackson, Crabbe, Harting, Meadowes . . .

Lamentably unmoved, a plain clothes policeman, posted against the canvas wall, took a pair of gloves from the pocket of his leather coat and stared blankly at a colleague. Hazel Bradfield, wife of the Head of Chancery, caught Crabbe's eye and smiled beautifully. Such a bore, she managed to imply, but it will soon be over, and then we might even have a drink. He looked quickly away. The only thing, he told himself fervently, is to know nothing and see nothing. Doggo, that's the word. Doggo. He glanced at his watch. Just one hour till the sun was over the yardarm. In Greenwich if not in Bonn. He'd have a beer first, just to keep his eye in; and afterwards he would have a little of the hard stuff. Doggo. See nothing and slip out the back way.

'Here,' said Cork into his ear, 'Listen. You remember that tip you gave me?'

'Sorry old boy?'

'South African Diamonds. Consols. They're down six bob.'

'Hang on to them,' Crabbe urged with total insincerity, and withdrew prudently to the edge of the marquee. He had barely found the kind of dark, protective crevice which naturally appealed to his submerged nature when a hand seized his shoulder and swung him roughly round on his heel. Recovering from his astonishment he found himself face to face with a plain clothes policeman. 'What the hell—' he broke out furiously, for he was a small man and hated to be handled. 'What the hell—' But the policeman was already shaking his head and mumbling an apology. He was sorry, he said, he had mistaken the gentleman for someone else.

Urbane or not, de Lisle was meanwhile growing quite angry.

The journey from the Embassy had irritated him considerably. He detested motor-bikes and he detested being escorted, and a noisy combination of the two was almost more than he could bear. And he detested deliberate rudeness, whether he or some one else was the object of it. And deliberate rudeness, he reckoned, was what they were getting. No sooner had they drawn up in the courtyard of the Ministry of the Interior than the doors of the car had been wrenched open by a team of young men in leather coats all shouting at once.

'Herr Siebkron will see you immediately! Now please! Yes! Immediately please!'

'I shall go at my own pace,' Bradfield had snapped as they were ushered into the unpainted steel lift. 'Don't you dare order me about.' And to de Lisle, 'I shall speak to Siebkron. It's like a trainload of monkeys.'

The upper floors restored them. This was the Bonn they knew: the pale, functional interiors, the pale, functional reproductions on the wall, the pale unpolished teak; the white shirts, the grey ties and faces pale as the moon. They were seven. The two who sat to either side of Siebkron had no names at all, and de Lisle wondered maliciously whether they were clerks brought in to make up the numbers. Lieff, an empty-headed parade horse from Protocol Department, sat on his left; opposite him, on Bradfield's right, an old *Polizeidirektor* from Bonn, whom de Lisle instinctively liked: a battle-scarred monument of a man, with white patches like covered bullet-holes in the leather of his skin. Cigarettes lay in packets on a plate. A stern girl offered decaffeinated coffee, and they waited until she had withdrawn.

What *does* Siebkron want? he wondered for the hundredth time since the terse summons at nine o'clock that morning.

The Conference began, like all conferences, with a résumé of what was said at a previous occasion. Lieff read the minutes in a tone of unctuous flattery, like a man awarding a medal. It was an occasion, he implied, of the greatest felicity. The *Polizei-direktor* unbuttoned his green jacket, and lit a length of Dutch cigar till it burned like a spill. Siebkron coughed angrily but the old policeman ignored him.

'You have no objection to these minutes, Mr Bradfield?' Siebkron usually smiled when he asked this question, and although his smile was as cold as the north wind, de Lisle could have wished for it today.

'Off the cuff, none,' Bradfield replied easily, 'But I must see them in writing before I can sign them.'

'No one is asking you to sign.'

De Lisle looked up sharply.

'You will allow me,' Siebkron declared, 'To read the following statement. Copies will be distributed.'

It was quite short.

The *doyen*, he said, had already discussed with Herr Lieff of Protocol Department, and with the American Ambassador, the question of the physical security of diplomatic premises in the event of civil unrest arising out of minority demonstrations in the Federal Republic. Siebkron regretted that additional measures were proving necessary, but it was desirable to anticipate unhappy eventualities rather than attempt to correct them when it was too late. Siebkron had received the *doyen*'s assurance that all diplomatic Heads of Mission would cooperate to the utmost with the Federal Authorities. The British Ambassador had already associated himself with this undertaking. Siebkron's voice had found a hard edge which was uncommonly close to anger. Lieff and the old policeman had turned deliberately to face Bradfield, and their expressions were frankly hostile.

'I am sure you subscribe to this opinion,' Siebkron said in English, handing a copy of the statement down the table.

Bradfield had noticed nothing. Taking his fountain pen from an inside pocket, he unscrewed the cap, fitted it carefully over the butt and ran the nib along line after line of the text.

'This is an *aide-memoire*?'

'A memorandum. You will find the German translation attached.'

'I can see nothing here that requires to be in writing at all,' Bradfield said easily. 'You know very well, Ludwig, that we always agree on such matters. Our interests are identical.'

Siebkron disregarded this pleasant appeal: 'You also understand that Doktor Karfeld is not well disposed towards the British. This places the British Embassy in a special category.'

Bradfield's smile did not flinch. 'It has not escaped our notice. We rely on you to see that Herr Karfeld's sentiments are not expressed in physical terms. We have every confidence in your ability to do so.'

'Precisely. Then you will appreciate my concern for the safety of all personnel of the British Embassy.'

Bradfield's voice came quite close to banter. 'Ludwig, what is this? A declaration of love?'

The rest came very fast, thrown down like an ultimatum: 'I must accordingly ask you that until further notice all British Embassy staff below the rank of Counsellor be confined to the area of Bonn. You will kindly instruct them that for their own safety they will please be in their residences—' he was reading again from the folder before him – 'Henceforth and until further notice, by eleven o'clock at night, local time.'

The white faces peered at them through the swathes of tobacco smoke like lamps through an anaesthetic. In the momentary confusion and bewilderment, only Bradfield's voice, fluent and decisive as the voice of a commander in battle, did not waver.

It was a principle of civil order which the British had learned by bitter experience in many parts of the world, he said, that unpleasant incidents were actually provoked by over-elaborate precautions.

Siebkron offered no comment.

While making every allowance for Siebkron's professional and personal concern, Bradfield felt obliged to warn him strongly against any gesture which might be misinterpreted by the outside world.

Siebkron waited.

Like Siebkron, Bradfield insisted, he himself had a responsibility to preserve Embassy morale and thus fortify the Junior Staff against strains yet to come. He could not support any measure at this stage which would look like a retreat in the face of an enemy who as yet had barely advanced . . . did Siebkron really wish it said that he could not control a handful of hooligans? . . .

Siebkron was standing up, the others with him. A terse inclination of the head replaced the obligatory handshake. The door opened and the leather coats led them briskly to the lift. They were in the wet courtyard. The roar of the motor-cycles deafened them. The Mercedes swept them into the carriage-way. What on earth have we done? de Lisle wondered. What on earth have we done to deserve this? Whoever has thrown the rock through teacher's window?

'It's nothing to do with last night?' he asked Bradfield at last, as they approached the Embassy.

'There is no conceivable connection,' Bradfield retorted. He was sitting bolt upright, his expression stiff and angry.

'Whatever the reason,' he added, more as a memorandum to himself than by way of a confidence to de Lisle, 'Siebkron is the one thread I dare not cut.'

'Quite,' said de Lisle and they got out. The sports were just ending.

Behind the English Church, on a wooded hill, in a semi-rural avenue away from the centre of Bad Godesberg, the Embassy has built itself a modest piece of suburban Surrey. Comfortable stockbrokers' houses with open fireplaces and long corridors for servants they no longer have, hide behind the exiguous privet and laburnum of splendid isolation. The air trembles to the gentle music of the British Forces Network. Dogs of un-mistakeably English breed ramble in the long gardens; the pavements are obstructed by the runabout cars of British Counsellors' wives. In this avenue, on each Sunday throughout the warmer months, a more agreeable ritual replaces the Chancery meeting. At a few minutes before eleven o'clock, dogs are summoned indoors, cats banished to the garden, as a dozen wives in coloured hats and matching handbags emerge from a dozen front doors, followed by their husbands in Sunday suits.

Soon a little crowd has gathered in the road; someone has made a joke; someone has laughed; they glance round anxiously for stragglers, and upwards at the nearer houses. Have the Crabbes overslept? Should someone give them a ring? No, here they come at last. Gently they begin the move downhill to the Church, the women leading, men following, their hands deep in their pockets. Reaching the Church steps they all pause, smiling invitingly at the senior wife present. She, with a little gesture of surprise, climbs the steps ahead of them and disappears through the green curtain, leaving her inferiors to follow, quite by accident, the order of succession which protocol, had they cared about such things, would exactly have demanded.

That Sunday morning, Rawley Bradfield, accompanied by Hazel, his beautiful wife, entered the Church and sat in their customary pew beside the Tills, who by the nature of things had gone ahead of them in the procession. Bradfield, though theoretically a Roman Catholic, regarded it as his iron duty to attend the Embassy Chapel; it was a matter on which he declined to consult either his Church or his conscience. They made a handsome couple. The Irish blood had come through richly in Hazel, whose auburn hair shone where the sunbeams touched it from the leaded window; and Bradfield had a way of deferring to her in public which was both gallant and commanding. Directly behind them, Meadowes the Registrar sat expressionless beside his blonde and very nervous daughter. She was a pretty girl, but the wives in particular were inclined to wonder how a man of her father's rectitude could tolerate such a quantity of make-up.

Having settled into his pew, Bradfield searched the hymnal for the advertised numbers – there were certain of them which he had proscribed on the grounds of taste – then glanced round the Church to check absentees. There being none, he was about to return to his hymnal when Mrs Vandelung, the Dutch Counsellor's wife, and currently Vice-President of the International Ladies, leaned over her pew to enquire in a breathy, somewhat hysterical undertone why there was no organist. Bradfield glanced at the little lighted alcove, at the empty stool with the embroidered cushion on the seat, and in the same instant he appeared to become aware of the embarrassed silence all round him which was accentuated by the creaking of the west door as Mickie Crabbe, whose turn it was to act as sidesman, closed it without benefit of a Voluntary. Rising quickly Bradfield walked down the aisle. From the front row of the choir, John Gaunt, the Chancery Guard, watched with veiled apprehension. Jenny Pargiter, upright as a bride, looked stiffly ahead of her, seeing nothing but the light of God. Janet Cork, wife of the cypher clerk, stood beside her, her mind upon her unborn child. Her husband was in the Embassy, serving a routine shift in the cypher room.

'Where the devil's Harting?' Bradfield asked, but one glance at Crabbe's expression told him that his question was wasted. Slipping out into the road, he hastened a short way up the hill and opened a small iron gate leading to the vestry, which he entered without knocking.

'Harting's failed to appear,' he said curtly. 'Who else plays the organ?'

The Chaplain, who found the Embassy a challenge but believed he was making headway, was a Low Church man with a wife and four children in Wales. No one knew why they would not join him.

'He's never missed before. Never.'

'Who else can play?'

'Perhaps the ferry isn't running. There's a lot of trouble about, I hear.'

'He could come the long way by the bridge. He's done it often enough. Can no one stand in for him?'

'Not that I know,' said the Chaplain, fingering the tip of his golden stole, his thoughts far away. 'But there's never been occasion to enquire, not really.'

'Then what are you going to do?'

'Perhaps someone could give a note,' the Chaplain suggested doubtfully, but his gaze had fixed on a baptismal postcard that was tucked behind a calendar. 'Maybe that would be the answer. Johnny Gaunt has a nice tenor, being Welsh.'

'Very well, the choir must lead. You'd better tell them at once.'

'Trouble *is* you see, they don't know the hymns, Mr Bradfield,' the Chaplain said. 'He wasn't at Friday's choir practice either you see. He didn't come, not really. We had to scrap it, see.'

Stepping back into the fresh air, Bradfield found himself face to face with Meadowes, who had quietly left his place beside his daughter and followed him to the back of the Church.

'He's vanished,' Meadowes said, dreadfully quietly. 'I've checked everywhere. Sick list, the doctor; I've been to his house. His car's in the garage; he's not used his milk. No one's seen or heard of him since Friday. He didn't come to Exiles. It was a special occasion for my daughter's birthday, but he didn't come to that either. He'd got engagements but he was going to look in. He'd promised her a hair-dryer as a present; it's not like him, Mr Bradfield, it's not his way at all.'

For one moment, just for one moment, Bradfield's composure seemed to desert him. He stared furiously at Meadowes, then back at the Church, as if undecided which to destroy; as if either in anger or despair he would rush down the path and burst open the doors and cry out the news to those who waited so complacently within.

'Come with me.'

Even as they entered the main gates of the Embassy and long before the police check cleared them, they could recognize the signs of crisis. Two army motor-cycles were parked on the front lawn. Cork, the cypher clerk on call, was waiting on the steps, an Everyman guide to investments still in his hand. A green German police van, its blue light flashing, had stationed itself beside the canteen, and they could hear the crackle of its radio.

'Thank the Lord you've come, sir,' said Macmullen the Head Guard, 'I sent the duty driver down; he must have passed you on the carriageway.'

All over the building bells were ringing.

'There's a message in from Hanover, sir, from the Consulate General; I didn't hear too well. The rally's gone mad, sir; all hell's broken loose. They're storming the library and they're going to march on the Consulate; I don't know what the world's coming to; worse than Grosvenor Square. I could hear their screaming on the telephone, sir.'

Meadowes followed Bradfield hastily up the stairs.

'You said a hair-dryer? He was giving your daughter a hair-dryer?'

It was a moment of deliberate inconsequence, of deliberate slowness perhaps, a nervous gesture before battle was joined. Meadowes at least construed it thus.

'He'd ordered it specially,' he said.

'Never mind,' said Bradfield, and was about to enter the cypher room when Meadowes addressed him once more.

'The file's gone,' he whispered. 'The green file for the special minutes. It's been gone since Friday.'

3
Alan Turner

IT WAS A day to be nearly free; a day to stay in London and dream of the country. In St James's Park, the premature summer was entering its third week. Along the lake, girls lay like cut flowers in the unnatural heat of a Sunday afternoon in May. An attendant had lit an improbable bonfire and the smell of burnt grass drifted with the echoes of the traffic. Only the pelicans, hobbling fussily round their island pavilion, seemed disposed to move; only Alan Turner, his big shoes crunching on the gravel, had anywhere to go; for once, not even the girls could distract him.

His shoes were of a heavy brown brogue and much repaired at the welts. He wore a stained tropical suit and carried a stained canvas bag. He was a big, lumbering man, fair-haired, plain-faced and pale, with the high shoulders and square fingers of an alpinist, and he walked with the thrusting slowness of a barge; a broad, aggressive, policeman's walk, wilfully without finesse. His age was hard to guess. Undergraduates would have found him old, but old for an undergraduate. He could alarm the young with age, and the aged with his youth. His colleagues had long ceased to speculate. It was known that he was a late entrant, never a good sign, and a former fellow of St Anthony's College, Oxford, which takes all kinds of people. The official Foreign Office publications were reserved. While they shed a merciless light on the origin of all their other Turners, in the matter of Alan they remained tight-lipped, as if, having considered all the facts, they felt that silence was the kindest policy.

'They've called you in too, then,' said Lambert, catching him up. 'I must say, Karfeld's really gone to town this time.'

'What the hell do they expect us to do? Man the barricades? Knit blankets?'

Lambert was a small, vigorous man and he liked it said of

him that he could mix with anyone. He occupied a senior position in Western Department and ran a cricket team open to all grades.

They began the ascent of Clive Steps.

'You'll never change them,' said Lambert. 'That's my view. A nation of psychopaths. Always think they're being got at. Versailles, encirclement, stab in the back; persecution mania, that's their trouble.'

He allowed time for Turner to agree with him.

'We're bringing in the whole of the Department. Even the girls.'

'Christ, that'll really frighten them. That's calling up the reserves, that is.'

'This could put paid to Brussels you know. Bang it clean on the nose. If the German Cabinet loses its nerve on the home front, we're all up a gum-tree.' The prospect filled him with relish. 'We shall have to find a quite different solution in that case.'

'I thought there wasn't one.'

'The Secretary of State has already spoken to their Ambassador; I am told they have agreed full compensation.'

'Then there's nothing to worry about is there? We can get on with our weekend. All go back to bed.'

They had reached the top of the steps. The founder of India, one foot casually upon a plateau of vanquished bronze, stared contentedly past them into the glades of the Park.

'They've kept the doors open.' Lambert's voice was tender with reverence. 'They're on the week-day schedule. My, they *are* going it. Well,' he remarked, receiving no admiring echo, 'You go your way, I go mine. Mind you,' he added shrewdly, 'It could do us a lot of good. Unite the rest of Europe behind us against the Nazi menace. Nothing like the stamp of jack-boots to stiffen the old alliances.' With a final nod of undeterred goodwill he was assumed into the imperial darkness of the main entrance. For a moment, Turner stared after him, measuring his slight body against the Tuscan pillars of the great portico, and there was even something wistful in his expression, as if actually he would quite like to be a Lambert, small and neat and adept and unbothered. Rousing himself at last, he continued towards a smaller door at the side of the building. It was a scruffy door with brown hardboard nailed to the inside of the glass and a notice denying entrance to unauthorized persons. He had some difficulty getting through.

'Mister Lumley's looking for you,' said the porter. '*When* you can spare a minute, I'm sure.'

He was a young, effeminate man and preferred the other side of the building. 'He was enquiring *most* particularly, as a matter of fact. All packed for Germany, I see.'

His transistor radio was going all the time; someone was reporting direct from Hanover and there was a roar in the background like the roar of the sea.

'Well, you'll get a nice reception by the sound of it. They've already done the library, and now they're having a go at the Consulate.'

'They'd done the library by lunchtime. It was on the one o'clock. The police have cordoned off the Consulate. Three deep. There's not a hope in hell of them getting anywhere near.'

'It's got worse since then,' the porter called after him. 'They're burning books in the market place; you wait!'

'I will. That's just what I bloody well will do.' His voice was awfully quiet but it carried a long way; a Yorkshire voice, and common as a mongrel.

'He's booked your passage to Germany. You ask Travel Section! Overland route and Second Class! Mr Shawn goes First!'

Shoving open the door of his room he found Shawn lounging at the desk, his Brigade of Guards jacket draped over the back of Turner's chair. The eight buttons glinted in the stray sunbeams which, bolder than the rest, had penetrated the coloured glass. He was talking on the telephone. 'They're to put everything in one room,' he said in that soothing tone of voice which reduces the calmest of men to hysteria. He had said it several times before, apparently, but was repeating it for the benefit of simpler minds. '*With* the incendiaries *and* the shredder. That's point one. Point two, *all* locally employed staff are to go *home* and lie low; we can't pay compensation to German citizens who get hurt on our behalf. Tell them that

42

first, then call me back. Christ Almighty!' he screamed to Turner as he rang off, 'Have you *ever* tried to deal with that man?'

'What man?'

'That bald-headed clown in E and O. The one in charge of nuts and bolts.'

'His name is Crosse.' He flung his bag into the corner. 'And he's not a clown.'

'He's mental,' Shawn muttered, losing courage, 'I swear he is.'

'Then keep quiet about it or they'll post him to Security.'

'Lumley's looking for you.'

'I'm not going,' Turner said. 'I'm bloody well not wasting my time. Hanover's a D post. They've no codes, no cyphers, nothing. What am I supposed to do out there? Rescue the bloody Crown Jewels?'

'Then why did you bring your bag?'

He picked up a sheaf of telegrams from the desk.

'They've known about that rally for months. Everyone has, from Western Department down to us. Chancery reported it in March. For once, we saw the telegram. Why didn't they evacuate staff? Why didn't they send the kids home? No money, I suppose. No third class seats available. Well sod them!'

'Lumley said immediately.'

'Sod Lumley too,' said Turner, and sat down. 'I'm not seeing him till I've read the papers.'

'It's *policy* not to send them home,' Shawn continued taking up Turner's point. Shawn thought of himself as *attached* rather than *posted* to Security Department; as resting, as it were, between appointments, and he missed no opportunity to demonstrate his familiarity with the larger political world. 'Business as usual, that's the cry. We can't allow ourselves to be stampeded by mob rule. After all, the Movement is a minority. The British lion,' he added, making an unconfident joke, 'can't allow itself to be upset by the pinpricks of a few hooligans.'

'Oh it can *not*; my God it can't.'

Turner put aside one telegram and began another. He read fast and without effort, with the confidence of an academic, arranging the papers into separate piles according to some undisclosed criterion.

'So what's going on? What have they got to lose apart from their honour?' he demanded, still reading. 'Why the hell call *us* in? Compensation's Western Department's baby, right? Evacuation's E and O's baby, right? If they're worried about the lease, they can go and cry at the Ministry of Works. So why the hell can't they leave us in peace?'

'Because it's Germany,' Shawn suggested weakly.

'Oh roll on.'

'Sorry if it *spoilt* something,' Shawn said with an unpleasant sneer, for he suspected Turner of a more colourful sex life than his own.

The first relevant telegram was from Bradfield. It was marked Flash; it had been despatched at eleven-forty and submitted to the Resident Clerk at two twenty-eight. Skardon, Consul General in Hanover, had summoned all British staff and families to the Residence, and was making urgent representations to the police. The second telegram consisted of a Reuter newsflash timed at eleven fifty-three: demonstrators had broken into the British Library; police were unequal to the situation; the fate of Fraulein Eick [*sic*] the librarian was unknown.

Hard upon this came a second rush telegram from Bonn: 'Norddeutscher Rundfunk reports Eick repeat Eick killed by mob.' But this was in turn immediately contradicted, for Bradfield, through the good offices of Herr Siebkron of the Ministry of the Interior, ('with whom I have a close relationship') had by then succeeded in obtaining direct contact with the Hanover police. According to their latest assessment, the British Library had been sacked and its books burned before a large crowd. Printed posters had appeared with anti-British slogans such as 'The Farmers won't Pay for your Empire!' and 'Work for your own bread, don't steal ours!' Fraulein Gerda Eich [*sic*] aged fifty-one of 4 Hohenzollernweg, Hanover, had been dragged down two flights of stone steps, kicked and punched in the face and made to throw her own books into the fire. Police with horses and anti-riot equipment were being brought in from neighbouring towns.

A marginal annotation by Shawn stated that Tracing Section had turned up a record of the unfortunate Fraulein Eich. She was a retired school teacher, sometime in British Occupational employment, sometime secretary of the Hanover Branch of the Anglo-German Society, who in 1962 had been awarded a British decoration for services to international understanding.

'Another anglophile bites the dust,' Turner muttered.

There followed a long if hastily compiled summary of broadcasts and bulletins. This, too, Turner studied with close application. No one, it seemed, and least of all those who had been present, was able to say precisely what had triggered off the riot, nor what had attracted the crowd towards the library in the first place. Though demonstrations were now a commonplace of the German scene, a riot on this scale was not; Federal authorities had confessed themselves 'deeply concerned'. Herr Ludwig Siebkron of the Ministry of the Interior had broken his habitual silence to remark to a Press Conference that there was 'cause for very real anxiety'. An immediate decision had been taken to provide additional protection for all official and quasi-official British buildings and residences throughout the Federal Republic. The British Ambassador, after some initial hesitation, had agreed to impose a voluntary curfew on his staff.

Accounts of the incident by police, press and even delegates themselves were hopelessly confused. Some declared it was spontaneous; a collective gesture aggravated by the word 'British' which happened to be exhibited on the side of the library building. It was natural, they said, that as the day of decision in Brussels drew rapidly closer, the Movement's policy of opposition to the Common Market should assume a specifically anti-British form. Others swore they had seen a sign, a white handkerchief that fluttered from a window; one witness even claimed that a rocket had risen behind the town hall and emitted stars of red and gold. For some the crowd had surged with a positive impulse, for others it had 'flowed'; for others again it had trembled. 'It was led from the centre,' one senior police officer reported. 'The periphery was motionless until the centre moved.' 'Those at the centre,' Western Radio maintained, 'kept their composure. The outrage was perpetrated by a few hooligans at the front. The others were then obliged to follow.' On one point only they seemed to agree: the incident had taken place when the music was loudest. It was even suggested by a woman witness that the music itself had been the sign which started the crowd running.

The *Spiegel* correspondent, on the other hand, speaking on Northern Radio, had a circumstantial account of how a grey omnibus chartered by a mysterious Herr Meyer of Luneburg conveyed 'a bodyguard of thirty picked men' to the town centre of Hanover one hour before the demonstration began and that this bodyguard, drawn partly from students and partly from young farmers, had formed a 'protective ring' round the Speaker's podium. It was these 'picked men' who had started the rush. The entire action had therefore been inspired by Karfeld himself. 'It is an open declaration,' he insisted, 'that from now on, the Movement proposes to march to its own music.'

'This Eich,' Turner said at last. 'What's the latest?'

'She's as well as can be expected.'

'How well's that?'

'That's all they said.'

'Oh fine.'

'Fortunately neither Eich nor the Library are a British responsibility. The Library was founded during the Occupation but handed over to the Germans quite soon afterwards. It's now controlled and owned exclusively by the *Land* authority. There's nothing British about it.'

'So they've burnt their own books.'

Shawn gave a startled smile.

'Well yes, actually,' he said. 'Come to think of it, they have. That's rather a useful point; we might even suggest it to Press Section.'

The telephone was ringing. Shawn lifted the receiver and listened.

'It's Lumley,' he said, putting his hand over the mouthpiece. 'The porter told him you're in.'

Turner appeared not to hear. He was studying another telegram; it was quite a short telegram, two paragraphs, not more; it was headed 'personal for Lumley' and marked 'immediate' and this was the second copy passed to Turner.

46

'He wants you, Alan.' Shawn held out the receiver.

Turner read the text once and then read it again. Rising, he went to the steel cupboard and drew out a small black notebook, unused, which he thrust into the recesses of his tropical suit.

'You stupid bugger,' he said very quietly, from the door. 'Why don't you learn to read your telegrams? All the time you've been bleating about fire extinguishers we've had a bloody defector on our hands.'

He held up the sheet of pink paper for Shawn to read.

'A planned departure, that's what they call it. Forty-three files missing, not one of them below Confidential. One green classified Maximum and Limit, gone since Friday. I'll say it was planned.'

Leaving Shawn with the telephone still in his hand, Turner thudded down the corridor in the direction of his master's room. His eyes were a swimmer's eyes, very pale, washed colourless by the sea.

Shawn stared after him. That's what happens, he decided, when you open your doors to the other ranks. They leave their wives and children, use filthy language in the corridors and play ducks and drakes with all the common courtesies. With a sigh, he replaced the receiver, raised it again and dialled News Department. This was Shawn, he said, S-H-A-W-N. He had had rather a good idea about the riots in Hanover, the way one might play it at Press Conference: it was nothing to do with *us* after all, if the Germans decided to burn their own books. . . . He thought that might go down pretty well as an example of cool English wit. Yes, Shawn, S-H-A-W-N. Not at all; they might even have lunch together some time.

Lumley had a folder open before him and his old hand rested on it like a claw.

'We know nothing about him. He's not even carded. As far as we're concerned, he doesn't exist. He hasn't even been vetted, let alone cleared. I had to scrounge his papers from Personnel.'

'And?'

'There's a smell, that's all. A foreign smell. Refugee background, emigrated in the thirties. Farm school, Pioneer Corps,

47

Bomb Disposal. He gravitated to Germany in forty-five. Temporary sergeant; Control Commission; one of the old carpet-baggers by the sound of it. Professional expatriate. There was one in every mess in Occupied Germany in those days. Some survived, some drifted into the consulates. Quite a few of them reverted; went into the night or took up German citizenship again. A few went crooked. No childhood, most of them, that's the trouble. Sorry,' Lumley said abruptly, and almost blushed.

'Any form?'

'Nothing to set the Thames on fire. We traced the next of kin. An uncle living in Hampstead; Otto Harting. Sometime adoptive father. No other relations living. He was in the pharmaceutical business. More an alchemist by the sound of it. Patent medicines, that kind of thing. He's dead now. Dead ten years. He was a member of the Hampstead Branch of the British Communist Party from forty-one to forty-five. One conviction for little girls.'

'How little?'

'Does it matter? His nephew Leo lived with him for a bit. Something may have rubbed off. The old man might even have recruited him then I suppose. . . . Long term penetration. That would fit the mould. Or someone may have reminded him of it later on. They never let you go, mind, once you've had a taste of it. Bad as Catholics.'

Lumley hated faith.

'What's his access?'

'Obscure. His function is listed as Claims and Consular, whatever that means. He has diplomatic rank, just. A Second Secretary. You know the kind of arrangement. Unpromotable, unpostable, unpensionable. Chancery gave him living space. Not a *proper* diplomat.'

'Lucky bloke.'

Lumley let that go.

'Entertainment allowance' – Lumley glanced at the file – 'A hundred and four pounds per annum, to be spread over fifty cocktail guests and thirty-four dinner guests. Accountable. Pretty small beer. He's locally employed. A temporary, of course. He's been one for twenty years.'

'That leaves me sixteen to go.'

'In fifty-six he put in an application to marry a girl called Aickman. Margaret Aickman. Someone he'd met in the Army. The application was never pursued, apparently. There's no record of whether he's married since.'

'Perhaps they've stopped asking. What are the missing files about?'

Lumley hesitated. 'Just a hotchpotch,' he said casually, 'a general hotchpotch. Bradfield's trying to put a list together now.' They could hear the porter's radio blaring again in the corridor.

Turner caught the tone and held on to it: 'What sort of hotchpotch?'

'Policy,' Lumley retorted. 'Not your field at all.'

'You mean I can't know?'

'I mean you needn't know.' He said this quite casually; Lumley's world was dying and he wished no one ill. 'He's chosen a good moment, I must say,' he continued, 'With all this going on. Perhaps he just took a handful and ran for it.'

'Discipline?'

'Nothing much. He got in a fight five years ago in Cologne. A night-club brawl. They managed to hush it up.'

'And they didn't sack him?'

'We like to give people a second chance.' Lumley was still deep in the file, but his tone was pregnant with innuendo.

He was sixty or more, coarse-spoken and grey; a grey-faced, grey-clothed owl of a man, hunched and dried out. Long ago he had been Ambassador to somewhere small, but the appointment had not endured.

'You're to cable me every day. Bradfield is arranging facilities. But don't ring me up, do you understand? That direct line is a menace.' He closed the folder. 'I've cleared it with Western Department, Bradfield's cleared it with the Ambassador. They'll let you go on one condition.'

'That's handsome of them.'

'The Germans mustn't know. Not on any account. They mustn't know he's gone; they mustn't know we're looking for him; they mustn't know there's been a leak.'

'What if he's compromised secret Nato material? That's as much their pigeon as ours.'

'Decisions of that kind are none of your concern. Your instructions are to go gently. Don't lead with your chin. Understand?'

Turner said nothing.

'You're not to disturb, annoy or offend. They're walking on a knife edge out there; *anything* could tilt the balance. Now, tomorrow, any time. There's even a danger that the Huns might think we were playing a double game with the Russians. If that idea got about it could balls everything up.'

'We seem to find it hard enough,' Turner said, borrowing from Lumley's vocabulary, 'Playing a single game with the Huns.'

'The Embassy have got one idea in their heads, and it's not Harting and it's not Karfeld and least of all is it you. It's Brussels. So just remember that. You'd better, because if you don't you'll be out on your arse.'

'Why not send Shawn? He's tactful. Charm them all, he would.'

Lumley pushed a memorandum across the desk. It contained a list of Harting's personal particulars. 'Because you'll find him and Shawn won't. Not that I admire you for that. You'd pull down the whole forest, you would, to find an acorn. What drives you? What are you looking for? Some bloody absolute. If there's one thing I really hate it's a cynic in search of God. Maybe a bit of failure is what you need.'

'There's plenty of it about.'

'Heard from your wife?'

'No.'

'You could forgive her, you know. It's been done before.'

'Jesus, you take chances,' Turner breathed. 'What the hell do you know about my marriage?'

'Nothing. That's why I'm qualified to give advice. I just wish you'd stop punishing us all for not being perfect.'

'Anything else?'

Lumley examined him like an old magistrate who had not many cases left.

'Christ, you're quick to despise,' he said at last. 'You frighten me, I'll tell you that for nothing. You're going to have to start liking people soon, or it'll be too late. You'll need us, you know, before you die. Even if we are a second best.' He thrust a file into Turner's hand. 'Go on then. Find him. But don't think you're off the leash. I should take the midnight train if I were you. Get in at lunchtime.' His hooded yellow eyes flickered towards the sunlit park. 'Bonn's a foggy bloody place.'

'I'll fly if it's all the same.'

Lumley slowly shook his head.

'You can't wait, can you. You can't wait to get your hands on him. Pawing the bloody earth, aren't you? Christ, I wish I had your enthusiasm.'

'You had once.'

'And get yourself a suit or something. Try and look as though you belong.'

'I don't though, do I?'

'All right,' said Lumley, not caring any more. 'Wear the cloth cap. Christ,' he added, 'I'd have thought your class was suffering from too much recognition already.'

'There's something you haven't told me. Which do they want most: the man or the files?'

'Ask Bradfield,' Lumley replied, avoiding his eye.

Turner went to his room and dialled his wife's number. Her sister answered.

'She's out,' she said.

'You mean they're still in bed.'

'What do you want?'

'Tell her I'm leaving the country.'

As he rang off he was again distracted by the sound of the porter's wireless. He had turned it on full and tuned it to the European network. A well-bred lady was giving a summary of the news. The Movement's next rally would be held in Bonn, she said; on Friday, five days from today.

Turner grinned. It was a little like an invitation to tea. Picking up his bag, he set off for Fulham, an area well known for boarding houses and married men in exile from their wives.

4
Decembers of Renewal

DE LISLE PICKED HIM up from the airport. He had a sports car that was a little too young for him and it rattled wildly on the wet cobble of the villages. Though it was quite a new car, the paintwork was already dulled by the chestnut gum of Godesberg's wooded avenues. The time was nine in the morning but the street lights still burned. To either side, on flat fields, farm-houses and new building estates lay upon the strips of mist like hulks left over by the sea. Drops of rain prickled on the small windscreen.

'We've booked you in at the Adler; I suppose that's all right. We didn't know quite what sort of subsistence you people get.'

'What are the posters saying?'

'Oh, we hardly read them any more. Reunification . . . alliance with Moscow. . . . Anti-America. . . . Anti-Britain.'

'Nice to know we're still in the big league.'

'You've hit a real Bonn day I'm afraid. Sometimes the fog is a little colder,' de Lisle continued cheerfully, 'Then we call it winter. Sometimes it's warmer, and that's summer. You know what they say about Bonn: either it rains or the level crossings are down. In fact, of course, both things happen at the same time. An island cut off by fog, that's us. It's a very *metaphysical* spot; the dreams have quite replaced reality. We live somewhere between the recent future and the not so recent past. Not *personally*, if you know what I mean. Most of us feel we've been here for ever.'

'Do you always get an escort?'

The black Opel lay thirty yards behind them. It was neither gaining nor losing ground. Two pale men sat in the front and the headlights were on.

'They're protecting us. That's the theory. Perhaps you heard of our meeting with Siebkron?' They turned right and the Opel followed them. 'The Ambassador is *quite* furious. And *now*, of course, they can say it's all vindicated by Hanover: no Englishman is safe without a bodyguard. It's not our view at all. Still, perhaps after Friday we'll lose them again. How are things in London? I hear Steed-Asprey's got Lima.'

'Yes, we're all thrilled about it.'

A yellow road sign said six kilometres to Bonn.

'I think we'll go round the city if you don't mind; there's liable to be rather a hold-up getting in and out. They're checking passes and things.'

'I thought you said Karfeld didn't bother you.'

'We all say that. It's part of our local religion. We're trained to regard Karfeld as an irritant, not an epidemic. You'll have to get used to that. I have a message for you from Bradfield, by the way. He's sorry not to have collected you himself, but he's been rather under pressure.'

They swung sharply off the main road, bumped over a tramline and sped along a narrow open lane. Occasionally a poster or photograph rose before them and darted away into the mist.

'Was that the whole of Bradfield's message?'

'There was the question of who knows what. He imagined you'd like to have that clear at once. *Cover*, is that what you'd call it?'

'I might.'

'Our friend's disappearance has been noticed in a *general* way,' de Lisle continued in the same amiable tone. 'That was inevitable. But fortunately Hanover intervened, and we've been able to mend a few fences. Officially, Rawley has sent him on compassionate leave. He's published no details; merely hinted at personal problems and left it at that. The Junior Staff can think what they like: nervous breakdown; family troubles; they can make up their own rumours. Bradfield mentioned the matter at this morning's meeting: we're all backing him up. As for yourself . . .'

'Well?'

'A general security check in view of the crisis? How would that sound to you? It seemed quite convincing to us.'

'Did you know him?'

'Harting?'

'That's right. Did you know him?'

'I think perhaps,' de Lisle said, pulling up at a traffic light, 'We ought to leave the first bite to Rawley, don't you? Tell me, what news of our little Lords of York?'

'Who the hell are they?'

'I'm *so* sorry,' de Lisle said in genuine discomfort. 'It's our local expression for the Cabinet. It was silly of me.'

They were approaching the Embassy. As they filtered left to cross the carriageway, the black Opel slid slowly past like an old nanny who had seen her children safely over the road. The lobby was in turmoil. Despatch riders mingled with journalists and police. An iron grille, painted a protective orange, sealed off the basement staircase. De Lisle led him quickly to the first floor. Someone must have telephoned from the desk because Bradfield was already standing as they entered.

'Rawley, this is Turner,' de Lisle said, as if there were not much he could do about it, and prudently closed the door on them.

Bradfield was a hard-built, self-denying man, thin-boned and well-preserved, of that age and generation which can do with very little sleep. Yet the strains of the last twenty-four hours were already showing in the small, uncommon bruises at the corners of his eyes, and the unnatural pallor of his complexion. He studied Turner without comment: the canvas bag clutched in the heavy fist, the battered fawn suit, the unyielding, classless features; and it seemed for a moment as if an impulse of involuntary anger would threaten his customary composure; of aesthetic objection that anything so offensively incongruous should have been set before him at such a time. Outside in the corridor Turner heard the hushed murmur of busy voices, the clip of feet, the faster chatter of the typewriters, and the phantom throb of code machines from the cypher room.

'It was good of you to come at such an awkward time. You'd better let me have that.' He took the canvas bag and dumped it behind the chair.

'Christ it's hot,' said Turner. Walking to the window, he rested his elbows on the sill and gazed out. Away to his right in the far distance, the Seven Hills of Königswinter, chalked over by fine cloud, rose like Gothic dreams against the colourless sky. At their feet he could make out the dull glint of water and the shadows of motionless vessels.

'He lived out that way didn't he? Königswinter?'

'We have a couple of hirings on the other bank. They are never much in demand. The ferry is a great inconvenience.'

On the trampled lawn, workmen were dismantling the marquee under the watchful eye of two German policeman.

'I imagine you have a routine in such cases,' Bradfield continued, addressing Turner's back. 'You must tell us what you want and we shall do our best to provide it.'

'Sure.'

'The cypher clerks have a dayroom where you'll be undisturbed. They are instructed to send your telegrams without reference to anyone else. I've had a desk and a telephone put in there for you. I have also asked Registry to prepare a list of the missing files. If there's anything more you want, I am sure de Lisle will do his best to provide it. And on the social side' – Bradfield hesitated – 'I am to invite you to dine with us tomorrow night. We would be very pleased. It's the usual Bonn evening. De Lisle will lend you a dinner jacket, I am sure.'

'There's lots of routines,' Turner replied at last. He was leaning against the radiator, looking round the room. 'In a country like this it should be dead simple. Call in the police. Check hospitals, nursing homes, prisons, Salvation Army hostels. Circulate his photograph and personal description and square the local press. Then I'd look for him myself.'

'Look for him? Where?'

'In other people. In his background. Motive, political associations, boy friends, girl friends, contacts. Who else was involved; who knew; who half-knew; who quarter-knew; who ran him; who did he meet and where; how did he communicate; safe houses, pick-up points; how long's it been going on. Who's protected him, may be. That's what I call looking. Then I'd write a report: point the blame, make new enemies.' He continued to examine the room, and it seemed that nothing was innocent under his clear, inscrutable eye. 'That's one routine. That's for a friendly country, of course.'

'Most of what you suggest is quite unacceptable here.'

55

'Oh sure. I've had all that from Lumley.'

'Perhaps before we go any further, you had better have it from me as well.'

'Please yourself,' said Turner, in a manner which might have been deliberately chosen to annoy.

'I imagine that in your world, secrets are an absolute standard. They matter more than anything. Those who preserve them are your allies; those who betray them are your quarry. Here, that is simply not the case. As of now, the local political considerations far exceed those of security.'

Suddenly, Turner was grinning. 'They always do,' he said. 'It's amazing.'

'Here in Bonn we have at present one contribution to make: to maintain at all costs the trust and good will of the Federal Government. To stiffen their resolve against mounting criticism from their own electorate. The Coalition is sick; the most casual virus could kill it. Our job is to pamper the invalid. To console, encourage and occasionally threaten him, and pray to God he survives long enough to see us into the Common Market.'

'What a lovely picture.' He was looking out of the window again. 'The only ally we've got, and he's on crutches. The two sick men of Europe propping one another up.'

'Like it or not, it happens to be the truth. We are playing a poker game here. With open cards and nothing in our hand. Our credit is exhausted, our resources are nil. Yet in return for no more than a smile, our partners bid and play. That smile is all we have. The whole relationship between HMG and the Federal Coalition rests upon that smile. Our situation is as delicate as that; and as mysterious. And as critical. Our whole future with Europe could be decided in ten days from now.' He paused, apparently expecting Turner to speak. 'It is no coincidence that Karfeld has chosen next Friday for his rally in Bonn. By Friday, our friends in the German Cabinet will be forced to decide whether to bow to French pressure or honour their promises to ourselves and their partners in the Six. Karfeld detests the Market and favours an opening to the East. In the short term he inclines to Paris; in the long term, to Moscow. By marching on Bonn and increasing the tempo of

56

his campaign, he is deliberately placing pressure on the Coalition at the most critical moment. Do you follow me?'

'I can manage the little words,' Turner said. A Kodachrome portrait of the Queen hung directly behind Bradfield's head. Her crest was everywhere: on the blue leather chairs, the silver cigarette box, even the jotting pads set out on the long conference table. It was as if the monarchy had flown here first class and left its free gifts behind.

'That is why I am asking you to move with the greatest possible circumspection. Bonn is a village,' Bradfield continued. 'It has the manners, vision and dimensions of the parish pump, and yet it is a State within a village. Nothing matters for us more than the confidence of our hosts. There are already indications that we have caused them offence. I do not even know how we have done that. Their manner, even in the last forty-eight hours, has become noticeably cool. We are under surveillance; our telephone calls are interrupted; and we have the greatest difficulty in reaching even our official ministerial contacts.'

'All right,' Turner said. He had had enough. 'I've got the message. I'm warned off. We're on tender ground. Now what?'

'Now this,' Bradfield snapped. 'We both know what Harting may be, or may have been. God knows, there are precedents. The greater his treachery here, the greater the potential embarrassment, the greater the shock to German confidence. Let us take the worst contingency. If it were possible to prove – I am not yet saying that it is, but there are indications – if it were possible to prove that by virtue of Harting's activities in this Embassy, our inmost secrets had been betrayed to the Russians over many years – secrets which to a great extent we share with the Germans – then that shock, trivial as it may be in the long term, could sever the last thread by which our credit here hangs. Wait.' He was sitting very straight at his desk, with an expression of controlled distaste upon his handsome face. 'Hear me out. There is something here that does not exist in England. It is called the anti-Soviet alliance. The Germans take it very seriously, and we deride it at our peril: *it is still our ticket to Brussels*. For twenty years or more, we have dressed ourselves in the shining armour of the defender. We may be bankrupt,

we may beg for loans, currency and trade; we may occasionally
. . . reinterpret . . . our Nato commitments; when the guns
sound, we may even bury our heads under the blankets; our
leaders may be as futile as theirs.'

What was it Turner discerned in Bradfield's voice at that
moment? Self-disgust? A ruthless sense of his own decline?
He spoke like a man who had tried all remedies, and would have
no more of doctors. For a moment the gap between them had
closed, and Turner heard his own voice speaking through the
Bonn mist.

'For all that, in terms of popular psychology, it is the one
great unspoken strength we have: that when the Barbarians
come from the East, the Germans may count on our support.
That Rhine Army will hastily gather on the Kentish hills and
the British independent nuclear deterrent will be hustled into
service. Now do you see what Harting could mean in the hand
of a man like Karfeld?'

Turner had taken the black notebook from his inside pocket.
It crackled sharply as he opened it. 'No. I don't. Not yet. You
don't want him found, you want him lost. If you had your way
you wouldn't have sent for me.' He nodded his large head in
reluctant admiration. 'Well, I'll say this for you: no one's ever
warned me off this early. Christ. I've hardly sat down. I hardly
know his full names. We've not heard of him in London, did
you know that? He's not even had any access, not in our book.
Not even one bloody military manual. He may have been
abducted. He may have gone under a bus, run off with a bird
for all *we* know. But *you*; Christ! You've really gone the bank,
haven't you? He's all the spies we've ever had rolled into one.
So what *has* he pinched? What do you know that I don't?'
Bradfield tried to interrupt but Turner rode him down implac-
ably. 'Or maybe I shouldn't ask? I mean I don't want to upset
anyone.'

They were glaring at one another across centuries of suspicion: Turner clever, predatory and vulgar, with the hard eye
of the upstart; Bradfield disadvantaged but not put down,
drawn in upon himself, picking his language as if it had been
made for him.

'Our most secret file has disappeared. It vanished on the

58

same day that Harting left. It covers the whole spectrum of our most delicate conversations with the Germans, formal and informal, over the last six months. For reasons which do not concern you, its publication would ruin us in Brussels.'

He thought at first that it was the roar of the aeroplane engines still ringing in his ears, but the traffic in Bonn is as constant as the mist. Gazing out of the window he was suddenly assailed by the feeling that from now on he would neither see nor hear with clarity; that his senses were being embraced and submerged by the cloying heat and the disembodied sound.

'Listen.' He indicated his canvas bag. 'I'm the abortionist. You don't want me but you've got to have me. A neat job with no aftermath, that's what you're paying for. All right; I'll do my best. But before we all go over the wall, let's do a bit of counting on our fingers, shall we?'

The catechism began.

'He was unmarried?'

'Yes.'

'Always has been?'

'Yes.'

'Lived alone?'

'So far as I know.'

'Last seen?'

'On Friday morning, at the Chancery meeting. In here.'

'Not afterwards?'

'I happen to know the pay clerk saw him, but I'm limited in whom I can ask.'

'Anyone else missing at all?'

'No one.'

'Had a full count have you? No little long-legged bird from Registry?'

'People are constantly on leave; no one is unaccountably absent.'

'Then why didn't Harting take leave? They usually do, you know. Defect in comfort, that's my advice.'

'I have no idea.'

'You weren't close to him?'

59

'Certainly not.'

'What about his friends? What do they say?'

'He has no friends worth speaking of.'

'Any not worth speaking of?'

'So far as I know, he has no close friends in the community. Few of us have. We have acquaintances, but few friends. That is the way of Embassies. With such an intensive social life, one learns to value privacy.'

'How about Germans?'

'I have no idea. He was once on familiar terms with Harry Praschko.'

'Praschko?'

'We have a parliamentary opposition here: the free Democrats. Praschko is one of its more colourful members. He has been most things in his time: not least a fellow traveller. There is a note on file to say they were once friendly. They knew one another during the Occupation, I believe. We keep an index of useful contacts. I once questioned him about Praschko as a matter of routine and he told me that the relationship was discontinued. That is all I can tell you.'

'He was once engaged to be married to a girl called Margaret Aickman. This Harry Praschko was named as a character reference. In his capacity as a member of the Bundestag.'

'Well?'

'You've never heard of Aickman?'

'Not a name to me, I'm afraid.'

'Margaret.'

'So you said. I never heard of any engagement, and I never heard of the woman.'

'Hobbies? Photography? Stamps? Ham radio?'

Turner was writing all the time. He might have been filling in a form.

'He was musical. He played the organ in Chapel. I believe he also had a collection of gramophone records. You would do better to enquire among the Junior Staff; he was more at home with them.'

'You never went to his house?'

'Once. For dinner.'

'Did he come to yours?'

60

There was the smallest break in the rhythm of their inter-rogation while Bradfield considered.

'Once.'

'For dinner?'

'For drinks. He wasn't quite dinner party material. I am sorry to offend your social instincts.'

'I haven't got any.'

Bradfield did not appear surprised.

'Still, you did go to him, didn't you? I mean you gave him hope.' He rose and ambled back to the window like a great moth lured to the light. 'Got a file on him, have you?' His tone was very detached; he might have been infected by Bradfield's own forensic style.

'Only paysheets, annual reports, a character reference from the Army. It's all very standard stuff. Read it if you want.' When Turner did not reply, he added: 'We keep very little here on staff; they change so often. Harting was the exception.'

'He's been here twenty years.'

'Yes. As I say, he is the exception.'

'And never vetted.'

Bradfield said nothing.

'Twenty years in the Embassy, most of them in Chancery. And never vetted once. Name never even submitted. Amazing really.' He might have been commenting on the view.

'I suppose we all thought it had been done already. He came from the Control Commission after all; one assumes they exacted a certain standard.'

'Quite a privilege being vetted, mind. Not the kind of thing you do for anyone.'

The marquee had gone. Homeless, the two German police-men paced the grey lawn, their wet leather coats flapping lazily round their boots. It's a dream, Turner thought. A noisy unwilling dream. 'Bonn's a very metaphysical place,' de Lisle's agreeable voice reminded him. 'The dreams have quite replaced reality.'

'Shall I tell you something?'

'I can hardly stop you.'

'All right: you've warned me off. That's usual enough. But where's the rest of it?'

'I've no idea what you mean.'

'You've no theory, that's what I mean. It's not like anything I've ever met. There's no panic. No explanation. Why not? He worked for you. You knew him. Now you tell me he's a spy; he's pinched your best files. He's garbage. Is it always like that here when somebody goes? Do the gaps seal that fast?' He waited. 'Let me help you, shall I? "He's been working here for twenty years. We trusted him implicitly. We still do." How's that?'

Bradfield said nothing.

'Try again. "I always had my suspicions about him ever since that night we were discussing Karl Marx. Harting swallowed an olive without spitting out the pip." Any good?'

Still Bradfield did not reply.

'You see, it's not usual. See what I mean? He's unimportant. How you wouldn't have him to dinner. How you washed your hands of him. And what a sod he is. What he's betrayed.'

Turner watched him with his pale, hunter's eyes; watched for a movement, or a gesture, head cocked waiting for the wind. In vain. 'You don't even *bother* to explain him, not to me, not to yourself. Nothing. You're just . . . blank about him. As if you'd sentenced him to death. You don't mind my being personal, do you? Only I'm sure you've not much time: that's the next thing you're going to tell me.'

'I was not aware,' Bradfield said, ice-cold, 'that I was expected to do your job. Nor you mine.'

'Capri. How about that? He's got a bird. The Embassy's in chaos, he pinches some files, flogs them to the Czechs and bolts with her.'

'He has no girl.'

'Aickman. He's dug her up. Gone off with Praschko, two on a bird. Bride, best man and groom.'

'I told you, he has no girl.'

'Oh. So you *do* know that? I mean there are some things you *are* sure of. He's a traitor and he's got no bird.'

'So far as anyone knows, he has no woman. Does that satisfy you?'

'Perhaps he's queer.'

'I'm sure he's nothing of the sort.'

'It's broken out in him. We're all a bit mad, aren't we, round about our age? The male menopause, how about that?'

'That is an absurd suggestion.'

'Is it?'

'To the best of my knowledge, yes.' Bradfield's voice was trembling with anger; Turner's barely rose above a murmur.

'We never know though, do we? Not till it's too late. Did he handle money at all?'

'Yes. But there's none missing.'

Turner swung on him. 'Jesus,' he said, his eyes bright with triumph. 'You checked. You *have* got a dirty mind.'

'Perhaps he's just walked into the river,' Turner suggested comfortingly, his eyes still upon Bradfield. 'No sex. Nothing to live for. How's that?'

'Ridiculous, since you ask.'

'Important to a bloke like Harting, though, sex. I mean if you're alone, it's the only thing. I mean I don't know how some of these chaps manage, do you? I know I couldn't. About a couple of weeks is as long as I can go, me. It's the only reality, if you live alone. Or that's what I reckon. Apart from politics of course.'

'Politics? Harting? I shouldn't think he read a newspaper from one year to the next. He was a child in such matters. A complete innocent.'

'They often are,' said Turner. 'That's the remarkable thing.' Sitting down again, Turner folded one leg over the other and leaned back in the chair like a man about to reminisce. 'I knew a man once who sold his birthright because he couldn't get a seat on the underground. I reckon there's more of that kind go wrong than was ever converted to it by the Good Book. Perhaps that *was* his problem? Not right for dinner parties: no room on the train. After all, he was a temporary, wasn't he?'

Bradfield did not reply.

'And he'd been here a long time. Permanent staff, sort of thing. Not fashionable, that isn't, not in an Embassy. They go native if they're around too long. But then he *was* native, wasn't he? Half. Half a Hun, as de Lisle would say. He never talked politics?'

'Never.'

'You sensed it in him, a political spin?'

'No.'

'No crack-up? No tension?'

'No.'

'What about that fight in Cologne?'

'What fight?'

'Five years back. In the night club. Someone worked him over; he was in hospital for six weeks. They managed to hush it up.'

'That was before my time.'

'Did he drink a lot?'

'Not to my knowledge.'

'Speak Russian? Take lessons?'

'No.'

'What did he do with his leave?'

'He seldom claimed any. If he did, I understand he stayed at his home in Königswinter. He took a certain interest in his garden, I believe.'

For a long time Turner frankly searched Bradfield's face for something he could not find.

'He didn't screw around,' he said. 'He wasn't queer. He'd no friends, but he wasn't a recluse. He wasn't vetted and you've no record of him. He was a political innocent but he managed to get his hands on the one file that really matters to you. He never stole money, he played the organ in Chapel, took a certain interest in his garden and loved his neighbour as himself. Is that it? He wasn't any bloody thing, positive or negative. What was he then, for Christ's sake? The Embassy eunuch? Haven't you any opinion at all' – Turner persisted in mock supplication – 'to help a poor bloody investigator in his lonely task?'

A watch chain hung across Bradfield's waistcoat, no more than a thread of gold, a tiny devotional token of ordered society.

'You seem deliberately to be wasting time on matters which are not at issue. I have neither the time nor the interest to play your devious games. Insignificant though Harting was, obscure though his motive may be, for the last three months he unfortunately had a considerable access to secret information. He obtained that access by stealth, and I suggest that instead of speculating on his sexual proclivities, you give some attention to what he has stolen.'

'Stolen?' Turner repeated softly. 'That's a funny word,' and he wrote it out with deliberate clumsiness in tall capital letters along the top of one page of the notebook. The Bonn climate had already made its mark upon him: dark dabs of sweat had appeared on the thin fabric of his disgraceful suit.

'All right,' he said with sudden fierceness, 'I'm wasting your bloody time. Now let's start at the beginning and find out why you love him so.'

Bradfield examined his fountain pen. You could be queer, Turner's expression said, if you didn't love honour more.

'Will you put that into English?'

'Tell me about him from your own point of view. What his work was, what he was like.'

'His sole task when I first arrived was handling German civilian claims against Rhine Army. Tank damage to crops; stray shells from the range; cattle and sheep killed on manoeuvres. Ever since the end of the war that's been quite an industry in Germany. By the time I took over Chancery two and a half years ago, he had made a corner of it.'

'You mean he was an expert.'

'As you like.'

'It's just the emotive terms, you see. They put me off. I can't help liking him when you talk that way.'

'Claims was his *métier* then, if you prefer. They got him into the Embassy in the first place; he knew the job inside out; he's done it for many years in many different capacities. First for the Control Commission, then for the Army.'

'What did he do *before* that? He came out in forty-five.'

'He came out in uniform, of course. A sergeant or something of the sort. His status was then altered to that of civilian assistant. I've no idea what his work was. I imagine the War Office could tell you.'

'They can't. I also tried the old Control Commission archive.

It's mothballs for posterity. They'll take weeks to dig out his file.'

'In any event, he had chosen well. As long as British units were stationed in Germany, there would be manoeuvres; and German civilians would claim reparations. One might say that his job, though specialized, was at least secured by our military presence in Europe.'

'Christ, there's not many would give you a mortgage on *that*,' said Turner with a sudden, infectious smile, but Bradfield ignored him.

'He acquitted himself perfectly adequately. More than adequately; he was good at it. He had a smattering of law from somewhere. German as well as military. He was naturally acquisitive.'

'A thief,' Turner suggested, watching him.

'When he was in doubt, he could call upon the Legal Attaché. It wasn't everybody's cup of tea, acting as a broker between the German farmers and the British Army, smoothing their feathers, keeping things away from the press. It required a certain instinct. He possessed that,' Bradfield observed, once more with undisguised contempt. 'On his own level, he was a competent negotiator.'

'But that wasn't your level, was it?'

'It was no one's,' Bradfield replied, choosing to avoid the innuendo. 'Professionally, he was a solitary. My predecessors had found it best to leave him alone and when I took over I saw no reason to change the practice. He was attached to Chancery so that we could exert a certain disciplinary control; no more. He came to morning meetings, he was punctual, he made no trouble. He was liked up to a point but not, I suppose, trusted. His English was never perfect. He was socially energetic at a certain level; mainly in the less discriminating Embassies. They say he got on well with the South Americans.'

'Did he travel for his work?'

'Frequently and widely. All over Germany.'

'Alone?'

'Yes.'

'And he knew the Army inside out: he'd get the manoeuvre

66

reports; he knew their dispositions, strengths, he knew the lot, right?'

'He knew far more than that; he heard the mess gossip up and down the country; many of the manoeuvres were inter-allied affairs. Some involved the experimental use of new weapons. Since they also caused damage, he was obliged to know the extent of it. There is a great deal of loose information he could have acquired.'

'Nato stuff?'

'Mainly.'

'How long's he been doing that work?'

'Since nineteen forty-eight or nine I suppose. I cannot say, without reference to the files, when the British first paid compensation.'

'Say twenty-one years, give or take a bit.'

'That is my own calculation.'

'Not a bad run for a temporary.'

'Shall I go on?'

'Do. Sure. Go on,' Turner said hospitably, and thought: if I was you I'd throw me out for that.

'That was the situation when I took over. He was a contract man; his employment was subject to annual revision. Each December his contract came up for renewal, each December renewal was recommended. That was how matters stood until eighteen months ago.'

'When Rhine Army pulled out.'

'We prefer to say here that Rhine Army has been added to our strategic reserve in the United Kingdom. You must remember the Germans are still paying support costs.'

'I'll remember.'

'In any event, only a skeleton force remained in Germany. The withdrawal occurred quite suddenly; I imagine it took us all by surprise. There had been disputes about offset agreements, there were riots in Minden. The Movement was just getting under way; the students in particular were becoming extremely noisy; the troops were becoming a provocation. The decision was taken at the highest level; the Ambassador was not even consulted. The order came; and Rhine Army had gone in a month. We had been making a great number of cuts around

67

that time. It's all the rage in London these days. They throw things away and call it economy.' Once more Turner glimpsed that inner bitterness in Bradfield, a family shame to which no guest alluded.

'And Harting was left high and dry.'

'For some time, no doubt, he had seen which way the wind was blowing. That doesn't lessen the shock.'

'He was still a temporary?'

'Of course. Indeed his chances of establishment, if they ever seriously existed, were diminishing rapidly. The moment it became apparent that Rhine Army must withdraw, the writing was on the wall. For that reason alone, I felt that it would have been quite mistaken to make any permanent arrangement for him.'

'Yes,' said Turner, 'I see that.'

'It is easily argued that he was unjustly treated,' Bradfield retorted. 'It could equally be argued that he had a damn good run for his money.' The conviction came through like a stain, suppress it as he might.

'You said he handled official cash.' Turner thought: this is what doctors do. They probe until they can diagnose.

'Occasionally he passed on cheques for the Army. He was a postbox, that was all. A middle man. The Army drew the money, Harting handed it over and obtained a receipt. I checked his accounts regularly. The Army Auditors, as you know, are notoriously suspicious. There were no irregularities. The system was watertight.'

'Even for Harting?'

'That's not what I said. Besides, he always seemed quite comfortably off. I don't think he's an avaricious person; I don't have that impression.'

'Did he live above his means?'

'How should I know what means he has? If he lived on what he got here, I suppose he lived up to them. His house in Königswinter was quite large; certainly it was above his grade. I gather he maintained a certain standard there.'

'I see.'

'Last night I made a point of examining his cash drawings for the last three months preceding his departure. On Friday,

68

after Chancery meeting, he drew seventy-one pounds and fourpence.'

'That's a bloody odd sum.'

'To the contrary, it's a very logical sum. Friday was the tenth of the month. He had drawn exactly one third of his monthly entitlement of pay and allowances, less tax, insurance, stoppages for dilapidation and personal telephone calls.' He paused. 'That is an aspect of him which perhaps I have not emphasized: he was a very self-sufficient person.'

'You mean he *is*.'

'I have never yet caught him in a lie. Having decided to leave, he seems to have taken what was owing to him and no more.'

'Some people would call that honourable.'

'Not to steal? I would call that a negative achievement. He might also know, from his knowledge of the law, that an act of theft would have justified an approach to the German police.'

'Christ,' said Turner, watching him, 'You won't even give him marks for conduct.'

Miss Peate, Bradfield's personal assistant, brought coffee. She was a middle-aged, under-decorated woman, stitched taut and full of disapproval. She seemed to know already where Turner came from, for she cast him a look of sovereign contempt. It was his shoes, he noticed to his pleasure, that she most objected to; and he thought: bloody good, that's what shoes are for.

Bradfield continued: 'Rhine Army withdrew at short notice and he was left without a job. That was the nub of it.'

'And without access to Nato military intelligence? That's what you're telling me.'

'That is my hypothesis.'

'Ah,' said Turner, affecting enlightenment, and wrote laboriously in his notebook *hypothesis* as if the very word were an addition to his vocabulary.

'On the day Rhine Army left, Harting came to see me. That was eighteen months ago, near enough.'

He fell silent, struck by his own recollection.

'He is so *trivial*,' he said at last, in a moment of quite uncharacteristic softness. 'Can't you understand that? So utterly lightweight.' It seemed to surprise him still. 'It's easy to lose sight of now: the sheer insignificance of him.'

'He never will be again,' Turner said carelessly, 'You might as well get used to it.'

'He walked in; he looked pale, that was all; otherwise quite unchanged. He sat down in that chair over there. That is his cushion, by the way.' He permitted himself a small, unloving smile. 'The cushion was a territorial claim. He was the only member of the Chancery who reserved his seat.'

'And the only one who might lose it. Who embroidered it?'

'I really have no idea.'

'Did he have a housekeeper?'

'Not to my knowledge.'

'All right.'

'He didn't say anything at all about his altered situation. They were actually listening to the radio broadcast in Registry, I remember. The regiments were being piped on to the trains.'

'Quite a moment for him, that.'

'I suppose it was. I asked him what I could do for him. Well, he said, he wanted to be useful. It was all very low-key, all very delicate. He'd noticed Miles Gaveston was under strain, what with the Berlin disturbances and the Hanover students and various other pressures: might he not help out? I pointed out to him he was not qualified to handle internal matters; they were the preserve of regular members of Chancery. No, he said, that wasn't what he meant at all. He wouldn't for a minute presume to trespass upon our major effort. But he had been thinking: Gaveston had one or two little jobs; could he not take them over? He had in mind for instance the Anglo-German Society, which was pretty well dormant by then but still entailed a certain amount of low-level correspondence. Then there was Missing Persons: might he not take over a few things of that kind in order to disencumber the busier Chancery officers? It made some sense, I had to admit.'

'So you said yes.'

'I agreed to it. On a purely provisional basis, of course. An interim arrangement. I assumed we would give him notice in

70

December when his contract ran out; until then, he could fill in his time with whatever small jobs he could find. That was the thin end of the wedge. I was no doubt foolish to listen to him.'

'I didn't say that.'

'You don't have to. I gave him an inch; he took the rest. Within a month he had gathered them all in; all the end-clippings of Chancery work, all the dross a big Embassy attracts: Missing Persons, Petitions to the Queen, Unannounced Visitors, Official Tours, the Anglo-German Society, letters of abuse, threats, all the things that should never have come to Chancery in the first place. By the same token, he spread his talents across the social field as well. Chapel, the choir, the Catering Committee, the Sports Committee. He even started up a National Savings group. At some point he asked to be allowed to use the title "Consular" and I consented. We have no Consular duties here, you understand; that all goes up to Cologne.' He shrugged. 'By December he had made himself useful. His contract was brought forward' – he had taken up his fountain pen and was again staring at the nib – 'and I renewed it. I gave him another year.'

'You treated him well,' Turner said, his eyes all the time upon Bradfield. 'You were quite kind to him really.'

'He had no standing here, no security. He was already on the doorstep and he knew it. I suppose that plays a part. We are more inclined to care for the people we can easily get rid of.'

'You were sorry for him. Why won't you admit it? It's a fair enough reason, for God's sake.'

'Yes. Yes I suppose I was. That first time, I was actually sorry for him.' He was smiling, but only at his own stupidity.

'Did he do the work well?'

'He was unorthodox, but not ineffectual. He preferred the telephone to the written word, but that was only natural; he had had no proper instruction in drafting. English was not his native language.' He shrugged. 'I gave him another year,' he said again.

'Which expired last December. Like a licence really. A licence to work; to be one of us.' He continued to watch

Bradfield. 'A licence to spy. And you renewed it a second time.'

'Yes.'

'Why?'

Once more Turner was aware of that hesitation which seemed to signify concealment.

'You weren't sorry for him, were you? Not this time?'

'My feelings are irrelevant.' He put down the pen with a snap. 'The reasons for keeping him on were totally objective.'

'I didn't say they weren't. But you can still be sorry for him.'

'We were understaffed and overworked. The Inspectors had already reduced us by two against my most strenuous advice. The allowances had been halved. Not just Europe was in flux. There were no constants anywhere any more. Rhodesia, Hong Kong, Cyprus. . . . British troops were running from one to the other trying to stamp out a forest fire. We were half-way into Europe and half-way out again. There was talk of a Nordic Federation; God knows what fool gave birth to that idea!' Bradfield declared with utter contempt. 'We were putting out feelers in Warsaw, Copenhagen and Moscow. One minute we were conspiring against the French, the next we were conspiring with them. While that was going on we found the energy to scrap three-quarters of the Navy and nine-tenths of our independent deterrent. It was our worst time; our most humiliating time, and our busiest. To crown everything, Karfeld had just taken over the Movement.'

'So Harting took you through the act again.'

'Not the same act.'

'What do you mean?'

A pause.

'It had more purpose. It had more urgency. I felt it and I did nothing about it. I blame myself. I was conscious of a new mood in him and I did not pursue it.' He continued: 'At the time I put it down to the general state of intensity in which we were all living. I realize now that he was playing his biggest card.'

'Well?'

'He began by saying he still didn't feel he was pulling his

weight. He had had a good year, but he felt he could do more. These were bad days; he would like to feel he was really helping to get things on an even keel. I asked him what he had in mind; I thought he'd just about swept the board by then. He said well, it *was* December – that was the nearest he ever came to referring to his contract – and he had naturally been wondering about the Personalities survey.'

'The what?'

'Biographies of prominent figures in German life. Our own confidential Who's Who. We prepare it every year, each of us takes a hand and contributes something on the German personalities with whom he deals. The Commercial people write about their commercial contacts, the Economists about the economists, the Attachés, Press, Information, they all add their bit. Much of the material is highly unflattering; some of it is derived from secret sources.'

'And Chancery edits?'

'Yes. Once again he had chosen very accurately. It was another of those chores which interfered with our proper duties. It was already overdue. De Lisle, who should have compiled it, was in Berlin; it was becoming a confounded nuisance.'

'So you gave him the job.'

'On a provisional basis, yes.'

'Until the next December, for instance?'

'For instance. It is easy now to think of reasons why he wanted that particular job. The survey provided him with a *laissez-passer* to any part of the Embassy. It runs across the board; it covers the whole range of Federal affairs: industrial, military, administrative. Once charged with the survey, he could call on whomever he liked without questions being asked. He could draw files from any other Registry: Commercial, Economic, Naval, Military, Defence – they all opened their doors to him.'

'And the question of vetting never crossed your mind?'

The self-critical note returned: 'Never.'

'Well we all have our moments,' said Turner quietly. 'And that's how he got his access?'

'There's more to it than that.'

'More? That's just about the lot, isn't it?'

'We not only have archives here; we have a Destruction programme as well. It has been running for years. The purpose is to keep Registry space available for new files and to get rid of old ones we no longer need. It sounds a somewhat academic project and in many ways it is; nevertheless, it happens to be vital. There is a clearly defined economic limit to the amount of paper Registry can handle, and to the amount of paper it will hold. The problem is akin to that of road traffic: we are constantly creating more paper than we can digest. Very naturally, it was another of those jobs we took up and put down as time allowed; it was also an absolute curse. For a while it would be forgotten; then the Office would write and ask for our latest figures.' He shrugged. 'As I say, it's very simple. We can't go on indefinitely, even in a place this size, building up more files than we destroy. Registry's bursting at the seams already.'

'So Harting proposed himself for the task.'

'Precisely.'

'And you agreed.'

'On a provisional basis. He should try his hand and see how it went. He has been working at it off and on for five months. When in doubt, I told him, he was to consult de Lisle. He never did so.'

'Where did he actually do this work? In his room?'

Bradfield barely hesitated. 'In Chancery Registry, where the most sensitive documents are kept. He had the run of the strongroom. He could draw whatever he wanted provided he didn't overplay his hand. There isn't even any record of what he did look at. There are also some letters missing; the Registrar will give you the details.'

Slowly Turner stood up, brushing his hands together as if they had sand on them.

'Of the forty-odd missing files, eighteen are drawn from the Personalities Survey and contain the most sensitive material on high-ranking German politicians. A careful reading would point clearly to our most delicate sources. The rest are Top Secret and cover Anglo-German agreements on a variety of subjects: secret treaties, secret codicils to published agreements. If he wished to embarrass us, he could hardly have chosen better. Some of the files go right back to forty-eight or nine.'

'And the one special file? "Conversations Formal and Informal"?'

'Is what we call a Green. It is subject to special procedures.'

'How many Greens are there in the Embassy?'

'This is the only one. It was in its place in Registry Strong-Room on Thursday morning. The Registrar noticed its absence on Thursday evening and assumed it was in operation. By Saturday morning he was deeply concerned. On Sunday he reported the loss to me.'

'Tell me,' said Turner at last. 'What happened to him during last year? What happened between the two Decembers? Apart from Karfeld.'

'Nothing specific.'

'Then why did you go off him?'

'I didn't,' Bradfield replied with contempt. 'Since I never had any feeling for him either way, the question does not arise. I merely learned during the intervening year to recognize his technique. I saw how he operated on people; how he wheedled his way in. I saw through him, that's all.'

Turner stared at him.

'And what did you see?'

Bradfield's voice was as crisp and as finite and as irreducible as a mathematical formula. 'Deceit. I'd have thought I had made that plain by now.'

Turner got up.

'I'll begin with his room.'

'The Chancery Guard has the keys. They're expecting you. Ask for Macmullen.'

'I want to see his house, his friends, his neighbours; if necessary I'll talk to his foreign contacts. I'll break whatever eggs I've got to, no more no less. If you don't like it, tell the Ambassador. Who's the Registrar?'

'Meadowes.'

'Arthur Meadowes?'

'I believe so.'

Something held him back: a reluctance, a hint of

uncertainty, almost of dependence, a middle tone quite out of character with anything that had gone before.

'Meadowes was in Warsaw, wasn't he?'

'That's correct.'

Louder now: 'And Meadowes has a list of the missing files, has he?'

'And letters.'

'And Harting worked for him, of course.'

'Of course. He is expecting you to call on him.'

'I'll see his room first.' It was a resolution he seemed to have reached already.

'As you wish. You mentioned you would also visit his house—'

'Well?'

'I am afraid that at present it is not possible. It is under police protection since yesterday.'

'Is that general?'

'What?'

'The police protection?'

'Siebkron insists upon it. I cannot quarrel with him now.'

'It applies to all hirings?'

'Principally the more senior ones. I imagine they have included Harting's because it is remote.'

'You don't sound convinced.'

'I cannot think of any other reason.'

'What about Iron Curtain Embassies; did Harting hang around them at all?'

'He went to the Russians occasionally; I cannot say how often.'

'This man Praschko, the friend he had, the politician. You said he used to be a fellow-traveller.'

'That was fifteen years ago.'

'And when did the association end?'

'It's on the file. About five years ago.'

'That's when he had the fight in Cologne. Perhaps it was with Praschko.'

'Anything is possible.'

'One more question.'

'Well?'

76

'That contract he had. If it had expired . . . say last Thursday?'

'Well?'

'Would you have renewed it? Again?'

'We are under great strain. Yes, I would have renewed it.'

'You must miss him.'

The door was opened from the outside by de Lisle. His gentle features were drawn and solemn.

'Ludwig Siebkron rang: the exchange had orders not to put through your calls. I spoke to him myself.'

'Well?'

'About the librarian, Eich: the wretched woman they beat up in Hanover.'

'About her?'

'I'm afraid she died an hour ago.'

Bradfield considered this intelligence in silence. 'Find out where the funeral is. The Ambassador must make a gesture; a telegram to the dependants rather than flowers. Nothing too conspicuous; just his deepest sympathy. Talk to them in Private Office, they'll know the wording. And something from the Anglo–German Society. You'd better handle that yourself. And send a cable to the Association of Assistant Librarians; they were enquiring about her. And ring Hazel will you, and tell her? She asked particularly to be kept informed.'

He was poised and perfectly in control. 'If you require anything,' he added to Turner, 'Tell de Lisle.'

Turner was watching him.

'Otherwise we shall expect you tomorrow night. About five to eight? Germans are very punctual. It is the local custom that we assemble before they arrive. And if you're going down to his room, perhaps you would take that cushion. I see no point in our having it up here.'

Albino Cork, stooped over the cypher machines while he coaxed the strips of print from the rollers, heard the thud and turned his pink eyes sharply towards the large figure in the doorway.

'That's my bag. Leave it where it is; I'll be in later.'

'Righty-ho,' said Cork and thought: a Funny. Just his luck,

with the whole ruddy world blowing up in his face, and Janet's baby due any minute, and that poor woman in Hanover turning up her toes, to be landed with a Funny in the dayroom. This was not his only grudge. The German steel strike was spreading nicely; if he had only thought of it on Friday and not Saturday, that little flutter on Swedish steel would have shown a four-bob capital profit in three days; and five per cent per day, in Cork's losing battle with clerical status, was what villas in the Adriatic were made of. Top Secret, he read wearily, Personal for Bradfield and Decypher Yourself: how much longer will *that* go on? Capri . . . Crete . . . Spetsai . . . Elba . . . *Give me an island to myself*, he sang, in a high-pitched pop improvisation – for Cork had dreams of cutting his own discs as well – *Give me an Island to myself, Any Island, Any Island but Bonn.*

5
John Gaunt

THE CROWD IN the lobby had thinned. The Post Office clock above the sealed lift said ten thirty-five; those who dared not risk a trip to the canteen had gathered at the front desk; the Chancery Guard had made mid-morning tea, and they were drinking it and talking in subdued voices when they heard his approaching footsteps. His heels had metal quarters and they echoed against the pseudo-marble walls like shots on a valley range. The despatch riders, with that nose for authority which soldiers have, gently set down their cups and fastened the buttons of their tunics.

'Macmullen?'

He stood on the lowest step, one hand propped massively on the banister, the other clutching the embroidered cushion. To either side of him, corridors, haunted with iron riot grilles and free-standing pillars of chrome, led into the dark like ghettos from a splendid city. The silence was suddenly important, making a fool of all that had gone before.

'Macmullen's off duty, sir. Gone down to Naafi.'

'Who are you?'

'Gaunt, sir. I'm standing in for him.'

'My name's Turner. I'm checking physical security. I want to see Room Twenty-one.'

Gaunt was a small man, a devout Welshman, with a long memory of the Depression inherited from his father. He had come to Bonn from Cardiff, where he had driven motor-cars for the police. He carried the keys in his right hand, low down by his side, and his gait was square and rather solemn, so that as he preceded Turner into the dark mouth of the corridor, he resembled a miner making for the pithead.

'Shocking really, all what they've been up to,' Gaunt chanted, talking ahead of him and letting the sound carry backwards. 'Peter Aldock, he's my stringer see, he's got a brother in

Hanover, used to be with the Occupation, married a German girl and opened a grocer's shop. Terrified he was for sure: well, he says, they all know my George is English. What'll happen to *him*? Worse than the Congo. Hullo there, Padre!'

The Chaplain sat at a portable typewriter in a small white cell opposite the telephone exchange, beneath a picture of his wife, his door wide open for confession. A rush cross was tucked behind the cord. 'Good morning John then,' he replied in a slightly reproving tone which recalled for both of them the granite intractability of their Welsh God; and Gaunt said, 'Hullo there' again but did not alter his pace. From all around them came the unmistakable sounds of a multi-lingual community: the lonely German drone of the Head Press Reader dictating a translation; the bark of the travel clerk shouting into the telephone; the distant whistling, tuneful and un-English, that seemed to come from everywhere, piped in from other corridors. Turner caught the smell of salami and second breakfasts, of newsprint and disinfectant and he thought: all change at Zurich, you're abroad at last.

'It's mainly the locally-employed down here,' Gaunt explained above the din, 'They aren't allowed no higher, being German.' His sympathy for foreigners was felt but controlled: a nurse's sympathy, tempered by vocation.

A door opened to their left; a shaft of white light broke suddenly upon them, catching the poor plaster of the walls and the tattered green of a bilingual noticeboard. Two girls, about to emerge from Information Registry, drew back to let them by and Turner looked them over mechanically, thinking: This was his world. Second class and foreign. One carried a thermos, the other laboured under a stack of files. Beyond them, through an outer window protected with jeweller's screens, he glimpsed the car park and heard the roar of a motor-bike as a despatch rider drove off. Gaunt had ducked away to the right, down another passage; he stopped, and they were at the door, Gaunt fumbling with the key and Turner staring over his shoulder at the notice which hung from the centre panel: 'Harting Leo, Claims and Consular', a sudden witness to the living man, or a sudden monument to the dead.

The characters of the first two words were a good two inches high, ruled at the edges and cross-hatched in red and green crayon; the word 'Consular' was done a good deal larger, and the letters were outlined in ink to give them that extra substance which the title evidently demanded. Stooping, Turner lightly touched the surface; it was paper mounted on hardboard, and even by that poor light he could make out the faint ruled lines of pencil dictating the upper and lower limits of each letter; defining the borders of a modest existence perhaps; or of a life unnaturally curtailed by deceit. 'Deceit. I'd have thought I'd have made that plain by now.'

'Hurry,' he said.

Gaunt unlocked the door. As Turner seized the handle and shoved it open, he heard his sister's voice on the telephone again and his own reply as he slammed down the receiver: 'Tell her I've left the country.' The windows were closed. The heat struck up at· them from the linoleum. There was a stink of rubber and wax. One curtain was slightly drawn. Gaunt reached out to pull it back.

'Leave it. Keep away from the window. And stay there. If anyone comes, tell them to get out.' He tossed the embroidered cushion on to a chair and peered round the room.

The desk had chrome handles; it was better than Bradfield's desk. The calendar on the wall advertised a firm of Dutch diplomatic importers. Turner moved very lightly, for all his bulk, examining but never touching. An old army map hung on the wall, divided into the original zones of military occupation. The British was marked in bright green, a fertile patch among the foreign deserts. It's like a prison cell, he thought, maximum security; maybe it's just the bars. What a place to break out of, and who wouldn't? The smell was foreign but he couldn't place it.

'Well, I *am* surprised,' Gaunt was saying. 'There's a lot gone I must say.'

Turner did not look at him.

'Such as what?'

'I don't know. Gadgets, All sorts. This is Mr Harting's room,' he explained. 'Very gadget-minded, Mr Harting is.'

'What sort of gadgets?'

'Well he had a *tea* machine, you know the kind that wakes

you up? Made a lovely cup of tea, that did. Pity that's gone, really.'

'What else?'

'A fire. The new fan type with the two bars over. And a lamp. A smashing one, Japanese. Go all directions, that lamp would. Turn it half-way and it burned *soft*. Very cheap to run as well, he told me. But I wouldn't have one, you know, not now they've cut the allowances. Still,' he continued consolingly, 'I expect he's taken them home, don't you, if that's where he's gone.'

'Yes. Yes, I expect he has.'

On the window-sill stood a transistor radio. Stooping until his eyes were on a level with the panel, Turner switched it on. At once they heard the mawkish tones of a British Forces announcer commenting on the Hanover riots and the prospects for a British victory in Brussels. Slowly Turner rolled the tuning needle along the lighted band, his ear cocked all the time to the changing babel of French, German and Dutch.

'I thought you said physical security.'

'I did.'

'You haven't hardly looked at the windows. Or the locks.'

'I will, I will.' He had found a Slav voice and he was listening with deep concentration. 'Know him well, did you? Come in here often for a cup?'

'Quite. Depends on how busy, really.'

Switching off the radio, Turner stood up. 'Wait outside,' he said. 'And give me the keys.'

'What's he done then?' Gaunt demanded, hesitating. 'What's gone wrong?'

'Done? Nothing. He's on compassionate leave. I want to be alone, that's all.'

'They say he's in trouble.'

'Who?'

'Talkers.'

'What sort of trouble?'

'I don't know. Car smash maybe. He wasn't at choir practice, see. Nor Chapel.'

'Does he drive badly?'

'Can't say really.'

Part defiant, part curious, Gaunt stayed by the door, watching as Turner pulled open the wooden wardrobe and peered inside. Three hair-dryers, still in their boxes, lay on the floor beside a pair of rubber overshoes.

'You're a friend of his, aren't you?'

'Not really. Only from choir, see.'

'Ah,' said Turner, staring at him now. 'You sang for him. I used to sing in choir myself.'

'Oh really now, where's that then?'

'Yorkshire,' Turner said with awful friendliness, while his pale gaze continued to fix upon Gaunt's plain face. 'I hear he's a lovely organist.'

'Not at all bad, I will say,' Gaunt agreed, rashly recognizing a common interest.

'Who's his *special* friend; someone else in the choir, was it? A lady perhaps?' Turner enquired, still not far from piety.

'He's not close to anyone, Leo.'

'Then who does he buy these for?'

The hair-dryers were of varying quality and complexity; the prices on the box ran from eighty to two hundred marks. 'Who for?' he repeated.

'All of us. Dips, non dips; it didn't signify. He runs a service see; works the diplomatic discounts. Always do you a favour Leo will. Don't matter what you fancy: radios, dishwashers, cars; he'll get you a bit off, like; you know.'

'Knows his way round, does he?'

'That's right.'

'Takes a cut too, I expect. For his trouble,' Turner suggested coaxingly. 'Quite right too.'

'I didn't say so.'

'Do you a girl as well, would he? Mister Fixit, is that it?'

'Certainly not,' said Gaunt, much shocked.

'What was in it for him?'

'Nothing. Not that I know of.'

'Just a little friend of all the world, eh? Likes to be liked. Is that it?'

'Well, we all do really, don't we?'

'Philosopher, are we?'

'Always *willing*,' Gaunt continued, very slow to follow the changes in Turner's mood. 'You ask Arthur Meadowes now, there's an example. The moment Leo's in Registry, not hardly a day after, he's down here collecting the mail. "Don't you bother," he says to Arthur. "Save your legs, you're not so young as you were and you've plenty to worry about already. I'll fetch it for you, look." That's Leo. Obliging. Saintly really, considering his disadvantages.'

'What mail?'

'Everything. Classified or Unclassified, it didn't make no difference. He'd be down here signing for it, taking it up to Arthur.'

Very still, Turner said, 'Yes, I see that. And maybe he'd drop in here on the way, would he? Check on his own room; brew up a cup of tea.'

'That's it,' said Gaunt, 'Always ready to oblige.' He opened the door. 'Well, I'll be leaving you to it.'

'You stay here,' said Turner, still watching him. 'You'll be all right. You stay and talk to me, Gaunt. I like company. Tell me about his disadvantages.'

Returning the hair-dryers to their boxes, he pulled out a linen jacket, still on its hanger. A summer jacket; the kind that barmen wear. A dead rose hung from the buttonhole.

'What disadvantages?' he asked, throwing the rose into the waste bag. 'You can tell me, Gaunt,' and he noticed the smell again, the wardrobe smell he had caught but not defined, the sweet, familiar, continental smell of male unguents and cigar.

'Only his childhood, that's all. He had an uncle.'

'Tell me about the uncle.'

'Nothing; only how he was daft. Always changing politics. He had a lovely way of narrative, Leo did. Told us how he used to sit down in the cellar in Hampstead with his uncle while the bombs were falling, making pills in a machine. Dried fruit. Squashed them all up and rolled them in sugar, then put them in the tins, see. Used to spit on them, Leo did, just to spite his uncle. My wife was very shocked when she heard that – I said don't be silly, that's deprivation. He hasn't had the love, see, not what you've had.'

Having felt the pockets, Turner cautiously detached the

84

jacket from the hanger and held the shoulders against his own substantial frame.

'Little bloke?'

'He's a keen dresser,' said Gaunt, 'Always well turned out, Leo is.'

'Your size?'

Turner held the jacket towards him, but Gaunt drew back in distaste.

'Smaller,' he said, his eyes still on the jacket. 'More the dancer type. Butterfly. You'd think he wore pumps all the time.'

'Pansy?'

'Certainly not,' said Gaunt, very shocked again, and colouring at the notion.

'How do you know?'

'He's a decent fellow, that's why,' said Gaunt, fiercely. 'Even if he has done something wrong.'

'Pious?'

'Respectful, very. And about religion. Never cheeky or brash, although he was foreign.'

'What else did he say about his uncle?'

'Nothing.'

'What else about his politics?' He was looking at the desk, examining the locks on the drawers.

Tossing the jacket on to a chair, he held out his hand for the keys. Reluctantly Gaunt released them.

'Nothing. I don't know nothing about his politics.'

'Who says anything about him doing something wrong?'

'You. All this hunting him. Measuring him; I don't fancy it.'

'What would he have done, I wonder? To make me hunt him like this?'

'God only knows.'

'In his wisdom.' He had opened the top drawers. 'Have you got a diary like this?'

It was bound in blue rexine and stamped in gold with the Royal crest.

'No.'

'Poor Gaunt. Too humble?' He was turning the pages,

working back. Once he stopped and frowned; once he wrote something in his black notebook.

'It was Counsellors and above, that's why,' Gaunt retorted. 'I wouldn't accept it.'

'He offered you one, did he? That was another of his fiddles, I suppose. What happened? He scrounged a bundle did he, from Registry, and handed them out to his old chums on the Ground Floor. "Here you are boys: the streets are paved with gold up there. Here's a keepsake from your old winger." Is that the way of it, Gaunt? And Christian virtue held you back, did it?' Closing the diary, he pulled open the lower drawers.

'What if he did? You've no call to go rifling through his desk there, have you? Not for a little thing like that! Pinching a handful of diaries; well that's hardly all the world, is it?' His Welsh accent had jumped all the hurdles and was running free.

'You're a Christian man, Gaunt. You know how the devil works better than I do. Little things lead to big things, don't they? Pinch an apple one day, you'll be hi-jacking a lorry the next. *You* know the way it goes, Gaunt. What else did he tell you about himself? Any more little childhood reminiscences?'

He had found a paper knife, a slim, silver affair with a broad, flat handle, and he was reading the engraving by the desk lamp.

'L.H. from Margaret. Now who was Margaret, I wonder?'
'I never heard of her.'
'He was engaged to be married once, did you know that?'
'No.'
'Miss Aickman. Margaret Aickman. Ring a bell?'
'No.'
'How about the Army. Did he tell you about that?'
'He loved the Army. In Berlin, he said, he used to watch the cavalry going over the jumps. He loved it.'
'He was in the infantry, was he?'
'I don't really know.'
'No.'
Turner had put the knife aside, next to the blue diary, made another note in his pocket-book and picked up a small flat tin of Dutch cigars.

'Smoker?'

'He liked a cigar. Yes. That's all he smoked, see. Always *carried* cigarettes mind. But I only ever saw him smoke those things. There was one or two in Chancery complained, so I hear. About the cigars. Didn't fancy them. But Leo could be stubborn when he had the mind, I will say.'

'How long have you been here, Gaunt?'

'Five years.'

'He was in a fight in Cologne. That in your time?'

Gaunt hesitated.

'Amazing the way things are hushed up here, I must say. You give a new meaning to the "need to know", you do. Everyone knows except the people who need to. What happened?'

'It was just a fight. They say he asked for it, that's all.'

'How?'

'I don't know. They say he deserved it, see. I heard from my predecessor: they brought him back one night, you couldn't hardly recognize him, that's what he said. Serve him right, he said; that's what they told him. Mind you, he could be pugnacious, I'm not denying it.'

'Who? Who told him?'

'I don't know. I didn't ask. That would be prying.'

'Often fighting, is he?'

'No.'

'Was there a woman involved? Margaret Aickman perhaps?'

'I don't know.'

'Then why's he pugnacious?'

'I don't know,' Gaunt said, torn once more between suspicion and a native passion for communication. 'Why are you then for that matter?' he muttered, venturing aggression, but Turner ignored him.

'That's right. Never pry. Never tell on a friend. God wouldn't like it. I admire a man who sticks to his principles.'

'I don't care what he's done,' Gaunt continued, gathering courage as he went. 'He wasn't a bad man. He was a bit sharp maybe, but so he would be, being continental, we all know that.' He pointed to the desk and the open drawers. 'But he wasn't bad like this.'

'No one is. Know that? No one's ever this bad. That's what

mercy's about. We're all lovely people, really. There's a hymn about that, isn't there? One of the hymns he used to play, and you and I used to sing, Gaunt, before we grew up and got elegant. That's a lovely thing about hymns: we never forget them, do we. Like limericks. God knew a thing or two when he invented rhyme I will say. What did he learn when he was a kid, tell me that? What did Leo learn on his uncle's knee, eh?'

'He could speak Italian,' Gaunt said suddenly, as if it were a trump card he had been holding back.

'He could, could he?'

'And he learnt it in England. At the Farm School. The other kids wouldn't speak to him, see, him being German, so he used to go out on a bicycle and talk to the Italian prisoners of war. And he's never forgotten it, never. He's got a lovely memory, I tell you. Never forgets a word you say to him, I'm sure.'

'Wonderful.'

'A real brain he could have been, if he'd had your advantages.'

Turner looked at him blankly. 'Who the hell says I've got any advantages?'

He had opened another drawer; it was filled with the small junk of any private life in any office: a stapler, pencils, elastic bands, foreign coins and used railway tickets.

'How often was choir, Gaunt? Once a week, was it? You'd have a nice sing-song and a prayer and afterwards you'd slip out and have a beer down the road, and he'd tell you all about himself. Then there was outings, I suppose. Coach trips, I expect. That's what we like, isn't it, you and I? Something corporate but spiritual. Coaches, institutions, choirs. And Leo came along, did he? Got to know everyone, hear their little confidences, hold their little hands. Quite the entertainer he must have been by the sound of it.'

All the while they spoke, he continued to record items in his notebook: sewing materials, a packet of needles, pills of different colours and descriptions. Fascinated despite himself, Gaunt drew nearer.

'Well not only that, see. Only I live on the top floor, there's a flat up there: it should have been Macmullen's but he can't occupy, him having too many children, they couldn't have *them* running wild up there now, could they? We practised in the Assembly Room first, Fridays, see, that's on the other side of the lobby next to the pay office, and then he'd come on up after, for a cup of tea, like. Well, you know, I had a few cups here too for that matter; quite a joy to pay back it was, after all he done for us; things he bought for us and that. He loved a cup of tea,' said Gaunt simply. 'He loved a fire too. I always had that feeling, he loved a family, him not having one.'

'He told you that, did he? He told you he'd no family?'

'No.'

'Then how do you know?'

'It was too evident to be talked about, really. He'd no education either; dragged up really, you could tell.'

Turner had found a bottle of long yellow pills and he was shaking them into the palm of his hand, sniffing cautiously at them.

'And that's been going on for years, has it? Cosy chats after practice?'

'Oh no. He didn't hardly notice me really, not till a few months ago and I didn't like to press him at all, him being a dip, see. It's only recently he took the interest. Same as Exiles.'

'Exiles?'

'Motoring Club.'

'How recent? When did he take you up?'

'New Year,' Gaunt said, now very puzzled. 'Yes. Since January I'd say. He seems to have had a change of heart January.'

'This January?'

'That's right,' Gaunt said, as if he were seeing it for the first time. 'Late January. Since he started with Arthur, really. Arthur's had a *great* influence on Leo. Made him more *contemplative*, you know. More the meditating kind. A great improvement, I'd say. And my wife agrees, you know.'

'I'll bet. How else did he change?'

'That's it really. More reflective.'

'Since January when he took you up. Bang: in comes the New Year and Leo's reflective.'

'Well, steadier. Like he was ill. We did wonder, you know. I said to my wife' – Gaunt lowered his voice in reverence at the notion – 'I wouldn't be surprised if the doctor hadn't warned him.'

Turner was looking at the map again, first directly and then sideways, noting the pin-holes of vanished units. In an old bookcase lay a heap of census reports, press cuttings and magazines. Kneeling, he began working through them.

'What else did you talk about?'

'Nothing serious.'

'Just politics?'

'I like serious conversation myself,' Gaunt said. 'But I didn't somehow fancy it with him, you didn't quite know where it would end.'

'Lost his temper, did he?'

The cuttings referred to the Movement. The census reports concerned the rise of public support for Karfeld.

'He was too gentle. Like a woman in that way; you could disappoint him dreadfully; just a word would do it. Vulnerable he was. *And* quiet. That's what I did never understand about Cologne, see. I said to my wife, well I don't know I'm sure, but if Leo started that fight, it was the devil got hold of him. But he had *seen* a lot, hadn't he?'

Turner had come upon a photograph of students rioting in Berlin. Two boys were holding an old man by the arms and a third was slapping him with the back of his hand. His fingers were turned upwards, and the light divided the knuckles like a sculpture. A line had been drawn round the frame in red ball point.

'I mean you never knew when you were being *personal*, like,' Gaunt continued, 'Touching him too near. I used to think sometimes, I said to my wife as a matter of fact, she was never quite at home with him herself, I said, "Well, I wouldn't like to have his dreams."'

Turner stood up. 'What dreams?'

'Just dreams. Things he's seen, I suppose. They say he saw a lot, don't they? All the atrocities.'

'Who does?'

'Talkers. One of the drivers, I think. Marcus. He's gone now. He had a turn with him up there in Hamburg in forty-six or that. Shocking.'

90

Turner had opened an old copy of *Stern* which lay on the bookcase. Large photographs of the Bremen riots covered both pages. There was a picture of Karfeld speaking from a high wooden platform; young men shouted in ecstasy.

'I think that bothered him you know,' Gaunt continued, looking over his shoulder. 'He spoke a lot about Fascism off and on.'

'Did he though?' Turner asked softly, 'Tell us about that, Gaunt. I'm interested in talk like that.'

'Well, just sometimes.' Gaunt sounded nervous. 'He could get very worked up about that. It could happen again, he said, and the West would just stand by; and the bankers all put in a bit, and that would be it. He said Socialist and Conservative, it didn't have no meaning any more, not when all the decisions were made in Zurich or Washington. You could see that, he said, from recent events. Well it was true really, I had to admit.'

For a moment, the whole sound-track stopped: the traffic, the machines, the voices, and Turner heard nothing but the beating of his own heart.

'What was the remedy then?' he asked softly.

'He didn't have one.'

'Personal action for instance?'

'He didn't say so.'

'God?'

'No, he wasn't a believer. Not truly, in his heart.'

'Conscience?'

'I told you. He didn't say.'

'He never suggested you might put the balance right? You and he together?'

'He wasn't *like* that,' Gaunt said impatiently. 'He didn't fancy company. Not when it came to . . . well, to his own *matters*, see.'

'Why didn't your wife fancy him?'

Gaunt hesitated.

'She liked to keep close to me when he was around, that's all. Nothing he ever said or did, mind; but she just liked to keep close.' He smiled indulgently. 'You know how they are,' he said. 'Very *natural*.'

'Did he stay long? Did he sit and talk for hours at a time? About nothing? Ogling your wife?'

'Don't say that,' Gaunt snapped.

Abandoning the desk, Turner opened the cupboard again and noted the printed number on the soles of the rubber overshoes.

'Besides he didn't stay long. He liked to go off and work night times, didn't he? Recently I mean. In Registry and that. He said to me: "John," he said, "I like to make my contribution." And he did. He was proud of his work these last months. It was beautiful; wonderful to see, really. Work half the night sometimes, wouldn't he? All night, even.'

Turner's pale, pale eyes rested on Gaunt's dark face.

'Would he?'

He dropped the shoes back into the cupboard and they clattered absurdly in the silence.

'Well he'd a lot to do, you know; a great lot. Loaded with responsibilities, Leo is. A fine man, really. Too good for this floor; that's what I say.'

'And that's what happened every Friday night since January. After choir. He'd come up and have a nice cup of tea and a chat, hang about till the place was quiet, then slip off and work in Registry?'

'Regular as clockwork. Come in prepared, he would. Choir practice first, then up for a cup of tea till the rest had cleared out like, then down to Registry. "John," he'd say. "I can't work when there's bustle, I can't stand it, I love peace and quiet to be truthful. I'm not as young as I was and that's a fact." Had a bag with him, all ready. Thermos, maybe a sandwich. Very efficient man, he was; handy.'

'Sign the night book, did he?'

Gaunt faltered, waking at long last to the full menace in that quiet, destructive monotone. Turner slammed together the wooden doors of the cupboard. 'Or didn't you bloody well bother? Well, not right really, is it? You can't come over all official, not to a guest. A dip too, at that, a dip who graced your parlour. Let him come and go as he pleased in the middle of the bloody night, didn't you? Wouldn't have been respectful to check up at all, would it? One of the family really, wasn't he?

92

Pity to spoil it with formalities. Wouldn't be Christian, that wouldn't. No idea what time he left the building, I suppose? Two o'clock, four o'clock?'

Gaunt had to keep very still to catch the words, they were so softly spoken.

'It's nothing *bad*, is it?' he asked.

'And that bag of his,' Turner continued in the same terribly low key. 'It wouldn't have been proper to look inside, I suppose? Open the thermos, for instance. The Lord wouldn't fancy that, would he? Don't you worry, Gaunt, it's nothing bad. Nothing that a prayer and a cup of tea won't cure.' He was at the door and Gaunt had to watch him. 'You were just playing happy families, weren't you; letting him stroke your leg to make you feel good.' His voice picked up the Welsh intonation and lampooned it cruelly. "Look how virtuous we are. . . . How much in love. . . . Look how grand, having the dips in. . . . Salt of the earth, we are. . . . Always something on the hod. . . . And sorry you can't have her, but that's my privilege." Well, you've bought it, Gaunt, the whole book. A guard they called you: he'd have charmed you into bed for half-a-crown.' He pushed open the door. 'He's on compassionate leave, and don't you forget it or you'll be in hotter water than you are already.'

'That may be the world you've come from,' Gaunt said suddenly, staring at him as if in revelation, 'But it isn't mine, Mr Turner, so don't come taking it out of me, see. I did my best by Leo and I would again, and I don't know what's all twisted in your mind. Poison, that's what it is: poison.'

'Go to hell.' Turner tossed him the keys, and Gaunt let them fall at his feet.

'If there's something else you know about him, some other gorgeous bit of gossip, you'd better tell me now. Fast. Well?'

Gaunt shook his head. 'Go away.'

'What else do the talkers say? A bit of fluff in the choir was there, Gaunt? You can tell me, I won't eat you.'

'I never heard.'

'What did Bradfield think of him?'

'How should I know? Ask Bradfield.'

93

'Did he like him?'

Gaunt's face had darkened with disapproval.

'I've no occasion to say,' he snapped. 'I don't gossip about my superiors.'

'Who's Praschko? Praschko a name to you?'

'There's nothing else. I don't know.'

Turner pointed at the small pile of Leo's possessions on the desk. 'Take those up to the cypher room. I'll need them later. And the press cuttings. Give them to the clerk and make him sign for them, understand? Whether you fancy him or not. And make a list of everything that's missing. Everything he's taken home.'

He did not go immediately to Meadowes, but went outside and stood on the grass verge beside the car park. A veil of mist hung over the barren field and the traffic stormed like an angry sea. The Red Cross building was dark with scaffolding and capped by an orange crane: an oil rig anchored to the tarmac. The policemen watched him curiously, for he remained quite still and his eyes seemed to be trained upon the horizon, though the horizon was obscure. At last – it might have been in response to a command they did not hear – he turned and walked slowly back to the front steps.

'You ought to get a proper pass,' the weasel-faced sergeant said, 'Coming in and out all day.'

Registry smelt of dust and sealing wax and printer's ink. Meadowes was waiting for him. He looked haggard and deeply tired. He did not move as Turner came towards him, pushing his way between the desks and files, but watched him dully and with contempt.

'Why did they have to send you?' he asked. 'Haven't they got anyone else? Who are you going to wreck this time?'

6

The Memory Man

THEY STOOD IN a small sanctum, a steel-lined tank which served both as a strong-room and an office. The windows were barred twice over, once with fine mesh and once with steel rods. From the adjoining room came the constant shuffle of feet and paper. Meadowes wore a black suit. The edges of the lapels were studded with pins. Steel lockers like sentinels stood along the walls, each with a stencilled number and a combination lock.

'Of all the people I swore I'd never see again—'

'Turner was at the top of the list. All right. All right, you're not the only one. Let's get it over, shall we?'

They sat down.

'She doesn't know you're here,' said Meadowes. 'I'm not going to tell her you're here.'

'All right.'

'He met her a few times; there was nothing between them.'

'I'll keep away from her.'

'Yes,' said Meadowes. He did not speak to Turner, but past him, at the lockers. 'Yes, you must.'

'Try and forget it's me,' Turner said. 'Take your time.' For a moment his expression seemed to yield, as the shadows formed upon his plain complexion, until in its way his face was as old as Meadowes', and as weary.

'I'll tell it you once,' Meadowes said, 'And that's all. I'll tell you all I know, and then you clear out.'

Turner nodded.

'It began with the Exiles Motoring Club,' Meadowes said. 'That's how I met him really. I like cars, always have done. I'd bought a Rover, Three Litre, for retirement—'

'How long have you been here?'

'A year. Yes, a year now.'

'Straight from Warsaw?'

'We did a spell in London in between. Then they sent me here. I was fifty-eight. I'd two more years to run and after Warsaw I reckoned I'd take things quietly. I wanted to look after her, get her right again—'

'All right.'

'I don't go out much as a rule but I joined this club, UK and Commonwealth it is mainly, but decent. I reckoned that would do us nicely: one evening a week, the rallies in the summer, get-togethers in the winter. I could take Myra, see; get her back into things, keep an eye on her. She wanted that herself, in the beginning. She was lost; she wanted company. I'm all she's got.'

'All right,' Turner said.

'They were a good lot when we joined, though it's like any other club, of course, it goes up and down; depends who runs it. Get a good crowd in and you have a lot of fun; get a bad crowd, there's jiving and all the rest.'

'And Harting was big there, was he?'

'You let me go at my own speed, right?' Meadowes' manner was firm and disapproving: a father corrects his son. 'No. He was not big there, not at that time. He was a member there, that's all, just a member. I shouldn't think he showed up, not once in six meetings. Well he didn't *belong* really. After all he was a diplomat, and the Exiles isn't meant for dips. Mid-November, we have the Annual General Meeting. Haven't you got your black notebook then?'

'November,' Turner said, not moving, 'The AGM. Five months ago.'

'It was a funny sort of do really. Funny atmosphere. Karfeld had been on the go about six weeks and we were all wondering what would happen next, I think. Freddie Luxton was in the chair and he was just off to Nairobi; Bill Aintree was Social Secretary and they'd warned him for Korea, and the rest of us were in a flutter trying to elect new officers, get through the agenda and fix up the winter outing. That's when Leo pipes up, and in a way that was his first step into Registry.'

Meadowes fell silent. 'I don't know what kind of fool I am,' he said. 'I just don't know.'

Turner waited.

'I tell you: we'd never *heard* of him, not really, not as somebody keen on the Exiles. And he had this reputation you see—'

'What reputation?'

'Well, they said he was a bit of a gypsy. Always on the fiddle. There was some story about Cologne. I didn't fancy what I'd heard, to be frank, and I didn't want him mixed up with Myra.'

'What story about Cologne?'

'Hearsay, that's all it is. He was in a fight. A night-club brawl.'

'No details?'

'None.'

'Who else was there?'

'I've no idea. Where was I?'

'The Exiles, AGM.'

'The winter outing. Yes. "Right," says Bill Aintree. "Any suggestions from the floor?" And Leo's on his feet straight away. He was about three chairs down from me. I said to Myra: "Here, what's *he* up to?" Well, Leo had a proposal, he said. For the winter outing. He knew an old man in Königswinter who owned a string of barges, very rich and very fond of the English, he said; quite high in the Anglo-German. And this old fellow had agreed to lend us two barges and two crews to run the whole club up to Koblenz and back. As some kind of *quid pro quo* for a favour the British had done him in the Occupation. Leo always knew people like that,' said Meadowes; and a brief smile of affection illuminated the sadness of his features. 'There'd be covered accommodation, rum and coffee on the way and a big lunch when we got to Koblenz. Leo had worked the whole thing out; he reckoned he could lay it on at twenty-one marks eighty a head including drinks and a present for his friend.' He broke off. 'I can't go any quicker, it's not my way.'

'I didn't say anything.'

'You're pressing all the time, I can feel it,' Meadowes said querulously, and sighed. 'They fell for it, we all did, Committee or not. You know what people are like: if one man knows what he wants . . .'

'And he did.'

'I suppose some reckoned he'd got an axe to grind, but no one cared. There was a few of us thought he was taking a cut to be honest, but well, maybe he deserved it. And the price was fair enough any time. Bill Aintree was getting out: *he* didn't care; he proposed it. Freddie Luxton was already packed: *he* didn't care. He seconded. The motion's carried and recorded without a word being said against, and as soon as the meeting's over, Leo comes straight across to me and Myra, smiling his head off. "She'll love that," he says, "Myra will. A nice trip on the river. Take her out of herself." Just as if he'd done it specially for her. I said yes, she would, and bought him a drink. It seemed wrong really, him doing so much and no one else paying him a blind bit of notice, whatever they say about him. I was sorry for him. *And* grateful,' he added simply. 'I still am: we had a lovely outing.'

Again he fell silent, and again Turner waited while the older man wrestled with private conflicts and private perplexities. From the barred window came the tireless throb of Bonn's iron heartbeat: the far thunder of drills and cranes, the moan of vainly galloping cars.

'I thought he was after Myra to be honest,' he said at last. 'I watched out for that, I don't mind admitting. But there wasn't a breath of it, not on either side. Goodness knows, I'm sharp enough on *that* after Warsaw.'

'I believe you.'

'I don't care whether you believe me or not. It's the truth.'

'He had a reputation for that as well, did he?'

'A bit.'

'Who with?'

'I'll go on with the story if you don't mind,' Meadowes said, looking at his hands. 'I'm not going to pass on that kind of muck. Least of all to you. There's more nonsense talked in this place than is good for any of us.'

'I'll find out,' Turner said, his face frozen like a dead man's. 'It'll take me longer, but that needn't worry you.'

'Dreadfully cold, it was,' Meadowes continued. 'Lumps of ice on the water, and beautiful, if that means anything to you. Just like Leo said: rum and coffee for the grown ups, cocoa for the kids, and everyone happy as a cricket. We started from Königs-winter and kicked off with a drink at his place before we went aboard, and from the moment we get there, Leo's looking after us. Me and Myra. He'd singled us out and that was it. We might have been the only people there for him. Myra loved it. He put a shawl round her shoulders, told her jokes. . . . I hadn't seen her laugh like it since Warsaw. She kept saying to me: "I haven't been so happy for years." '

'What sort of jokes?'

'About himself mainly . . . running on. He had a story about Berlin, him shoving a cartload of files across the parade ground in the middle of a cavalry practice, and the sergeant-major on his horse, and Leo down there with the handcart. . . . He could do all the voices, Leo could; one minute he was up on his horse, the next minute he's the Guard corporal. . . . He could even do the trumpets and that. Wonderful really; wonderful gift. Very entertaining man, Leo . . . very.'

He glanced at Turner as if he expected to be contradicted, but Turner's face was without expression. 'On the way back, he takes me aside. "Arthur, a quiet word," he says; that's him, a quiet word. You know the way he talks.'

'No.'

'Confiding. Everyone's special. "Arthur," he says, "Rawley Bradfield's just sent for me; they want me to move up to Registry and give you a hand up there, and before I tell him yes or no, I'd like to hear what *you* feel." Putting it in my hands, you see. If I didn't fancy the idea, he'd head it off; that's what he was hinting at. Well it came as a surprise, I don't mind telling you. I didn't quite know what to think; after all he was a Second Secretary . . . it didn't seem right, that was my first reaction. And to be frank I wasn't sure I believed him. So I asked him: "Have you any experience of archives?" Yes, but long ago, he said, though he'd always fancied going back to them.'

'When was that then?'

'When was what?'

When was he dealing with archives?'

'Berlin I suppose. I never asked. You didn't ask Leo about his background really; you never knew what you might hear.'

99

Meadowes shook his head. 'So here he was with this suggestion. It didn't seem right, but what could I say? "It's up to Bradfield," I told him. "If he sends you, and you want to come, there's work enough." Well it worried me for a bit to be honest. I even thought of talking to Bradfield about it but I didn't. Best thing is, I thought, let it blow over; I'll probably hear no more of it. For a time that's just what happened. Myra was bad again, there was the leadership crisis at home and the gold row in Brussels. And as for Karfeld, he was going hammer and tongs all over the place. There were deputations out from England, Trade Union protests, old comrades and I don't know what. Registry was a beehive, and Harting went clean out of my mind. He was Social Secretary of the Exiles by then, but otherwise I hardly saw him. I mean he didn't rate. There was too much else to think of.'

'I get it.'

'The next thing I knew was, Bradfield sends for me. It was just before the holiday – about 20th December. First, he asks me how I'm getting along with the Destruction programme. I was a bit put out; we'd really been going it those last months. Destruction was about the last thing anyone had been bothering with.'

'Go carefully now: I want the fat as well as the lean.'

'I said it was hanging fire. Well, he says, how would I feel if he sent me someone to help out with it, come and work in Registry and bring it up to date? There'd been the suggestion, he said, nothing definite, and he wanted to sound me out first, there'd been the suggestion Harting might be able to lend a hand.'

'Whose suggestion?'

'He didn't say.'

It was suddenly upon them; and each in his way was mystified:

'Whoever suggested anything to Bradfield,' Meadowes asked. 'It makes no sense.'

'That's rather what I wondered,' Turner confessed, and the silence returned.

'So you said you'd have him?'

'No, I told him the truth. I said I didn't need him.'

'You didn't *need* him? You told Bradfield that?'

'Don't press me like that. Bradfield knew very well I didn't need anyone. Not for Destruction anyway. I'd been on to Library in London and spoken to them, back in November that was, once the Karfeld panic began. I'd told them I was worried about the programme, I was way behind, could I let it go till the crisis was over? Library told me to forget it.'

Turner stared at him.

'And Bradfield knew that? You're certain Bradfield knew?'

'I'd sent him a minute of the conversation. He never even referred to it. Afterwards I asked that PA of his and she was certain she'd put it up to him.'

'Where is it? Where's the minute now?'

'Gone. It was a loose minute: it was Bradfield's responsibility whether he preserved it or not. But they'll know about it in Library all right; they were quite surprised later on to find we'd bothered with Destruction at all.'

'Who did you speak to in Library?'

'Once to Maxwell, once to Cowdry.'

'Did you remind Bradfield of that?'

'I began to, but he just cut me off. Closed right down on me. "It's all arranged," he says. "Harting's joining you mid-January and he'll manage Personalities and Destruction." So lump it, in other words. "You can forget he's a diplomat," he said. "Treat him as your subordinate. Treat him how you like. But he's coming mid-January and that's a fact." You know how he throws people away. Specially Harting.'

Turner was writing in his notebook but Meadowes paid no attention.

'So that's how he came to me. That's the truth. I didn't want him, I didn't trust him, not completely anyway, and to begin with I suppose I let him know it. We were just too busy: *I* didn't want to waste time breaking in a man like Leo. What was I supposed to do with him?'

A girl brought tea. A brown woolly cosy covered the pot and the cubes of sugar were individually wrapped and stamped with the Naafi's insignia. Turner grinned at her but she ignored him. He could hear someone shouting about Hanover.

'They do say things are bad in England too,' Meadowes said.

'Violence; demonstrations; all the protests. What is it that gets into your generation? What have we *done* to you? That's what I don't understand.'

'We'll start with when he arrived,' Turner said. That's what it would be like, he thought, to have a father you believed in: values for their own sake and a gap as wide as the Atlantic.

'I said to Leo when he came, "Leo, just keep out of the way. Don't get between my feet, and don't go bothering other people." He took it like a lamb. "Right-ho Arthur, whatever you say." I asked him whether he'd got something to get on with. Yes, he said, Personalities would keep him going for a bit.'

'It's like a dream,' Turner said softly looking up at last from his notebook. 'It's a lovely dream. First of all he takes over the Exiles. A one man takeover, real Party tactics; I'll do the dirty work, you go back to sleep. Then he cons you, then he cons Bradfield, and within a couple of months he's got the pick of Registry. How was he? Cocky? I should think he could hardly stand up for laughing.'

'He was quiet. Not cocky at all. Subdued I'd say. Not at all what they told me he was like.'

'Who?'

'Oh . . . I don't know. There's a lot didn't like him; there's a lot more were jealous of him.'

'Jealous?'

'Well, he was a diplomat, wasn't he. Even if he was a temporary. They said he'd be running the place in a fortnight, taking ten per cent on the files. You know the way they talk. But he'd changed. They all admitted that, even young Cork and Johnny Slingo. You could almost date it, they said, from when the crisis began. It sobered him down.' Meadowes shook his head as if he hated to see a good man go wrong. 'And he was useful.'

'Don't tell me. He took you by surprise.'

'I don't know how he managed it. He knew nothing about archives, not our kind anyway; and I can't for the life of me see how he got near enough to anyone in Registry to ask; but by mid-February, that Personalities Survey was drafted, signed off and away, and the Destruction programme was back on the rails. We were working all round him: Karfeld, Brussels, the Coalition crisis and the rest of it. And there was Leo, still as a rock, working away at his own bits and pieces. No one told him anything twice, I think that was half the secret. He'd a lovely memory. He'd scrounge a bit of information, tuck it away, and bring it out weeks later when you'd forgotten all about it. I don't think he forgot a word anyone ever said to him. He could listen with his eyes, Leo could.' Meadowes shook his head at the reminiscence: 'The memory man, that's what Johnny Slingo used to call him.'

'Handy. For an archivist of course.'

'You see it all differently,' Meadowes said at last. 'You can't distinguish the good from the bad.'

'You tell me when I go wrong,' Turner replied, writing all the time. 'I'll be grateful for that. Very.'

'Destruction's a weird game,' Meadowes said, in the reflective tone of a man reviewing his own craft. 'To begin with, you'd think it was simple. You select a file, a big one, say a subject file with twenty-five volumes. I'll give you an example: *Disarmament*. There's a real rag-bag. You turn up the back numbers first to check the dates and the material, all right? So what do you find? Industrial dismantling in the Ruhr, 1946; Control Commission policy on the allocation of shotgun licences, 1949. Re-establishment of German military potential, 1950. Some of it's so old you'd laugh. You take a look at the current columns to compare, and what do you find? Warheads for the Bundeswehr. It's a million miles away. All right, you say, let's burn the back papers, they're irrelevant. There's fifteen volumes at least we can chuck out. Who's the desk officer for disarmament? Peter de Lisle: put it up to him: "Please may we destroy up to nineteen-sixty?" No objection, he says, so you're off.' Meadowes shook his head. 'Only you're not. You're not even half-way to off. You can't just carve off the back ten volumes and shove them in the fire. There's the ledger for a start: who's going to cancel all the entries? There's the card index; that's got to be weeded. Were there treaties? Right: clear with legal department. Is there a military interest? Clear it with the MA. Are there duplicates in London? No. So we all sit back and wait another two months: no destruction of originals without written permission from Library. See what I mean?'

'I get the idea,' said Turner, waiting.

'Then there's all the cross references, the sister files in the same series: will *they* be affected? Should they be destroyed as well? Or should we make up residuals to be on the safe side? Before you know where you are, you're wandering all over Registry, looking in every nook and cranny; there's no end to it once you start; nothing's holy.'

'I should think it suited him down to the ground.'

'There's no *restriction*,' Meadowes observed simply, as if replying to a question. 'It may offend you, but it's the only system I can understand. Anyone can look at anything, that's my rule. Anyone sent up here, I trust them. There's no other way to run the place. I can't go sniffing round asking who's looking at what, can I?' he demanded, ignoring Turner's bewildered gaze.

'He took to it like a duck to water. I was amazed. He was happy, that was the first thing. It tickled him, working in here, and quite soon it tickled me having him. He liked the company.' He broke off. 'The only thing we ever *really* minded,' he said with an unexpected smile, 'was those ruddy cigars he smoked. Javanese Dutch I believe they were. Stank the place out. We used to tease him about them but he wouldn't budge. Still, I think I miss them now.' He continued quietly: 'He'd been out of his depth in Chancery, he's not their sort at all, and the ground floor didn't have much for him either in my opinion, but this place was just right.' He inclined his head towards the closed door. 'It's like a shop in there, sometimes: you have the customers and you have one another. Johnny Slingo, Valerie . . . well, they took to him too and that's all there is to it. They were all against him when he came, and they all took to him within a week, and that's the truth of it. He'd got a *way* with him. I know what you're thinking: it flattered my ego, I suppose you'd say. All right, it did. Everyone wants to be liked and he liked us. All right, I'm lonely; Myra's a worry, I've failed as a parent and I never had a son; there was a bit of that about it too, I suppose, although there's only ten years between us. Perhaps it's him being little that makes the difference.'

'Go for the girls, did he?' Turner asked, more to break the uncomfortable silence than because he had been preparing questions in his mind.

'Only banter.'

'Ever hear of a woman called Aickman?'

'No.'

'Margaret Aickman. They were engaged to be married, her and Leo.'

'No.'

Still they did not look at one another.

'He liked the work too,' Meadowes continued. 'In those first weeks. I don't think he'd ever realized till then how much he *knew* by comparison with the rest of us. About Germany, I mean, the *soil* of it.'

He broke off, remembering, and it might have been fifty years ago. 'He knew *that* world too,' he added. 'He knew it inside out.'

'What world?'

'Post-war Germany. The Occupation; the years they don't want to know about any more. He knew it like the back of his hand. "Arthur," he said to me once, "I've seen these towns when they were car parks. I've heard these people talk when even their language was forbidden." It used to knock him clean off course sometimes. I'd catch sight of him deep in a file, still as a mouse, just fascinated. Or he'd look away, look round the room, for someone with a moment to spare, just so he could tell them about something he'd come across: "Here," he'd say. "See that? We disbanded that firm in 1947. Look at it now!" Other times, he'd go right off into a dream, and then you'd lost him altogether; he was on his own. I think it bothered him to *know* so much. It was queer. I think he almost felt guilty sometimes. He went on quite a lot about his memory. "You're making me destroy my childhood," he says one time – we were breaking up some files for the machine – "You're making an old man of me." I said, "If that's what I'm doing you're the luckiest man alive." We had a good laugh about that.'

'Did he ever mention politics?'

'No.'

'What did he say about Karfeld?'

'He was concerned. Naturally. That's why he was so glad to be helping out.'

'Oh sure.'

'It was trust,' Meadowes said defiantly. 'You wouldn't understand that. And that was true, what he said: it *was* the old stuff we were trying to get rid of; it *was* his childhood; it *was* the old stuff that meant the most to him.'

'All right.'

'Listen: I'm not holding any brief for him. He's ruined my career for all I know, what there was left after you finished with it. But I'm telling you: you've got to see the *good* in him too.'

'I'm not arguing with you.'

'It did *bother* him, his memory. I remember once with the music: he got me listening to gramophone records. Mainly so that he could sell them to me, I suppose; he'd worked some deal he was very proud of, with one of the shops in town. "Look," I said. "It's no good Leo; you're wasting your time. I get to know one record so I learn another. By that time I've forgotten the first one." He comes right back at me, very fast: "Then you ought to be a politician, Arthur," he says. "That's what they do." He meant it, believe me.'

Turner grinned suddenly. 'That's quite funny.'

'It would have been,' said Meadowes, 'if he hadn't looked so darned fierce with it. Then another time we're talking about Berlin, something to do with the crisis, and I said, "Well never mind, no one thinks of Berlin any more," which is true really. Files I mean; no one draws the files or bothers with the contingencies; not like they used to, anyway. I mean *politically* it's a dead duck. "No," he says. "We've got the big memory and the small memory. The small memory's to remember the small things and the big memory's to forget the big ones." That's what he said; it touched me, that did. I mean there's a lot of us think that way, you can't help it these days.'

'He came home with you, did he, sometimes? You'd make an evening of it?'

'Now and then. When Myra was out. Sometimes I'd slip over there.'

'Why when Myra was out?' Turner pounced quite hard on that: 'You *still* didn't trust him did you?'

'There's rumours,' Meadowes said evenly. 'There was talk about him. I didn't want her connected.'

'Him and who?'

'Just girls. Girls in general. He was a bachelor and he liked his fun.'

'*Who?*'

Meadowes shook his head. 'You've got it wrong,' he said. He was playing with a couple of paper clips, trying to make them interlock.

'Did he ever talk about England in the war? About an uncle in Hampstead?'

'He told me once he arrived at Dover with a label round his neck. That wasn't usual either.'

'What wasn't—'

'Him talking about himself. Johnny Slingo said he'd known him four years before he came to Registry and he'd never got a word out of him. He was all opened up, that's what Johnny said, it must be old age setting in.'

'Go on.'

'Well that was all he had, a label: Harting Leo. They shaved his head and deloused him and sent him to a Farm School. He was allowed to choose apparently: domestic science or agriculture. He chose agriculture because he wanted to own land. It seemed daft to me, Leo wanting to be a farmer, but there it is.'

'Nothing about Communists? A left-wing group of kids in Hampstead? Nothing like that at all?'

'Nothing.'

'Would you tell me if there was something?'

'I doubt it.'

'Did he ever mention a man called Praschko? In the Bundestag.'

Meadowes hesitated. 'He said one night that Praschko had walked out on him.'

'How? Walked out *how?*'

'He wouldn't say. He said they'd emigrated to England together, and returned here together after the war; Praschko had chosen one path and Leo had chosen another.' He shrugged. 'I didn't press him. Why should I? After that night he never mentioned him again.'

'All that talk about his *memory*: what do you think he had in mind?'

'Something historical, I suppose. He thought a lot about history, Leo did. Mind you, that's a couple of months back now.'

'What difference does that make?'

'That was before he went on his track.'

'His what?'

'He went on a track,' Meadowes said simply. 'That's what I'm trying to tell you.'

'I want to hear about the missing files,' Turner said. 'I want to check the ledgers and the mail.'

'You'll wait your turn. There's some things that aren't just *facts*, and if you'll only pay attention you'll maybe hear about them. You're like Leo, you are: always wanting the answer before you've even heard the question. What I'm trying to tell you is, I knew from the day he came here that he was looking for something. We all did. You felt it with Leo. You felt he was looking for something. Well we all are in a way, but Leo was looking for something real. Something you could almost touch, it meant so much to him. That's rare in this place, believe me.'

It was a whole life which Meadowes seemed to draw upon.

'An archivist is like an historian; he has time-periods he's faddy about; places, Kings and Queens. All the files here are related, they're bound to be. Give me any file from next door; any file you want, I could trace you a path clean through the whole Registry, from Icelandic shipping rights to the latest guidance on gold prices. That's the fascination of files; there's nowhere to stop.'

Meadowes ran on. Turner studied the grey, parental face, the grey eyes clouded with concern, and he felt the dawning of excitement.

'You think you run an archive,' Meadowes said. 'You don't. It runs you. There's qualities to an archive that just get you,

and there's not a thing you can do about it. Take Johnny
Slingo now. You saw him as you came in, on the left there, the
old fellow in the jacket. He's the intellectual type, college and
all the rest. Johnny's only been at it a year, came to us from
Admin as a matter of fact, but he's stuck with the nine-nine
fours: Federal Germany's relations with Third Parties. He
could sit where you are and recite the date and place of every
single negotiation there's ever been about the Hallstein Doc-
trine. Or take my case, I'm mechanical. I like cars, inventions,
all that world. I reckon I know more about German infringe-
ment of patent rights than any desk officer in Commercial
Section.'

'What was Leo's track?'

'Wait. It's important what I'm telling. I've spent a lot of
time thinking about it in the last twenty-four hours, and you're
going to hear it *right*, whether you like it or not. The files get
hold of you; you can't help it. They'd rule your life if you ever
let them. They're wife and child to some men, I've seen it
happen. And times they just *take* you, and then you're on a
track and you can't get off it; and that's what they did to Leo.
I don't know how it happens. A paper catches your eye, something silly: a threatened strike of sugar-workers in Surabaya,
that's our favourite joke at the moment. "Hullo," you say to
yourself, "Why hasn't Mr So-and-So signed that off?" You
check back: Mr So-and-So never saw it. He never read the
telegram at all. Well he must see it then, mustn't he? Only it
all happened three years ago, and Mr So-and-So is Ambassador
in Paris. So you start trying to find out what action was taken,
or wasn't taken. Who was consulted? Why didn't they inform
Washington? You chase the cross references, draw the original
material. By then it's too late; you've lost your sense of propor-
tion; you're away, and by the time you shake yourself out of
it you're ten days older and none the wiser, but maybe you're
safe again for a couple of years. Obsession, that's what it is. A
private journey. It happens to all of us. It's the way we're
made.'

'And it happened to Leo?'

'Yes. Yes, it happened to Leo. Only from the first day he
came here, I had that feeling he was . . . well, that he was

109

waiting. Just the way he looked, the way he handled paper. . .
Always peering over the hedge. I'd glance up and catch sight of
him and there was those little brown eyes looking all the time.
I know you'll say I'm fanciful; I don't care. I didn't make a lot
of it, why should I? We all have problems, and besides it was
like a factory in here by then. But it's true all the same. I've
thought about it and it's true. It was nothing much to begin
with; I just noticed it. Then gradually he got on his track.'

A bell rang suddenly; a long, assertive peal up and down the
corridors. They heard the slamming of doors and the sound of
running feet. A girl was calling: 'Where's Valerie, where's
Valerie?'

'Fire practice,' Meadowes said. 'We're running to two or
three a week at present. Don't worry. Registry's exempt.'

Turner sat down. He looked even paler than before. He ran
a big hand through his tufted, fair hair.

'I'm listening,' he said.

'Ever since March now he's been working on a big project:
all the seven-o-sevens. That's Statutes. There's about two
hundred of them or more, and mainly to do with the handover
when the Occupation ended. Terms of withdrawal, residual
rights, rights of evocation, phases of autonomy and God knows
what. All forty-nine to fifty-five stuff, not relevant here at all.
He might have started in half a dozen places on the Destruction, but the moment he saw the seven-o-sevens, they were the
ones for him. "Here," he said. "That's just right for me
Arthur, I can cut my milk teeth on them. I know what they're
talking about; it's familiar ground." I shouldn't think anyone
had looked at it for fifteen years. But *tricky*, even if it was
obsolete. Full of technical talk. Surprising what Leo knew,
mind. All the terms, German and English, all the legal
phrases.' Meadowes shook his head in admiration. 'I saw a
minute of his go to the Legal Attaché, a résumé of a file; *I*
couldn't have put it together I'm sure, and I doubt whether
there's anyone in Chancery could either. All about the Prussian
Criminal Code and regional sovereignty of justice. And half of
it in German, too.'

'He knew more than he was prepared to let on: is that what
you're saying?'

'No it's not,' said Meadowes. 'And don't you go putting words into my mouth. He was being *used*, that's what I mean; he had a lot of knowledge in him that he hadn't done anything with for a long time. All of a sudden, he could put it to work.'

Meadowes resumed: 'With the seven-o-sevens there wasn't any real question of *destruction*: more of sending it back to London and getting it stored out of the way, but it all had to be read and submitted the same as everything else, and he'd been getting very deep in it these last few weeks. I told you he was quiet up here; well he was. And once he got tucked into the Statutes he got quieter and quieter. He was on a track.'

'When did this happen?'

At the back of Turner's notebook there was a diary; he had it open before him.

'Three weeks ago. He went further and further *in*. Still jolly, mind; still bouncing up and down to get the girls a chair or help them with a parcel. But something had got hold of him, and it meant a lot to him. Still quizzy: no one will ever cure him of that: he had to know exactly what each of us was up to. But subdued. And he got worse. More and more thoughtful; more and more *serious*. Then on Monday, last Monday, he changed.'

'A week ago today,' said Turner, 'The fifth.'

'Seven days. Is that all? My God.' There was a sudden smell of hot wax from next door, and the muffled thud of a large seal being pressed on to a packet.

'That'll be the two o'clock bag they're getting ready,' he muttered inconsequentially, and glanced at his silver pocket watch. 'It's due down there at twelve thirty.'

'I'll come back after lunch if you like.'

'I'd rather be done with you before,' Meadowes said. 'If you don't mind.' He put the watch away. 'Where is he? Do *you* know? What's happened to him? He's gone to Russia, is that it?'

'Is that what you think?'

'He might have gone anywhere, you couldn't tell. He wasn't like us. He tried to be, but he wasn't. More like you, I suppose, in some ways. Perverse. Always busy but always doing things back to front. Nothing was simple, I reckon that was his trouble.

Too much childhood. Or none. It comes to the same thing really. I like people to grow *slowly*.'

'Tell me about last Monday. He changed: how?'

'Changed for the better. He'd shaken himself out of it, whatever it was. The track was over. He was smiling when I came in, really happy. Johnny Slingo, Valerie, they both noticed it, same as I did. We'd all been going full tilt of course; I'd been in most of Saturday, all Sunday; the others had been coming and going.'

'What about Leo?'

'Well, he'd been busy too, there was no doubt to that, but we didn't see him around an awful lot. An hour up here, three hours down there—'

'Down where?'

'In his own room. He did that sometimes, took a few files downstairs to work on. It was quieter. "I like to keep it warm." he said. "It's my old room, Arthur, and I don't like to let it grow cold." '

'And he took his files down there, did he?' Turner asked, very quiet.

'Then there was Chapel: that took up a part of Sunday, of course. Playing the organ.'

'How long's he been doing that, by the way?'

'Oh, years and years. It was reinsurance,' Meadowes said with a little laugh. 'Just to keep himself indispensable.'

'So Monday he was happy.'

'Serene. There's no other word for it. "I like it here, Arthur," he said. "I want you to know that." Sat down and got on with his work.'

'And he stayed that way till he left?'

'More or less.'

'What do you mean, "More or less"?'

'Well, we had a bit of a row. That was Wednesday. He'd been all right Tuesday, happy as a sandboy, then Wednesday I caught him at it.' He had folded his hands before him on his lap and he was looking at them, head bowed.

'He was trying to look at the Green File. The Maximum Limit.' He touched the top of his head in a small gesture of nervousness. 'He was always quizzy, I told you. Some people are like that, they can't help it. Didn't matter what it was; I could leave a letter from my own mother on the desk: I'm damn sure that if Leo had half a chance he'd have read it. Always thought people were conspiring against him. It drove us mad to begin with; look in anything, he would. Files, cupboards, anywhere. He hadn't been here a week before he was signing for the mail. The whole lot, down in the bagroom. I didn't care for that at all at first, but he got all huffy when I told him to stop and in the end I let it go.' He opened his hands, seeking an answer. 'Then in March we had some Trade Contingency papers from London – special guidance for Econ on new alignments and forward planning, and I caught him with the whole bundle on his desk. "Here," I said. "Can't you read? They're subscription only, they're not for you." He didn't turn a hair. In fact he was really angry. "I thought I could handle anything!" he says. He'd have hit me for two pins. "Well you thought wrong," I told him. That was March. It took us both a couple of days to cool down.'

'God save us,' said Turner softly.

'Then we had this Green. A Green's rare. *I* don't know what's in it; Johnny doesn't, Valerie doesn't. It lives in its own despatch box. H.E.'s got one key, Bradfield's got the other and he shares it with de Lisle. The box has to come back here to the strong-room every night. It's signed in and signed out, and only I handle it. So anyway: lunchtime Wednesday it was. Leo was up here on his own; Johnny and me went down to the canteen.'

'Often here on his own lunchtimes, was he?'

'He liked to be, yes. He liked the quiet.'

'All right.'

'There was a big queue at the canteen and I can't stand queuing, so I said to Johnny, "You stay here, I'll go back and do a spot of work and try again in half an hour." So I came in unexpectedly. Just walked in. No Leo, and the strong-room was open. And there he was; standing there, with the Green despatch box.'

'What do you mean, *with* it?'

'Just holding it. Looking at the lock as far as I could make out. Just curious. He smiled when he saw me, cool as anything.

He's sharp, I've told you that. "Arthur," he says, "you've caught me at it, you've discovered my guilty secret." I said, "What the hell are you up to? Look what you've got there in your hands!" Like that. "You know me," he says, very disarming. "I just can't help it." He puts down the box. "I was *actually* looking for some seven-o-sevens, you don't happen to have seen them anywhere, do you? For March and February fifty-eight." Something like that.'

'So then what?'

'I read him the Riot Act. What else could I do? I said I'd report him to Bradfield, the lot. I was furious.'

'But you didn't?'

'No.'

'Why not?'

'You wouldn't understand,' Meadowes said at last. 'You think I'm soft in the head, I know. It was Myra's birthday Friday; we were having a special do at the Exiles. Leo had choir practice and a dinner party.'

'Dinner party? Where?'

'He didn't say.'

'There's nothing in his diary.'

'That's not my concern.'

'Go on.'

'He'd promised to drop in sometime during the evening and give her her present. It was going to be a hair-dryer; we'd chosen it together.' He shook his head again. 'How can I explain it? I've told you: I felt responsible for him. He was that kind of bloke. You and I could blow him over with one puff if we wanted.'

Turner gazed at him incredulously.

'And I suppose there was something else too.' He looked Turner full in the face. 'If I tell Bradfield, that's it. Leo's had it. There's nowhere for him to go, is there? See what I mean. Like now, for instance: I mean I hope he *has* gone to Moscow, because there's nowhere else going to take him.'

'You mean you suspected him?'

'I suppose so, yes. Deep down I suppose I did. Warsaw's done that for me, you know. I'd like Myra to have settled there. With her student. All right, they put him up to it; they made

114

him seduce her. But he did say he'd marry her, didn't he? For the baby. I'd have loved that baby more than I can say. That's what you took away from me. From her as well. That's what it was all about. You shouldn't have done that you know.'

He was grateful for the traffic then, for any noise to fill that damned tank and take away the accusing echo of Meadowes' flat voice.

'And on Thursday the box disappeared?'

Meadowes shrugged it away. 'Private Office returned it Thursday midday. I signed it in myself and left it in the strong-room. Friday it wasn't there. That was that.'

He paused.

'I should have reported it at once. I should have gone running to Bradfield Friday afternoon when I noticed. I didn't. I slept on it. I brooded about it all Saturday. I chewed Cork's head off, went for Johnny Slingo, made their lives hell. It was driving me mad. I didn't want to raise a hare. We'd lost all manner of things in the crisis. People get light-fingered. Someone's pinched our trolley, I don't know who: one of the Military Attachés' clerks, that's my guess. Someone else has lifted our swivel chair. There's a long-carriage typewriter from the Pool; diaries, all sorts, cups from the Naafi even. Anyway, those were the excuses. I thought one of the users might have taken it: de Lisle, Private Office . . .'

'Did you ask Leo?'

'He'd gone by then, hadn't he?'

Once more Turner had slipped into the routine of interrogation.

'He carried a briefcase, didn't he?'

'Yes.'

'Was he allowed to bring it in here?'

'He brought in sandwiches and a thermos.'

'So he was allowed?'

'Yes.'

'Did he have the briefcase Thursday?'

'I think so. Yes, he would have done.'

'Was it big enough to hold the despatch box?'

'Yes.'

'Did he have lunch in here Thursday?'

'He went out at about twelve.'

'And came back?'

'I told you: Thursday's his special day. Conference day. It's a left-over from his old job. He goes to one of the Ministries in Bad Godesberg. Something to do with outstanding claims. Last Thursday he had a lunch date first I suppose. Then went on to the meeting.'

'Has he always been to that meeting? Every Thursday?'

'Ever since he came into Registry.'

'He had a key, didn't he?'

'What for? Key to where?'

Turner was on unsure ground. 'To let himself in and out of Registry. Or he knew the combination.'

Meadowes actually laughed.

'There's me and Head of Chancery knows how to get in and out of here, and no one else. There's three combinations and half a dozen burglar switches and there's the strong-room as well. Not Slingo, not de Lisle, *no one* knows. Just us two.'

Turner was writing fast.

'Tell me what else is missing,' he said at last.

Meadowes unlocked a drawer of his desk and drew out a list of references. His movements were brisk and surprisingly confident.

'Bradfield didn't tell you?'

'No.'

Meadowes handed him the list. 'You can keep that. There's forty-three of them. They're all box files, they've all disappeared since March.'

'Since he went on his track.'

'The security classifications vary from Confidential to Top Secret, but the majority are plain Secret. There's Organization files, Conference, Personality and two Treaty files. The subjects range from the dismantling of chemical concerns in the Ruhr in 1947 to minutes of unofficial Anglo-German exchanges at working level over the last three years. Plus the Green and that's Formal and Informal Conversations—'

'Bradfield told me.'

'They're like pieces, believe me, pieces in a puzzle . . . that's what I thought at first . . . I've moved them round in my mind. Hour after hour. I haven't slept. Now and then—' he broke off. 'Now and then I thought I had an idea, a sort of picture, a half picture, I'd say . . .' Stubbornly he concluded:

'There's no clear pattern to it, and no reason. Some are marked out by Leo to different people; some are marked 'certified for destruction' but most are just plain missing. You can't tell, you see. You just can't keep tabs, it's impossible. Until someone *asks* for the file you don't know you haven't got it.'

'*Box* files?'

'I told you. All forty-three. They weigh a couple of hundred-weights between them I should think.'

'And the letters? There are letters missing too.'

'Yes,' Meadowes said reluctantly. 'We're short of thirty-three incoming letters.'

'Never entered, were they? Just lying about for anyone to pick up? What were the subjects? You haven't put it down.'

'We don't know. That's the truth. They're letters from German Departments. We know the references because the Bag Room's written them in the log. They never reached Registry.'

'But you've checked the references?'

Very stiffly Meadowes said: 'The missing letters belong on the missing files. The references are the same. That's all we can tell. As they're from German Departments, Bradfield has ruled that we do not ask for duplicates until the Brussels decision is through: in case our curiosity alerts them to Harting's absence.'

Having returned his black notebook to his pocket, Turner rose and went to the barred window, touching the locks, testing the strength of the wire mesh.

'There was something about him. He was special. Something *made* you watch him.'

From the carriageway they heard the two-tone wail of an emergency horn approach and fade again.

'He was special,' Turner repeated. 'All the time you've been talking, I've heard it. Leo this, Leo that. You had your eye on him; you *felt* him, I know you did. Why?'

'There was nothing.'

'What were these rumours? What was it they said about him that frightened you? Was he somebody's fancy-boy, Arthur? Something for Johnny Slingo, was he, in his old age? Working the queers' circuit was he, is that what all the blushing's for?'

Meadowes shook his head. 'You've lost your sting,' he said. 'You can't frighten me any more. I know you; I know your worst. It's nothing to do with Warsaw. He wasn't that kind. I'm not a child and Johnny's not a homosexual either.'

Turner continued to stare at him. 'There's something you heard. Something you knew. You watched him, I know you did. You watched him cross a room; how he stood, how he reached for a file. He was doing the silliest bloody job in Registry and you talk about him as if he was the Ambassador. There was chaos in here, you said so yourself. Everyone except Leo chasing files; making up, entering, connecting, all standing on your heads to keep the ball rolling in a crisis. And what was Leo doing? Leo was on Destruction. He could have been making flax for all his work mattered. You said so, not me. So what *was* it about him? *Why* did you watch him?'

'You're dreaming. You're twisted and you can't see anything straight. But if by any chance you were right, I wouldn't even whisper it to you on my deathbed.'

A notice outside the cypher room said: 'Back at two fifteen. Phone 333 for emergencies.' He banged on Bradfield's door and tried the handle; it was locked. He went to the banister and looked angrily down into the lobby. At the front desk a young Chancery Guard was reading a learned book on engineering. He could see the diagrams on the right-hand page. In the glass-fronted waiting-room, the Ghanaian Chargé in a velvet collar was staring thoughtfully at a photograph of Clydeside taken from very high up.

'All at lunch, old boy,' a voice whispered from behind him. 'Not a Hun will stir till three. Daily truce. Show must go on.' A hanging, vulpine figure stood among the fire extinguishers. 'Crabbe,' he explained, 'Mickie Crabbe, you see,' as if the name itself were an excuse. 'Peter de Lisle's just back, if you don't mind. Been down at the Ministry of the Interior, saving women and children. Rawley's sent him to feed you.'

'I want to send a telegram. Where's room three double three?'

'Proles' rest room, old boy. They're having a bit of a kip after all the hoohah. Troubled times. Give it a break,' he suggested. 'If it's urgent it'll keep, if it's important it's too late, that's what I say.' Saying it, Crabbe led him along the silent corridor like a decrepit courtier lighting him to bed. Passing the lift, Turner paused and stared at it once more. It was firmly padlocked and the notice said 'Out of order.'

Jobs are separate, he told himself, why worry, for God's sake? Bonn is not Warsaw. Warsaw was a hundred years ago. Bonn is today. We do what we have to do and move on. He saw it again, the Rococo room in the Warsaw Embassy, the chandelier dark with dust, and Myra Meadowes alone on the daft sofa. 'Another time they post you to an Iron Curtain country,' Turner was shouting, 'you bloody well choose your lovers with more care!'

Tell her I'm leaving the country, he thought; I've gone to find a traitor. A full-grown, four-square, red-toothed, paid-up traitor.

Come on, Leo, we're of one blood, you and I: underground men, that's us. I'll chase you through the sewers, Leo; that's why I smell so lovely. We've got the earth's dirt on us, you and I. I'll chase you, you chase me and each of us will chase ourselves.

7

de Lisle

THE AMERICAN CLUB was not as heavily guarded as the Embassy. 'It's no one's gastronomic dream,' de Lisle explained, as he showed his papers to the GI at the door, 'but it does have a gorgeous swimming-pool.' He had booked a window table overlooking the Rhine. Fresh from their bathe, they drank Martinis and watched the giant brown helicopters wavering past them towards the landing-strip up river. Some were marked with red crosses, others had no markings at all. Now and then white passenger ships, sliding through the mist, bore huddled groups of tourists towards the land of the Nibelungs; the boom of their own loudspeakers followed them like small thunder. Once a crowd of schoolchildren passed, and they heard the strains of the Lorelei banged out on an accordion, and the devoted accompaniment of a heavenly, if imperfect, choir. The seven hills of Königswinter were much nearer now, though the mist confused their outline.

With elaborate diffidence de Lisle pointed out the Petersberg, a regular wooded cone capped by a rectangular hotel. Neville Chamberlain had stayed there in the thirties, he explained: 'That was when he gave away Czechoslovakia, of course. The first time, I mean.' After the war it had been the seat of the Allied High Commission; more recently the Queen had used it for her State Visit. To the right of it was the Drachenfels, where Siegfried had slain the dragon and bathed in its magic blood.

'Where's Harting's house?'

'You can't quite see it,' de Lisle said quietly, not pointing any more. 'It's at the foot of the Petersberg. He lives, so to speak, in Chamberlain's shadow.' And with that he led the conversation into more general fields.

'I suppose the trouble with being a visiting fireman is that you so often arrive on the scene after the fire's gone out. Is that it?'

'Did he come here often?'

'The smaller Embassies hold receptions here; if their drawing-rooms aren't big enough. That was rather his mark, of course.'

Once again his tone became reticent, though the dining-room was empty. Only in the corner near the entrance, seated in their glass-walled bar, the inevitable group of foreign correspondents mimed, drank and mouthed like sea horses in solemn ritual.

'Is *all* America like this?' de Lisle enquired. 'Or worse?' He looked slowly round. 'Though it does give a sense of *dimension*, I suppose. And optimism. That's the trouble with Americans, isn't it, really? All that emphasis on the future. So dangerous. It makes them destructive of the present. Much kinder to look *back*, I always think. I see no hope at all for the future, and it gives me a *great* sense of freedom. And of caring: we're much nicer to one another in the condemned cell aren't we? Don't take me too seriously, will you?'

'If you wanted Chancery files late at night, what would you do?'

'Dig out Meadowes.'

'Or Bradfield?'

'Oh, that would be really going it. Rawley has the combinations, but only as a long stop. If Meadowes goes under a bus, Rawley can still get at the papers. You really *have* had a morning of it, haven't you,' he added solicitously. 'I can see you're still under the ether.'

'What would *you* do?'

'Oh, I'd draw the files in the afternoon.'

'Now; with all this working at night?'

'If Registry's open on a crisis schedule there's no problem. If it's closed, well, most of us have safes and strong-boxes, and they're cleared for overnight storage.'

'Harting didn't have one.'

'Shall we just say *he* from now on?'

'So where would he work? If he drew files in the evening, classified files, and worked late: what would he do?'

'He'd take them to his room I suppose, and hand in the files to the Chancery Guard when he left. If he's not working in Registry. The Guard has a safe.'

'And the Guard would sign for them?'

'Oh Lordy, yes. We're not *that* irresponsible.'

'So I could tell from the Guard's night-book?'

'You could.'

'He left without saying good-night to the Guard.'

'Oh my,' said de Lisle, clearly very puzzled. 'You mean he took them home?'

'What kind of car did he have?'

'A mini shooting-brake.'

They were both silent.

'There's nowhere else he might have worked, a special reading room, a strong-room on the ground floor?'

'Nowhere,' de Lisle said flatly. 'Now I think you'd better have another of those things, hadn't you, and cool the brain a little?'

He called the waiter.

'Well I've had a simply *ghastly* hour at the Ministry of the Interior with Ludwig Siebkron's faceless men.'

'What doing?'

'Oh, mourning the poor Miss Eich. That was gruesome. It was also very *odd*,' he confessed. 'It really was very odd indeed.' He drifted away. 'Did you know that blood plasma came in tins? The Ministry now say that they want to store some in the Embassy canteen, just in case. It's the most Orwellian thing I've ever heard; Rawley's going to be quite furious. He thinks they've gone much too far already. Apparently none of us belongs to groups any more: *uniblood.* I suppose it makes for equality.' He continued, 'Rawley's getting pretty cross about Siebkron.'

'Why?'

'The lengths he insists on going to, just for the sake of the poor English. All right, Karfeld is desperately anti-British and anti-Common Market. And Brussels is crucial, and British entry touches the nationalist nerve and maddens the Movement, and the Friday rally is alarming and everyone's very much on edge. One accepts all that wholeheartedly. And nasty things happened in Hanover. But we still don't deserve *so* much attention, we really don't. First the curfew, then the bodyguards, and now these wretched motor-cars. I think we feel he's crowding us on purpose.' Reaching past Turner, de Lisle took the enormous menu in his slender, woman's hand. 'How about oysters? Isn't that what real people eat? They have them in all seasons here. I gather they get them from Portugal or somewhere.'

'I've never tried them,' Turner said with a hint of aggression.

'Then you must have a dozen to make up,' de Lisle replied easily and drank some more Martini. 'It's so nice to meet some-one from *outside*. I don't suppose you can understand that.'

A string of barges chased up river with the current.

'The unsettling thing is, I suppose, one doesn't feel that ultimately all these precautions are for our own good. The Germans seem suddenly to have their horns drawn in, as if we were being deliberately provocative; as if *we* were doing the demonstrating. They barely talk to us down there. A *total* freeze up. Yes. That's what I mean,' he concluded. 'They're treating us as if we were hostile. Which is doubly frustrating when all we ask is to be loved.'

'He had a dinner party on Friday night,' Turner said suddenly.

'Did he?'

'But it wasn't marked in his diary.'

'Silly man.' He peered round but no one came. 'Where *is* that wretched boy?'

'Where was Bradfield on Friday night?'

'Shut up,' said de Lisle crisply. 'I don't like that kind of thing. And then there's Siebkron himself,' he continued as if nothing had happened, 'Well, we all know *he's* shifty; we all know he's juggling with the Coalition and we all know he had political aspirations. We also know he has an appalling security problem to cope with next Friday, and a lot of enemies waiting to say he did it badly. Fine—' he nodded his head at the river, as if in some way it were involved in his perplexities – 'So why spend six hours at the deathbed of poor Fraülein Eich? What's so fascinating about watching her die? And why go to the ridiculous lengths of putting the sentries on every tiny British hiring in the area? He's got an obsession about us, I swear he has; he's worse than Karfeld.'

'Who is Siebkron? What's his job?'

'Oh, muddy pools. Your world in a way. I'm sorry, I shouldn't have said that.' He blushed, acutely distressed. Only the timely arrival of the waiter rescued him from his embarrassment. He was quite a young boy, and de Lisle addressed him with inordinate courtesy, seeking his opinion on matters beyond his competence, deferring to his judgment in the selection of the Moselle and enquiring minutely after the quality of the meat.

'They say in Bonn,' he continued when they were alone again, 'to borrow a phrase, that if you have Ludwig Siebkron for a friend you don't need an enemy. Ludwig's very much a local species. Always someone's left arm. He keeps saying he doesn't want any of us to die. That's exactly why he's frightening: he makes it so possible. It's easy to forget,' he continued blandly, 'that Bonn may be a democracy but it's *frightfully* short of democrats.' He fell silent. 'The trouble with *dates*,' he reflected at last, 'is that they create compartments in time. Thirty-nine to forty-five. Forty-five to fifty. Bonn isn't pre-war, or war, or even post-war. It's just a small town in Germany. You can no more slice it up than you can the Rhine. It plods along, or whatever the song says. And the mist drains away the colours.'

Blushing suddenly, he unscrewed the cap of the tabasco and applied himself to the delicate task of allocating one drop to each oyster. It claimed his entire attention. 'We all apologize for Bonn. That's how you recognize the natives. I wish I collected model trains,' he continued brightly. 'I would like to place *far* greater emphasis on trivia. Do you have anything like that: a hobby, I mean?'

'I don't get the time,' said Turner.

'*Nominally* he heads something called the Ministry of the Interior Liaison Committee; I understand he chose the name himself. I asked him once: liaison with whom, Ludwig? He thought that was a great joke. He's our age of course. Front generation minus five; slightly cross at having missed the war, I suspect, and can't *wait* to grow old. He also flirts with CIA, but that's a status symbol here. His principal occupation is knowing Karfeld. When anyone wants to conspire with the Movement, Ludwig Siebkron lays it on. It *is* a bizarre life,' he conceded, catching sight of Turner's expression. 'But Ludwig revels in it. Invisible Government: that's what he likes. The fourth estate. Weimar would have suited him down to the ground. And you have to understand about the Government here: *all* the divisions are very artificial.'

Compelled, apparently, by a single urge, the foreign correspondents had left their bar and were floating in a long shoal towards the centre table already prepared for them. A very large man, catching sight of de Lisle, pulled a long strand of black hair over his right eye, and extended his arm in a Nazi greeting. De Lisle lifted his glass in reply.

'That's Sam Allerton,' he explained in an aside. 'He really *is* rather a pig. Where was I? Artificial divisions. Yes. They absolutely bedevil us here. Always the same: in a grey world we reach frantically for absolutes. Anti-French, pro-French, Communist, anti-Communist. Sheer nonsense, but we do it time and again. That's why we're so wrong about Karfeld. So dreadfully wrong. We argue about *definitions* when we should be arguing about *facts*. Bonn will go to the gallows arguing about the width of the rope that hangs us. *I* don't know how you define Karfeld; who does? The German Poujade? The middle-class revolution? If that's what he is then we *are* ruined, I agree, because in Germany they're *all* middle class. Like America: reluctantly equal. They don't want to be equal, who does? They just are. Uniblood.'

The waiter had brought the wine, and de Lisle pressed Turner to taste it. 'I'm sure your palate is fresher than mine.' Turner declined, so he sampled it himself, elaborately. 'How very clever,' he said appreciatively to the waiter. 'How *good*.'

'All the smart definitions apply to him, every one, of course they do; they apply to anyone. Just like psychiatry: presume the symptoms and you can *always* find a name for them. He's isolationist, chauvinist, pacifist, revanchist. And he wants a trade alliance with Russia. He's progressive, which appeals to the German old, he's reactionary, which appeals to the German young. The young are so *puritanical* here. They want to be cleansed of prosperity; they want bows and arrows and Barbarossa.' He pointed wearily towards the Seven Hills. 'They want all that in modern dress. No wonder the old are hedonistic. But the young—' He broke off. 'The young,' he said, with deep distaste, 'have discovered the cruellest of all truths: that the most effective way of punishing their parents is to imitate them. Karfeld is the students' adopted grown-up . . . I'm sorry. This is my hobby-horse. *Do* tell me to shut up.'

Turner appeared not to have heard. He was staring at the policemen who stood at intervals along the footpath. One of them had found a dinghy tethered under the bank, and he was playing with the sheet, swinging it round and round like a skipping rope.

'They keep asking us in London: who are his supporters? Where does he get his money from? Define, define. What am I to tell them? "The man in the street," I wrote once, "traditionally the most elusive social class." They adore that kind of answer until it reaches Research Department. "The disenchanted," I said, "the orphans of a dead democracy, the casualties of coalition government." Socialists who think they've been sold out to conservatism, anti-socialists who think they're been sold out to the reds. People who are just too intelligent to vote at all. Karfeld is the one hat that covers all their heads. How do you *define* a mood? *God* they are obtuse. We get no instructions any more: just questions. I told them: "Surely you have the same kind of thing in England? It's all the rage everywhere else." And after all, no one suspected a world plot in Paris: why look for it here? Mood . . . ignorance . . . boredom.' He leaned across the table. 'Have *you* ever voted? I'm sure you have. What's it like? Did you feel altered? Was it like Mass? Did you walk away ignoring everybody?' De Lisle ate another oyster. 'I think London has been bombed. Is that the answer? And you're just a blind to cheer us up. Perhaps only Bonn is left. What a frightful thought. A world in exile. That's what we are though. Inhabited by exiles, too.'

'Why does Karfeld hate the British?' Turner asked. His mind was far away.

'That, I confess, is one of life's unsolved mysteries. We've all tried our hand at it in Chancery. We've talked about it, read about it, argued about it. No one has the answer.' He shrugged. 'Who believes in motive these days, least of all in a politician? We did *try* to define that. Something we once did to him, perhaps. Something he once did to us. It's the childhood impressions that last the longest they say. Are you married, by the way?'

'What's that got to do with it?'

'*My*,' said de Lisle admiringly, 'you *are* prickly.'

'What does he do for money?'

'He's an industrial chemist; he runs a big plant outside Essen. There's a theory the British gave him a rough time during the Occupation, dismantled his factory and ruined his business. I don't know how true it all is. We've attempted a certain amount of research but there's very little to go on and Rawley, quite rightly, forbids us to enquire outside. God knows,' he declared with a small shudder, 'what Siebkron would think of us if we started *that* game. The press just says he hates us, as if it required no explanations. Perhaps they're right.'

'What's his record?'

'Predictable. Graduated before the war, drafted into the Engineers. Russian front as a demolitions expert; wounded at Stalingrad but managed to get out. The disillusionment of peace. The hard struggle and the slow build-up. All very romantic. The death of the spirit, the gradual revival. There are the usual boring rumours that he was Himmler's aunt or something of the sort. No one pays them much heed; it's a sign of arriving in Bonn these days, when the East Germans dig up an improbable allegation against you.'

'But there's nothing to it?'

'There's always something; there's never enough. Anyway, it doesn't impress anyone except us, so why bother? He came by degrees to politics, he says; he speaks of his years of sleep and his years of awakening. He has a rather Messianic turn of phrase, I fear, at least when he talks about himself.'

'You've never met him, have you?'

'Good God no. Just read about him. Heard him on the radio. He's very *present* in our lives in some ways.'

Turner's pale eyes had returned to the Petersberg; the sun, slanting between the hills, glinted directly upon the windows of the grey hotel. There is one hill over there that is broken like a quarry; small engines, white with dust, shuffle at its feet.

'You have to hand it to him. In six months he's changed the whole *galère*. The cadre, the organization, the jargon. They were cranks before Karfeld; gypsies, wandering preachers, Hitler's risen, all that nonsense. Now they're a patrician, graduate group. No shirt-sleeved hordes for him, thank you; none of your socialist nonsense, apart from the students, and he's very clever about tolerating them. He knows what a narrow line there is between the pacifist who attacks the policeman and the policeman who attacks the pacifist. But for most of us Barbarossa wears a clean shirt and has a doctorate in chemical engineering. *Herr Doktor Barbarossa*, that's the cry these days. Economists, historians, statisticians . . . above all, lawyers, of course. Lawyers are the great German gurus, always have been; you know how illogical lawyers are. But not *politicians*: politicians aren't a bit respectable. And for Karfeld of course, they smack far too much of representation; Karfeld doesn't want anyone representing him, thank you. Power without rule, that's the cry. The right to know better, the right not to be responsible. It's the *end*, you see, not the beginning,' he said, with a conviction quite disproportionate to his lethargy. 'Both we and the Germans have been through democracy and no one's given us credit for it. Like shaving. No one *thanks* you for shaving, no one *thanks* you for democracy. Now we've come out the other side. Democracy was only possible under a class system, that's why: it was an indulgence granted by the privileged. We haven't time for it any more: a flash of light between feudalism and automation, and now it's gone. What's left? The voters are cut off from parliament, parliament is cut off from the Government and the Government is cut off from everyone. Government by silence, that's the slogan. Government by alienation. I don't need to tell *you* about that; it's a British product.'

He paused, expecting Turner to make some further interjection but Turner was still lost in thought. At their long

128

table, the journalists were arguing. Someone had threatened to hit someone else; a third was promising to bang their heads together.

'*I* don't know what I'm defending. Or what I'm representing; who does? "A gentleman who lies for the good of his country," they told us with a wink in London. "Willingly," I say. "But first tell me what truth I must conceal." They haven't the least idea. Outside the Office, the poor world dreams we have a book bound in gold with POLICY written on the cover. . . . God, if only they knew.' He finished his wine. 'Perhaps *you* know? I am supposed to obtain the maximum advantage with the minimum of friction. What do they mean by advantage, I wonder: power? I doubt whether power is to our advantage. Perhaps we *should* go into decline. Perhaps we need a Karfeld? A new Oswald Mosley? I'm afraid we would barely notice him. The opposite of love isn't hate; it's apathy. Apathy is our daily bread here. Hysterical apathy. Have some more Moselle.'

'Do you think it's possible,' Turner said, his gaze still upon the hill, 'that Siebkron already *knows* about Harting? Would that make them hostile? Would that account for the extra attention?'

'Later,' de Lisle said quietly. 'Not in front of the children if you don't mind.'

The sun landed upon the river, lighting it from nowhere like a great gold bird, spreading its wings over the whole valley, frisking the water's surface into the light-hearted movements of a new spring day. Ordering the boy to bring two of his *nicest* brandies to the tennis garden, de Lisle picked his way elegantly between the empty tables to the side door. At the centre of the room the journalists had fallen silent; sullen with drink, slumped in their leather chairs, they gracelessly awaited the stimulus of new political catastrophe.

'Poor old thing,' he observed as they entered the fresh air. 'What a bore I've been. Do you get this wherever you go? I suppose we all unburden our hearts to the stranger, do we? And do we all finish up like little Karfelds? Is that it? Middle-class patriotic anarchists? How awfully dreary for you.'

'I've got to see his house,' Turner said. 'I've got to find out.'

'You're out of court,' de Lisle replied evenly. 'Ludwig Siebkron's got it picketed.'

It was three o'clock; a white sun had broken through the clouds. They sat in the garden under beach umbrellas, sipping their brandy and watching the diplomatic daughters volley and laugh in the wet, red clay of the tennis courts.

'Praschko, I suspect, is a baddie,' de Lisle declared. 'We used to have him on the books long ago, but he went sour on us.' He yawned. 'He was quite dangerous in his day; a political pirate. No conspiracy was complete without him. I've met him a few times; the English still bother him. Like all converts, he does hanker for the lost loyalties. He's a Free Democrat these days; or did Rawley tell you? That's a home for lost causes if ever there was one; they've got some *very* weird creatures over there.'

'But he was a friend.'

'You are innocent,' de Lisle said drowsily, 'Like Leo. We can know people all our lives without becoming friends. We can know people five minutes and they're our friends for life. Is Praschko so important?'

'He's all I've got,' said Turner. 'He's all I've got to go on. He's the only person I've heard of who knew him outside the Embassy. He was going to be best man at his wedding.'

'*Wedding? Leo?*' de Lisle sat bolt upright, his composure gone.

'He was engaged long ago to someone called Margaret Aickman. They seem to have known one another in Leo's pre-Embassy days.'

De Lisle fell back in apparent relief.

'If you're thinking of approaching Praschko—' he said.

'I'm not, don't worry; that's one message I have got.' He drank. 'But someone tipped Leo off. *Someone* did. He went mad. He knew he was living on borrowed time and he took whatever he could get his hands on. Anything. Letters, files . . . and when he finally ran for it, he didn't even bother to apply for leave.'

'Rawley wouldn't have granted it; not in this situation.'

'Compassionate leave; he'd have got that all right, it was the first thing Bradfield thought of.'

'Did he pinch the trolley too?'

Turner did not answer.

'I suppose he helped himself to my nice electric fan. He'll need *that* in Moscow for sure.' De Lisle leaned even farther back into his chair. The sky was quite blue, the sun as hot and intense as if it came through glass. 'If *this* keeps up, I'll have to get a new one.'

'Someone tipped him off,' Turner insisted. 'It's the only explanation. He panicked. That's why I thought of Praschko, you see: he's got a left-wing past. Fellow traveller was Rawley's term. He was old chums with Leo; they'd even spent the war together in England.' He stared at the sky.

'You're going to advance a *theory*,' de Lisle murmured. 'I can hear it ticking.'

'They come back to Germany in forty-five; do some army service; then part. They go different ways: Leo stays British and covers *that* target, Praschko goes native and gets himself mixed up in German politics. They'd be a useful pair, those two, as long-term agents, I must say. Maybe they were both at the same game . . . recruited by the same person back in England when Russia was the ally. Gradually they run down their relationship. That's standard, that is. Not safe to associate any more . . . bad security to have our names linked: but they keep it up; keep it up in secret. Then one day Praschko gets word. Just a few weeks ago. Out of the blue perhaps. He hears it on the Bonn grapevine you're all so proud of: Siebkron's on the trail. Some old trace has come up; someone's talked; we're betrayed. Or maybe they're only after Leo. Pack your bags, he says, take what you can and run for it.'

'What a horrid mind you must have,' de Lisle said luxuriously. 'What a nasty, inventive mind.'

'The trouble is, it doesn't work.'

'Not really, does it? Not in *human* terms. I'm glad you recognize that. Leo wouldn't *panic*, that's not his way. He had himself much under control. And it sounds very silly, but he loved us. Modestly, he loved us. He was *our* kind of man, Alan. Not theirs. He expected dreadfully little from life. Pit pony.

That's how I used to think of him in those wretched ground-floor stables. Even when he came upstairs, he seemed to bring a bit of the dark with him. People thought of him as *jolly*. The jolly extrovert . . .'

'No one I've talked to thought he was jolly.'

De Lisle turned his head and looked at Turner with real interest.

'Didn't they? What a horrifying thought. Each of us thought the other was laughing. Like clowns at the tragedy. That's very nasty,' he said.

'All right,' Turner conceded. 'He wasn't a believer. But he might have been when he was younger, mightn't he?'

'Might.'

'Then he goes to sleep . . . his conscience goes to sleep, I mean—'

'Ah.'

'Until Karfeld wakes him up again – the new Nationalism . . . the old enemy. . . . Wakes him with a bang. "Hey, what's going on?" He saw it all happening again; he told people that: history repeating itself.'

'Was it really Marx who said that: "History repeats itself, but the first time it's tragedy, and the second time it's comedy?" It seems *far* too witty for a German. Though I will admit: Karfeld does make Communism awfully inviting.'

'What was he *like*?' Turner insisted, 'What was he really *like*?'

'Leo? God, what are any of us like?'

'You knew him. I didn't.'

'You won't interrogate me, will you?' he asked, not altogether as a joke; 'I'm damned if I'll buy you lunch for you to unmask me.'

'Did Bradfield like him?'

'Who does Bradfield like?'

'Did he keep a close eye on him?'

'On his work, no doubt, where it was relevant. Rawley's a professional.'

'He's Roman Catholic too, isn't he?'

'My goodness,' de Lisle declared with quite unexpected vehemence, 'What an awful thing to say. You really musn't compartment people like that, it won't do. Life just isn't made up of so many cowboys and so many Red Indians. Least of all diplomatic life. If *that's* what you think life is, you'd better defect yourself.' With this he threw back his head and closed his eyes, letting the sun restore him. 'After all,' he added, his equability quite revived, 'that's what you object to in Leo, isn't it? He's gone and attached himself to some silly faith. God is dead. You can't have it both ways, that would be *too* mediaeval.' He lapsed once more into a contented silence.

'I have a particular vision of Leo,' he said at last. 'Here's something for your little notebook. What do you make of this ? One gorgeous winter afternoon. I'd been to a boring German conference and it was half past four and I'd nothing much to do, so I took myself for a drive up into the hills behind Godesberg. Sun, frost, a bit of snow, a bit of wind . . . it was how I imagine ascending into Heaven. Suddenly, there was Leo. Indisputably, unquestionably, positively Leo, shrouded to the ears in Balkan black, with one of those dreadful Homburg hats they wear in the Movement. He was standing at the edge of a football field watching some kids kicking a ball and smoking one of those little cigars everyone complained about.'

'Alone?'

'All alone. I thought of stopping but I didn't. He hadn't any car that I could see and he was miles from anywhere. And suddenly I thought, no; don't stop; he's at Church. He's looking at the childhood he never had.'

'You were fond of him, weren't you?'

De Lisle might have replied, for the question did not seem to disconcert him, but he was interrupted by an unexpected intruder.

'Hullo. A new flunkey?' The voice was slurred and gritty. As its owner was standing directly in the sun, Turner had to screw up his eyes in order to make him out at all; at length he discerned the gently swaying outline and the black unkempt hair of the English journalist who had saluted them at lunch. He was pointing at Turner, but his question, to judge by the cast of his head, was addressed to de Lisle.

'What is he,' he demanded, 'pimp or spy?'

'Which do you want to be, Alan?' de Lisle asked cheerfully,

but Turner declined to answer. 'Alan Turner, Sam Allerton,' he continued, quite unbothered. 'Sam represents a lot of newspapers, don't you, Sam? He's enormously powerful. Not that he cares for power of course. Journalists never do.'

Allerton continued to stare at Turner.

'Where's he come from then?'

'London Town,' said de Lisle.

'What part of London Town?'

'Ag and Fish.'

'Liar.'

'The Foreign Office, then. Hadn't you guessed?'

'How long's he here for?'

'Just visiting.'

'How long for?'

'You know what visits are.'

'I know what *his* visits are,' said Allerton. 'He's a bloodhound.' His dead, yellow eyes slowly took him in: the heavy shoes, the tropical suit, the blank face and the pale, unblinking gaze.

'Belgrade,' he said at last. 'That's where. Some bloke in the Embassy screwed a female spy and got photographed. We all had to hush it up or the Ambassador wasn't going to give us any more port. *Security* Turner, that's who you are. The Bevin boy. You did a job in Warsaw, didn't you? I remember that too. That was a balls-up, wasn't it? Some girl tried to kill herself. Someone you'd been too rough with. We had to sweep that under the carpet as well.'

'Run away, Sam,' said de Lisle.

Allerton began laughing. It was quite a terrible noise, mirthless and cancered; indeed it seemed actually to cause him pain, for as he sat down, he interrupted himself with low, blasphemous cries. His black, greasy mane shook like an ill-fitted wig; his paunch, hanging forward over his waistband, trembled uncertainly.

'Well, Peter, how was Luddi Siebkron? Going to keep us safe and sound, is he? Save the Empire?'

Without a word, Turner and de Lisle got up and made their way across the lawn towards the car park.

'Heard the news, by the way?' Allerton called after them.

'What news?'

'You chaps don't know a thing, do you? Federal Foreign Minister's just left for Moscow. Top level talks on Soviet-German trade treaty. They're joining Comecon and signing the Warsaw pact. All to please Karfeld and bugger up Brussels. Britain out, Russia in. Non-aggressive Rappallo. What do you think of that?'

'We think you're a bloody liar,' said de Lisle.

'Well, it's nice to be fancied,' Allerton replied, with a deliberate homosexual lisp. 'But don't tell me it won't happen, lover boy, because one day it will. One day they'll do it. They'll have to. Slap Mummy in the face. Find a Daddy for the Fatherland. It isn't the West any more, is it? So who's it going to be?' He raised his voice as they continued walking. 'That's what you stupid flunkies don't understand! Karfeld's the only one in Germany who's telling the truth: the Cold War's over for everyone except the fucking diplomats!' His Parthian shot reached them as they closed the doors. 'Never mind darlings,' they heard him say. 'We can all sleep soundly now Turner's here.'

The little sports car nosed its way slowly down the sanitary arcades of the American Colony. A church bell, much amplified, was celebrating the sunlight. On the steps of the New England chapel, a bride and groom faced the flashing cameras. They entered the Koblenzerstrasse and the noise hit them like a gale. Overhead, electronic indicators flashed out theoretical speed checks. The photographs of Karfeld had multiplied. Two Mercedes with Egyptian lettering on their number plates raced past them, cut in, swung out again and were gone.

'That lift,' Turner said suddenly. 'In the Embassy. How long's it been out of action?'

'God, when was anything? Mid-April I suppose.'

'You're sure of that?'

'You're thinking of the trolley? Which also disappeared in mid-April?'

'You're not bad,' Turner said. 'You're not bad at all.'

'And you would be making a most terrible mistake if you ever thought you were a specialist,' de Lisle retorted, with that same unpredictable force which Turner had discerned in him before. 'Just don't go thinking you're in a white coat, that's all; don't go thinking we're all laboratory specimens.' He swung violently to avoid a double lorry and at once a motorized scream of fury rose from behind them. 'I'm saving your soul though you may not notice it.' He smiled. 'Sorry. I've got Siebkron on my nerves, that's all.'

'He put P. in his diary,' Turner said suddenly. 'After Christmas: meet P. Give P. dinner. Then it faded out again. It could have been Praschko.'

'It could have been.'

'What Ministries are there in Bad Godesberg?'

'Buildings, Scientific, Health. Just those three so far as I know.'

'He went to a conference every Thursday afternoon. Which one would that be?'

De Lisle pulled up at the traffic lights and Karfeld frowned down on them like a cyclops, one eye ripped off by a dissenting hand.

'I don't think he *did* go to a conference,' de Lisle said cautiously. 'Not recently anyway.'

'What do you mean?'

'Just that.'

'For Christ's sake?'

'Who told you he went?'

'Meadowes. And Meadowes got it from Leo and Leo said it was a regular weekly meeting and cleared with Bradfield. Something to do with claims.'

'Oh my God,' said de Lisle softly. He pulled away, holding the left-hand lane against the predatory flashing of a white Porsche.

'What does "Oh God" mean?'

'I don't know. Not what you think perhaps. There was no conference, not for Leo. Not in Bad Godesberg, not anywhere else; not on Thursdays, not on any other day. Until Rawley came, it's true, he attended a low-level conference at the Buildings Ministry. They discussed private contracts for repairing German houses damaged by Allied manoeuvres. Leo rubber stamped their proposals.'

'Until Bradfield came?'

'Yes.'

'Then what happened? The conference had run down, had it? Like the rest of his work.'

'More or less.'

Instead of turning right into the Embassy gateway, de Lisle filtered to the left bay and prepared to make the circuit a second time.

'What do you mean? "*More or less*"?'

'Rawley put a stop to it.'

'To the conference?'

'I told you: it was mechanical. It could be done by correspondence.'

Turner was almost in despair. 'Why are you fencing with me? What's going on? Did he stop the conference or not? What part's he playing in this?'

'Take care,' de Lisle warned him, lifting one hand from the steering-wheel. 'Don't rush in. Rawley sent me instead of him. He didn't like the Embassy to be represented by someone like Leo.'

'Someone like—'

'By a temporary. That's all! By a temporary without full status. He felt it was wrong so he got me to go along in his place. After that, Leo never spoke to me again. He thought I'd intrigued against him. Now that's enough. Don't ask me any more.' They were passing the Aral garage again, going north. The petrol attendant recognized the car and waved cheerfully to de Lisle. 'That's your mede or measure. I'm not going to discuss Bradfield with you if you bully me till you're blue in the face. He's my colleague, my superior and—'

'And your friend! Christ forgive me: who do you represent out here? Yourselves or the poor bloody taxpayer? I'll tell you who: the Club. *Your* Club. The bloody Foreign Office; and if you saw Rawley Bradfield standing on Westminster Bridge hawking his files for an extra pension, you'd bloody well look the other way.'

Turner was not shouting. It was rather the massive slowness of his speech which gave it urgency.

'You make me puke. All of you. The whole sodding circus.

You didn't give a twopenny damn for Leo, any of you, while he was here. Common as dirt, wasn't he? No background, no childhood, no nothing. Shove him the other side of the river where he won't be noticed! Tuck him away in the catacombs with the German staff! Worth a drink but not worth dinner! What happens now? He bolts, and he takes half your secrets with him for good measure, and suddenly you've got the guilts and you're blushing like a lot of virgins holding your hands over your fannies and not talking to strange men. Everybody: you, Meadowes, Bradfield. You *know* how he wormed his way in there, how he conned them all; how he stole and cheated. You know something else too: a friendship, a love affair, something that made him special for you, made him interesting. There's a whole world he lived in and none of you will put a name to it. What was it? Who was it? Where the hell did he go on Thursday afternoons if he didn't go to the Ministry? Who ran him? Who protected him? Who gave him his orders and his money and took his information off him? Who held his hand? He's a spy, for Christ's sake! He's put his hand in the till! And the moment you find out, you're all on his side!'

'No,' said de Lisle. They were pulling up at the gate; the police were converging on them, tapping on the window. He let them wait. 'You've got it wrong. You and Leo form a team of your own. You're the other side of the wire. Both of you. That's your problem. Whatever definitions, whatever labels. That's why you're beating the air.'

They entered the car park and de Lisle drove round to the canteen side where Turner had stood that morning, staring across the field.

'I've got to see his house,' Turner said. 'I've got to.' They were both looking ahead of them, through the windscreen.

'I thought you'd ask me that.'

'All right, forget it.'

'Why should I? I've no doubt you'll go anyway. Sooner or later.'

They got out and walked slowly over the tarmac. The despatch riders were lying on the lawn, their motor-bikes

138

stacked round the flagpole. The geraniums, martially arranged, glinted like tiny guardsmen along the verges.

'He loved the Army,' de Lisle said, as they climbed the steps. 'He really loved it.'

As they paused to show their passes yet again to the weasel sergeant, Turner chanced to look back at the carriageway.

'Look!' he said suddenly. 'That's the pair that picked us up at the airport.'

A black Opel had lumbered into the filter bay; two men sat in the front; from his vantage point on the steps, Turner could make out easily the multiple reflectors of the long driving mirror glittering in the sunlight.

'Ludwig Siebkron took us to lunch,' de Lisle said with a dry smile, 'and now he's brought us home. I told you: don't go thinking you're a specialist.'

'Then where were you on Friday night?'

'In the woodshed,' de Lisle snapped, 'waiting to murder Lady Ann for her priceless diamonds.'

The cypher room was open again. Cork lay on a truckle bed, a handbook on Caribbean bungalows lay beside him on the floor. On the desk in the dayroom was a blue Embassy envelope addressed to Alan Turner Esquire. His name was typewritten; the style was stiff and rather gauche. There was a number of things, the writer said, which Mr Turner might care to know about in connexion with the matter which had brought him to Bonn. If it were convenient, the writer continued, he might care to call for a glass of sherry wine at the above address at half past six o'clock. The address was in Bad Godesberg and the writer was Miss Jenny Pargiter of Press and Information Section, presently on attachment to Chancery. She had signed her name and typed it beneath the signature for reasons of clarity; the P was written rather large, Turner decided; and as he opened the blue rexine diary he permitted himself a rare if puzzled smile of anticipation. P for Praschko; P for Pargiter. And P was the initial on the diary. Come on, Leo, let's have a look at your guilty secret.

8

Jenny Pargiter

'I ASSUME,' Jenny Pargiter began, in a prepared statement, 'that you are used to dealing in delicate matters.'

The sherry stood between them on the glass-topped sofa table. The flat was dark and ugly: the chairs were Victorian wicker, the drapes German and very heavy. Constable reproductions hung in the dining alcove.

'Like a doctor, you have standards of professional confidence.'

'Oh sure,' said Turner.

'It was mentioned at Chancery meeting this morning that you were investigating Leo Harting's disappearance. We were warned not to discuss it, even among ourselves.'

'You're allowed to discuss it with me,' said Turner.

'No doubt. But I naturally would wish to be told how much further any confidence might go. What, for instance, is the relationship between yourselves and Personnel Department?'

'It depends on the information.'

She had raised the sherry glass to the level of her eye and appeared to be measuring the fluid content. It was an attitude evidently designed to demonstrate her sophistication and her ease of mind.

'Supposing someone – supposing I myself had been injudicious. In a personal matter.'

'It depends who you've been injudicious *with*,' Turner replied, and Jenny Pargiter coloured suddenly.

'That is not what I meant at all.'

'Look,' said Turner, watching her, 'if you come and tell me in confidence that you've left a bundle of files in the bus, I'll have to give details to Personnel Department. If you tell me you've been going out with a boy friend now and then, I'm not going to fall over in a faint. Mainly,' he said, pushing his sherry glass across the table for her to replenish, 'Personnel Department don't want to know we exist.' His manner was very casual, as if he barely cared. He sat impassively, filling the whole chair.

'There is the question of protecting other people, third parties who cannot necessarily speak for themselves.'

Turner said, 'There's also the question of security. If you didn't think it was important, you wouldn't ask to see me in the first place. It's up to you. I can't give you any guarantees.'

She lit a cigarette with sharp, angular movements. She was not an ugly girl, but she seemed to dress either too young or too old, so that whatever Turner's age, she was not his contemporary.

'I accept that,' she said and regarded him darkly for a moment, as if assessing how much Turner could take. 'However, you have misunderstood the reason why I asked you to call here. It is this. Since you are quite certain to be told all manner of rumours about Harting and myself, I thought it best if you heard the truth from me.'

Turner put down his glass and opened his notebook.

'I arrived here just before Christmas,' Jenny Pargiter said, 'from London. Before that I was in Djakarta. I returned to London intending to be married. You may have read of my engagement?'

'I think I must have missed it,' said Turner.

'The person to whom I was engaged decided at the last minute that we were not suited. It was a very courageous decision. I was then posted to Bonn. We had known one another for many years; we had read the same subject at University and I had always assumed we had much in common. The person decided otherwise. That is what engagements are for. I am perfectly content. There is no *reason* for anyone to be sorry for me.'

'You got here at Christmas?'

'I asked particularly to be here in time for the holiday. In previous years, we had always spent Christmas together. Unless I was in Djakarta of course. The . . . separation on this occasion was certain to be painful to me. I was most anxious to mitigate the distress with a new atmosphere.'

'Quite.'

'As a single woman in an Embassy, one is very often overcome with invitations at Christmas. Almost everyone in Chancery invited me to spend the festive days with them. The Bradfields, the Crabbes, the Jacksons, the Gavestons: they all asked me. I was also invited by the Meadowes. You have met Arthur Meadowes no doubt.'

'Yes.'

'Meadowes is a widower and lives with his daughter, Myra. He is in fact a B3, though we no longer use those grades. I found it very touching to be invited by a member of the Junior Staff.'

Her accent was very slight, provincial rather than regional, and for all her attempts at disowning it, it mocked her all the time.

'In Djakarta we always had that tradition. We *mixed* more. In a larger Embassy like Bonn, people tend to remain in their groups. I am not suggesting there should be total assimilation: I would even regard that as *bad*. The A's, for instance, tend to have different tastes as well as different intellectual interests to the B's. I am suggesting that in Bonn the distinctions are too *rigid*, and too many. The A's remain with the A's and the B's with the B's even inside the different sections: the economists, the attachés, Chancery; they all form cliques. I do not consider that right. Would you care for more sherry?'

'Thanks.'

'So I accepted Meadowes' invitation. The other guest was Harting. We spent a pleasant day, stayed there till evening, then left. Myra Meadowes was going out – she has been very ill, you know; she had a liaison in Warsaw, I understand, with a local undesirable and it very nearly ended in tragedy. Personally I am against anticipated marriages. Myra Meadowes was going to a young people's party and Meadowes himself was invited to the Corks, so there was no question of our remaining. As we were leaving, Harting suggested we went for a walk. He knew a place not far away; it would be nice to drive up there and get some fresh air after so much food and drink. I am very fond of exercise. We had our walk and then he proposed that I should go back with him for supper. He was very insistent.'

142

She was no longer looking at him. Her fingertips were pressed together on her lap, making a basket of her hands.

'I felt it would be wrong to refuse. It was one of those decisions which women find extremely difficult. I would have been quite glad of an early night, but I did not wish to cause offence. After all, it was Christmas Day, and his behaviour during the walk had been perfectly unobjectionable. On the other hand it must be said that I had barely seen him before that day. In the event, I agreed, but I said that I would not wish to be late home. He accepted this provision and I followed him to Königswinter in my car. To my surprise I found that he had prepared everything for my arrival. The table was laid for two. He had even persuaded the boilerman to come and light the fire. After supper, he told me that he loved me.' Picking up her cigarette she drew sharply upon it. Her tone was more factual than ever: certain things had to be said. 'He told me that in all his life he had never felt such emotion. From that first day that I had appeared at Chancery meeting, he had been going out of his mind. He pointed to the lights of the barges on the river. "I stand at my bedroom window," he said, "and I watch every one of them, right through the night. Morning after morning, I watch the dawn rise on the river." It was all due to his obsession for me. I was dumbfounded.'

'What did you say?'

'I had no chance to say anything. He wished to give me a present. Even if he never saw me again, he wished me to have this Christmas gift as a token of his love. He disappeared into the study and came back with a parcel, all wrapped up and ready, with a label, "To my love." I was naturally completely at a loss. "I can't accept this," I said. "I refuse. I can't allow you to give me things. It puts me at a disadvantage." I explained to him that though he was completely English in many ways, in this respect the English did things differently. On the Continent, it was quite customary to take women by storm, but in England courtship was a long and thoughtful matter. We would have to get to know one another, compare our views. There was the discrepancy in our ages; I had my career to consider. I didn't know what to do,' she added helplessly. The brittleness had vanished from her voice: she was helpless and a little pathetic. 'He kept saying, after all it was *Christmas*; I should think of it as just an ordinary Christmas present.'

'What was in the parcel?'

'A hair-dryer. He said he admired my hair above everything. He watched the sun shine on it in the mornings. During Chancery meeting you understand. He must have been speaking figuratively; we were having a wretched winter.' She took a short breath. 'It must have cost him twenty pounds. No one, not even my ex-fiancé during our most intimate period, has ever given me anything so valuable.'

She performed a second ritual with the cigarette box, ducking her hand forward and arresting it suddenly, selecting a cigarette as if it were a chocolate, not this one but that one, lighting it with a heavy frown. 'We sat down and he put on a gramophone record. I am afraid I am not musical, but I thought that music might distract him. I was extremely sorry for him, and most reluctant to leave him in that condition. He just stared at me. I didn't know where to look. Finallly he came over and tried to embrace me, and I said I had to go home. He saw me to the car. He was very correct. Fortunately we had two more days of holiday. I was able to decide what to do. He telephoned twice to invite me to supper and I refused. By the end of the holiday, I had made up my mind. I wrote him a letter and returned the gift. I felt no other course was open to me. I went in early and left the parcel with the Chancery Guard. I explained in my letter that I had given great thought to all he had said and I was convinced I would never be able to return his affection. It would therefore be wrong for me to encourage him, and since we were colleagues and would be seeing a lot of each other, I felt it was only prudent to tell him this immediately, before—'

'Before what?'

'The gossip started,' she said with sudden passion. 'I've never known anywhere for such gossip. You can't move without them making up some wicked story about you.'

'What story have they made up about you?'

'God knows,' she said uselessly. 'God knows.'

'Which Guard did you leave the parcel with?'

'Walter, the younger one. Macmullen's son.'

'Did he tell other people?'

'I particularly asked him to regard the matter as confidential.'

'I should think that impressed him,' Turner said.

She stared at him angrily, her face red with embarrassment.

'All right. So you gave him the bird. What did he do about it?'

'That day he appeared at Chancery meeting and wished me good morning as if nothing had happened. I smiled at him and that was that. He was pale but brave . . . sad but in command. I felt that the worst was over. . . . Fortunately he was about to begin a new job in Chancery Registry and I hoped that this would take his mind off other things. For a couple of weeks I barely spoke to him. I saw him either in the Embassy or at social functions and he seemed quite happy. He made no allusion to Christmas evening or to the hair-dryer. Occasionally at cocktail parties he would come and stand quite close to me and I knew that . . . he wished for my proximity. Sometimes I would be conscious of his eyes on me. A woman can tell these things; I knew that he had still not completely given up hope. He had a way of catching my eye that was . . . beyond all doubt. I cannot imagine why I had not noticed it before. However, I continued to give him no encouragement. That was the decision I had taken, and whatever the short-term temptations to alleviate his distress, I knew that in the long term no purpose could be served by . . . leading him on. I was also confident that anything so sudden and . . . irrational would quickly pass.'

'And did it?'

'We continued in this way for about a fortnight. It was beginning to get on my nerves. I seemed unable to go to a single party, to accept a single invitation without seeing him. He didn't even address me any more. He just looked. Wherever I went, his eyes followed me. . . . They are very dark eyes. I would call them soulful. Dark brown, as one would expect, and they imparted a remarkable sense of dependence. . . . In the end I was almost frightened to go out. I'm afraid that at that stage, I even had an unworthy thought. I wondered whether he was reading my mail.'

'Did you now?'

'We all have our own pigeonholes in Registry. For telegrams and mail. Everyone in Registry takes a hand at sorting the incoming papers. It is of course the custom here as in England that invitations are sent unsealed. It would have been quite possible for him to look inside.'

'Why was the thought unworthy?'

'It was untrue, that's why,' she retorted. 'I taxed him with it and he assured me it was quite untrue.'

'I see.'

Her voice became even more pedagogic; the tones came very crisply, brooking no question whatever.

'He would never do such a thing. It was not in his nature, it had not crossed his mind. He assured me categorically that he was not . . . stalking me. That was the expression I used; it was one I instantly regretted. I cannot imagine how I came on such a ridiculous metaphor. To the contrary, he said, he was merely following his usual social pattern; if it bothered me he would change it, or decline all further invitations until I instructed him otherwise. Nothing was further from his mind than to be a burden to me.'

'So after that you were friends again, were you?'

He watched her search for the wrong words, watched her balance awkwardly at the edge of truth, and awkwardly withdraw.

'Since the twenty-third of January he has not spoken to me again,' she blurted. Even in that sad light, Turner saw the tears running down her rough cheeks as her head fell forward and her hand rose quickly to cover them. 'I can't go on. I think of him all the time.'

Rising, Turner opened the door of the drinks cupboard and half filled a tumbler with whisky.

'Here,' he said gently, 'This is what you like; drink it up and stop pretending.'

'It's overwork.' She took the glass. 'Bradfield never relaxes. He doesn't like women. He hates them. He wants to drive us all into the ground.'

'Now tell me what happened on the twenty-third of January.'

She was sitting sideways in the chair, her back towards him, and her voice had risen beyond her control.

'He ignored me. He pretended to lose himself in work. I'd go into Registry to collect my papers and he wouldn't even look up. Not for me. Not any more. He might for other people, but not for me. Oh no. He had never taken much interest in work – you only had to watch him in Chancery meetings to realize that. He was idle at heart. Glib. But the moment he heard me come along, he couldn't work hard enough. He saw through me, even if I greeted him. Even if I walked straight into him in the corridor, it was the same. He didn't notice me. I didn't exist. I thought I'd go off my head. It wasn't right: after all, he's only a B you know, and a temporary; he's nothing really. He carries no weight at all, you only have to hear how they talk about him. . . . Cheap, that's what they say of him. A quick mind but quite unsound.' For a moment she was far above his grade. 'I wrote him letters. I rang his number at Königswinter.'

'They all knew did they? You made a display of it did you?'

'First of all he chases after me . . . besieges me with declarations of love . . . like a gigolo really. Of course, I mean there's part of me that sees through *that* all right, don't you worry. Running hot and cold like that: who does he think he is?'

She lay across the chair, her head buried in the crook of her elbow, her shoulders shaking to the rhythm of her sobbing.

'You've got to tell me,' Turner said. He was standing over her, his hand on her arm. 'Listen. You've got to tell me what happened at the end of January. It was something important wasn't it? Something he asked you to do for him. Something political. Something special you're afraid of. First of all he made up to you. He worked on you, took you by surprise . . . then he got what he wanted; something very simple he couldn't get for himself. And when he'd got it he didn't want you any more.'

The sobbing started.

'You told him something he needed to know; you did him a favour: a favour to help him along the line. All right, you're not unique. There's a good few others have done the same thing one way or the other, believe me. So what is it?' He knelt down beside her. 'What was it that was injudicious? What was it that involved third parties? Tell me! it was something that frightened the life out of you! *Tell me what it was!*'

'Oh God, I lent him the keys. I lent him the keys,' she said.

'Hurry.'

'The Duty Officer's. The whole lot. He came to me and begged me . . . no, not begged. No.'

She was sitting up, white in the face. Turner refilled her glass and put it back in her hand.

'I was on duty. Night Duty Officer. Thursday January the twenty-third. Leo wasn't allowed to be Duty Officer. There are things temporaries can't see: special instructions . . . contingency plans. I'd stayed in to cope with a rush of telegrams; it must have been half past seven, eight o'clock. I was leaving the cypher room . . . just going to Registry, and I saw him standing there. As if he'd been waiting. Smiling. "Jenny," he said, "What a nice surprise." I was so happy.'

The sobbing broke out again.

'I was so happy. I'd been longing for him to speak to me again. He'd been waiting for me, I knew he had; he was pretending it was an accident. And I said to him: "Leo." I'd never called him that before. Leo. We just talked, standing in the corridor. What a *lovely* surprise he kept saying. Perhaps he could give me dinner? I reminded him, in case he had forgotten, that I was on duty. That didn't bother him either. What a pity, how about tomorrow night? Then the weekend? He would ring me on Saturday morning, how would that be? That would be fine, I said, I'd like that. And we could go for a walk first, he said, up on the football field? I was so happy. I still had the telegrams in my arms, a whole bundle, so I said well, I'd better get along, post these into Arthur Meadowes. He wanted to take them for me but I said no, I could manage them, it was all right. I was just turning away. . . . I wanted to be first to go, you see, I didn't want him walking away from me. I was just going and he said, "Oh Jenny, look here, by the way . . ." You know the way he talks. "Well, a ridiculous thing has happened, the choir are all hanging around downstairs and no one can unlock the Assembly Room door. Somebody's locked it and we can't find the key and we wondered whether you had one." It seemed a bit odd really; I couldn't think why anyone should *want* to lock it in the first place. So I said, yes, I'd come down and open it; I'd just have to check in some telegrams for distribution. I mean he knew I'd got a key; the Duty Officer has a spare key for every room in the Embassy. "Don't bother to come down," he says. "Just give me the key and I'll do it for you. It won't take two minutes." And he saw me hesitate.'

She closed her eyes.

'He was so *little*,' she burst out. 'You could hurt him so easily. I'd already accused him of opening my letters. I loved him. . . . I swear I've never loved anyone . . .' Gradually her crying stopped.

'So you gave him the keys? The whole bunch? That's room keys, safe keys—'

'Keys to all desks and steel cupboards; to the front and rear doors of the building and the key to turn off the alarm in Chancery Registry.'

'Lift keys?'

'The lift wasn't bolted by then . . . the grilles weren't up. . . . They did that the next weekend.'

'How long did he have them for?'

'Five minutes. Maybe less. It's not long enough, is it?' She had seized his arm beseeching him. 'Say it's not long enough.'

'To take an impression? He could take fifty impressions if he knew what he was about.'

'He'd need wax or plasticine or something: I asked. I looked it up.'

'He'd have had it ready in his room,' Turner said indifferently. 'He lived on the ground floor. Don't worry,' he added gently. 'He may just have been letting in the choir. Don't let your imagination run away with you.'

She had stopped crying. Her voice calmed. She spoke with a sense of private recognition: 'It wasn't choir practice night. Choir practice is on Fridays. This was Thursday.'

'You found out did you? Asked the Chancery Guard?'

'I knew already! I knew when I handed him the keys! I tell myself I didn't, but I did. But I had to trust him. It was an act of giving. Don't you see? An act of giving, an act of love. How can I expect a man to understand that?'

'And after you'd given,' Turner said, getting up, 'he didn't want you any more, did he?'

'That's like all men, isn't it?'

'Did he ring you Saturday?'

'You know he didn't.' Her face was still buried in her fore-arm. He closed the notebook. 'Can you hear me?'

'Yes.'

'Did he ever mention a woman to you; a Margaret Aickman? He was engaged to her. She knew Harry Praschko as well.'

'No.'

'No other woman?'

'No.'

'Did he ever talk politics?'

'No.'

'Did he ever give you any cause to suppose he was a person of strong left-wing leanings?'

'No.'

'Ever see him in the company of suspicious persons?'

'No.'

'Did he talk about his childhood? His uncle? An uncle who lived in Hampstead. A communist who brought him up?'

'No.'

'Uncle Otto?'

'No.'

'Did he ever mention Praschko? Well, did he? Did he ever mention Praschko, do you hear?'

'He said Praschko was the only friend he'd ever had.' She broke down again, and again he waited.

'Did he mention Praschko's politics?'

'No.'

'Did he say they were still friends?'

She shook her head.

'Somebody had lunch with Harting last Thursday. The day before he left. At the Maternus. Was that you?'

'I told you! I swear to you!'

'Was it?'

'No!'

'He's marked it down as you. It's marked P. That's how he wrote you down other times.'

'It wasn't me!'

'Then it was Praschko, was it?'

'How should I know?'

'Because you had an affair with him! You told me half and not the rest! You were sleeping with him up to the day he left!'

'It's not true!'

'Why did Bradfield protect him? He hated Leo's guts: why did he look after him like that? Give him jobs? Keep him on the payroll?'

'Please go,' she said. 'Please go. Never come back.'

'Why!'

She sat up.

'Get out,' she said.

'You had dinner with him Friday night. The night he left. You were sleeping with him and you won't admit it!'

'No!'

'He asked you about the Green File! He made you get the Despatch Box for him!'

'He didn't! He didn't! Get out!'

'I want a cab.'

He waited while she telephoned. '*Sofort*,' she said, '*Sofort*,' come at once and take him away.

He was at the door.

'What will you do when you find him?' she asked with that slack voice that follows passion.

'Not my business.'

'Don't you care?'

'We never will find him, so what does it matter?'

'Then why look for him?'

'Why not? That's how we spend our lives, isn't it? Looking for people we'll never find.'

He walked slowly down the stairs to the hall. From another flat came the growl of a cocktail party. A group of Arabs, very drunk, swept past him pulling off their coats and shouting. He waited on the doorstep. Across the river, the narrow lights of Chamberlain's Petersberg hung like a necklace in the warm dark. A new block stood directly before him. It seemed to have been built from the top, beginning with the crane and working downwards. He thought he had seen it before from a different angle. A railway bridge straddled the end of the avenue. As the express thundered over it, he saw the silent diners grazing at their food.

'The Embassy,' he said. 'British Embassy.'

'*Englische Botschaft ?*'

'Not English. British. I'm in a hurry.'

The driver swore at him, shouting about diplomats. They drove extremely fast and once they nearly hit a tram.

'Get a bloody move on, can't you?'

He demanded a receipt. The driver kept a rubber stamp and a pad in his glove tray, and he hit the paper so hard that it crumpled. The Embassy was a ship, all its windows blazing. Black figures moved in the lobby with the slow coupling of a ballroom dance. The car park was full. He threw away the receipt. Lumley didn't countenance taxi fares. It was a new rule since the last cut. There was no one he could claim from. Except Harting, whose debts appeared to be accumulating.

Bradfield was in conference, Miss Peate said. He would probably be flying to Brussels with the Ambassador before morning. She had put away her papers and was fiddling with a blue leather *placement* tray, fitting the names round a dinner table in order of precedence, and she spoke to him as if it were her duty to frustrate him. And de Lisle was at the Bundestag, listening to the debate on Emergency Legislation.

'I want to see the Duty Officer's keys.'

'I'm afraid you can only have *them* with Mr Bradfield's consent.'

He fought with her and that was what she wanted. He overcame her and that was what she wanted too. She gave him a written authority signed by Administration Section and countersigned by the Minister (Political). He took it to the front desk where Macmullen was on duty. Macmullen was a big, steady man, sometime sergeant of Edinburgh constabulary, and whatever he had heard about Turner had given him no pleasure.

'And the night book,' Turner said. 'Show me the night book since January.'

'Please,' said Macmullen and stood over him while he looked through it in case he took it away. It was half past eight and the Embassy was emptying. 'See you in the morning,' Mickie Crabbe whispered as he passed. 'Old boy.'

There was no reference to Harting.

'Mark me in,' Turner said, pushing the book across the counter. 'I'll be in all night.'

As Leo was, he thought.

9

Guilty Thursday

THERE WERE ABOUT fifty keys and only half a dozen were labelled. He stood in the first floor corridor where Leo had stood, drawn back into the shadow of a pillar, staring at the cypher room door. It was about seven thirty, Leo's time, and he imagined Jenny Pargiter coming out with a bundle of papers in her arm. The corridor was very noisy now, and the steel trap on the cypher room door was rising and falling like a guillotine for the Registry girls to hand in telegrams and collect them; but that Thursday night had been a quiet time, a lull in the mounting crisis, and Leo had spoken to her *here*, where Turner stood now. He looked at his watch and then at the keys again and thought: five minutes. What *would* he have done? The noise was deafening; worse than day; not only the voices but the very pounding of the machines proclaimed a world entering emergency. But that night was calm, and Leo was a creature of silence, waiting here to draw his quarry and destroy. In five minutes.

He walked along the corridor as far as the lobby and looked down into the stair well and watched the evening shift of typists slip into the dark, survivors from a burning ship, letting the night recover them. Brisk but nonchalant would be his manner, for Jenny would watch him all the way till here; and Gaunt or Macmullen would see him descend these stairs; brisk but not triumphant.

He stood in the lobby. But *what* a risk, he thought suddenly: what a hazardous game. The crowd parted to admit two German officials. They were carrying black briefcases and they walked portentously as though they had come to perform an operation. They wore grey scarves put on before the overcoat, and folded broad and flat like Russian tunics. *What* a risk. She could revoke; she could pursue him; she would know within minutes, if she had not known already, that Leo was lying, she would know the moment she reached the lobby and heard no singing from the Assembly Room, saw no trace at all of a dozen singers entered in the night book, saw no hats and coats on those very pegs beside the door where the German officials were even now disencumbering themselves; she would know that Harting Leo, refugee, fringe-man, lover *manqué* and trader in third-rate artifices, had lied to her to get the keys.

'A gift of love, an act of love: how can I expect a *man* to understand that?'

Before entering the corridor, he stopped and examined the lift. The gold-painted door was bolted; the central panel of glass was black, boarded from the inside. Two heavy steel bars had been fastened horizontally for added security.

'How long's that been there?'

'Since Bremen, sir,' Macmullen said.

'When was Bremen?'

'January, sir. Late January. The Office advised it, sir. They sent a man out specially. He did the cellars and the lift, sir.' Macmullen gave information as if it were evidence before the bailies of Edinburgh, in a series of verbal drill movements, breathing at regulation intervals. 'He worked the whole weekend,' Macmullen added with awe; for he was a self-indulgent man and readily exhausted by work.

He made his way slowly through the gloom to Harting's room thinking: *these* doors would be closed; these lights extinguished, these rooms silent. Was there a moon to shine through the bars? Or only these blue night lights burning for a cheaper Britain, and his own footsteps echoing in the vaults?

Two girls passed him, dressed for the emergency. One wore jeans and she looked at him very straight, guessing his weight. Jesus, he thought, quite soon I'm going to grab one, and he unlocked the door to Leo's room and stood there in the dark. What *were* you up to, he wondered, you little thief?

Tins. Cigar tins would do, filled with white hardening putty; a child's plasticine from that big Woolworths in Bad Godesberg would do; a little white talc to ensure a clean imprint. Three movements of the key, this side, that side, a straight stab into the flesh, and make sure the shoulders are clearly visible. It may not be a perfect fit; that depends on the blanks and the print, but a nice soft metal will yield a little in the womb and form itself to fit the inner walls. . . . Come on Turner, the sergeant used to say, you'd find it if it had hairs round it. He had them ready, then. All fifty tins? Or just one?

Just one key. Which? Which Aladdin's cave, which secret chamber hid the secret treasures of this grumbling English house?

Harting, you thief. He began on Harting's own door, just to annoy him, to bring it home to an absent thief that *his* door can be fiddled with as well, and he worked slowly along the passage fitting the keys to the locks, and each time he found a key that matched he took it off the ring and dropped it into his pocket and thought, What good did *that* one do you? Most of the doors were not even locked, so that the keys were redundant anyway: cupboards, lavatories, washrooms, restrooms, offices, a first-aid room that stank of alcohol and a junction box for electric cables.

A microphone job? Was that the nature of your technical interest, thief? The gimmicks, the flex, the hair-dryers, the bits and pieces: was that all a lovely cover for carting in some daft conjuring set for eavesdropping? 'Balls,' he said out loud, and with a dozen keys already tapping against his thigh, he plodded up the stairs again straight into the arms of the Ambassador's private secretary, a strutting, fussy man who had borrowed a good deal of his master's authority.

'H.E. will be leaving in a minute; I should make yourself scarce if I were you,' he said with chilling ease. 'He's not awfully keen on you people.'

In most of the corridors it was daytime. Commercial Section was celebrating Scottish week. A mauve grousemoor, draped in Campbell tartan, hung beside a photograph of the Queen in highland dress. Miniatures of Scotch Whisky were mounted in a *collage* with dancers and bagpipes, and framed in plywood battens. In the Open Plan, under radiant exhortations to buy from the North, pale-faced clerks struck doggedly at machines for adding and subtracting. *Deadline Brussels!* A placard warned them, but the machines seemed unimpressed. He climbed a floor and was in Whitehall with the Service Attachés, each with his tiny Ministry and his stencilled title on the door.

'What the hell are you up to?' a sergeant clerk demanded, and Turner told him to keep a civil tongue in his head. Somewhere a military voice wrestled gallantly with dictation. In the Typing Pool, the girls sat forlornly in schoolroom lines: two juniors in green overalls gently nursed a mammoth duplicator while a third laid out the coloured telegrams as if they were fine linen for going away. Raised above them all, the Head Girl, blue haired and fully sixty, sat on a separate dais checking stencils. She alone, scenting the enemy, looked up sharply, nose towards the wind. The walls behind here were lined with Christmas cards from Head Girls in other missions. Some depicted camels, others the royal crest.

'I'm going over the locks,' he muttered, and her look said 'Go over what you like, but not my girls.'

Christ, I could do with one, I'm telling you. Surely you could spare just one for a quick drop into paradise? Harting, you thief.

It was ten o'clock. He had visited every room to which Harting had acquired access; he had gained nothing but a headache for his trouble. Whatever Harting wanted was no longer there, or else so hidden as to require weeks of searching; or so obvious as to be invisible. He felt the sickness which follows tension and his mind was racing with unco-ordinated recollections. Christ: one single day. From enthusiasm to frustration in one day. From an aeroplane to the day-room desk, all the clues and none; I've lived a whole bloody life and it's only Monday. He stared at the blank foolscap pages of the telegram form, wondering what the hell to write. Cork was asleep and the robots were silent. The keys lay in a heap before him. One by one he began threading them back on to the ring. Put together, he thought; *construct*. You will not go to bed until you are at least aware of the trail you must follow. The task of an intellectual, his fart-arsed tutor brayed, is to make order out of chaos. Define anarchy. It is a mind without a system. Please teacher, what is a system without a mind? Taking a pencil he lazily drew a chart of the days of the week and divided each day into panels of one hour. He opened the blue diary. Re-form the fragments, make of all the pieces one piece. You'll find him and Shawn won't. Harting Leo, Claims and Consular, thief and hunter, will hunt you down.

'You don't know anything about shares by any chance?' Cork enquired, waking with a start.

'No, I don't.'

'My query is, you see,' he continued, rubbing his pink eyes, 'If there's a slump on Wall Street and a slump in Frankfurt and we don't make the Market on this run, how will it affect Swedish steel?'

'If I were you,' Turner said, 'I'd put the whole lot on red and forget it.'

'Only I have this firm intention,' Cork explained. 'We've got a bit of land lined up in the Caribbean—'

'Shut up.'

Construct. Put your ideas on a blackboard and *then* see what happens to them. Come on, Turner, you're a philosopher, tell us how the world goes round. What little absolute will we put into Harting's mouth, for instance? Facts. Construct. Did you not, after all, my dear Turner, abandon the *contemplative* life of the academic in favour of the *functional* life of the civil servant? Construct; put your theories to work and de Lisle will call you a real person.

Mondays first. Mondays are for invitations out. Buffet parties are favoured, de Lisle had told him in an aside at luncheon; they eliminate the pains of *placement*. Mondays are reserved for away matches. England plays the wogs. Away to a different kind of slavery. Harting was essentially a second division man. The minor Embassies. Embassies with small drawing rooms. The B team played away on Mondays.

' – and if it's a girl, I reckon we could get a coloured nanny, an Amah; she could do the teaching, up to O-level at least.'

'Can't you keep quiet?'

'Provided we have the funds,' Cork added. 'You can't get them for nothing, I'm sure.'

'I'm working, can't you understand?'

I'm trying, he thought and his mind drifted into other fields. He was with the little girl in the corridor, whose full unpainted lips faded so reluctantly into the feathery skin; he imagined that long appraising stare upon his nascent paunch and he heard her laughing as his own wife had laughed: Alan darling, you're supposed to take me, not fight me. It's rhythm, it's like dancing, can't you understand? And Tony's such a *beautiful* dancer, Alan darling, and I shall be a little late tonight, and I shall be away tomorrow, playing an away match with my Monday lover. Alan stop. Stop! Alan please don't hit me! I'll never touch him again, I swear. Until Tuesday.

Harting, you thief.

Tuesdays were for entertaining at home. Home is a Tuesday; home is having people in. He made a list of them and thought: it's worse than Blackheath. It's worse than her bloody mother fighting for her fragment of power; it's worse than Bournemouth and seed cake for the minister; it's worse than black Sundays in Yorkshire and weddings timed for six o'clock tea; it is a custom built, unassailable preventive detention of vacuous social exchange. The Vandelungs (Dutch) . . . the Canards (Canadian) . . . the Obutus (Ghanaian) . . . the Cortezanis (Italian) . . . the Allertons, the Crabbes, and once, sure enough, the Bradfields; this happy band was mingled with no fewer than forty-eight accountable bores defined only by their quantity: the Obutus plus six . . . the Allertons plus two . . . the Bradfields alone. You gave them your *full* attention, didn't you? 'I understand he maintains a certain standard there.' Champagne and two veg *that* night. Plover's eggs paid for by the Russian taxpayer. His wife interrupted him: darling why don't we go out tonight? The Willoughbys won't mind, they know I loathe cooking and Tony *adores* Italian food. Oh sure, sure: anything to please Tony.

' – And if it's a boy,' Cork said, 'I'll take it on myself. There must be *some* facilities for boys, even in a place like that. I mean it's a paradise, isn't it, specially for teachers.'

Wednesday was welfare. Ping pong night. Sing song night. The sergeants' mess: 'Have a little something in that gin and whisky, Mr Turner, sir, just to give it bite. The boys say one thing about you, sir, and I'm sure you won't mind me repeating it, sir, seeing it's Christmas: Mr Turner, they say – they always give you the Mister, sir, it's not something they do for everyone – Mr Turner is tough; Mr Turner is firm. But Mr Turner is *fair*. Now, sir, about my leave . . .' Exiles night. A night for worming an inch or two further into the flesh of the Embassy; come back little girl and just slip off those jeans. A night strictly for business. He studied the engagements in detail and thought: you really did work for your secrets, I will admit. You really hawked yourself, didn't you? Scottish Dancing, Skittles Club, Exiles Motoring, Sports Committee. Sooner you than me, boy: you really believed. I'll say that for you too. You really went for goal, didn't you? You kept the ball and you went through the lot of them, you thief.

Which left – since the weekends were not marked with anything but references to gardening and a couple of trips to Hanover – which left Thursdays.

Guilty Thursdays.

Draw a box round Thursday, telephone the Adler and find out what time they lock up. They don't. Draw another box round *that* box, measuring one and a half inches by half an inch and decorate the margins in between with sinuous snakes; cause their forked tongues to lick suggestively at the sweet Gothic curves of the letter T, and wait for the throbbing of a tormented head to be assumed into the waking drumbeat of the cypher machines. And the result?

Silence. Bloody silence.

The result is a Thursday shrouded in sexual mystery, tantalized by abstinence. A Thursday surrounded by meticulous entries written in a swollen, boring mayoral hand by a man with nothing to do and a lot of time to do it in. 'Remember Mary Crabbe's coffee grinder,' the worshipful mayor of Turner's home town in Yorkshire warned his fortunate biographer; remember to grind Mary Crabbe, you thief. 'Speak to Arthur about Myra's birthday,' Mr Crail the Minister, well known throughout all Yorkshire for the inanity of his sermons, whispered in a benevolent aside; 'Anglo-German Society Buffet Luncheon for Friends of the Free City of Hamburg,' 'International Ladies Subscription Luncheon, Costumes of All Nations, DM. 15.00. Incl. wine,' the Master of Ceremonies proclaimed, puffing his Mess-Night capitals over the lined pages. And make a mental note to ruin Jenny Pargiter's career. And Meadowes' retirement. And Gaunt? And Bradfield? And who else along the path? Myra Meadowes? You wrecker, Harting.

'Can't you turn those bloody things off?'

'I wish I could,' said Cork. 'Something's up, don't ask me what. Personal for Bradfield decypher yourself. Following for Bradfield by hand of officer . . . it must be his bloody birthday.'

'Funeral more likely,' Turner growled and returned to the diary.

But on Thursdays Harting *did* have something to do, something real; and not yet realized. Something he kept quiet about. Very. Something urgent and constructive; something secret. Something that made all the other days worthwhile, something to believe in. On Thursdays, Leo Harting touched the hem; and kept his mouth shut. Not even the weekly lie was recorded. Only last Thursday carried any entry at all, and that read: '*Maternus. One o'clock. P.*' The rest were as blank, as innocent and as unrevealing as the little virgins in the ground floor corridor.

Or as guilty.

All Harting's life took place that day. He had lived from Thursday to Thursday as others live from year to year. What *kind* of meeting did they have, Harting and his master? What kind of relationship after all these years of collaboration? Where did they meet? Where did he unpack those files and letters and breathlessly recite his intelligence? In the tower room of a slate-roofed villa? In a soft, linen bed with a soft silk girl and the jeans hanging on the bedpost? Under the bridge where the train went over? Or in the crumbling Embassy with a dusty chandelier, and old father Meadowes holding his little hand on the gilded sofa? In a pretty baroque bedroom of a Godesberg Hotel? In a grey block on the new housing estates? In a coy bungalow with a wrought iron name and stained glass let into the door? He tried to imagine them, Harting and his master, furtive yet assured, the whispered jokes and the whispered laughter. Here: this is a good one the porno seller whispers; I hardly like to part with this myself. You do *like* it straight don't you? 'Well, it's nice to be fancied,' Allerton lisped. Did they sit over a bottle as they casually planned their next assault upon the citadel, while in the background the camera clicked and the assistant gently shuffled the papers? Give it me once more darling but gently, like Tony. You're not confident, dear, you haven't read the manuals and learned the parts of the rifle.

Or was it a hasty pick-up? A back-street encounter, a frantic exchange as they drove through the small alleys and prayed to God they had no accident? Or on a hilltop? By a football field, where Harting wore the Balkan hat and the grey uniform of the Movement?

Cork was on the telephone to Miss Peate, and a note of awe had entered his voice:

'Stand by for seven hundred groups from Washington. London please pass and decypher yourself. You'd better warn him now: He's going to be in all night. Look dear, I don't care whether he's conferring with the Queen of England. This one's top priority, and it's my job to let him know so if you won't I will. *Ooh*, she is a bitch.'

'I'm glad you think that,' Turner said with one of his rare grins.

'I reckon she captains the team.'

'England versus the Rest of the World,' Turner agreed and they both laughed.

Was it with Praschko, then, that he had lunched at the *Maternus*? If so, Praschko could hardly be his regular contact, for *he* would not add the tell-tale P, that Harting, who covered his tracks so well; and would not lunch with Praschko in public either, after the trouble he had taken to sever his relationship. Was there, in that case, a middle-man, a cut-out, between Praschko and Harting? Or was this the day the system failed? Hold the line Turner, hold on to reason, for unreason will be your downfall. Make order out of chaos. Was this P the sign that Praschko proposed to see him in person, to warn him perhaps that Siebkron was on his trail? To order him – here was a chance – to order him *at any risk* and *at all costs* to steal the Green File before he ran?

Thursday.

He lifted the keys and swung them gently from his finger. Thursday was the day for meeting . . . pressure day . . . the day he was warned . . . the day before he left . . . the day of the weekly briefing and de-briefing . . . the day he borrowed the keys from Pargiter.

Christ: had he really slept with Pargiter? There are certain sacrifices, General Shlobodovitch, which not even Leo Harting will make in the service of Mother Russia.

The useless keys. What did he suppose he would get from them? Entry to the coveted despatch box? Balls. He would have observed the procedure; Meadowes had even instructed him in it. He would know very well there were no spare keys to the despatch box in the Duty Officer's bunch. Entry to Registry itself then? Balls again. He would know at a glance that Registry was protected with better locks than these.

So what key did he want?

What key did he want so desperately that he imperilled his whole career as a spy in order to get a copy of it? What key did he want, that he made up to Jenny Pargiter and risked the disapproval of the Embassy – incurred it, indeed, if Meadowes and Gaunt were anything to go by. What key? The key to the lift, so that he could smuggle out his files, dump them in some hideaway on an upper floor and remove them singly and at leisure in his briefcase? Was that what the missing trolley meant?

Fantastic visions presented themselves. He saw the little figure of Harting sprinting down the dark corridor, pushing the trolley ahead of him into the open lift, saw the pyramid of box files trembling on the upper shelf, and on the lower shelf the accidental by-product: the stationery, the seal, the diaries, the long-carriage typewriter from the pool. . . . He saw the mini van waiting at the side entrance and Harting's nameless master holding the door and he said: 'Oh bugger it,' schoolboy-style at the very moment when Miss Peate came to fetch the telegrams, and Miss Peate's sigh was a statement of sexual abstinence.

'He'll want his code books too,' Cork warned her.

'He happens to be quite aware of the decoding procedure thank you.'

'Here, what's up then, what's going on in Brussels?' Turner asked.

'Rumours.'

'What of?'

'If they wanted you to know *that*, they would hardly use the person to person procedure would they?'

'You don't know London,' said Turner.

As she left she managed even in her walk – in her loping, English touch-nothing, feel-nothing, sex-is-for-the-lower-classes walk – to convey her particular contempt for Turner and all his works.

'I could murder her,' Cork said confidently, 'I could cut her nasty throat. I wouldn't have a moment's regret. Three years she's been here and the only time she smiled was when the Old Man creased his Rolls Royce.'

It was absurd. No questions; he knew it was absurd. Spies of Harting's calibre do not steal; they record, memorize, photograph; spies of Harting's calibre act by graft and calculation, not by impulse. They cover their tracks and survive to deceive again tomorrow.

Nor do they tell transparent lies.

They do not tell Jenny Pargiter that choir practice takes place on Thursdays when she can find out within five minutes that they take place on Fridays. They do not tell Meadowes that they are attending conferences in Bad Godesberg, when both Bradfield and de Lisle know that they are not; and have not done so for two years or more. They do not draw their balance of pay and allowances before they defect, as a signal to anyone who happens to be interested; they do not risk the curiosity of Gaunt in order to work late at night.

Work *where*?

He wanted privacy. He wanted to do by night things he could not do by day. What things? Use his camera in some remote room where he had concealed the files, where he could turn the lock upon himself? Where *was* the trolley? Where *was* the typewriter? Or was their disappearance, as Meadowes had assumed, really unconnected with Harting? At present there was only one answer: Harting had hidden the files in a cache

164

during the day, he had photographed them at night in privacy, and he returned them the next morning. . . . Except that he hadn't returned them. So why steal?

A spy does not steal. Rule one. An Embassy, discovering a loss, can change its plans, re-make or revoke treaties, take a dozen prophylactic measures to anticipate and minimize the harm that has been done. The best girl is the girl you don't have. The most effective deceit is the deceit which is never discovered. Then why steal? The reason was already clear. Harting was under pressure. Calculated though his actions might be, they had all the marks of a man racing against time. What was the hurry? What was the deadline?

Slowly, Alan; gently Alan; be like Tony, Alan. Be like lovely, slow, willowy, rhythmical, anatomically conversant, friendly Tony Willoughby, well known in the best clubs and famous for his copulative technique.

'I'd rather have a boy really, first,' said Cork. 'I mean, when you've got one behind you, you can branch out. Mind you, I don't hold with large families I will say. Not unless you can solve the servant problem. Are you married by the by? Oh dear, sorry I asked.'

Suppose for a moment that that furious private journey in Registry was the result of a dormant Communist sympathy re-awakened by the events of last autumn; suppose that was what had driven him. Then to what hasty end was his fury *directed*? Merely to the deadline dictated by a greedy master? The first stage was easily deduced: Karfeld came to power in October. From then on, a popular nationalist party was a reality; even a nationalist government was not impossible. For a month, two months, Harting broods. He sees Karfeld's face on every hoarding, hears the familiar slogans, 'He really *is* an invitation to Communism,' de Lisle had said. . . . The awakening is slow and reluctant, the old associations and sympathies lie deep and are slow in coming to the surface. Then the moment of decision, the turning point. Either alone, or as a result of Praschko's persuasion, he determines to betray. Praschko approaches him: the Green File. Get the Green File and our old cause will be served. . . . Get the Green File by decision-day in Brussels. . . . The contents of that file, Bradfield had said, could effectively compromise our entire posture in Brussels. . . .

Or was he being blackmailed? Was that the nature of the race? Must he choose between satisfying a greedy master or being compromised by an unknown indiscretion? Was there something in the Cologne incident, for example, which reflected to his discredit: a woman, an involvement in some seedy racket? Had he embezzled Rhine Army funds? Was he selling off tax-free whisky and cigarettes? Had he drifted into a homosexual entanglement? Had he, in fact, succumbed to any one of the dozen classic temptations which are the staple diet of diplomatic espionage? Girl, replace those jeans immediately.

It was not in character. De Lisle was right: there was a thrust, a driving purpose to Harting's actions which went beyond self-preservation; an aggression, a ruthlessness, a fervour which was infinitely more positive than the reluctant compliance of a man under threat. In this underworld life which Turner was now investigating, Harting was not a servant but a principal. He was not deputed but appointed; he was not oppressed, but an oppressor, a hunter, a pursuer. In that, at least, there was an identity between Turner and Harting. But Turner's quarry was named. His tracks, up to a point, were clear. Beyond that point they vanished into the Rhine mist. And most confusing of all was this; though Harting hunted alone, Turner reflected, he had not wanted for patronage . . .

Was Harting blackmailing Bradfield?

Turner asked the question suddenly, sitting up quite straight. Was that the explanation of Bradfield's reluctant protection? Was that why he had found him work in Registry, allowed him to vanish without explanation on Thursday afternoons, to wander round the corridors with a briefcase?

He looked once more at the diary and thought: question fundamentals. Madam, show this tired schoolboy your fundamentals, learn the parts, read the book from scratch . . . that was your tutor's advice and who are you to ignore the advice of your tutor. Do not ask *why* Christ was born on Christmas Day, ask whether he was born at all. If God gave us our wit, my dear Turner, He gave us also the wit to see through His simplicity. So why Thursday at all? Why the afternoon? Why *regular* meetings? However desperate, why did Harting meet his contact in the daylight, in working hours, in Godesberg, when his absence from the Embassy had to be the occasion of a lie in the first place? It was absurd: Balls, Turner, such as they are. Harting could meet his contact at any time. At night in Königswinter: on the forest slopes of Chamberlain's Petersberg; in Cologne, Koblenz, in Luxembourg or over the Dutch border at weekends when no excuse, truthful or untruthful, need be offered to anyone.

He dropped his pencil and swore out loud.

'Trouble?' Cork enquired. The robots were chattering wildly and Cork was tending them like hungry children.

'Nothing that prayer won't cure,' said Turner, recalling something he had said to Gaunt that morning.

'If you want to send that telegram,' Cork warned him, unperturbed, 'You'd better hurry.' He was moving quickly from one machine to the other, tugging at papers and knobs as if his task were to keep them all at work. 'The balloon's going up in Brussels by the look of it. Threat of a complete Hun walk-out if we don't raise our ante on the Agricultural Fund. Haliday-Pride says he thinks it's a pretext. In half an hour I'll be taking bookings for June if we go on at this rate.'

'What sort of pretext?'

Cork read out loud. 'A convenient door by which to leave Brussels until the situation in the Federal Republic returns to normal.'

Yawning, Turner pushed the telegram forms aside. 'I'll send it tomorrow.'

'It is tomorrow,' said Cork gently.

If I smoked I'd smoke one of your cigars. I could do with a bit of soma just now, he thought; if I can't have one of *those*, I'll have a cigar instead. From beginning to end, he knew the whole thesis was wrong.

Nothing worked, nothing interlocked, nothing explained the *energy*, nothing explained itself. He had constructed a chain of which no one link was capable of supporting the others. Holding his head in his hand, he let the Furies loose and watched them posture in grotesque slow motion before his tired imagination: the faceless Praschko, master spy, controlling from a position of parliamentary impregnability a network of refugee agents; Siebkron, the self-seeking custodian of public security, suspecting the Embassy of complicity in a massive betrayal to Russia, alternately guarding and persecuting those whom he believes to be responsible. Bradfield, rigorous, upper-class academic, hater and protector of spies, inscrutable for all his guilty knowledge, keeper of the keys to Registry, to the lift and the despatch box, about to vanish to Brussels after staying up all night; fornicating Jenny Pargiter, compelled into far more sinister complicity by an illusory passion which had already blackened her name all over the Embassy; Meadowes, blinded by a frustrated father's love for the little Harting, precariously loading the last of the forty files on to his trolley; de Lisle, the ethical queer, fighting for Harting's right to betray his friends. Each, magnified and distorted, looked towards him, danced, twisted and vanished in the face of Turner's own derisive objections. The very facts which only hours before had brought him to the brink of revelation now threw him back into the forests of his own doubt.

Yet how else, he told himself, as he locked away his posses-sions in the steel cupboard and abandoned Cork to the protest-ing machines; how else, the minister would ask, breaking the seed cake on the little plate with his soft, enormous hand, how else do fancies multiply, how else is wisdom forged, and a course of Christian action finally resolved upon, if not through doubt? Surely, my dear Mrs Turner, doubt is Our Lord's greatest gift to those in need of faith? As he walked into the corridor feeling giddy and very sick, he asked himself once more: what secrets are kept in the magic Green File? And who the hell is going to tell me: me, Turner, a temporary?

The dew was rising out of the field and rolling on to the carriageway like steam. The roads glistened under the wet grey clouds, the wheels of the traffic crackled in the heavy damp. Back to the grey, he thought wearily. No more hunt today. No little angel to submit to this old hairless ape. No absolutes yet at the end of the trail; nothing to make a defector of me.

The night porter at the Adler looked at him kindly. 'You were entertained?' he asked, handing him the key.

'Not much.'

'One should go to Cologne. It is like Paris.'

De Lisle's dinner jacket was draped carefully over his arm-chair with an envelope pinned to the sleeve. A bottle of Naafi whisky stood on the table. 'If you want to take a look at that property,' Turner read, 'I'll collect you on Wednesday morning at five.' A postscript wished him a pleasant evening at the Bradfields, and requested him in a facetious aside not to pour tomato soup down the lapels as de Lisle did not wish to have his politics misread; particularly, he added, since Herr Ludwig Siebkron of the Federal Ministry of the Interior was expected to be of the company.

Turner ran a bath, took the tumbler from the basin and half filled it with whisky. Why had de Lisle relented? Out of compassion for a lost soul? Save us. And since this was the end to a night of silly questions, why was he being invited to meet Siebkron? He went to bed and half slept until afternoon, dreaming of Bournemouth and the spiky, unclimbable conifers that ran along the bare cliffs at Branksome; and he heard his wife say, as she packed the children's clothes into the suitcase, 'I'll find my road, you find yours, and let's see who gets to Heaven first.' And he heard Jenny Pargiter's crying again, on and on, a call for pity in an empty world. Don't worry, Arthur, he thought, I wouldn't go near Myra to save my life.

10

Kultur at the Bradfields

'YOU SHOULD FORBID them more, Siebkron,' Herr Saab
declared recklessly, his voice thick with burgundy. 'They are
crazy damn fools, Siebkron. Turks.' Saab had out-talked and
out-drunk them all, forcing them into embarrassed silence.
Only his wife, a little blonde doll of unknown origin and a
sweet, revealed bosom, continued to vouchsafe him admiring
glances. Invalids, incapable of retaliation, the remaining guests
sat dying under the sheer tedium of Herr Saab's diatribe.
Behind them, two Hungarian servants moved like nurses along
the beds, and they had been told – there was no doubt in
Turner's mind – that Herr Ludwig Siebkron merited more
attention than all the other patients put together. And needed
it. His pale, magnified eyes were already drained of all but the
last drops of life; his white hands were folded like napkins
beside his plate, and his entire listless manner was that of a
person waiting to be moved.

Four silver candlesticks, 1729, by Paul de Lamerie, octagonal
based and, in the words of Bradfield's father, quite decently
marked, joined Hazel Bradfield to her husband like a line of
diamonds down the long table. Turner sat at the centre, midway between the second and third, held rigid by the iron bands
of de Lisle's dinner jacket. Even the shirt was too small for
him. The head porter had obtained it for him in Bad Godesberg
for more money than he had ever paid for a shirt in his life, and
now it was choking him and the points of the half-starched
collar were stabbing the flesh of his neck.

'Already they are coming in from the villages. Twelve
thousand people they will have in that damn Market Place.
You know what they are building? They are building a
Schaffott.' His English had once more defeated him. 'What the
hell is *Schaffott*?' he demanded of the company at large.

Siebkron stirred as if he had been offered water. 'Scaffold,' he murmured, and the dying eyes, lifting in Turner's direction, flickered and went out.

'Siebkron's English is fantastic!' Saab cried happily. 'Siebkron dreams of Palmerston in the daytime and Bismarck in the dark. Now is evening, you see: he is in the middle!' Siebkron heard the diagnosis and it gave him no comfort at all. 'A *scaffold*. I hope they maybe hang the damn fellow on it. Siebkron, you are too kind to him.' He lifted his glass to Bradfield and proposed a long toast pregnant with unwelcome compliments.

'Karl-Heinz also has fantastic English,' the little doll said. 'You are too modest, Karl-Heinz. It is just as good as Herr Siebkron's.' Between her breasts, deep down, Turner glimpsed a tiny flash of white. A handkerchief? A letter? Frau Saab did not care for Siebkron; she cared for no man, indeed, whose virtue was extolled above her husband's. Her interjection had cut the thread: once more the conversation lay like a fallen kite, and for a moment not even her husband had the wind to lift it.

'You said forbid him.' Siebkron had picked up a silver nutmeg grater in his soft hand and was gently turning it in the candlelight, searching for tell-tale flaws. The plate before him was licked quite clean, a cat's plate on a Sunday. He was a sulky, pale man, well-scrubbed and no more than Turner's age, with something of the hotelier about him, a man used to walking on other people's carpets. His features were rounded but unyielding; his lips autonomous, parting to perform one function, closing to perform another. His words were not a help but a challenge, part of a silent interrogation which only fatigue, or the deep cold sickness of his heart, prevented him from conducting aloud.

'*Ja*. Forbid him,' Saab assented, leaning well across the table in order to reach his audience. 'Forbid the meetings, forbid the marching, forbid it all. Like the Communists, that's the only damn thing they understand. *Siebkron, Sie waren ja auch in Hanover!* Siebkron was there also: why don't he forbid it? They are wild beasts out there. They have a power, *nicht wahr Siebkron?* My God, I have also made my experiences.' Saab was an older man, a journalist who had served a number of newspapers in his time, but most of them had disappeared since the war. No one seemed in much doubt what sort of experiences Herr Saab had made. 'But I have never hated the English. Siebkron, you can confirm that. *Das können sie ja bestätigen.* Twenty years I have written about this crazy Republic. I have been critical – sometimes damn critical – but I have never been *hard* against the English. That I never was,' he concluded, jumbling his last words in a way which at once cast doubt upon the whole assertion.

'Karl-Heinz is fantastically strong for the English,' the little doll said. 'He eats English, he drinks English.' She sighed as if the rest of his activities were rather English too. She ate a great deal, and some of it was still in her mouth as she spoke, and her tiny hands held other things that she would eat quite soon.

'We owe you a debt,' said Bradfield with heavy cheerfulness, 'Long may you keep it up, Karl-Heinz.' He had arrived back from Brussels half an hour ago, and his eye was on Siebkron all the time.

Mrs Vandelung, the wife of the Dutch Counsellor, drew her stole more snugly over her ample shoulders. 'We are going to England every year,' she said complacently, apropos of nothing at all. 'Our daughter is at school in England, our son is at school in England . . . ' She ran on. Nothing she loved, cherished or possessed was not of an English character. Her husband, a shrivelled, nautical man, touched Hazel Bradfield's beautiful wrist and nodded with reflected fervour.

'Always,' he whispered, as if it were a pledge. Hazel Bradfield, waking from her reverie, smiled rather solemnly at him while her eyes regarded with detachment the grey hand that still held her. 'Why, Bernhard,' she said gently, 'what a darling you are tonight. You will make the women jealous of me.' It was not, all the same, a comfortable joke. Her voice had its ugly edge; she could be one of several daughters, Turner decided, intercepting her angry glance as Saab resumed his monologue; but she was not merciful to her plainer sisters. 'Am I sitting in Leo's place?' he wondered, 'Eating Leo's portion?' But Leo stayed at home on Tuesdays . . . and besides, Leo was not allowed here, he reminded himself, raising his glass to answer a toast from Saab, except for a drink.

Saab's subject, miraculously, was still the British, but he had enriched it with autobiographical matter on the discomforts of bombing: 'You know what they say about Hamburg? Question: what is the difference between an Englishman and a man of Hamburg? Answer: the man of Hamburg speaks German. You know in those cellars, what we were saying? *Thank God they are British bombs!* Bradfield prosit! Never again.'

'Never again indeed,' Bradfield replied, and wearily toasted him in the German style, looking at him over the brim of his glass, drinking and looking again.

'Bradfield, you are the *best piece*. Your ancestors fought at Waterloo, and your wife is as beautiful as the Queen. You are the best piece in the British Embassy and you didn't invite the damn Americans and you didn't invite the damn Franch. You are a good fellow. Frenchmen is bastards,' he concluded to everyone's alarm, and there was a moment's startled silence.

'Karl-Heinz, I'm sure that isn't very loyal,' said Hazel and a little laugh went up at her end of the table, originated by a pointless elderly Gräfin summoned at the last moment to partner Alan Turner. An unwelcome shaft of electric light broke upon the company. The Hungarians marched in from the kitchen like the morning shift and cleared away bottles and china with inconsiderate *panache*.

Saab leaned still further across the table and pointed a big, not very clean finger at the guest of honour. 'You see this fellow Ludwig Siebkron here is a damn odd fellow. We all admire him in the Press Corps, because we can't never damn well get hold of him, and in journalism we admire only what we cannot have. And do you know why we cannot have Siebkron?'

The question amused Saab very much. He looked happily round the table, his dark face glistening with delight. 'Because he is so damn busy with his good friend and . . . *Kumpan*.' He snapped his fingers in frustration. '*Kumpan*,' he repeated. '*Kumpan?*'

'*Drinking companion*,' Siebkron suggested. Saab stared at him lamely, bewildered by assistance from such an unexpected quarter.   'Drinking companion,' he muttered; 'Klaus Kar-feld,' and fell silent.

'Karl-Heinz, you must remember *Kumpan*,' his wife said softly, and he nodded and smiled at her valiantly.

'You have come to join us, Mister Turner?' Siebkron enquired, addressing the nutmeg grater. Suddenly the lights were on Turner, and Siebkron, risen from his bed, was conducting the rare surgery of a private practice.

'For a few days,' Turner said. The audience was slow in gathering, so that for a moment the two men faced one another in secret communion while the others continued their separate pursuits. Bradfield had engaged in a desultory cross-talk with Vandelung; Turner caught a reference to Vietnam. Saab, suddenly returning to the field, took up the subject and made it his own.

'The Yanks would fight in Saigon,' he declared, 'but they wouldn't fight in Berlin. Seems a bit of a pity they didn't build the Berlin Wall in Saigon.' His voice was louder and more offensive, but Turner heard it out of the dark that was beyond Siebkron's unflinching gaze. 'All of a sudden the Yanks are going crazy about self-determination. Why don't they try it in East Germany a little bit? Everyone fights for the damn Negroes. Everyone fights for the damn jungle. Maybe it's a pity we don't wear no feathers.' He seemed to be challenging Vandelung, but without effect: the old Dutchman's grey skin was as smooth as a coffin, and nothing would sprout there any more. 'Maybe it's a pity we don't have no palm trees in Berlin.' They heard him pause to drink. 'Vietnam is shit. But at least this time maybe they can't say we started it,' he added with more than a trace of self-pity.

'War is terrible,' the Gräfin whickered, 'We lost everything,' but she was talking after the curtain had gone up. Herr Ludwig Siebkron proposed to speak, and had put down the silver nutmeg grater in order to signify his will.

'And where do you come from, Mister Turner?'

'Yorkshire.' There was silence. 'I spent the war in Bourne-mouth.'

'Herr Siebkron meant which Department,' Bradfield said crisply.

'Foreign Office,' said Turner. 'Same as everyone else,' and looked at him indifferently across the table. Siebkron's white eyes neither condemned nor admired, but waited for the moment to insert the scalpel.

'And may we ask Mr Turner which section of the Foreign Office is so fortunate as to have his services?'

'Research.'

'He's also a distinguished mountaineer,' Bradfield put in from far away, and the little doll cried out with the sharp surprise of sexual delight. '*Die Berge!*' Out of the corner of his eye Turner saw one china hand touch the halter of her dress as if she would take it clean off in her enthusiasm. 'Karl-Heinz—'

'Next year,' Saab's brown voice assured her in a whisper. 'Next year we go to the mountains,' and Siebkron smiled to Turner as if that were one joke they could surely share.

'But now Mr Turner is in the valley. You are staying in Bonn, Mr Turner?'

'Godesberg.'

'In a hotel, Mr Turner?'

'The Adler. Room Ten.'

'And what kind of research, I wonder, is conducted from the Hotel Adler, Room Ten?'

'Ludwig, my dear chap,' Bradfield interposed – his jocularity was not so very hollow – 'Surely you recognize a spy when you see one. Alan's our Mata Hari. He entertains the Cabinet in his bedroom.'

Laughter, Siebkron's expression said, does not last for ever; he waited until it had subsided. 'Alan,' he repeated quietly. 'Alan Turner from Yorkshire, working in Foreign Office Research Department and staying at the Adler Hotel, a distinguished mountaineer. You must forgive my curiosity, Mr Turner. We are all on edge here in Bonn, you know. As, for my sins, I am charged with the physical protection of the British Embassy, I have naturally a certain interest in the people I protect. Your presence here is reported to Personnel Department no doubt? I must have missed the bulletin.'

'We put him down as a technician,' Bradfield said, clearly irritated now to be questioned before his own guests.

'How sensible,' said Siebkron. 'So much simpler than Research. He does research but you put him down as a technician. Your technicians on the other hand are all engaged in research. It's a perfectly simple arrangement. But your research is of a practical nature, Mr Turner? A statistician? Or you are an academic perhaps?'

'Just general.'

'General research. A very catholic responsibility. You will be here long?'

'A week. Maybe more. Depends how long the project lasts.'

'The research project? Ah. Then you have a project. I had imagined at first you were replacing someone. Ewan Waldebere for instance; he was engaged in commercial research, was he not, Bradfield? Or Peter McCreedy, on scientific development. Or Harting: you are not replacing Leo Harting for instance? Such a pity he's gone. One of your oldest and most valuable collaborators.'

'Oh Harting!' Mrs Vandelung had taken up the name, and it was already clear she had strong views. 'You know what they are saying now already? That Harting is drunk in Cologne. He goes on *fits* you know.' She was much entertained to hold their interest. 'All the week he wears angels' wings and plays the organ and sings like a Christian; but at weekends he goes to Cologne and fights the Germans. He is quite a Jekyll and Hyde I assure you!' She laughed indulgently. 'Oh he is very wicked. Rawley, you remember André de Hoog I am sure. He has heard it all from the police here: Harting made a great fight in Cologne. In a night club. It was all to do with a bad woman. Oh, he is *very* mysterious I assure you. And now we have no one to play the organ.'

Through the mist Siebkron repeated his question.

'I'm not replacing anyone,' Turner said and he heard Hazel Bradfield's voice, quite steady from his left, but vibrant for all that with anger unexpressed.

'Mrs Vandelung, you know our silly English ways. We are supposed to leave the men to their jokes.'

Reluctantly the women departed. Little Frau Saab, desolated to leave her husband, kissed his neck and made him promise to be sober. The Gräfin said that in Germany one expected a cognac after a meal: it aided the digestion. Only Frau Siebkron followed without complaint; she was a quiet, deserted beauty who had learned very early in her marriage that it paid not to resist.

Bradfield was at the sideboard with decanters and silver coasters; the Hungarians had brought coffee in a Hester Bateman jug which sat in unremarked magnificence at Hazel's end of the table. Little Vandelung was lost in memories; he was standing at the French windows, staring down the sloping dark lawn at the lights of Bad Godesberg.

'Now we will get port,' Saab assured them all. 'With Bradfield that is always a fantastic experience.' He selected Turner. 'I have had ports here, I can tell you, that are older than my father. What are we getting tonight, Bradfield? A Cockburn? Maybe he will give us a Cruft's. Bradfield knows all the brands. *Ein richtiger Kenner*: Siebkron, what is *Kenner auf Englisch?*'

'Connoisseur.'

'French!' Saab was outraged. 'The English have no word for *Kenner?* They use a French word? Bradfield! Telegram! Tonight! *Sofort an Ihre Majestät!* Personal recommendation top secret to the damn Queen. All Connoisseurs are forbidden. Only Kenner permitted! You are married, Mister Turner?'

Bradfield, having sat himself in Hazel's chair, now passed the port to his left. The coaster was a double one, joined elaborately with silver cords.

'No,' said Turner, and it was a word thrown down hard for anyone to pick up who wanted it. Saab, however, heard no music but his own.

'Crazy! The English should breed! Many babies. Make a culture. England, Germany and Scandinavia! To hell with the French, to hell with the Americans, to hell with the Africans. *Klein-Europa*, do you understand me, Turner?' He held up his clenched fist, stiff from the elbow. 'Tough and good. What can speak and think. I am not so damn crazy. *Kultur*. You know what that means, *Kultur?*' He drank. 'Fantastic!' he cried. 'The best ever! Number one.' He held up his glass to the candle. 'The best damn port I ever had. You can see the blood in the heart. Bradfield, what is it? A Cockburn for sure, but he always contradicts me.'

Bradfield hesitated, caught in a genuine dilemma. His eye turned first to Saab's glass, then to the decanters, then to his glass again.

'I'm delighted you enjoyed it. Karl-Heinz,' he said. 'I rather think, as a matter of fact, that what you are drinking is Madeira.'

Vandelung, from the French windows, began laughing. It was a cracked, vengeful laugh and it went on for a long time, while his whole little body shook to the tune of it, rising and falling with the bellows of his old lungs.

'Well now, Saab,' he said at last, walking slowly back to the table, 'Maybe you will bring a little of your culture to the Netherlands as well.'

He began laughing again like a schoolboy, holding his knobbly hand to his mouth in order to conceal the gaps, and Turner was sorry for Saab just then, and did not care for Vandelung at all.

Siebkron had taken no port.

'You went to Brussels today. I hope very much that you had a successful journey, Bradfield? I hear there are renewed difficulties. I am sorry. My colleagues tell me New Zealand presents a serious problem.'

'Sheep!' Saab cried. 'Who will eat the sheep? The English have made a damn farm out there and now no one won't eat the sheep.'

Bradfield's voice was all the more deliberate. 'No new problem has been raised at Brussels. The questions of New Zealand and the Agricultural Fund have both been on the table for years. They present no problems that cannot be ironed out between friends.'

'Between good friends. Let us hope you are right. Let us hope the friendship is good enough and the difficulties small enough. Let us hope so.' Siebkron's gaze was on Turner again. 'So Harting is gone,' he remarked, laying his hands flatly together in prayer. 'Such a loss to our community. Particularly for the Church.' And looking directly at Turner he added: 'My colleagues tell me you know Mr Sam Allerton, the distinguished British journalist. You spoke with him today, I believe.'

Vandelung had given himself a glass of Madeira and was sampling it ostentatiously. Saab, sullen and dark faced, stared from one of them to the other, comprehending little.

'Ludwig, what an extraordinary idea. What do you mean, "Harting is gone"? He's on leave. I cannot imagine how all these silly rumours have got about. Poor fellow, his only crime was not to tell the Chaplain.' Bradfield's laughter was wholly artificial, but it was an act of courage in itself. 'Compassionate leave. It is not like you, Ludwig, to get your information wrong.'

'You see, Mr Turner, I have great difficulties here. For my sins, I am responsible for civil order during the demonstrations. Responsible to my Minister, you understand; and only in a modest capacity. But responsible all the same.'

His modesty was saintly. Put a ruff on him and a surplice and he could sing in Harting's choir any time. 'We are expecting a little demonstration on Friday. I am afraid that among certain minority groups the English are at present not very popular. You will appreciate that I don't want anybody to get hurt; anybody at all. Naturally therefore I like to know where everybody is. So that I can protect them. But poor Mister Bradfield is often so overworked he does not tell me.' He broke off and glanced once at Bradfield, and then no more. 'Now I am not *blaming* Bradfield that he does not tell me. Why should he?' The white hands parted in concession. 'There are many little things and there are even one or two big things which Bradfield does not tell me. Why should he? That would not be consistent with his vocation as a diplomat. I am correct, Mister Turner?'

'It's not my problem.'

'But it is mine. Let me explain what happens. My colleagues are observant people. They look around, count heads, and notice that somebody is missing. They make enquiries, question servants and friends perhaps, and they are told that he has disappeared. Immediately I am worried for him. So are my colleagues. My colleagues are compassionate people. They don't like anyone to go astray. What could be more human? They are boys, some of them. Just boys. Harting has gone to England?'

The last question was spoken directly to Turner, but Bradfield took it on himself and Turner blessed him.

'He has family problems. Clearly we cannot advertise them. I don't propose to put a man's private life upon the table in order to satisfy your files.'

'That is a very excellent principle. And one we must all follow. Do you hear that, Mr Turner?' His voice was remarkably emphatic. 'What is the point of a paper chase? What *is* the point?'

'Why on earth are you so bothered about Harting?' Bradfield demanded, as if it were a joke of which he had tired. 'I'm astonished you even know of his existence. Let's go and get some coffee, shall we?'

He stood up; but Siebkron remained where he was.

'But of *course* we know of his existence,' he declared. 'We admire his work. We admire it very much indeed. In a department such as mine, Mr Harting's ingenuity finds many admirers. My colleagues speak of him constantly.'

'What are you talking about?' Bradfield had coloured in anger. 'What *is* all this? What work?'

'He used to be with the Russians, you know,' Siebkron explained to Turner. 'In Berlin. That was a long time ago, of course, but I am sure that he learnt a great deal from them, don't you think so, Mr Turner? A little technique, a little ideology perhaps? And *grip*. The Russians *never* let go.'

Bradfield had put the two decanters on a tray and was standing at the doorway waiting for them to go ahead of him.

'What work was that?' Turner asked gruffly, as Siebkron reluctantly rose from his chair.

'Research. Just general research, Mr Turner. Like yourself, you see. It is nice to think that you and Harting have common interests. As a matter of fact that is why I asked whether you would replace him. My colleagues understand from Mr Allerton that you and Harting have *many* things in common.'

Hazel Bradfield looked up anxiously as they entered, and the glance she exchanged with Bradfield was eloquent of the emergency. Her four women guests sat on a single sofa. Mrs Vandelung was working at a sampler; Frau Siebkron in church black had laid her hands on her lap and was staring in private fascination at the open fire. The Gräfin, consoling herself for the untitled company she was obliged to keep, sipped morosely at a large brandy. Her parsimonious face was lit with small red flowers like poppies on a battlefield. Only little Frau Saab, her bosom freshly powdered, smiled to see them enter.

They were settled, resigned to boredom.

'Bernhard,' said Hazel Bradfield, patting the cushion beside her, 'Come and sit by me. I find you *specially* cosy this evening.' With a foxy smile the old man took his place obediently beside her. 'Now you're to tell me *all* the horrors I am to expect on Friday.' She was playing the spoilt beauty, and playing it well, but there was an undercurrent of anxiety in her voice which not even Bradfield's tuition had taught her wholly to suppress.

At a separate table, Siebkron sat alone like a man who travelled by a better class. Bradfield talked to his wife. No, she conceded, she had not been to Brussels; she did not go often with her husband. 'But you must insist!' he declared and launched at once upon a description of a favourite Brussels hotel. The Amigo; one should stay at the Amigo; it had the best service he had ever encountered. Frau Siebkron did not care for large hotels; she took her holidays in the Black Forest; that was what the children liked best. Yes; Bradfield loved the Black Forest himself; he had close friends at Dornstetten.

Turner listened in grudging admiration to Bradfield's inexhaustible flow of small-talk. He expected no help from anyone. His eyes were dark with fatigue, but his dialogue was as fresh, as considerate and as aimless as if he were on holiday.

'Come along, Bernhard; you're just a wise old owl and nobody ever tells me anything. I'm just the Hausfrau. I'm supposed to look at *Vogue* and make canapés all day.'

'You know the saying,' Vandelung replied. 'What else must happen in Bonn before something happens? They can do nothing we have not seen before.'

'They can trample all over my roses,' Hazel remarked,

lighting herself a cigarette. 'They can steal my husband away at all hours of the night. Day trips to Brussels indeed! It's quite absurd. And look what they did in Hanover. Can you imagine what would happen if they broke *these* windows? Dealing with that wretched Works Department? We'd all be sitting here in overcoats while they worked out who pays. It's *too* bad, it really is. Thank goodness we have Mr Turner to protect us.' As she said this her gaze rested upon him, and it seemed to him both anxious and enquiring. 'Frau Saab, does *your* husband travel all over the place these days? I am sure journalists make *far* better husbands than diplomats.'

'He is very true.' The little doll blushed unhappily.

'She means *loyal*.' Saab kissed her hand with love.

Opening her tiny handbag, she took out a powder compact and parted its gold petals one by one. 'We have been married one year tomorrow. It is so beautiful.'

'*Du bist noch schöner*,' Saab cried and the conversation disintegrated into an exchange of domestic and financial intelligence on the Saabs' newly-formed household. Yes, they had bought a plot of land up by Oberwinter. Karl-Heinz had bought it last year for the engagement and already the value had risen four marks per *quadratmeter*.

'Karl-Heinz, how do you say *quadratmeter*?'

'The same,' Saab asserted, ' Quadrate meter,' and glowered at Turner in case he should dare to contradict him.

Suddenly Frau Saab was talking and no one could stop her any more. Her whole little life was spread before them in an oriental tinkle of hopes and disappointments; the colour which had mounted so prettily to her cheeks stayed there like the warm flush of sexual success.

They had hoped that Karl-Heinz would get the Bonn *Büro* of his newspaper. Bonn editor: that had been their expectation. His salary would go up another thousand and he would have a real *position*. What had happened instead? The paper had appointed *den Flitzdorf* and the Flitzdorf was just a boy, with no experience and nothing and *completely* homosexual and Karl-Heinz, who had worked now eighteen years for the paper and had so many contacts, was still only second man and was having to make extra by writing for all the cheese-papers.

'Yellow press,' said her husband, but for once she quite ignored him.

Well, when that had happened they had had a long discussion and decided they would go ahead with their building plans although the *Hypothek* was appalling; and no sooner had they paid over the money to the *Makler* than a really terrible thing happened: the Africans had come to Oberwinter. It was quite awful. Karl-Heinz was always very sharp against Africans, but now they had actually taken the next door plot and were building a *Residenz* for one of their Ambassadors, and twice a week they all came up and climbed like monkeys over the bricks and shouted they wanted it different; and in no time they would have a whole colony up there, with Cadillacs and children and music all night, and as for herself, she would be all alone when Karl-Heinz was working late, and they were already putting special bolts on the doors so that she would not be—

'They talk fantastic!' Saab shouted, loudly enough for Siebkron and Bradfield to look round at him sharply; for the two men had drawn away to the window and were murmuring quietly into the night. 'But we don't get nothing to drink!'

'Karl-Heinz, my poor chap, we are completely neglecting you.' With a final word to Siebkron, Bradfield walked down the room to where the decanters stood on their bright-cut silver tray. 'Who else would like a nightcap?'

Vandelung would have joined him, but his wife forbade it.

'And take *great* care,' she warned the young Frau Saab in a dreadfully audible aside, 'Or he will have a heart attack. So much eating and drinking and shouting: it affects the heart. And with a young wife not easily satisfied,' she added contentedly, 'he could die easy.' Taking her little grey husband firmly by the wrist, Frau Vandelung led him into the hall. In the same instant Hazel Bradfield leaned purposefully across the abandoned chair. 'Mr Turner,' she said quietly, 'there is a matter in which you can help me. May I take you away a moment?'

They stood in the sun room. Potted plants and tennis rackets lay on the window sills; a child's tractor, a pogo stick and a bundle of garden canes were strewn over the tiled floor. There was a mysterious smell of honey.

'I understand you're making enquiries about Harting,' she said. Her voice was crisp and commanding; she was very much Bradfield's wife.

'Am I?'

'Rawley's worrying himself to death. I'm convinced that Leo Harting's at the back of it.'

'I see.'

'He doesn't sleep and he won't even discuss it. For the last three days he's hardly spoken to me. He even sends messages by way of other people. He's cut himself off entirely from everything except his work. He's near breaking point.'

'He didn't give me that impression.'

'He happens to be my husband.'

'He's very lucky.'

'What's Harting taken?' Her eyes were bright with anger or determination. 'What's he stolen?'

'What makes you think he's stolen anything?'

'Listen. I, not you, am responsible for my husband's welfare. I have a *right* to know if Rawley is in trouble; tell me what Harting has done. Tell me where he is. They're all whispering about it; everyone. This ridiculous story about Cologne; Siebkron's curiosity: why can't *I* know what's going on?'

'That's what I was wondering myself,' Turner said.

He thought she might hit him, and he knew that if she did, he would hit her back. She was beautiful, but the arch corners of her mouth were drawn down in the frustrated fury of a rich child, and there were things about her voice and manner which were dreadfully familiar.

'Get out. Leave me alone.'

'I don't care who you are. If you want to know official secrets you can bloody well get them at source,' Turner said, and waited for her to rise to him again.

Instead, she swept past him into the hall and ran upstairs. For a moment he remained where he was, staring confusedly at the muddle of children's and adult toys, the fishing rods, the croquet set and all the casual, wasteful equipment of a world he had never known. Still lost in thought, he made his way slowly back to the drawing-room. As he entered, Bradfield and Siebkron, side by side at the French window, turned as one man to stare at him, the object of their shared contempt.

It was midnight. The Gräfin, drunk and quite speechless, had been loaded into a taxi. Siebkron had gone; his farewell had been confined to the Bradfields. His wife must have gone with him, though Turner had not noticed her departure; the cushion where she had sat was barely depressed. The Vandelungs had also gone. Now the five of them sat round the fire in a state of post-festive depression, the Saabs on the sofa holding hands and staring at the dying coals, Bradfield quite silent sipping his thin whisky; while Hazel herself, in her long skirt of green tweed, curled like a mermaid into an armchair, played with the Blue Russian cat in self-conscious imitation of an eighteenth-century dream. Though she rarely looked at Turner, she did not trouble to ignore him; occasionally she even addressed a remark to him. A tradesman had been impertinent, but Hazel Bradfield would not do him the compliment of taking away her custom.

'Hanover was fantastic,' Saab muttered.

'Oh not again, Karl-Heinz,' Hazel pleaded, 'I think I've heard enough of that to last forever.'

'*Why* did they run?' he asked himself. 'Siebkron was also there. They *ran*. From the front. They ran like crazy for that library. Why did they do that? All at once: *alles auf einmal*.'

'Siebkron keeps asking me the same question,' Bradfield said, in an exhausted moment of frankness. 'Why did they run? *He* should know if anyone does: he was at Eich's bedside; I wasn't. He heard what she had to say, I suppose; I didn't. What the hell's got into him? On and on: "What happened at Hanover mustn't happen in Bonn." Of course it mustn't, but he seems to think it's my fault it happened in the first place. I've never known him like that.'

'You?' Hazel Bradfield said with undisguised contempt. 'Why on earth should he ask *you*? You weren't even there.'

'He asks me all the same,' said Bradfield, standing up, in a moment so utterly passive and tender that Turner was moved suddenly to speculate on their relationship. 'He asks me all the

185

same.' He put his empty glass on the sideboard. 'Whether you like it or not. He asks me repeatedly: "Why did they run?" Just as Karl-Heinz was asking now. "What made them run? What was it about the library that attracted them?" All I could say was that it was British, and we all know what Karfeld thinks about the British. Come on, Karl-Heinz: we must put you young people to bed.'

'And the grey buses,' Saab muttered. 'You read what they found about the buses for the bodyguard? They were *grey*, Bradfield, *grey*!'

'Is that significant?'

'It *was*, Bradfield. About a thousand years ago, it was damn significant, my dear.'

'I'm afraid I'm missing the point,' Bradfield observed with a weary smile.

'As usual,' his wife said; no one took it as a joke.

They stood in the hall. Of the two Hungarians, only the girl remained.

'You have been damn good to me, Bradfield,' Saab said sadly as they took their leave. 'Maybe I talk too much. *Nicht wahr, Marlene:* I talk too much. But I don't trust that fellow Siebkron. I am an old pig, see? But Siebkron is a young pig. Pay attention!'

'Why shouldn't I trust him, Karl-Heinz?'

'Because he don't never ask a question unless he knows the answer.' With this enigmatic reply, Karl-Heinz Saab fervently kissed the hand of his hostess and stepped into the dark, steadied by the young arm of his adoring wife.

Turner sat in the back while Saab drove very slowly on the left hand side of the road. His wife was asleep on his shoulder, one little hand still scratching fondly at the black fur which decorated the nape of her husband's neck.

'Why did they run at Hanover?' Saab repeated, weaving happily between the oncoming cars, 'Why those damn fools run?'

At the Adler, Turner asked for morning coffee at half past four, and the porter noted it with an understanding smile, as if that were the sort of time he expected an Englishman to rise. As he went to bed, his mind detached itself from the distasteful and mystifying interrogations of Herr Ludwig Siebkron in order to dwell on the more agreeable person of Hazel Bradfield. It was just as mysterious, he decided as he fell asleep, that a woman so beautiful, desirable and evidently intelligent, could tolerate the measureless tedium of diplomatic life in Bonn. If darling upper-class Anthony Willoughby ever took a shine at her, he thought, what on earth would Bradfield do then? And why – the chorus that sang him to sleep was the same chorus which had kept him awake throughout the long, tense, meaningless evening – why the hell was he invited in the first place?

And *who* had asked him? 'I am to invite you to dinner on Tuesday,' Bradfield had said: don't blame *me* for what happens.

And Bradfield, I *heard*! I heard you submit to pressure; I felt the softness of you for the first time; I took a step in your direction, I saw the knife in your back and I heard you speak with my own voice. Hazel you bitch; Siebkron you swine; Harting you thief: if *that's* what you think about life, queer de Lisle simpered in his ear, why don't you defect yourself.' God is dead. You can't have it both ways, that would be too medieval. . . .

He had set his alarm for four o'clock, and it seemed to be ringing already.

11

Königswinter

IT WAS STILL dark when de Lisle collected him and Turner had to ask the night porter to unlock the hotel door. The street was cold, friendless and deserted; the mist came at them in sudden patches.

'We'll have to go the long way over the bridge. The ferry's not running at this hour.' His manner was short to the point of abruptness.

They had entered the carriageway. To either side of them, new blocks, built of tile and armoured glass, sprang like night weeds out of the untilled fields, crested by the lamps of small cranes. They passed the Embassy. The dark hung upon the wet concrete like the smoke of a spent battle. The Union Jack swung limply from its standard, a single flower on a soldier's grave. Under the weary light of the front porch, the lion and the unicorn, their profiles blurred with repeated coats of red and gold, fought bravely on. In the waste land, the two rickety goalposts leaned drunkenly in the twilight.

'Things are warming up in Brussels,' de Lisle remarked in a tone which promised little elaboration. A dozen cars were parked in the forecourt, Bradfield's white Jaguar stood in its private bay.

'For us or against us?'

'What do you think?' He continued: 'We have asked for private talks with the Germans; the French have done the same. Not that they want them; it's the tug-of-war they enjoy.'

'Who wins?'

De Lisle did not reply.

The deserted town hung in the pink unearthly glow which cradles every city in the hour before dawn. The streets were wet and empty, the houses soiled like old uniforms. At the University arch, three policemen had made a lane of barricades and they flagged them down as they approached. Sullenly they walked round the small car, recording the licence number, testing the suspension by standing on the rear bumper, peering through the misted windscreen at the huddled occupants within.

'What was that they shouted?' Turner asked as they drove on.

'Look out for the one-way signs.' He turned left, following the blue arrow. 'Where the hell are they taking us?'

An electric van was scrubbing the gutter; two more police-men in greatcoats of green leather, their peak caps bent, sus-piciously surveyed its progress. In a shop window a young girl was fitting beach clothes to a model, holding one plastic arm and feeding the sleeve along it. She wore boots of heavy felt and shuffled like a prisoner. They were in the station square. Black banners stretched across the road and along the awning of the station. 'Welcome to Klaus Karfeld!' 'A hunter's greet-ing, Klaus!' 'Karfeld! You stand for our self-respect!' A photograph, larger than any which Turner had so far seen, was raised on a massive new hoarding. '*Freitag !*' said the legend: Friday. The floodlights shone upon the world and left the face in darkness.

'They're arriving today. Tilsit, Meyer-Lothringen; Karfeld. They're coming down from Hanover to prepare the ground.'

'With Ludwig Siebkron playing host.'

They were running along some tramlines, still following the diversion signs. The route took them left and right again. They had passed under a small bridge, doubled back, entered another square, halted at some improvised traffic lights and suddenly they were both sitting forward in their cramped seats, staring ahead of them in astonishment, up the gentle slope of the market place towards the Town Hall.

Immediately before them, the empty stalls stood in lines like beds in a barrack hut. Beyond the stalls, the gingerbread houses offered their jagged gables to the lightening sky. But de Lisle and Turner were looking up the hill at the single pink and grey building which dominated the whole square. Ladders had been laid against it; the balcony was festooned in swathes of black; a flock of Mercedes was parked before it on the cobble. To its left, in front of a chemist's shop, floodlit from a dozen places, rose a white scaffolding like the outline of a medieval storming tower. The pinnacle reached as high as the dormer windows of the adjacent building; the giant legs, naked as roots grown in the dark, splayed obscenely over their own black shadows. Workmen were already swarming at its base. Turner could hear the piping echo of hammers and the whine of powered saws. A stack of timber struggled upwards on a silent pulley.

'Why are the flags at half mast?'

'Mourning. It's a gimmick. They're in mourning for national honour.'

They crossed the long bridge. 'That's better,' said de Lisle with a small grunt of satisfaction, and pushed down his collar as if he had entered a warmer world.

He was driving very fast. They passed a village and another. Soon they had entered the country and were following a new road along the eastern bank. To their right the tor of Godesberg, divided by tiers of mist, stood grimly over the sleeping town. They skirted the vineyard. The furrows, picked out by the mysterious darkness, were like seams stitched to the zig-zag patterns of the staves. Above the vineyard, the forests of the Seven Hills; above the forests, broken castles and Gothic follies black against the skyline. Abandoning the main road, they entered a short avenue which led directly to an esplanade bordered by unlit lamps and pollarded trees. Beyond it lay the Rhine, smouldering and undefined.

'Next on the left,' de Lisle said tersely. 'Tell me if there's anyone on guard.'

A large white house loomed before them. The lower windows were shuttered, the front gates open. Turner left the car and walked a short way along the pavement. Picking up a stone, he flung it hard and accurately against the side of the house. The sound echoed crookedly across the water, and upwards towards the black slopes of the Petersberg. Scanning the mist, they waited for a cry or a footstep. There was none.

'Park up the road and come back,' said Turner.

'I think I'll just park up the road. How long will you need?'

'You know the house. Come and help me.'

'Not my form. Sorry. I don't mind bringing you but I'm not coming in.'

'Then why bring me?'

De Lisle did not reply.

'Don't dirty your fingers, will you.'

Keeping to the grass verge, Turner followed the drive towards the house. Even by that light, he was conscious of the same sense of order which had characterized Harting's room. The long lawn was very tidy, the rose beds trimmed and weeded, the roses ringed with grass-cuttings and separately labelled with metal tags. At the kitchen door, three dustbins, numbered and licensed according to the local regulation, stood in a concrete bay. About to insert the key, he heard a footstep.

It was unmistakeably a footstep. It had the double imprint, slurred yet infallibly human, of a heel falling on gravel and the toe immediately following. A cautious footstep perhaps; a gesture half made and then withheld, a message sent and revoked; but beyond all argument a footstep.

'Peter?' He's changed his mind again, he thought. He's being soft hearted. 'Peter!'

There was still no answer.

'Peter, is that you?' He stooped, quickly picked up an empty bottle from the wooden crate beside him and waited, his ears tuned to the lightest sound. He heard the crowing of a cock in the Seven Hills. He heard the prickling of the sodden earth, like the tingling of pine needles in a wood; he heard the rustling of tiny waves along the river's shore; he heard the distant throbbing of the Rhine itself, like the turning of an unearthly machine, one tone made of many, breaking and joining like the unseen water; he heard the mutter of hidden barges, the shoot of anchor chains suddenly released; he heard a cry, like the lowing of lost cattle on a moor, as a lonely siren echoed on the cliff face. But he did not hear another footstep, nor the comfortable tones of de Lisle's courteous voice. Turning the key he pushed open the door, hard; then stood still and listened again, the bottle rigid in his hand, while the faint aroma of stale cigar rose lovingly to his nostrils.

He waited, letting the room come to him out of the cold

gloom. Gradually, the new sounds began. First from the direction of the serving hatch came the chink of glass; from the hall, the creak of wood; in the cellar, a hollow box was dragged over a concrete floor; a gong rang, one tone, imperious and distinctive; and from everywhere now, all about him there rose a vibrant, organic hum, obscure yet very close, pressing upon him, louder with every minute, as if the whole building had been struck with a flat hand and were trembling from the blow. Running to the hall, he charged into the dining-room, put on the lights with a single sweeping movement of his palm and glared savagely round him, shoulders haunched, bottle clenched in his considerable fist.

'Harting!' he shouted now, 'Harting?' He heard the shuffle of scattering feet, and thrust back the partition door.

· 'Harting!' he called again, but his only answer was the soot slipping in the open hearth, and the banging of an errant shutter on the poor stucco outside. He went to the window and looked across the lawn towards the river. On the far bank, the American Embassy, brilliant as a power house, drove yellow shafts through the mist deep into the elusive water. Then at last he recognized the nature of his tormentor: a chain of six barges, flags flying, radar-lights glittering above them like the blue stars nailed to the mast, was swiftly disappearing into the fog. As the last vessel vanished, so the strange domestic orchestra put aside its instruments. The glass ceased to chime, the stairs to creak, the soot to fall, the walls to tremble. The house settled again, ruminative but not yet reassured, waiting for the next assault.

Putting the bottle on the windowsill, Turner straightened himself and walked slowly from room to room. It was a wasteful, thinly built barrack of a place, built for a colonel out of reparation costs, at a time when the High Commission was stationed on the Petersberg; one of a colony, de Lisle had said, but the colony was never completed, for by then the Occupation had ended and the project was abandoned. A left-over house for a left-over man. It had a light side and a dark side according to whether the rooms looked on to the river or the Petersberg; the plaster was rough and belonged out of doors.

The furniture was equivocal, as if no one had ever decided how much prestige Harting was entitled to. If there was emphasis, it fell upon the gramophone. Flexes ran from it in all directions and speakers to either side of the chimney had been set upon pivots to assist directional adjustment.

The dining table was laid for two.

At the centre, four porcelain cherubs danced in a circle. Spring pursued Summer, Summer recoiled from Autumn, Winter drew them all forward. To either side, two places were set for dinner. Fresh candles, matches, a bottle of Burgundy, unopened, in the wine basket; a cluster of roses withering in a silver bowl. Over it all lay a thin layer of dust.

He wrote quickly in his notebook, then continued to the kitchen. It might have been confected for a woman's magazine. He had never seen so many gadgets. Mixers, cutters, toasters, openers. A plastic tray lay on the counter, the remnants of a single breakfast. He lifted the lid of the teapot. It was a herbal tea, bright red. Dregs of it remained in the teacup, staining the spoon. A second cup lay upside down in the plate rack. A transistor radio, similar to the one he had seen in the Embassy, stood on top of the refrigerator. Having once again noted the wavelengths, Turner went to the door, listened, then began pulling open cupboards, extracting tins and bottles, peering inside. Occasionally he recorded what he found. In the refrigerator half-litre cartons of Naafi milk stood in neat order along the inside shelf. Taking out a bowl of pâté he gently sniffed it, testing its age. On a white plate, two steaks were set side by side. Strips of garlic had been threaded into the flesh. He prepared it on the Thursday night, he thought suddenly. On Thursday night he *still* didn't know he was going to defect on Friday.

The upstairs corridor was carpeted with thin runners of coco-nut matting. The pine furniture was very rickety. He pulled out the suits one by one, thrusting his hands into the pockets, then throwing them aside as if they were spent. Their cut, like that of the house, was military; the jackets were waisted, with a small pocket midway on the right side; the trousers were tapered and had no turn-ups. Occasionally, as he continued his search, he drew out a handkerchief, a scrap of paper or a bit of pencil, and these he would examine, and perhaps record, before tossing the suit aside and seizing another from the rickety wardrobe. The house was trembling again. From somewhere – it seemed this time to be from the very depths of the building – came the sound of clanking metal like a goods train braking, one place calling and another answering, ascending from floor to floor. Barely had it died before he heard another footfall. Dropping the suit he sprang to the window. He heard it again. Twice. Twice he had heard the solid tread of feet. Pushing back the shutter he leaned into the twilight and stared down at the driveway.

'Peter?'

Was it the dark that moved, or a man? He had left the lights on in the hall and they cast a patchwork of shadows on the drive. There was no wind to set the beech trees nodding. A man then? A man hurrying past the window on the inside? A man whose shape had flickered on the gravel?

'Peter?'

Nothing. No car, no guard. The neighbouring houses still lay in darkness. Above him, Chamberlain's mountain woke slowly to the dawn. He closed the window.

He worked faster now. In the second wardrobe another half dozen suits confronted him. Recklessly he dragged them from their hangers, struck at the pockets and cast them away; and then that extra sense warned him: go slowly. He had come upon a suit of dark blue gabardine, a summer suit but very much for formal wear, more creased than the others and set aside from them as if it were awaiting the cleaner, or tomorrow. He weighed it cautiously in his hand. Laying it on the bed, he felt in the pockets and drew out a brown envelope carefully folded upon itself. A brown OHMS envelope, the kind of thing they use for income tax. There was no writing on the outside and the flap had been sealed and ripped open. It was a key: a Yale key of dull, leaden colour, not newly cut but worn with age or use, a long, old fashioned, complicated key for a deep and complicated lock, quite unlike the standard keys which comprised the Duty Officer's bunch. A despatch box key? Returning it to the envelope, he put it between the pages of his notebook and carefully examined the remaining pockets. Three cocktail sticks, one with grime at the point as if he had used it for cleaning his nails. Olive stones. Some loose change, four marks eighty, made up in small denominations. And a bill for drinks, undated, from a hotel in Remagen.

He left the study till last. It was a mean room, filled with cartons of whisky and tinned food. An ironing board stood beside the shuttered window. On an old card table, piles of catalogues, trade brochures and diplomatic price lists lay in uncharacteristic confusion. A small notebook recorded the commodities which Harting was evidently pledged to obtain. Turner glanced through it, then put it in his pocket. The tins of Dutch cigars were in a wooden box; there must have been a gross of them or more.

The glass-fronted bookcase was locked. Crouching, Turner studied the titles, rose, listened again, then fetched a screwdriver from the kitchen and with a single powerful wrench ripped the wood so that the brass came through suddenly like a bone through flesh, and the door swung uselessly open. The first half dozen volumes were German bound and pre-war, heavily ribbed and gilded. He could not read all the titles precisely, but some he guessed; Stundinger's *Leipziger Kommentar zum Strafgesetzbuch; Verwaltungsrecht*; and someone else on the Statute of Limitations. In each was written the name, Harting Leo, like the name on the coathanger; and once he came upon the printed emblem of a Berlin bear overwritten in a spiky German hand, very faint on the curves and very bold on the downstrokes '*Für meinen geliebten Sohn Leo*'. The lower shelf was a medley: a Code of Conduct for British Officers in Germany, a German paperback on the flags of the Rhine, and an English–German phrase book published in Berlin before the war, annotated and very fingered. Reaching right to the back, he drew out a handful of slim, cloth-bound monthly newsletters of the Control Commission of Germany for the years forty-nine to fifty-one; some volumes were missing. As he opened the first volume the spine creaked and the dust rose swiftly to his nostrils. 'No. 18 Field Investigation Unit Hanover,' the inscription read, written out, every word, in a good clerical hand, very bold on the downstrokes and refined at the curves, in a black, powdery ink which only governments can buy. A thin line cancelled the title and a second title replaced it: 'No. 6 General Enquiry Unit, Bremen.' Beneath it again (for Bremen too had been crossed out) he read the words: 'Property of the Judge Advocate General's Department, Moenchengladbach,' and beneath that again, 'Amnesty Commission, Hanover. Not to be taken away.' Selecting a page at random, he found himself suddenly arrested by a retrospective account of the operation of the Berlin airlift. Salt should be slung under the wings of the aircraft and on no account carried inside the fuselage . . . the transportation of petrol presented high risks on landing and taking off . . . it was found preferable, in the interests of morale if not of economy, to fly-in coal and corn rather than to make the bread in advance and deliver it ready-baked . . . by using dehydrated instead of fresh potatoes, seven hundred and twenty tons could be saved on a daily ration of nine hundred tons for the civilian population. Fascinated, he slowly turned the yellow pages, his eye halting at phrases of unexpected familiarity. '*The first meeting of the Allied High Commission was held on 21st September at the Petersberg, near Bonn* . .' A German Tourist Office was to be opened in New York. . . . The festivals of Bayreuth and Oberammergau were to be resuscitated as swiftly as time allowed. . . . He glanced at the summary of minutes of the High Commission meetings: '*Methods of broadening opportunities and responsibilities of the Federal Republic of Germany in the field of foreign and economic activity were considered. . . . The wider powers for the German Federal Republic in the field of foreign trade, decided upon under the Occupation statute, were defined. . . . Direct German participation in two more international organizations was authorized . . .*'

The next volume opened naturally at a page dealing with the release of German prisoners detained under certain arrest categories. Once again, he found himself compelled to read on: Three million Germans presently in captivity . . . those detained were faring better than those at liberty . . . the Allies faced with the impossibility of separating the wheat from the chaff. . . . Operation Coalscuttle would send them down the mines, Operation Barleycorn would send them to the harvest. . . . One passage was sharply sidelined in blue ballpoint: *On 31st May, 1948, therefore, as an act of clemency, an amnesty was granted from proceedings under Ordinance 69 to all members of the SS not in automatic arrest categories, except for those who had been active as concentration camp guards.* The words 'act of clemency' had been underscored, and the ink looked uncommonly fresh.

Having examined each, he grasped hold of the covers and with a savage twist wrenched them from the binding as if he were breaking the wings of a bird; then turned over what remained and shook it, searching for hidden matter; then rose and went to the door.

The clanking had begun again and it was far louder than before. He remained motionless, his head to one side, his colourless eyes vainly searching the gloom: and he heard a low whistle, a long monotone, resonant and mournful, patiently summoning, softly coaxing, eerily lamenting. A wind had risen; it was the wind for sure. He could hear the shutter again, slamming against the wall: yet surely he had closed the shutter? It was the wind: a dawn wind which had come up the river valley. A strong wind, though, for the creaking of the stairs was taut, and mounted its own scale like the creaking of a ship's ropes as the sails fill; and the glass, the dining-room glass, it was jingling absurdly; far louder than before.

'Hurry,' Turner whispered. He was talking to himself.

He pulled open the drawers of the desk. They were not locked. Some were empty. Light bulbs, fuse wire, sewing materials; socks, spare cuffs for shirts; an unframed print of a galleon in full sail. He turned it over and read: 'To darling Leo from Margaret, Hanover 1949. With fondest affection.' The script was clearly continental. Folding it roughly, he put it in his pocket. Under the print was a box. It was a square, hard box by the feel of it, bound in a black silk handkerchief, wrapped like a parcel and pinned upon itself. Unfastening the pins he cautiously drew out a tin of dull silvery metal; it must have been painted once, for the metal had the matt uneven texture of a surface scratched clean with a fine instrument. Loosening the lid, he looked inside, then gently, almost reverently, emptied the contents on to the handkerchief. Five buttons lay before him. They were each about one inch in diameter, wooden and hand-made to the same pattern, crudely but with the greatest care, as if the maker wanted for instruments but not for application, and they were pierced twice, generously, to admit a very broad thread. Under the tin was a German text book, the property of a Bonn library, stamped and annotated by the librarian. He could not understand it very well, but it seemed to be a technical treatise on the use of military gases. The last borrower had taken it out in February of that year. Certain passages were sidelined and there were small notes in the margin: 'Toxic effect immediate . . . symptoms delayed by cold weather.' Training the light full upon them, Turner sat at the desk, his head cupped in his hand and studied them with the greatest concentration; so that only instinct made him swing round and face the tall figure in the doorway.

He was quite an elderly man. He wore a tunic and a peaked cap of the kind that German students used to wear, or merchant sailors in the First World War. His face was dark with coaldust; he held a rusted riddling-iron like a trident across his body, and it trembled dreadfully in his old hands; but his red, stupid eyes were turned downwards to the pile of desecrated books, and he looked very angry indeed. Very slowly, Turner stood up. The old man did not move, but the riddling-iron shook wildly, and the white of his knuckles shone white through the soot. Turner ventured a pace forward.

'Good morning,' he said.

One black hand detached itself from the shaft and rose mechanically to the peak of his hat. Turner strode to the corner where the cartons of whisky were stacked. He ripped open the top carton, pulled out a bottle, tore off the lid. The old man was mumbling, shaking his head, still staring at the books.

'Here,' said Turner softly, 'Have a drink,' and held the bottle forward into the old man's line of sight.

Listlessly he let the iron fall, took the bottle and held it to his thin lips while Turner charged past him to the kitchen. Opening the door, he shouted at the top of his voice.

'De Lisle!'

The echo carried wildly into the deserted street and out-wards to the river.

'De Lisle!'

Even before he had returned to the study, the lights were going on in the windows of neighbouring houses.

Turner had pulled open the wooden shutters to let in the new daylight, and now the three of them stood in a baffled group, the old man blinking at the broken books and clutching the whisky in his shaking hand.

'Who is he?'

'The boilerman. We all have them.'

'Ask him when he last saw Harting.'

The old man did not immediately reply, but instead, waking again to the whisky, drank a little more, then passed it to de Lisle, whom he appeared instinctively to trust. De Lisle set it on the desk beside the silk handkerchief and quietly repeated his question, while the old man stared from one to the other, and then at the books.

'Ask him when he last saw Harting.'

At last he spoke. His voice was timeless: a slow peasant drawl, the murmur of the confessional, querulous yet sub-jugate, the voice of an underdog in the hopeless quest for consideration. Once he reached out his black fingers to touch the smashed beading of the bookcase; once he nodded towards the river, as if the river was where he lived; but the murmur continued through his gestures as if it came from someone else.

'He sells tickets for a pleasure cruise,' de Lisle whispered. 'He comes at five in the evening on the way home, and first thing in the morning on the way to work. He stokes the boilers, does the dustbins and the empties. In summer he cleans the boats before the charabancs arrive.'

'Ask him again. When did he last see Harting? Here' – he produced a fifty mark note – 'Show him this – say I'll give it him if he tells me what I want to know.'

Seeing the money, the old man examined Turner carefully with his dry, red eyes. His face was lined and hollow, starved at some-time and held up by the long cords of his shrivelled skin, and the soot was worked into it like pigment into canvas. Folding the banknote carefully down the centre he added it to the wad from his hip pocket.

'When?' Turner demanded. '*Wann?*'

Cautiously the old man began putting his words together, picking them one by one, articles in the bargain. He had taken off his hat; a sooty stubble covered his brown skull.

'Friday,' de Lisle quietly interpreted. His eye was on the window and he seemed distracted. 'Leo paid him on Friday afternoon. He went round to his house and paid him on the doorstep. He said he was going on a long journey.'

'Where to?'

'He didn't say where.'

'When will he come back? Ask him that.'

Once more, as de Lisle translated and Turner caught the half familiar words: *kommen . . . zurück.*

'Leo gave him two months' pay. He says he has something to show us. Something that is worth another fifty marks.'

The old man was glancing quickly from one to the other of them, fearful but expectant, while his long hands nervously explored the canvas tunic. It was a sailor's tunic, shapeless and bleached, and it hung without relation to his narrow frame. Finding what he was looking for, he cautiously rolled back the lower hem, reached upward and detached something from his neck. As he did so he began murmuring again, but faster than before, nervous and voluble.

'He found it on Saturday morning in the rubbish.'

It was a holster made of green webbing, army issue, suitable for a three-eight pistol. It had 'Harting Leo' stencilled on the inside and it was empty.

'In the dustbin, right on top; the first thing he saw when he lifted the lid. He didn't show it to the others. The others shouted at him and threatened to kick his face in. The others reminded him of what they'd done to him in the war and they said they'd do it again.'

'What others? Who?'

'Wait.'

Going to the window, de Lisle peered casually out. The old man was still talking.

'He says he distributed anti-Nazi pamphlets in the war,' he called, still watching. 'By mistake. He thought they were ordinary newspapers and the others caught him and hung him upside down. That's who the others seem to be. He says he likes the English best. He says Harting was a real gentleman. He says he wants to keep the whisky too. Leo always gave him Scotch. And cigars. Little Dutch cigars, a kind you can't get in the shops. Leo had them sent specially. And last Christmas he gave his wife a hair-dryer. He would also like fifty marks for the holster,' he added, but by then the cars had entered the drive, and the little room was filled with the double wail of a police horn and the double flash of a blue light. They heard the shout and the stamp of feet as the green figures gathered at the windows, pointing their guns into the room. The door was open and a young man in a leather coat held a pistol in his hand. The boilerman was crying, wailing, waiting to be hit and the blue light was rolling like a light for dancing. 'Do nothing,' de Lisle had said. 'Obey no orders.'

He was talking to the boy in the leather coat, offering his red diplomatic card for examination. His voice was quiet but very firm, a negotiator's voice, neither flippant nor concessive, stiffened with authority and hinting at injured privilege. The young detective's face was as blank as Siebkron's. Gradually de Lisle appeared to be gaining the ascendancy. His tone changed to one of indignation. He began asking questions, and the boy became conciliatory, even evasive. Gradually Turner gathered the trend of de Lisle's complaint. He was pointing at Turner's notebook and then at the old man. A list, he was saying, they were making a list. Was it forbidden for diplomats to make a list? To assess delapidation, to check the inventory of Embassy furniture? It was surely a natural enough thing to do at a time when British property was in danger of destruction. Mr Harting had gone on extended leave of absence; it was expedient to make certain dispositions, to pay the boilerman his fifty marks. . . . And since when, de Lisle wished to know, were British diplomats forbidden entry to British Embassy livings? By what right, de Lisle wished to know, had this great concourse of militia burst upon the privacy of extra-territorial persons?

More cards were exchanged, more documents mutually examined; names and numbers mutually recorded. The detective was sorry, he said; these were troubled times, and he stared at Turner for a long time as if he recognized a colleague. Troubled times or not, de Lisle appeared to reply, the rights of diplomats must be respected. The greater the danger, the more necessary the immunity. They shook hands. Somebody saluted. Gradually they all withdrew. The green uniforms dispersed, the blue lights vanished, the vans drove away. De Lisle had found three glasses and was pouring a little whisky into each. The old man was whimpering. Turner had returned the buttons to their tin and put the tin in his pocket together with the little book on military cases.

'Was that them?' he demanded. 'Were those the ones who questioned him?'

'He says: *like* the detective, but a little older. Whiter, he says: a richer kind of man. I think we both know who he's talking about. Here, you'd better look after this yourself.'

Tugging the holster from the folds of his brown overcoat, de Lisle thrust it without pride into Turner's waiting hand.

The ferry was hung with the flags of the German Federation. The crest of Königswinter was nailed to the bridge. Militia packed the bow. Their steel helmets were square, their faces pale and sad. They were very quiet for such young men and their rubber boots made no sound on the steel deck, and they stared at the river as if they had been told to remember it. Turner stood apart from them, watching the crew cast away, and he perceived everything very clearly because he was tired and frightened and because it was still early morning: the heavy vibration of the iron deck as the cars thumped over the ramp and pressed forward to the best berth; the howl of the engines and the clatter of chains as the men shouted and cast away, the strident bell that put out the fading chimes of the town's churches, the uniform hostility of the drivers as they rose from their cars and picked the change from their pigskin purses as if men were a secret society and could not acknowledge each other in public; and the pedestrians, the bronzed and the poor, coveting the cars from which they were kept apart. The river bank receded; the little town drew its spires back into the hills like scenery at the opera. Gradually they described their awkward course, steering a long arc with the current to avoid the sister ferry from the opposite bank. Now they slowed almost to a halt, drifting down river as the *John F. Kennedy*, loaded with equal pyramids of fine coal, bore swiftly down upon them, the children's washing sloping in the wet air. Then they were rocking in its wake and the women passengers were calling in amusement.

'He told you something else. About a woman. I heard him say *Frau* and *Auto*. Something about a woman and a car.'

'Sorry old boy,' de Lisle said coolly, 'It's the Rhineland accent. Sometimes it simply defeats me.'

Turner stared back at the Königswinter bank, shielding his eyes with his gloved hand because even in that miserable spring the light came sharply off the water. At last he saw what he was looking for: to each side, like mailed hands pointing to the Seven Hills of Siegfried, turreted brown villas built with the wealth of the Ruhr; between them a splash of white against the trees of the esplanade. It was Harting's house receding in the mist.

'I'm chasing a ghost,' he muttered. 'A bloody shadow.'

'Your own,' de Lisle retorted, his voice rich with disgust.

'Oh, sure, sure.'

'I shall drive you back to the Embassy,' de Lisle continued. 'From then on, you find your own transport.'

'Why the hell did you bring me if you're so squeamish?' And suddenly he laughed. 'Of course,' he said. 'What a bloody fool I am! I'm going to sleep! You were frightened I might find the Green File and you thought you'd wait in the wings. Unsuitable for temporaries. Christ!'

Cork had just heard the eight o'clock news. The German delegation had withdrawn from Brussels during the night. Officially the Federal Government wished to 'reconsider certain technical problems which had arisen in the course of discussions'. Unofficially, as Cork put it, they had run away from school. Blankly he watched the coloured paper stutter out of the rollers and fall into the wire basket. It was about ten minutes before the summons came. There was a knock on the door and Miss Peate's stupid head appeared at the little trap. Mr Bradfield would see him at once. Her mean eyes were alive with pleasure. Once and for all, she meant. As he followed her into the corridor, he caught sight of Cork's brochure on plots of land in the Bahamas and he thought: that's going to be useful by the time he's done with me.

12

'And there was Leo. In the second class'

'I HAVE ALREADY spoken to Lumley. You go home tonight. Travel section will attend to your tickets.' Bradfield's desk was piled high with telegrams. 'And I have apologized in your name to Siebkron.'

'*Apologized?*'

Bradfield dropped the latch on the door. 'Shall I spell it out for you? Like Harting, you are evidently something of a political primitive. You are here on a temporary diplomatic footing; if you were not, you would undoubtedly be in prison.' He was pale with anger. 'God alone knows what de Lisle thought he was up to. I shall speak to him separately. You have deliberately disobeyed my instruction; well, you people have your own code, I suppose, and I am as suspect as the next man.'

'You flatter yourself.'

'In this case, however, you were placed specifically under my authority, by Lumley, by the Ambassador and by the necessities of the situation here, and specifically ordered to make no move which could have repercussions outside the Embassy. Be quiet and listen to me! Instead of showing the minimal consideration that was asked of you, however, you go round to Harting's house at five in the morning, frighten the wits out of his servant, wake the neighbours, bellow for de Lisle, and finally attract a full-scale police raid which, in a matter of hours, will no doubt be the talking point of the community. Not content with that, you are party to a stupid lie to the police about conducting an inventory; I imagine that will bring a smile even to Siebkron's lips, after the description you offered him of your work last night.'

'Any more?'

'A great deal thank you. Whatever Siebkron suspected that Harting had done, you have by now delivered the proof. You saw his attitude for yourself. Heaven knows what he does not think we are up to.'

'Then tell him,' Turner suggested. 'Why not? Ease his mind. Christ, he knows more than we do. Why do we make a secret of something they all know? They're in full cry. The worst we can do is spoil their kill.'

'I will not have it *said*! Anything is better, any doubts, any suspicions on their part, than our admission at this moment in time that for twenty years a member of our diplomatic staff has been in Soviet employment. Is there nothing you will understand of this? I will not have it *said*! Let them think and do what they like, without our cooperation they can *only* surmise.'

It was a statement of personal faith. He sat as still and as upright as a sentry guarding a national shrine.

'Is that the lot?'

'You people are supposed to work in secret. One calls upon you expecting a standard of discretion. I could tell you a little about your behaviour here, had you not made it abundantly clear that manners mean nothing to you whatever. It will take a long time to sweep up the mess you have left behind you in this Embassy. You seem to think that nothing reaches me. I have already warded off Gaunt and Meadowes; no doubt there are others I shall have to soothe.'

'I'd better go this afternoon,' Turner suggested. He had not taken his eyes from Bradfield's face. 'I've ballsed it up, haven't I? Sorry about that. Sorry you're not satisfied with the service. I'll write and apologize; that's what Lumley likes me to do. A bread and butter letter. So I'll do that. I'll write.' He sighed, 'I seem to be a bit of a Jonah. Best thing to do really, chuck me out. Be a bit of a wrench for you, that will. You don't like getting rid of people do you? Rather give them a contract.'

'What are you suggesting?'

'That you've a damn good reason for insisting on discretion! I said to Lumley – Christ that was a joke – I asked him, see: does he want the files of the man? What the hell *are* you up to? Wait! One minute you give him a job, the next you don't want to know him. If they brought his body in now you couldn't care bloody less: you'd pat the pockets for papers and wish him luck!'

He noticed, quite inconsequentially, Bradfield's shoes. They were hand-made and polished that dark mahogany which is only captured by servants, or by those who have been brought up with them.

'What the devil do you mean?'

'I don't know who's putting the finger on you: I don't care. Siebkron, I would guess, from the way you crawl to him. Why did you bring us together last night if you were so bloody worried about offending him? What was the point to that, for one? *Or did he order you to?* Don't answer yet, it's my turn. You're Harting's guardian angel, do you realize that? It sticks out a mile, and I'll write it six foot high when I get back to London. You renewed his contract, right? Just that, for a start. Although you despised him. But you didn't just *give* him work; you *made* work for him. You knew bloody well the Foreign Office didn't give a damn about the Destruction programme. Or for the Personalities Index either, I shouldn't wonder. But you pretended; you built it up for him. Don't tell me it was compassion for a man who didn't belong.'

'Whatever there was of *that* has worn pretty thin by now,' Bradfield remarked, with a hint of that dismay, or self-contempt, which Turner now occasionally discerned in him.

'Then what about the Thursday meeting?'

A look of sheer pain crossed Bradfield's face.

'My God you are insufferable,' he said, more as a mental note, a privately recorded judgment, than an insult directly intended.

'The Thursday conference that never was! It was you who took Harting off that conference; you who gave the job to de Lisle. But Harting still went out Thursday afternoons all right. Did you stop him? Did you hell. I expect you even know where he went, don't you.' He held up the gunmetal key he had taken from Harting's suit. 'Because there's a special place, you see. A hideaway. Or maybe I'm telling you something you know already. Who did he meet out there? Do you know that too? I used to think it was Praschko, until I remembered *you* fed me that idea, you yourself. So I'm going bloody carefully with Praschko.'

Turner was leaning across the desk, shouting at Bradfield's

bowed head. 'As to Siebkron, he's rolling up a whole bloody network, like as not. Dozens of agents, for all we know: Harting was just one link in a chain. You can't begin to control what Siebkron knows and doesn't know. We're dealing with reality you know, not diplomacy.' He pointed to the window and the blurred hills across the river. 'They sell horses over there! They screw around, talk to friends, make journeys; they've been beyond the edge of the forest, they know what the world looks like!'

'It requires very little, in an intelligent person, to know that,' said Bradfield.

'And that's what I'm going to tell Lumley when I get back to the smoke. Harting didn't work alone! He had a patron as well as a controller and for all I know, they were the same man! And for all I bloody well know, Leo Harting was Rawley Bradfield's fancy boy! Having a bit of public school vice on the side!'

Bradfield was standing up, his face contracted with anger. 'Tell Lumley what you like,' he whispered, 'but get out of here and don't ever come back,' and it was then that Mickie Crabbe put his red, bubbling face round Miss Peate's connecting door.

He was looking puzzled and slightly indignant, and he was chewing absurdly at his ginger moustache. 'Rawley, I say,' he said and began again, as if he had started in the wrong octave. 'Sorry to burst in, Rawley. I tried the door in the corridor but the latch was down. Sorry Rawley. It's about Leo,' he said. The rest came out with rather a rush, 'I've just seen him down at the railway station. Bloody well having a beer.'

'Be quick,' said Bradfield.

'Doing a favour for Peter de Lisle. That's all,' Crabbe began defensively. Turner caught the smell of drink on his breath, mingling with the smell of peppermint. 'Peter had to go down to the Bundestag. Debate on Emergency Legislation, big thing apparently, second day, so he asked me to cover the jamboree at the railway station. The Movement's leaders, coming in from Hanover. Watch the arrivals, see who turned up. I often do odd jobs for Peter,' he added apologetically. 'Turned out to be a Lord Mayor's Show. Press, television lights, masses of cars lined up in the road' – he glanced nervously at Bradfield – 'where the taxis stand, Rawley, *you* know. And crowds. All singing rah-rah and waving the old black flags. Bit of music.' He shook his head in private wonder. 'That square is *plastered* with slogans.'

'And you saw Leo,' Turner said, pressing. 'In the crowd?'

'Sort of.'

'What do you mean?'

'Well the back of his head. Head and shoulders. Just a glimpse. No time to grab him: gone.'

Turner seized him with his big, stone hands. 'You said you saw him having a beer!'

'Let him go,' said Bradfield.

'Hey steady!' For a moment Crabbe looked almost ferocious. 'Well I saw him later, you see. After the show was over. Face to face sort of thing.'

Turner released him.

'The train came in and everyone started cheering pretty loud, and shoving about and trying to get a glimpse of Karfeld. There was even a bit of fighting at the edges, I think, but that was mainly the journalists. *Sods*,' he added with a spark of real hatred. 'That shit Sam Allerton was there, by the way. I should think *he* started it.'

'For Christ's sake!' Turner shouted, and Crabbe regarded him quite straightly, with an expression which spoke of bad form.

'First of all Meyer-Lothringen came out – the police had made a gangway for him out of cattle pens – then Tilsit, then Halbach, and everyone shouting like gyppos. Beatles,' he said, incomprehendingly. 'Kids mainly they were, long-haired student types, leaning over the railings trying to touch the chaps' shoulders. Karfeld didn't make it. Some fellow near me said he must have gone out the other side, gone down the passage to avoid the crowd. He doesn't like people coming too close, that's what they say; that's why he builds these damn great stands everywhere. So half the crowd charges off to see if they can find him. The rest hang around in case, and then there's this announcement over the blower: we can all go home because Karfeld's still in Hanover. Lucky for Bonn, that's what I thought.' He grinned. 'What?'

Neither spoke.

'The journalists were furious and I thought I'd just give Rawley a ring to let him know Karfeld hadn't turned up. London likes to keep track, you see. Of Karfeld.' This for Turner. 'They like to keep tabs on him, not have him talking to strange men.' He resumed: 'There's an all-night Post Office by the hall there, and I was just coming out when it occurred to me' – he made a feeble attempt to drag them into the conspiracy – 'that maybe I ought to have a quick cup of coffee to collect my thoughts, and I happened to look through the glass door of the waiting-room. Doors are side by side you see. Restaurant one side, waiting-room the other. It's a sort of buffet in there with a few places to sit as well. I mean sit and not drink,' he explained, as if that were a particular type of eccentricity he had occasionally met with. 'There's the first class on the left and the second class on the right, both glass doors.'

'For pity's sake!' Turner breathed.

'And there was Leo. In the second class. At a table. Wearing a trench coat, a sort of army looking thing. Seemed in rather bad shape.'

'Drunk?'

'I don't know. Christ, that would be going it, wouldn't it: eight in the morning.' He looked very innocent. 'But tired out and well, not dapper, you know, not like he usually is. Gloss, bounce: all gone. Still,' he added stupidly, 'Comes to all of us I suppose.'

'You didn't speak to him?'

'No thanks. I know him in that mood. I gave him a wide berth and came back and told Rawley.'

'Was he carrying anything,' Bradfield said quickly. 'Did he have a briefcase with him? Anything that could hold papers?'

'Nothing *about*,' Crabbe muttered, 'Rawley old boy. Sorry.'

They stood in silence, all three, while Crabbe blinked from one face to the other.

'You did well,' Bradfield muttered at last. 'All right, Crabbe.'

'*Well?*' Turner shouted. 'He did bloody badly! Leo's not in quarantine. Why didn't he talk to him, drag him here by the neck, reason with him? God Almighty you're not bloody well alive, either of you! *Well?* He may be gone by now; that was our last chance! He was probably waiting for his final contact; they've dirtied him up for the journey out! Did he have anyone with him?' He pulled open the door. 'I said did he have anyone with him? Come on!'

'A kid,' said Crabbe. 'Little girl.'

'A *what*?'

'Six or seven years old. Someone's kid. He was talking to it.'

'Did he recognize you?'

'Doubt it. Seemed to look through me.'

Turner seized his raincoat from the stand.

'I'd rather not,' said Crabbe, answering the gesture rather than the exhortation. 'Sorry.'

'And you! What are *you* standing there for? *Come on!*'

Bradfield did not move.

'*For God's sake!*'

'I'm staying here. Crabbe has a car. Let him take you. It must be nearly an hour since he saw him, or thought he did, with all that traffic. He'll be gone by now. I don't propose to waste my own time.' Ignoring Turner's astonished gaze, he continued, 'The Ambassador has already asked me not to leave the building. We expect word from Brussels any minute; it is highly likely that he will wish to call upon the Chancellor.'

'Christ, what do you think this is? A tripartite conference. He may be sitting there with a caseful of secrets! No wonder he looks under the weather! What's got into you now? Do you *want* Siebkron to find him before we do? Do you want him to be caught red-handed?'

'I have already told you: secrets are not sacrosanct. We would prefer them kept, it is true. In relation to what I have to do here—'

'*Those* secrets are, aren't they? What about the bloody Green File?'

Bradfield hesitated.

'*I've* no authority over him,' Turner cried. 'I don't even know what he looks like! What am *I* supposed to do when I see him?

Tell him you'd like a word with him? You're his boss, aren't you? Do you *want* Ludwig Siebkron to find him first?' Tears had started absurdly to his eyes. His voice was one of utter supplication. 'Bradfield!'

'He was all alone,' Crabbe muttered, not looking at Bradfield, 'just him and himself, old boy. And the kid. I'm sure of that.'

Bradfield stared at Crabbe, and then at Turner, and once again his face seemed crowded by private pains scarcely held at bay.

'It's true,' he said at last, very reluctantly, 'I am his superior. I am responsible. I had better be there.' Carefully double-locking the outer door, he left word with Miss Peate that Gaveston should stand in for him, and led the way downstairs.

New fire extinguishers, just arrived from London, stood like red sentinels along the corridor. At the landing, a consignment of steel beds awaited assembly. A file-trolley was loaded with grey blankets. In the lobby two men, mounted on separate ladders, were erecting a steel screen. Dark Gaunt watched them in bewilderment as they swept through the glass doors into the car park, Crabbe leading. Bradfield drove with an arrogance which took Turner by surprise. They raced across the lights on amber, keeping to the left lane to make the turn into the station road. At the traffic check he barely halted; both he and Crabbe had their red cards ready at the window. They were on wet cobble, skidding on the tramlines and Bradfield held the wheel still, waiting patiently for the car to come to its senses. They approached an intersection where the sign said 'Yield', and ran straight over it under the wheels of an oncoming bus. The cars were fewer, the streets were packed with people.

Some carried banners, others wore the grey gabardine rain-coats and black Homburg hats which were the uniform of the Movement's supporters. They yielded reluctantly, scowling at the number plates and the glittering foreign paintwork. Bradfield neither sounded his horn nor changed gear, but let them wake to him and avoid him as they might. Once he braked for an old man who was either deaf or drunk; once a boy slapped the roof of the car with his bare hand, and Bradfield became very still and pale. Confetti lay on the steps, the pillars were covered with slogans. A cab driver was yelling as if he had been hit. They had parked in the cab rank.

'Left,' Crabbe called as Turner ran ahead of him. A high doorway admitted them to the main hall.

'Keep left,' Turner heard Crabbe shout for the second time.

Three barriers led to the platform; three ticket collectors sat in their glass cages. Notices warned him in three languages not to ask them favours. A group of priests, whispering, turned to eye him disapprovingly: haste, they said, is not a Christian quality. A blonde girl, her face chestnut brown, swung dangerously past him with a rucksack and well-worn skis, and he saw the trembling of her pullover.

'He was sitting just there,' Crabbe whispered, but by then Turner had flung open the glazed swing door and was standing inside the restaurant, glaring through the cigarette smoke at each table in turn. A loudspeaker barked a message about changing at Cologne. 'Gone,' Crabbe was saying, 'Sod's flown.'

The smoke hung all around, lifting in the glow of the long tube lights, curling into the darker corners. The smell was of beer and smoked ham and municipal disinfectant; the far counter, white with Dutch tiles, glinted like an ice wall in the fog. In a brown-wood cubicle sat a poor family on the move; the women were old and dressed in black, their suitcases were bound with rope; the men were reading Greek newspapers. At a separate table a little girl rolled beermats to a drunk, and that was the table Crabbe was pointing at.

'Where the kiddie is, you see. He was having a Pils.'

Ignoring the drunk and the child, Turner picked up the glasses and stared at them uselessly. Three small cigar ends lay in the ashtray. One was still slightly smouldering. The child watched him as he stooped and searched the floor and rose again empty handed; she watched him stride from one table to the next, glaring into the faces, seizing a shoulder, pushing down a newspaper, touching an arm.

'Is this him?' he yelled. A lonely priest was reading *Bildzeitung* in a corner; beside him, hiding in his shadow, a darkfaced gypsy ate roast chestnuts out of a bag.

'No.'

'This?'

'Sorry old boy,' said Crabbe, very nervous now, 'No luck. I say, go easy.'

By the stained-glass window two soldiers were playing chess. A bearded man was making the motions of eating, but there was no food before him. Outside on the platform a train was arriving, and the vibration shook the crockery. Crabbe was addressing the waitress. He was hanging over her, whispering and his hand was on the flesh of her upper arm. She shook her head.

'We'll try the other one,' he said, as Turner joined them. They walked across the room together, and this woman nodded, proud to have remembered, and made a long story, pointing at the child and talking about '*der kleine Herr*', the little gentleman, and sometimes just about '*der Kleine*', as if 'gentleman' were a tribute to her interrogators rather than to Harting.

'He was here till a few minutes ago,' Crabbe said in some bewilderment. 'Her version, anyway.'

'Did he leave alone?'

'Didn't see.'

'Did he make any impression on her?'

'Steady. She's not a big thinker, old boy. Don't want her to fly away.'

'What made him leave? Did he see someone? Did someone signal to him from the door?'

'You're stretching it old son. She didn't see him leave. She didn't worry about him, he paid with every order. As if he might leave in a hurry. Catch a train. He went out to watch the hoo-hah, when the boys arrived, then came back and had another cigar and a drink.'

'What's the matter then? Why are you looking like that?'

'It's bloody odd,' Crabbe muttered, frowning absurdly.

'What's bloody odd?'

'He's been here all night. Alone. Drinking but not drunk. Played with the kid part of the time. Greek kid. That was what he liked best: the kid.' He gave the woman a coin and she thanked him laboriously.

'Just as well we missed him,' Crabbe declared. 'Pugnacious little sod when he gets like this. Go for anyone when he's got his dander up.'

'How do you know?'

Crabbe grimaced in painful reminiscence: 'You should have seen him that night in Cologne,' he muttered, still staring after the waitress. 'Jesus.'

'In the fight? You were there?'

'I tell you,' Crabbe repeated. He spoke from the heart. 'When that lad's really going, he's best avoided altogether. Look.' He held out his hand. A wooden button lay in the palm and it was identical to the buttons in the scratched tin in Königswinter. 'She picked this up from the table,' he said. 'She thought it might be something he needed. She was hanging on to it in case he came back, you see.'

Bradfield came slowly through the doorway. His face was taut but without expression.

'I gather he's not here.'

No one spoke.

'You still say you saw him?'

'No mistake, old boy. Sorry.'

'Well, I suppose we must believe you. I suggest we go back to the Embassy.' He glanced at Turner. 'Unless you prefer to stay. If you have some further theory to test.' He looked round the buffet. Every face was turned towards them. Behind the bar, a chrome machine was steaming unattended. Not a hand moved. 'You seem to have made your mark here anyway.' As they walked slowly back to the car, Bradfield said, 'You can come into the Embassy to collect your possessions but you must be out by lunchtime. If you have any papers, leave them with Cork and we'll send them on by bag. There's a flight at seven. Take it. If you can't get a seat, take the train. But go.'

They waited while Bradfield spoke to the policemen and showed them his red card. His German sounded very English in tone but the grammar was faultless. The policeman nodded, saluted and they took their leave. Slowly they returned to the Embassy through the sullen faces of the aimless crowd.

'Extraordinary place for Leo to spend the night,' Crabbe muttered, but Turner was fingering the gunmetal key in the OHMS envelope in his pocket, and still wondering, for all his sense of failure, whose door it had unlocked.

13

The strain of being a pig

HE SAT AT the cypher room desk, still in his raincoat, packing together the useless trophies of his investigation, the army holster, the folded print, the engraved paper knife from Margaret Aickman; the blue-bound diary for counsellors and above, the little notebook for diplomatic discounts, and the scratched tin of five wooden buttons cut to size; and now the sixth button and the three stubs of cigar.

'Never mind,' said Cork kindly. 'He'll turn up.'

'Oh sure. Like the investments and the Caribbean dream. Leo's everybody's darling. Everybody's lost son, Leo is. We all love Leo, although he cut our throats.'

'Mind you, he couldn't half tell the tale.' He was sitting on the trucked bed in his shirt sleeves, pulling on his outdoor shoes. He wore metal springs above the elbows and his shirt was like an advertisement on the underground. There was no sound from the corridor. 'That's what *got* you about him. Quiet, but a sod.'

A machine stammered and Cork frowned at it reprovingly.

'Blarney,' he continued. 'That's what he had. The magic. He could tell you *any* bloody tale and you believed it.'

He had put them into a paper waste-bag. The label on the outside said 'SECRET. Only to be disposed of in the presence of two authorized witnesses.'

'I want this sealed and sent to Lumley,' he said, and Cork wrote out a receipt and signed it.

'I remember the first time I met him,' Cork said, in the cheerful voice which Turner associated with funeral breakfasts. 'I was *green*. I was really *green*. I'd only been married six months. If I hadn't twigged him I'd have—'

'You'd have been taking his tips on investment. You'd have been lending him the code books for bedside reading.' He stapled the mouth of the bag, folding it against itself.

'Not the code books. Janet. He'd have been reading *her* in bed.' Cork smiled happily. 'Bloody neck! You wouldn't credit it. Come on then. Lunch.'

For the last time Turner savagely clamped together the two arms of the stapler. 'Is de Lisle in?'

'Doubt it. London's sent a brief the size of your arm. All hands on deck. The dips are out in force.' He laughed. 'They ought to have a go with the old black flags. Lobby the deputies. Strenuous representations at all levels. Leave no stone unturned. *And* they're going for another loan. I don't know where the Krauts get the stuff from sometimes. Know what Leo said to me once? "I tell you what, Bill, we'll score a big diplomatic victory. We'll go down to the Bundestag and offer them a million quid. Just you and me. I reckon they'd fall down in a faint." He was right, you know.'

Turner dialled de Lisle's number but there was no reply.

'Tell him I rang to say goodbye,' he said to Cork, and changed his mind. 'Don't worry.'

He called Travel Section and enquired about his ticket. It was all in order, they assured him; Mr Bradfield had sent down personally and the ticket was waiting for him at the desk. They seemed impressed. Cork picked up his coat.

'And you'd better cable Lumley and give him my time of arrival.'

'I'm afraid H. of C.'s done that already,' Cork said, with something quite near to a blush.

'Well. Thanks.' He was at the door, looking back into the room as if he would never see it again. 'I hope it goes all right with the baby. I hope your dreams come true. I hope everyone's dream comes true. I hope they all get what they're looking for.'

'Look: think of it this way,' Cork said sympathetically. 'There's things you just don't give up, isn't there?'

'That's right.'

'I mean you can't pack everything up neat and tidy. Not in life, you can't. That's for girls, that is. That's just romantic. You get like Leo otherwise: you can't leave a thing alone. Now what are you going to do with yourself this afternoon? There's a nice matinee at the American cinema. . . . No. Wouldn't be right for you: lot of screaming kids.'

'What do you mean, he can't leave a thing alone?'

Cork was drifting round the room, checking the machines, the desks and the secret waste.

'Vindictive. Vindictive wasn't in it. He had a feud with Fred Anger once; Fred was Admin. They say it ran five years till Fred was posted.'

'What about?'

'Nothing.' He had picked a scrap of paper from the floor and was reading it. 'Absolutely sweet Fanny Adams. Fred cut down a lime tree in Leo's garden, said it was endangering the fence. Which it was. Fred told me: "Bill," he said, "that tree would have *fallen* down in the autumn." '

'He had a thing about land,' Turner said. 'He wanted his own patch. He didn't like being in limbo.'

'Know what Leo did? He made a wreath out of leaves. Brought it into the Embassy and nailed it on to Fred's office door. With bloody great two-inch nails. Crucified it near enough. The German staff thought Fred had snuffed it. Leo didn't laugh though. He wasn't joking; he really meant it. He was *violent*, see. Now dips don't notice that. All oil and how-d' you-do, he was to them. And helpful, I'm not saying he wasn't helpful. I'm just saying that when Leo had a grudge, I wouldn't fancy being the other end of it. That's all I'm saying.'

'He went for your wife, did he?'

'I put a stop to that,' said Cork. 'Just as well. Seeing what happened elsewhere. The Welfare Dance, that was. A couple of years back. He started coming it. Nothing *nasty*, mind. Wanted to give her a hair-dryer and that. Meet me up on the hill, that lark. I said to him, "You find your own hair to dry," I said. "She's mine." You can't blame him though, can you? Know what they say about refugees: they lose everything except their accents. Dead right, you know. Trouble with Leo was, he wanted it all back. So I suppose that's it: take the pick of the files and run for it. Flog them to the highest bidder. It's no more than what we owe him, I don't suppose.' Satisfied with his security check, Cork stacked together his brochures and came towards the door where Turner stood. 'You're from the North, aren't you?' he asked. 'I can tell by your voice.'

'How well did you know him?'

'Leo? Oh, like all of us really. I'd buy this and that, give him a saucer of milk now and then; put an order in for the Dutchman.'

'Dutchman?'

'Firm of diplomatic exporters. From Amsterdam. Cheaper if you can be bothered; you know. Do you anything: butter, meat, radios, cars, the lot.'

'Hair-dryers?'

'Anything. There's a rep. calls every Monday. Fill in your form one week, chuck it into Leo and you get the order the next. I expect there was a bit in it for him: *you* know. Mind you, you could never catch him out. I mean you could check up till you were blue in the face: you'd never find out where he took his divi. Though I *think* it was those bloody cigars. They were really shocking, you know. I don't think he enjoyed them; he just smoked them because they were free. And because we pulled his leg about them.' He laughed simply. 'He conned the lot of us, that's the truth of it. You too, I suppose. Well, I'll be slipping on then. So long.'

'You were saying about that first time you met him.'

'Was I? Oh well, yes.' He laughed again. 'I mean you couldn't believe *anything*. My first day: Mickie Crabbe took me down there. We done the round by then. "Here," says Mickie, "just one more port of call," and takes me downstairs to see Leo. "This is Cork," he says. "Just joined us in Cyphers." So then Leo moves in.' Cork sat down on the swivel chair beside the door and leaned back like the rich executive he longed to be. ' "Glass of sherry," he says. We're supposed to be dry here, but that never bothered Leo; not that he drank himself, mind. "We must celebrate the new arrival. You don't *sing* by any chance, do you, Cork?" "Only in the bath," I says and we all have a nice laugh. Recruiting for the choir, see: that always impressed them. Very pious gentleman, Mr Harting, I thought. Not half. "Have a cigar, Cork?" No thanks. "A fag then?" Don't mind if I do, Mr Harting. So then we sit there like a lot of dips, sipping our sherry, and I'm thinking, "Well, I must say you're quite the little king round here." Furniture, maps, carpet . . . all the trappings. Fred Anger cleared a lot of it out, mind, before he left. Nicked, half of it was. *Liberated*, you know. Like in the old Occupation days. "So how are things in London, Cork?" he asks, "Everything much the same I suppose?" Putting me at my ease, cheeky sod. "That old porter at the main door: still saucy with the visiting Ambassadors, is he, Cork?" He really came it. "And the coal fires: still lighting the coal fires every morning, are they, Cork?" "Well," I says, "They're not doing too bad, but it's like everything else, it takes its time." Some crap like that. "Oh, ah, really," he says, "because I had a letter from Ewan Waldebere only a few months back telling me they were putting in the central heating. And that old bloke who used to pray on the steps of Number Ten, still there is he, Cork, morning and night, saying his prayers? Doesn't seem to have done us much good, does he? I tell you: I was practically calling him sir. Ewan Waldebere was Head of Western Department by then, all set to be God. So then he comes on about the choir again and the Dutchman and a few other things besides, anything he can do to help, and when we get outside I look at Mickie Crabbe and Mickie's *pissing* himself. Doubled up, Mickie is. "Leo?" he says, "Leo? He's never been inside the Foreign Office in his life. He hasn't even been back to England since forty-five." ' Cork broke off, shaking his head. 'Still,' he repeated, with an affectionate laugh, 'You can't blame him, can you?' He got up. 'And I mean, we all saw through him, but we still fell for it, didn't we? I mean Arthur and . . . I mean everybody. It's like my villa,' he added simply, 'I know I'll never get there, but I believe in it all the same. I mean you have to really . . . you couldn't live, not without illusions. Not here.'

Taking his hands out of his mackintosh pocket, Turner stared first at Cork and then at the gunmetal key in his big palm, and he seemed to be torn and undecided.

'What's Mickie Crabbe's number?'

Cork watched with apprehension as he lifted the receiver, dialled and began talking.

'They don't *expect* you to go on looking for him,' Cork said anxiously. 'I don't really think they do.'

'I'm not bloody well looking for him, I'm having lunch with Crabbe and I'm catching the evening flight and nothing on God's earth would keep me in this dream box for an hour longer than I need.' He slammed down the receiver and stalked out of the room.

De Lisle's door was wide open but his desk was empty. He wrote a note: 'Called in to say goodbye. Goodbye. Alan Turner,' and his hand was shaking with anger and humiliation. In the lobby, small groups were sauntering into the sunlight to eat their sandwiches or lunch in the canteen. The Ambassador's Rolls-Royce stood at the door; the escort of police outriders waited patiently. Gaunt was whispering to Meadowes at the front desk and he fell suddenly quiet as Turner approached.

'Here,' he said, handing him the envelope. 'Here's your ticket.' His expression said, 'Now go back to where you belong.'

'Ready when you are old son,' Crabbe whispered from his habitual patch of darkness. 'You see.'

The waiters were quiet and awfully discreet. Crabbe had asked for snails which he said were very good. The framed print in their little alcove showed shepherds dancing with nymphs, and there was just a suggestion of expensive sin.

'You were with him that night in Cologne. The night he got into the fight.'

'Extraordinary,' said Crabbe, 'Really. Do you like water?' he asked, and added a little to each of their glasses, but it was no more than a tear shed for the sober. 'Don't know what came over him.'

'Did you often go out with him?'

He grinned unsuccessfully and they drank.

'That was five years ago, you see. Mary's mother was ill; kept on flogging back to England. I was a grass widower, so to speak.'

'So you'd push off with Leo occasionally; have a drink and chase a few pussycats.'

'More or less.'

'In Cologne?'

'Steady, old boy,' said Crabbe. 'You're like a bloody lawyer.' He drank again and as the drink went into him he shook like a poor comedian reacting late. 'Christ,' he said. 'What a day. Christ.'

'Night clubs are best in Cologne, are they?'

'You can't do it *here*, old boy,' Crabbe said with a nervous start. 'Not unless you want to screw half the Government. You've got to be *bloody* careful in Bonn.' He added needlessly, '*Bloody* careful.' He jerked his head in wild confirmation. 'Cologne's the better bet.'

'Better girls?'

'Can't make it, old boy. Not for years.'

'But Leo went for them, did he?'

'He liked the girls,' said Crabbe.

'So you went to Cologne that night. Your wife was in England, and you went on the razzle with Leo.'

'We were just sitting at a table. Drinking, you see.' He suited the gesture to the word. 'Leo was talking about the Army: remember old so-and-so. That game. Loved the Army, Leo did, loved it. Should have stayed in, that's my feeling. Not that they'd have had him, not as a regular. He needed the discipline, in my opinion. Urchin really. Like me. It's all right when you're young, you don't mind. It's later. They knocked hell out of me at Sherborne. Hell. Used to hold the taps, head in the basin, while the bloody prefects hit me. I didn't care then. Thought it was life.' He put a hand on Turner's arm. 'Old boy,' he whispered. 'I *hate* them now. Didn't know I had it in me. It's all come to the surface. For two pins I'd go back there and shoot the buggers. Truth.'

'Did you know him in the Army?'

'No.'

'Then who were you remembering?'

'I ran across him in the CCG a bit. Moenchengladbach. Four Group.'

'When he was on Claims?'

Crabbe's reaction to harassment was unnerving. Like his namesake he seemed in some mysterious way to draw the extremities of his presence under a protective shell, and to lie passive until the danger had passed. Ducking his head into his glass he kept it there, shoulders hunched, while he peered at Turner with pink, hooded eyes.

'So you were drinking and talking.'

'Just quietly. Waiting for the cabaret. I like a good cabaret.' He drifted away into a wholly incredible account of an attempt he had made upon a girl in Frankfurt on the occasion of the last Free Democrats' Conference: 'Fiasco,' he declared proudly. 'Climbing over me like a bloody monkey and I couldn't do a thing.'

'So the fight came after the cabaret?'

'Before. There was a bunch of Huns at the bar kicking up a din; singing. Leo took offence. Started glaring at them. Pawing the earth a bit. Suddenly he'd called for the bill. "*Zahlen!*" Just like that. Bloody loud too. I said "Hoi! old boy, what's up?" Ignored me. "I don't want to go," I said. "Want to see the tit show." Blind bit of notice. The waiter brings the bill, Leo tots it up, shoves his hand in his pocket and puts a button on the plate.'

'What kind of button?'

'Just a button. Like the one the dolly found down at the Bahnhof. Bloody wooden button with holes in it.' He was still indignant. 'You can't pay bloody bills with a *button*. Can you? Thought it was a joke at first. Had a bit of a laugh. "What happened to the rest of her?" I said. Thought he was joking, see. He wasn't.'

'Go on.'

' "Here you are," he said. "Keep the change," and gets up cool as anything. "Come on Mickie, this place stinks." Then they go for him. Jesus. Fantastic. Never thought he had it in him. Three down and one to go and then somebody cracks him with a bottle. All the blows; East End stuff. He could really mix it. Then they got him. They bent him over the bar backwards and just worked him over. Never seen anything like it. No one said a word. No how d'you do, nothing. System. Next thing we knew was, we were out in the street. Leo was on his hands and knees and they came out and gave him a few more for luck, and I was coughing my guts out on the pavement.'

'Pissed?'

'Sober as a bloody judge, old boy. They'd kicked me in the stomach, you see.'

'You?'

His head shook dreadfully as it sank to meet the glass: 'Tried to bail him out,' he muttered. 'Tried to mix it with the other chaps while he got away. Trouble is,' he explained, taking a deep draught of whisky. 'I'm not the fellow I used to be. Praschko had hoofed it by then.' He giggled. 'He was half-way out of the door by the time the button hit the plate. He seemed to know the form. Don't blame him.'

Turner might have been asking after an old friend. 'Praschko came often, did he? Back in those days?'

'First time I met him, old boy. And the last. Parted brass rags after that. Don't blame him. MP and all that. Bad for business.'

'What did *you* do?'

'Jesus. Trod gently, old boy.' He shuddered. 'Home posting loomed large. Bloody flea pit in Bushey or somewhere. With Mary. No thanks.'

'How did it end?'

'I reckon Praschko got on to Siebkron. Coppers dumped us at the Embassy. Guard got us a cab and we sloped off to my place and called a doctor. Then Ewan Waldebere turned up, he was Minister Political. Then Ludwig Siebkron in a dirty great Mercedes. Christ knows what didn't happen. Siebkron grilled him. Sat in my drawing-room and grilled him no end. Didn't care for it I must say. All the same, pretty serious when you think of it. Bloody diplomat tearing the arse off nightclubs, assaulting citizenry. Lot of fences to mend.'

The waiter brought some kidneys cooked in vinegar and wine.

'God,' said Crabbe. 'Look at that. Delicious. Lovely after snails.'

'What did Leo tell Siebkron?'

'Nix. Nothing. You don't know Leo. Close isn't the word. Waldebere, me, Siebkron: not a syllable to any of us. Mind you, they'd really gone for him. Waldebere faked him some leave; new teeth, stitches, Christ knows what. Told everybody he'd done it swimming in Yugoslavia. Diving into shallow water. Bashed his face in. Some water: Christ.'

'Why do you think it happened?'

224

'No idea, old boy. Wouldn't go out with him after that. Not safe.'

'No opinions?'

'Sorry,' said Crabbe. His face sank beneath the surface, misted with meaningless wrinkles.

'Ever seen this key?'

'Nope.' He grinned affectionately. 'One of Leo's, was it? Screw anything in the old days, Leo would. Steadier now.'

'Any names attached to that?'

He continued staring at the key.

'Try Myra Meadowes.'

'Why?'

'She's willing. She's had one baby already. In London. They say half the drivers go through her every week.'

'Did he ever mention a woman called Aickman? Someone he was going to marry?'

Crabbe assumed an expression of puzzled recollection.

'Aickman,' he said. 'Funny. That was one of the old lot. From Berlin. He did talk about her. When they worked with the Russkies. That's it. She was another of those inbetweeners. Berlin, Hamburg, all that game. Stitched those bloody cushions for him. Care and attention.'

'What was he *doing* with the Russians,' Turner asked after a pause. 'What work was it?'

'Quadrupartite, bi-partite . . . one of them. Berlin's on its own, see. Different world, specially in those days. Island. Different sort of island.' He shook his head. 'Not like him,' he added. 'All that Communist kick. Not his book at all. Too bloody hard-nosed for all that balls.'

'And this Aickman?'

'Miss Brandt, Miss Etling and Miss Aickman.'

'Who are they?'

'Three dollies. In Berlin. Came out with them from England. Pretty as pictures, Leo said. Never seen girls like it. Never seen girls at all if you ask me. Emigré types going back to Germany. Join the Occupation. Same as Leo. Croydon airport, sitting on a crate, waiting for the plane, and these three dollies come along in uniform, waggling their tails. Miss Aickman, Miss Brandt and Miss Etling. Posted to the same unit. From then on he

225

never looked back. Him and Praschko and another fellow. All went out together from England in forty-five. With these dollies. They made up a song about it: Miss Aickman, Miss Etling and Miss *Brandt* . . . drinking song, saucy rhymes. They sang it that night as a matter of fact. Going along in the car, happy as sandboys. Jesus.'

He'd have sung it himself for two pins.

'Leo's girl was Aickman. His first girl. He'd always go back to her, that's what he said. "There'll never be another like the first one," that's what he said. "All the rest are imitations." His very words. You know the way Huns talk. Introspective beggars.'

'What became of her?'

'Dunno old boy. Fizzled away. What they all do, isn't it? Grow old. Shrivel up. Whoopsadaisy.' A piece of kidney fell from his fork and the gravy splashed on his tie.

'Why didn't he marry her?'

'She took the other road, old boy.'

'Which other road?'

'She didn't like him being English, he said. Wanted him to be a Hun again and face facts. Big on metaphysics.'

'Perhaps he's gone to find her.'

'He always said he would one day. "I've drunk at a good few pools, Mickie," he said. "But there'll never be another girl like Aickman." Still, that's what we all say, isn't it?' He dived into the Moselle as if it were a refuge.

'Is it?'

'You married, old boy, by the by? Keep away from it.' He, shook his head. 'It would be all right if I could manage the bedroom. But I can't. It's like a bloody grease-pot for me. I can't make it.' He sniggered. 'Marry at fifty-five, my advice. Little sixteen-year-old dolly. Then they don't know what they're missing.'

'Praschko was up there, was he? In Berlin? With the Russians and Aickman?'

'Stable companions.'

'What else did he tell you about Praschko?'

'He was a Bolshie in those days. Nothing else.'

'Was Aickman?'

'Could be, old boy. Never said; didn't interest him that much.'

'Was Harting?'

'Not Leo, old boy. Didn't know his arse from his elbow where politics are concerned. Restful that was. Trout,' he whispered. 'I'd like trout next. Kidneys are just in between. If it's on the secret vote, I mean.'

The joke entertained him off and on for the remainder of the meal. Only once would he be drawn on the subject of Leo, and that was when Turner asked him whether he had had much to do with him in recent months.

'Not bloody likely,' Crabbe whispered.

'Why not?'

'He was getting broody, old boy. I could tell. Sizing up for another crack at someone. Pugnacious little beast,' he said, baring his teeth in a sudden grimace of alcoholic cramp. 'He'd started leaving those buttons about.'

He got back to the Adler at four; he was fairly drunk. The lift was occupied so he used the stairs. That's it, he thought. That is the sweet end. He would go on drinking through the afternoon and he would drink on the plane and with any luck by the time he saw Lumley he would be speechless. The Crabbe answer: snails, kidneys, trout and scotch and keep your head down while the big wheels roll over. As he reached his own floor he noticed vaguely that the lift had been wedged with a suitcase and he supposed the porter was collecting more luggage from someone's bedroom. We're the only lucky people in the place, he thought. We're leaving. He tried to open the door to his room but the lock was jammed; he wrestled with the key but it wouldn't give. He stepped back quite quickly when he heard the footsteps, but he didn't really have much chance. The door was pulled open from inside. He had a glimpse of a pale round face and fair hair carefully combed back, a bland brow furrowed with anxiety, he saw the stitching of the leather as it moved down on him in slow motion and he wondered whether the stitches cut the scalp the way they cut the face. He felt the nausea strike him and his stomach fold, and the wooden club buffet at the back of his knees; he heard the soft

227

surgeon's voice calling from the darkness as the warm grass of the Yorkshire dales prickled against his child's face. He heard the taunting voice of Tony Willoughby, soft as velvet, clinging like a lover, saw his pianist's hands drift over her white hips, and heard Leo's music whining to God in every red timber tabernacle of his own childhood. He smelt the smoke of the Dutch cigars, and there was Willoughby's voice again offering him a hair-dryer: I'm only a temporary, Alan old boy, but there's ten per cent off for friends of the family. He felt the pain again, the thudding as they began slapping him and he saw the wet black granite of the orphanage in Bournemouth and the telescope on Constitution Hill. 'If there's one thing I really hate,' Lumley observed, 'It's a cynic in search of God.' He had a moment's total agony as they hit him in the groin, and as it slowly subsided he saw the girl who had left him drifting in the black streets of his own defiant solitude. He heard the screaming of Myra Meadowes as he broke her down, lie for lie, the scream as they took her from her Polish lover, and the scream as she parted from her baby; and he thought he might be crying out himself until he recognized the towel they had shoved into his mouth. He felt something cold and iron hard hit the back of his head and stay there like a lump of ice, he heard the door slam and knew he was alone; he saw the whole damned trail of the deceived and the uncaring; heard the fool voice of an English Bishop praising God and war; and fell asleep. He was in a coffin, a smooth cold coffin. On a marble slab with polished tiles and the glint of chrome at the far end of a tunnel. He heard de Lisle muttering to him in kindly moderation and Jenny Pargiter's sobbing like the moan of every woman he had left; he heard the fatherly tones of Meadowes exhorting him to charity and the cheerful whistling of unencumbered people. Then Meadowes and Pargiter slipped away, lost to other funerals, and only de Lisle remained, and only de Lisle's voice offered any comfort.

'My dear fellow,' he was saying, as he peered curiously downward, 'I dropped in to say goodbye, but if you're going to take a bath, you might at least take off that dreadful suit.'

'Is it Thursday?'

De Lisle had taken a napkin from the rail and was soaking it under the hot tap.

'Wednesday. Wednesday as ever was. Cocktail time.'

He bent over him and began gently dabbing the blood from his face.

'That football field. Where you saw him. Where he took Pargiter. Tell me how I get there.'

'Keep still. And don't talk or you'll wake the neighbours.'

With the gentlest possible movements he continued touching away the caked blood. Freeing his right hand Turner cautiously felt in the pocket of his jacket for the gunmetal key. It was still there.

'Have you ever seen this before?'

'No. No, I haven't. Nor was I in the greenhouse at 3 AM on the morning of the second. But how *like* the Foreign Office,' he said, standing back and critically surveying his handiwork, 'to send a bull to catch a matador. You won't mind my reclaiming my dinner jacket, will you?'

'Why did Bradfield ask me?'

'Ask you what?'

'To dinner. To meet Siebkron. Why did he invite me on Tuesday?'

'Brotherly love; what else?'

'What's in that despatch box that Bradfield's so frightened of?'

'Poisonous snakes.'

'That key wouldn't open it?'

'No.'

De Lisle sat down on the edge of the bath. 'You shouldn't be doing this,' he said. 'I know what you'll tell me; somebody had to get their hands dirty. Just don't expect me to be pleased it's you. You're not just *somebody*: that's your trouble. Leave it to the people who were born with blinkers.' His grey, tender eyes were shadowed with concern. 'It is totally absurd,' he declared. 'People crack up every day under the strain of being saints. You're cracking up under the strain of being a pig.'

'Why doesn't he go? Why does he hang around?'

'They'll be asking that about you tomorrow.'

Turner was stretched out on de Lisle's long sofa. He held a whisky in his hand and his face was covered in yellow antiseptic from de Lisle's extensive medicine chest. His canvas bag lay in a corner of the room. De Lisle sat at his harpsichord, not playing it but stroking the keys. It was an eighteenth-century piece, satinwood, and the top was bleached by tropical suns.

'Do you take that thing everywhere?'

'I had a violin once. It fell to pieces in Leopoldville. The glue melted. It's awfully hard,' he observed dryly, 'to pursue culture when the glue melts.'

'If Leo's so damn clever, why doesn't he go?'

'Perhaps he likes it here. He'd be the first, I must say.'

'And if *they're* so damned clever, why don't they take him away?'

'Perhaps they don't know he's on the loose.'

'What did you say?'

'I said perhaps they don't know he's run for it. I'm not a spy, I'm afraid, but I am human and I do know Leo. He's extremely perverse. I can't imagine for a moment he would do exactly what they told him. If there is a "they", which I doubt. He wasn't a *natural* servant.'

Turner said, 'I try all the time to force him into the mould. He won't fit.'

De Lisle struck a couple of notes with his finger.

'Tell me, what do you *want* him to be? A goodie or a baddie? Or do you just want the freedom of the search? You want *something*, don't you? Because anything's better than nothing. You're like those beastly students: you can't stand a vacuum.'

Turner had closed his eyes and was lost in thought.

'I expect he's dead. That would be very macabre.'

'He wasn't dead this morning, was he?' Turner said.

'And you don't like him to be in limbo. It annoys you. You want him to land or take off. There are no *shades* for you, are there? I suppose that's the fun of searching for extremists: you search for their convictions, is that it?'

'He's still on the run,' Turner continued. 'Who's he running *from*? Us or them?'

'He could be no his own.'

'With fifty stolen box files? Oh sure. Sure.'

De Lisle examined Turner over the top of the harpsichord.

'You complement one another. I look at you and I think of Leo. You're Saxon. Big hands, big feet, big heart and that lovely reason that grapples with ideals. Leo's the other way round. He's a performer. He wears our clothes, uses our language but he's only half tamed. I suppose I'm on your side, really: you and I are the concert audience.' He closed the harpsichord. 'We're the ones who glimpse, and reach, and fall back. There's a Leo in all of us but he's usually dead by the time we're twenty.'

'What are you then?'

'Me? Oh, reluctantly, a conductor.' Standing up, he carefully locked the keyboard with a small brass key from his chain. 'I can't even play the thing,' he said, tapping the bleached lid with his elegant fingers. 'I tell myself I will one day; I'll take lessons or get a book. But I don't really care: I've learnt to live with being half-finished. Like most of us.'

'Tomorrow's Thursday,' Turner said. 'If they don't know he's defected, they'll be expecting him to turn up, won't they?'

'I suppose so,' de Lisle yawned. 'But then they know where to go, don't they, whoever they are? And you don't. That is something of a drawback.'

'It might not be.'

'Oh.'

'We know where *you* saw him, at least, that Thursday afternoon, don't we, when he was supposed to be at the Ministry? Same place as he took Pargiter. Seems quite a hunting-ground for him.'

De Lisle stood very still, the keychain still in his hand.

'It's no good telling you not to go, I suppose?'

'No.'

'Asking you? You're acting against Bradfield's instructions.'

'Even so.'

'And you're sick. All right. Go and look for your untamed half. And if you *do* find that file, we shall expect you to return it unopened.'

And that, quite suddenly, was an order.

14

Thursday's Child

THE WEATHER ON the plateau was stolen from other seasons and other places. It was a sea wind from March which sang in the wire netting, bending the tufts of coarse grass and crashing into the forest behind him; and if some mad aunt had planted a monkey-puzzle in the sandy earth, Turner could have hopped straight down the path and caught the trolley-bus to Bournemouth Square. It was the frost of November whose icy pipes encased the bracken stems; for there the cold had hidden from the wind and it gripped like arctic water at his ankles; the frost of a stone crevice on a north face, when only fear will set your hands to work, and life is treasured because it is won. The last strips of an Oxford sun lay brav ly dying on the empty playing-field; and the sky was a Yorkshire evening in autumn, black and billowing and fringed with grime. The trees were curved from childhood, bent by the blustering wind, Mickie Crabbe's boyhood bent at the taps in the washroom, and when the gusts had gone they waited still, backs arched for the next assault.

The cuts on his face were burning raw and his pale eyes were bright with sleepless pain. He waited, staring down the hill. Far below to his right lay the river, and for once the wind had silenced it, and the barges called in vain. A car was climbing slowly towards him; a black Mercedes, Cologne registration, woman driver; and did not slow down as it passed. On the other side of the wire, a new hut was shuttered and padlocked. A rook had settled on the roof and the wind tugged at its feathers. A Renault, French diplomatic registration, woman driver, one male passenger: Turner noted the number in his black book. His script was stiff and childish, and the letters came to him unnaturally. He must have hit back after all, for two knuckles on his right hand were badly cut, as if he had punched an open mouth and caught the front teeth. Harting's handwriting was neat, rounding the rough corners, but Turner's was big and downright, promising collision.

'You are both *movers*, you and Leo,' de Lisle had said some time last night, as they sat in their deep armchairs. 'Bonn is stationary but you are movers. . . . You are fighting one another, but it is you against us. . . . The opposite of love is not hate but apathy. . . . You must come to terms with apathy.'

'For Christ's sake,' Turner complained.

'This is your stop,' de Lisle had said, opening the car door for him. 'And if you're not back by tomorrow morning I shall tell the coastguards.'

He had bought a spanner in Bad Godesberg, a monkey wrench, heavy at the head, and it lay like a lead weight against his hip. A Volkswagen bus, dark grey, Registration SU, full of children, stopping at the changing hut. Their noise came at him suddenly, a flock of birds racing with the wind, a tattered jingle of laughter and complaint. Someone blew a whistle. The sun hit them low down, like torch beams shining along a corridor. The hut swallowed them. 'I have never known anyone,' de Lisle had cried in despair, 'make such a meal of his disadvantages.'

He drew back quickly behind the tree. One Opel Rekord; two men. Registration Bonn. The spanner nudged him as he wrote. The men were wearing hats and overcoats and were professionally without expression. The side windows were of smoked glass. The car continued, but at a walking pace. He saw their blank blond faces turned towards him, twin moons in the artificial dark. *Your* teeth? Turner wondered. Was it your teeth I knocked in? I can't tell you apart. Trust you to come to the ball. All the way up the hill, they could not have touched ten miles an hour. A van passed, followed by two lorries. Somewhere a clock chimed; or was it a school bell? Or Angelus, or Compline, or sooty sheep in the Dales, or the ring of the ferry from the river? He would never hear it again; yet there is no truth, as Mr Crail would say, that cannot be confirmed. No, my child; but the sins of others are a sacrifice to God. Your sacrifice. The rook had left the roof. The sun had gone. A little Citroën was wandering into sight. A *deux chevaux*, dirty as fog, with one bashed wing, one illegible number plate, one driver hidden in the shadow, and one headlight flashing on and off and one horn blaring for the hunt. The Opel had disappeared. Hurry moons or you will miss His coming. The wheels jerk like dislocated limbs as the little car turns off the road and bumps towards him over the frozen mud ruts of the timber track, the pert tail rocking on its axle. He hears the blare of dance music as the door opens, and his mouth is dry from the tablets, and the cuts on his face are a screen of twigs. One day, when the world is free, his fevered mind assured him, clouds will detonate as they collide and God's angels will fall down dazed for the whole world to look at. Silently he dropped the spanner back into his pocket.

She was standing not ten yards away, her back towards him, quite indifferent to the wind, or the children who now burst upon the playground.

She was staring down the hill. The engine was still running, shaking the car with inner pains. A wiper juddered uselessly over the grimy windscreen. Fot an hour she barely moved.

For an hour she waited with oriental stillness, heeding nothing but whoever would not come. She stood like a statue, growing taller as the light left her.

The wind dragged at her coat. Once her hand rose to gather in the errant strands of hair, and once she walked to the end of the timber-track to look down into the river valley, in the direction of Königswinter; then slowly returned, lost in thought, and Turner dropped to his knees behind the trees, praying that the shadows protected him.

Her patience broke. Getting noisily back into the car she lit a cigarette and slapped the horn with her open hand. The children forgot their game and grinned at the hoarse burp of the exhausted battery. The silence returned.

The windscreen wiper had stopped but the engine was still running and she was revving it to encourage the heater. The windows were misting up. She opened her handbag and took out a mirror and a lipstick.

She was leaning back in the seat, eyes closed, listening to dance music, one hand gently beating time on the steering wheel. Hearing a car, she opened the door and looked idly out, but it was only the black Rekord going slowly down the hill again and though the moons were turned towards her, she was quite indifferent to their interest.

The playing-field was empty. The shutters were closed on the changing hut. Turning on the overhead lamp, she read the time by her watch, but by then the first lights were coming up in the valley and the river was lost in the low mist of dusk. Turner stepped heavily on to the path and pulled open the passenger door.

'Waiting for someone?' he asked and sat down beside her, closing the door quickly so that the light went out again. He switched off the wireless.

'I thought you'd gone,' she said hotly, 'I thought my husband had got rid of you.' Fear, anger, humiliation seized hold of her. 'You've been spying on me all the time! Crouching in the bushes like a detective! How dare you? You vulgar, bloody little man!' She drew back her clenched fist and perhaps she hesitated when she saw the mess his face was in, but it wouldn't have made much difference because at the same moment Turner hit her very hard across the mouth so that her head jerked back against the pillar with a snap. Opening his door he walked round the car, pulled her out and hit her again with his open hand.

'We're going for a walk,' he said, 'And we'll talk about your vulgar bloody lover.'

He led her along the timber path to the crest of the hill. She walked quite willingly, holding his arm with both her hands, head down, crying silently.

They were looking down on to the Rhine. The wind had fallen. Already above them, the early stars drifted like sparks of phosphorus on a gently rocking sea. Along the river the lights kindled in series, faltering at the moment of their birth and then miraculously living, growing to small fires fanned by the black night breeze. Only the river's sounds reached them; the chugging of the barges and the nursery chime of the clocks telling off the quarters. They caught the mouldering smell of the Rhine itself, felt its cold breath upon their hands and cheeks.

'It began as a dare.'

She stood apart from him, gazing into the valley, her arms clutching round her body as if she were holding a towel.

'He won't come any more. I've had it. I know that.'

'Why won't he?'

'Leo never *said* things. He was far too much of a puritan.' She lit a cigarette. 'Because he'll never stop searching, that's why.'

'What for?'

'What do any of us look for? Parents, children, a woman.' She turned to face him. 'Go on,' she challenged. 'Ask the rest.'

Turner waited.

'When intimacy took place, isn't that what you want to know? I'd have slept with him that same night if he'd asked me, but he didn't get round to it because I'm Rawley's wife and he knew that good men were scarce. I mean he knew he *had* to survive. He was a creep, don't you realize? He'd have charmed the feathers off a goose.' She broke off. 'I'm a fool to tell you anything.'

'You'd be a bigger fool not to. You're in big trouble,' Turner said, 'in case you don't know.'

'I can't remember when I haven't been. How else do I beat the system? We were two old tarts and we fell in love.'

She was sitting on a bench, playing with her gloves.

'It was a buffet. A bloody Bonn buffet with lacquered duck and dreadful Germans. Someone's welcome to someone. Someone's farewell. Americans I should think. Mr and Mrs Somebody the Third. Some dynastic feast. It was appallingly provincial.' Her voice was her own, swift and falsely confident, but for all her efforts it still possessed that note of hard-won dexterity which Turner had heard in British diplomatic wives all over the world: a voice to talk through silences, cover embarrassments, retrieve offences; a voice that was neither particularly cultured nor particularly sophisticated but, like a nanny in pursuit of lost standards, doggedly trod its course. 'We'd come straight from Aden and we'd been here exactly a year. Before that we were in Peking and now we were in Bonn. Late October: Karfeld's October. Things had just hotted up.

In Aden we'd been bombed, in Peking we were mobbed and now we were going to be burned in the Market Place. Poor Rawley: he seems to attract humiliation. He was a prisoner of war as well, you know. There ought to be a name for him: the humiliated generation.'

'He'd love you for that,' said Turner.

'He loves me without it.' She paused. 'The funny thing is, I'd never noticed him before. I thought he was just a rather dull little . . .temporary. The prissy little man who played the organ in Chapel and smoked those filthy cigars at cocktail parties. . . . Nothing there. . . . Empty. And that night, the moment he came in, the moment he appeared at the doorway I felt him choose me and I thought: "Look out. Air raid." He came straight over to me. "Hullo, Hazel." He'd never called me Hazel in my life and I thought: "You cheeky devil, you'll have to work for this." '

'Good of you to take the risk,' said Turner.

'He began to talk. I don't know what about; I never much noticed *what* he said; any more than he did. Karfeld I suppose. Riots. All the stamping and shouting. But I noticed *him*. For the first time, I really did.' She fell silent. 'And I thought, "Hoi: where have you been all my life?" It was like looking in an old bank book and finding you've got a credit instead of an overdraft. He was *alive*.' She laughed. 'Not like you a bit. *You're* about the deadest thing I ever met.'

Turner might have hit her again, were it not for the awful familiarity of her mockery.

'It was the tension you noticed first. He was *patrolling* himself. His language, his manners . . . it was all a fake. He was on guard. He listened to his own voice the way he listened to yours, getting the cadence right, putting the adverbs in the right order. I tried to place him: who would I *think* you were if I didn't *know*? South American German? . . . Argentine trade delegate? One of those. Glossy latinized Hun.' Again she broke off, lost in recollection – 'He had those velvety German end-bits of language and he used them to trim the balance of every sentence. I made him talk about himself, where he lived, who cooked for him, how he spent his weekends. The next thing I knew, he was giving me advice.

Diplomatic advice: where to buy cheap meat. The Post Report. The Dutchman was best for this, the Naafi for that; butter from the Economat, nuts from the Commissary. Like a woman. He had a thing about herbal teas; Germans are mad about digestion. Then he offered to sell me a hair-dryer. Why are you laughing?' She asked in sudden fury.

'Was I?'

'He knew some way of getting a discount: twenty-five per cent, he said. He'd compared all the prices, he knew all the models.'

'He'd been looking at your hair too.'

She rounded on him: 'You keep your place,' she snapped.

'You're not within shouting distance of him.'

He hit her again, a long swinging blow deep into the flesh of the cheek and she said 'You bastard' and went very pale in the darkness, shivering with anger.

'Get on with it.'

At last she began again: 'So I said yes. I was fed up anyway. Rawley was buried with a French Counsellor in the corner; everyone else was fighting for food at the buffet. So I said yes, I *would* like a hair-dryer. At twenty-five per cent off. I was afraid I hadn't got the money on me; would he take a cheque? I might just as well have said, yes I'll go to bed with you. That was the first time I saw him smile; he didn't smile often as a rule. His whole face was lit up. I sent him to get some food, and I watched him all the way, wondering what it was going to be like. He had that egg walk . . . *Eiertanz* they call it here . . . just like in Chapel really, but *harder*. The Germans were crowding the bar, fighting for the asparagus, and he just darted between them and came out with two plates loaded with food and the knives and forks sticking out of his handkerchief pocket; grinning like mad. I've got a brother called Andrew who plays scrum-half at rugger. You could hardly have told the difference. From then on, I didn't worry. Some foul Canadian was trying to get me to listen to a lecture on agriculture and I bit his head off. They're about the only ones left who still believe in it all, the Canadians. They're like the British in India.'

Hearing some sound she turned her head sharply and stared

back along the path. The tree trunks were black against the low horizon; the wind had dropped; a night dew had damped their clothes.

'He won't come. You said so yourself. Get on with it. Hurry.'

'We sat on a stair and he started talking about himself again. He didn't need any prompting. It just came out . . . it was fascinating. About Germany in the early days after the war. "Only the rivers were whole." I never knew whether he was translating German or using his imagination or just repeating what he'd picked up.' She hesitated, and again glanced down the path. 'How at night the women built by arclight . . . passing stones as if they were putting out a fire. . . . How he learnt to sleep in a fifteen hundredweight using a fire extinguisher as a pillow. He did a little act, putting his head on one side and twisting his mouth to show his stiff neck. Bedroom games.' She stood up abruptly. 'I'm going back. If he finds the car empty, he'll run away; he's as nervous as a kitten.'

He followed her to the timber track, but the plateau was deserted except for the Opel Rekord parked in the lay-by with its lights out.

'Sit in the car,' she said. 'Never mind them.' For the first time she really noticed the marks on his face by the interior light and she drew in her breath sharply.

'Who did that?'

'They'll do it to Leo if they find him first.'

She was leaning back in the seat, her eyes closed. Someone had torn the cloth on the roof and it hung down in beggar's shreds. There was a child's driving wheel on the floor with a plastic tube attached to it and Turner pushed it out of the way with his foot.

'Sometimes I thought: "You're empty. You're just imitating life." But you daren't think that of a lover. He was a negotiator, an actor, I suppose. He was caught between all those worlds: Germany and England, Königswinter and Bonn, Chapel and the discounts, the first floor and the ground floor. You can't expect anyone to fight all those battles and stay alive. Sometimes he just served us,' she explained simply. 'Or me. Like a headwaiter. We were all his customers; whatever he wanted. He didn't live, he survived. He's always survived. Till now.' She lit another cigarette. The car was very cold. She tried to start the engine and put the heater on, but the ignition failed.

'After that first evening it was all over bar bed. Rawley came and found me and we were the last to go. He'd been having a row with Lésère about something and he was pleased at having come off best. Leo and I were still sitting on the stairs, drinking coffee, and Rawley just came over and kissed me on the cheek. What was that?'

'Nothing.'

'I saw a light down the hill.'

'It was a bicycle crossing the road. It's gone now.'

'I hate him kissing me in public; he knows I can't stop him. He never does it in private. "Come on my dear, it's time to go." Leo stood up when he saw him coming, but Rawley didn't even notice him. He took me over to Lésère. "This is the person you should really apologize to," he said. "She's been sitting alone on the stairs all evening." We were going out of the door and Rawley stopped to collect his coat, and there was Leo, holding it for him.' She smiled, and it was the smile of real love, rejoicing at the memory. 'He didn't seem to notice me any more. Rawley turned his back on him and put his arms into the sleeves and I actually saw Leo's own arms stiffen and his fingers curl. Mind you, I was glad. I *wanted* Rawley to behave like that.' She shrugged. 'I was hooked,' she said. 'I'd been looking for a fly and now I'd got one, feathers and all. Next day I looked him up in the Red Book. You know what that is by now: nothing. I rang up Mary Crabbe and asked her about him. Just for fun. "I ran into an extraordinary little man last night," I said. Mary had a fit. "My dear, he's poison. Keep *right* away from him. He dragged Mickie to a night club once and got him into *awful* trouble. Mercifully," she said, "his contract's running out in December and he'll be gone." I tried Sally Askew, she's terrifically worthy. I could have died' – she broke out laughing, then drew her chin down into her chest to copy the sonorous tones of the Economic Minister's wife: ' "A useful bachelor, if Huns are in short supply." They often are here, you know; there are more of us than them. Too many diplomats chasing too few Germans: that's Bonn. The trouble was, Sally said, the Germans were getting rather old school again about Leo's kind, so she and Aubrey had reluctantly given him up. "He's an unconscious irritant, my dear, if you know what I mean." I was absolutely thrilled. I put down the receiver and I shot into the drawing-room and I wrote him a great long letter about absolutely nothing.'

She tried the engine again but it didn't even cough. She gathered her coat more tightly round her.

'Cor,' she whispered. 'Come on, Leo. You don't half put a strain on friendship.'

In the black Opel a tiny light went on and off like a signal. Turner said nothing, but his thick fingertips lightly touched the spanner in his pocket.

'A schoolgirl letter. Thank you for being so attentive. Sorry for claiming all your time and please remember about the hair-dryer. Then a lovely long made-up story about how I went shopping in the *Spanischer Gerten* and an old lady dropped a two-Mark piece into an orange-crate and no one could find it and she said it was payment because she'd left it in the shop. I delivered the letter to the Embassy myself and he rang up that afternoon. There were two models, he said, the more expensive one had different speeds and you didn't need an adapter.'

'Transformer.'

'What about colour? I just listened. He said it would be very difficult to make a decision for me, what with the speeds and the colour. Couldn't we meet and discuss it? It was a Thursday and we met up here. He said he came up every Thursday to get some fresh air and watch the children. I didn't believe him, but I was very happy.'

'Is that all he said about coming up here?'

'He said once they owed him time.'

'Who did?'

'The Embassy. Something Rawley had taken away from him and given to someone else. A job. So he came up here instead.' She shook her head in real admiration. 'He's as stubborn as a mule,' she declared. '"They owe it me," he said, "so I take it. And that's the only way I live." '

'I thought you said he didn't say things?'

'Not the best things.'

He waited.

'We just walked and looked at the river and on the way back we held hands. As we were leaving he said, "I forgot to show you the hair-dryer," So I said, "What a pity. We'll have to meet here next Thursday too, won't we." He was *enormously* shocked.' She had a special voice for him as well: it was both mocking and possessive and it seemed to exclude Turner rather than draw him in. ' "My *dear* Mrs Bradfield—" I said, "If you come next week I'll let you call me Hazel." I'm a whore,' she explained. 'That's what you're thinking.'

'And after that?'

'Every Thursday. Here. He parked his car down the lane and I left mine in the road. We were lovers but we hadn't been to bed. It was very grown-up. Sometimes he talked; sometimes he didn't. He kept showing me his house across the river as if he wanted to sell it me. We'd go all along the path from one little hilltop to another so that we could see it. I teased him once. "You're the devil. You're showing me the whole kingdom." He didn't care for that. He never forgot anything, you see. That was the survivor in him. He didn't like me to talk about evil, or pain or anything. He knew all *that* inside out.'

'And the rest?'

He saw her face tilt and the smile break.

'Rawley's bed. A Friday. There's an avenger in Leo, not far down. He always knew when Rawley was going away: he used to check in the Travel Office, look at the Travel Clerk's bookings. He'd say to me: he's in Hanover next week . . . he's in Bremen.'

'What did Bradfield go there for?'

'Oh God. Visiting the Consulates. . . . Leo asked me the same question: how should *I* know? Rawley never tells *me* anything. Sometimes I thought he was following Karfeld round Germany . . . he always seemed to go where the rallies were.'

'And from then on?'

She shrugged. 'Yes. From then on. Whenever we could.'

'Did Bradfield know?'

'Oh God. Know? Don't know? You're worse than the Germans. It was in between. You want things spelt out for you, don't you? Some things can't be. Some things aren't true till they're said. Rawley knows that better than anyone.'

'Christ,' Turner whispered. 'You give yourself all the chances,' and he remembered he had said the same thing to Bradfield three days ago.

She stared ahead of her through the windscreen.

'What are people *worth*? Children, husbands, careers. You go under and they call it sacrifice. You survive and they call you a bitch. Chop yourself in bits. For what? I'm not God. I can't hold them all up on my shoulders. I live for them; they live for someone else. We're all saints. We're all fools. Why don't we live for ourselves and call *that* service for a change?'

'*Did he know?*'

He had seized her arm.

'Did he!'

The tears trickled sideways over the bridge of her nose. She wiped them away.

'Rawley's a diplomat,' she said at last. 'The art of the possible, that's Rawley. The limited aim, the trained mind. "Let's not get overheated. Let's not put a name to things. Let's not negotiate without knowing what we want to achieve." He can't . . . he can't go mad, it isn't in him. He can't live for anything. Except me.'

'But he knew.'

'I should think so,' she said wearily. 'I never asked him. Yes, he knew.'

'Because you made him renew that contract, didn't you. Last December. You worked on him.'

'Yes. That was awful. That was quite awful. But it had to be done,' she explained, as if she were referring to a higher cause of which they were both aware. 'Or he'd have sent Leo away.'

'And that was what Leo wanted. That's why he picked you up.'

'Leo married me for my money. For what he could get out of me,' she said. 'He stayed with me for love. Does that satisfy you?'

243

Turner did not reply.

'He never put it into words. I told you. He never said the big things. "One more year is all I need. Just one year, Hazel. One year to love you, one year to get what they owe me. One year from December and then I'll go. They don't realize how much they need me." So I invited him for drinks. When Rawley was there. It was early on, before the gossip started. We were just the three of us; I made Rawley come back early. "Rawley this is Leo Harting, he works for you and he plays the organ in Chapel." "Of course. We've met," he said. We talked about nothing. Nuts from the Commissary. Spring leave. What it was like in Königswinter in the summer. "Mr Harting has asked us to dinner," I said. "Isn't he kind?" Next week we went to Königswinter. He gave us all the bits and pieces: ratafia biscuits with the sweet, halva with the coffee. That was all.'

'What was all?'

'Oh Christ, can't you see? I'd shown him! I'd shown Rawley what I wanted him to buy me!'

It was quite still now. The rooks had perched like sentinels on slowly rocking branches, and there was no wind any more to stir their feathers.

'Are they like horses?' she asked. 'Do they sleep standing up?'

She turned her head to look at him but he did not reply.

'He hated silence,' she said dreamily. 'It frightened him. That's why he liked music; that's why he liked his house . . . it was full of noise. Not even the dead could have slept there. Let alone Leo.'

She smiled remembering.

'He didn't live in it, he manned it. Like a ship. All night he'd be hopping up and down fixing a window or a shutter or something. His whole life was like that. Secret fears, secret memories; things he would never tell but expected you to know about.' She yawned. 'He won't come now,' she said. 'He hated the dark too.'

'Where is he?' Turner said urgently. 'What's he doing?'

She said nothing.

'Listen: he whispered to you. In the night he boasted, told you how he made the world turn for him. How clever he was, the tricks he played, the people he deceived!'

'You've got him wrong. Utterly wrong.'

'Then tell me!'

'There's nothing to tell. We were pen friends, that's all. He was reporting from another world.'

'*What* world? Bloody Moscow and the fight for peace?'

'I was right. You are vulgar. You want all the lines joined up and all the colours flat. You haven't got the guts to face the half tones.'

'Has he?'

She seemed to have put him out of her mind. 'Let's go, for God's sake,' she said shortly, as if Turner had been keeping her waiting.

He had to push the car quite a distance along the track before it started. As they careered down the hill, he saw the Opel pull out from the lay-by and hurriedly take up its position thirty yards behind them. She drove to Remagen, to one of the big hotels along the waterfront run by an old lady who patted her arm as she sat down. Where was the little man? she asked, *der nette kleine Herr* who was always so jolly and smoked cigars and spoke such excellent German.

'He talked it with an accent,' she explained to Turner. 'A slight English accent. It was something he'd taught himself.'

The sun room was quite empty except for a young couple in the corner. The girl had long, blonde hair. They stared at him oddly because of the cuts on his face. From their window table Turner saw the Opel park in the esplanade below them. The number plate had changed but the moons were just the same. His head was aching terribly. He had not taken more than half his whisky before he wanted to vomit. He asked for water. The old lady brought a bottle of local health water and told him all about it. They had used it in both wars, she explained, when the hotel was a first-aid post for those who were wounded while trying to cross the river.

'He was going to meet me here last Friday,' she said. 'And take me home to dinner. Rawley was leaving for Hanover. Leo cried off at the last minute.'

245

'On the Thursday afternoon he was late. I didn't bother. Sometimes he didn't turn up at all. Sometimes he worked. It was different. Just the last month or so. He'd changed. I thought at first he'd got another woman. He was always slipping off to places—'

'What places?'

'Berlin once. Hamburg. Hanover. Stuttgart. Rather like Rawley. So he said anyway; I was never sure. He wasn't strong on truth. Not your kind.'

'He arrived late. Last Thursday. *Come on*!'

'He'd had lunch with Praschko.'

'At the Maternus,' Turner breathed.

'They'd had a *discussion*. That was another Leo-ism. It didn't commit you. Like the Passive Voice, that was another favourite. A *discussion* had taken place. He didn't say what about. He was preoccupied. Broody. I knew him better than to try and jerk him out of it so we just walked around. With *them* watching us. And I knew this was it.'

'This was what?'

'This was the year he'd wanted. He'd found it, whatever it was, and now he didn't know what to do with it.' She shrugged. 'And by then, I'd found it too. He never realized. If he'd lifted a finger I'd have packed and gone with him.' She was looking at the river. 'Not children, husbands or any bloody thing would have stopped me. Not that he would have wanted me.'

'*What's* he found?' Turner whispered.

'I don't know. He found it and he talked to Praschko and Praschko was no good. Leo knew he wouldn't be any good; but he had to go back and find out. He had to make sure he was on his own.'

'How do you know that? How much did he tell you?'

'Less than he thought, perhaps. He assumed I was part of him and that was that.' She shrugged. 'I was a friend and friends don't ask questions. Do they?'

'Go on.'

'Rawley was going to Hanover, he said; Friday night Rawley would go to Hanover. So Leo would give me dinner at Königswinter. A special dinner. I said "to celebrate?" "No. No. Hazel, not a *celebration*." But everything was special now, he said, and there wasn't much time anymore. He wouldn't be getting another contract. No more years after December. So why not have a good dinner once in a while? And he looked at me in a frightfully shifty way and we plodded round the course again, him leading. We'd meet in Remagen, he said: we'd meet here. And then: "I say, Hazel, what the devil is Rawley *up to*, look here, in Hanover? I mean, two days before the rally?" '

She had a ready-made face for Leo as well, a frown, a heavy German frown of exaggerated sincerity with which she surely teased him when they were together.

'What *was* Rawley up to, then?' Turner demanded.

'Nothing as it turned out. He didn't go. And Leo must have got wind of that, because he cried off.'

'When?'

'He rang up on Friday morning.'

'What did he say? *Exactly* what did he say?'

'Exactly, he said he couldn't make it that night. He didn't give a reason. Not a real one. He was awfully sorry; there was something he had to do. It had become urgent. It was his boardroom voice: "Awfully sorry, Hazel." '

'That was all?'

'I said all right.' She was acting against tragedy. 'And good luck.' She shrugged. 'I haven't heard from him since. He disappeared and I was worried. I rang his house day and night. That's why you came to dinner. I thought you might know something. You didn't. Any fool could see that.'

The blonde girl was standing up. She wore a long suit of fitted suède and she had to pull tightly at the crotch to straighten the sharp creases. The old lady was writing a bill. Turner called to her and asked for more water and she left the room to get it.

'Ever seen this key?'

Clumsily he drew it from the official buff envelope and laid it on the tablecloth before her. She picked it up and held it cautiously in her palm.

'Where did you get this from?'

'Königswinter. It was in a blue suit.'

'The suit he wore on Thursday,' she said examining it.

'It's one you gave him, is it?' he asked with unconcealed distaste. 'Your house-key?'

'Perhaps it's the one I wouldn't give him,' she replied at last. 'That was the only thing I wouldn't do for him.'

'Go on.'

'I suppose that's what he wanted from Pargiter. That bitch Mary Crabbe told me he'd had a fling with *her*.' She stared down at the esplanade, at the waiting Opel parked in the shadow between the lights; then across the river to Leo's side.

'He said the Embassy had got something that belonged to him. Something from long ago. "They *owe* me, Hazel." He wouldn't say what it was. Memories, he said. It was to do with long ago, and I could get him the key so that he could take it back. I told him: "Talk to them. Tell Rawley, he's human." He said, No, Rawley was the last person on earth he could talk to. It wasn't anything valuable. It was locked away and they didn't even know they had it. You're going to interrupt. Don't. Just listen. I'm telling you more than you deserve.'

She drank some whisky.

'About the third time . . . in *our* house. He lay in bed and just went on about it: "Nothing *bad*," he said, "nothing *political*, but something owed." If he was Duty Officer it wouldn't matter, but he wasn't allowed to do Duty, being what he was. There was one key, they'd never miss it, no one knew how many there were anyway. One key he must have.' She broke off. 'Rawley fascinated him. He loved his dressing-room. All the trappings of a gent. He loved to *see*. Sometimes that's what I was to him: Rawley's wife. The cuff links, the Edward Lear. . . . He wanted to know all the backstairs things like who cleaned his shoes, where he had his suits made. That was when he played his card: while he was dressing. He pretended to remember what he'd been talking about all night. "I say Hazel, look here. *You* could get me the key. When Rawley's working late one night, couldn't you? I mean, call on him, say you'd left something in the Assembly Room. It would be *frightfully* simple. It's a different key," he said. "It's not like the others. Very easily recognized, Hazel." That key,' she remarked flatly handing it back to him. ' "You're clever," I said, "You'll find a way." '

'That was before Christmas?'

'Yes.'

'What a bloody fool I am,' Turner whispered. 'Jesus Christ!'

'Why? What is it?'

'Nothing.' His eyes were bright with success. 'Just for a moment, I forgot he was a thief, that's all. I thought he'd copy that key, and he just stole it. Of course he would!'

'He's not a thief! He's a man. He's ten times the man you are.'

'Oh sure, sure. You were big scale you two. I've heard all that crap, believe me. You lived in the big unspoken part of life, didn't you? You were the artists, and Rawley was the poor bloody technician. You had souls, you two, you heard voices; Rawley just picked up the bits because he loved you. And all the time I thought they were sniggering about Jenny Pargiter. Christ Almighty! Poor sod,' he said, looking out of the window. 'Poor bastard. I'll never like Bradfield, that's for sure; but Christ, he has my full sympathy.'

Leaving some money on the table he followed her down the stone steps. She was frightened.

'He never mentioned Margaret Aickman to you, I suppose? He was going to marry her, you know. She was the only woman he loved.'

'He never loved anyone but me.'

'But he didn't mention her? He did to other people, you see. Everyone except you. She was his *big* love!'

'I don't believe it, I'll never believe it!'

He pulled open the car door and leaned in after her. 'You're all right, aren't you? You've touched the hem. He *loved* you. The whole bloody world can go to war as long as you have your little boy!'

'Yes. I've touched the hem. He was real with me. I made him real. He's real whatever he's doing now. That was our time, and I'm not going to let you destroy it; you or anyone else. He found me.'

'What else did he find?'

Miraculously, the car started.

'He found me, and whatever he found down there was the other part of coming alive.'

'*Down?* Down where? Where did he go? Tell me! You know! What was it he said to you?'

She drove away, not looking back, quite slowly, up the esplanade into the evening and the small lights.

The Opel drew out, preparing to follow her. Turner let it pass, then ran across the road and jumped into a taxi.

The Embassy car park was full, the guard was doubled at the gate. Once more, the Ambassador's Rolls Royce waited at the door like an ancient ship to bear him to the storm. As Turner ran up the steps, his raincoat flying behind him, he held the key ready in his hand.

15

The Glory Hole

TWO QUEEN'S MESSENGERS stood at the desk, their black leather pouches hung like parachute harnesses over their regimental blazers.

'Who's Duty Officer?' Turner snapped.

'I thought you'd gone,' said Gaunt. 'Seven o'clock yesterday, that's what—'

There was a creak of leather as the messengers hastily made room for him.

'I want the keys.'

Gaunt saw the cuts on Turner's face and his eyes opened wide.

'Ring the Duty Officer.' Turner picked up the receiver and offered it to him across the desk. 'Tell him to come down with the keys. Now!'

Gaunt was protesting. The lobby swung a little and held still. Turner heard his silly Welsh bleat, half complaining, half flattering and he grasped him roughly by the arm and pulled him into the dark corridor.

'If you don't do as I say, I'll see they post the hell out of you for the rest of your natural life.'

'The keys aren't drawn, I tell you.'

'Where are they?'

'I've got them here. In the safe. But you can't have them, not without a signature, you know that very well!'

'I don't want them. I want you to count them, that's all. Count the bloody keys!'

The messengers, ostentatiously discreet, were talking to one another in awkward undertones, but Turner's voice cut through them like an axe: 'How many should there be?'

'Forty-seven.'

Summoning the younger guard, Gaunt unlocked the safe that was built into the corner and drew out the familiar bunch of bright-cut brass keys. Overcome by curiosity, the two messengers watched while the square, miner's fingers told off each key like a bead on the abacus. He counted them once and he counted them a second time, and he handed them to the boy who counted them again.

'Well?'

'Forty-six,' said Gaunt grudgingly. 'No doubt.'

'Forty-six,' the boy echoed. 'One short.'

'When were they last counted?'

"Tisn't hardly possible to say,' Gaunt muttered, 'They've been going in and out for weeks.'

Turner pointed to the shining new grille that cut off the basement stairway.

'How do I get down there?'

'I told you. Bradfield has the key. It's a riot gate, see. Guards don't have the authority.'

'How do the cleaners get down there then? What about the boilermen?'

'The boiler-room's separate access, now, ever since Bremen see. They've put grilles down there as well. They can use the outside stairs but they can't go no further than the boiler on account of being prevented.' Gaunt was very scared.

'There's a fire escape . . . a service lift.'

'Only the back staircase, but that's locked too, see. Locked.'

'And the keys?'

'With Bradfield. Same as for the lift.'

'Where does it lead from?'

'Top floor.'

'Up by your place?'

'What of it then?'

'Up by your place or not?'

'Near.'

'Show me!'

Gaunt looked down, looked at the boy, looked at Turner and then back at the boy again. Reluctantly he dropped the keys into the boy's hand and without a word to the messengers led Turner quickly upstairs.

It might have been daytime. All the lights were on, doors open. Secretaries, clerks and diplomats, hastening down corridors, ignored them as they passed. The talk was of Brussels. The city's name was whispered like a password. It lay on every tongue and was stammered out by every typewriter; it was cut into the white wax of the stencils and rung on every telephone. They climbed another flight to a short corridor that smelt of a swimming-pool. A draught of fresh air struck them from their left. The door ahead of them said 'Chancery Guard Private' and the label underneath, 'Mr and Mrs J. Gaunt, British Embassy, Bonn.'

'We don't have to go in, do we?'

'This is where he came and saw you? Friday evenings after choir? He came up here?'

Gaunt nodded.

'What happened when he left? Did you see him out?'

'He wouldn't let me. "You stay there my boy and watch your telly, I'll see myself off the premises." '

'And that's the door: the back staircase.'

He was pointing to his left where the draught came from.

'It's locked though, see. Hasn't been opened for years.'

'That's the only way in?'

'Straight down to the basement it goes. They were going to have a rubbish chute till the money ran out so they put stairs instead.'

The door was solid and unrelieved, with two stout locks that had not been disturbed for a long time. Shining a pencil torch on to the lintels, Turner gently fingered the wooden beading that ran down the two sides, then took a firm grip on the handle.

'Come here. You're his size. You try. Take the handle. Don't turn it. Push. Push hard.'

The door yielded without a sound.

The air was suddenly very cold and stale; American air when the conditioners fail. They stood on a half landing. The stairs under them were very steep. A small window gave on to the Red Cross field. Directly below, the cowl of the canteen chimney puffed floodlit smoke into the darkness. The plaster was peeling in large blisters. They heard the drip of water. On the reverse side of the door post, the wood had been neatly sawn away. By the thin light of the torch they began their descent.

The steps were of stone; a narrow strip of coconut matting ran down the centre. 'Embassy Club this way,' a very old poster ran. 'All welcome.' They caught the sound of a kettle bobbing on a ring and heard a girl's voice reading back a passage of dictation: 'While the official statement of the Federal Government describes the reason for the withdrawal as merely technical, even the most sober commentators . . .' and instinctively they both stopped, heart in mouth, listening to the clear words precisely spoken in to the stairwell.

'It's the ventilation,' Gaunt whispered. 'It's coming through the shaft, see.'

'Shut up.'

They heard de Lisle's voice languidly correcting her. '*Moderate*,' he said. '*Moderate* would be *much* better. Change *sober* to *moderate*, will you, my dear? We don't want them to think we're drowning our sorrows in drink.'

The girl giggled.

They must have reached the ground floor, for a bricked doorway stood ahead of them, and fragments of wet plaster lay on the linoleum. A makeshift noticeboard advertised vanished entertainments: the Embassy Players would present a Christmas performance of Gogol's *Government Inspector*. A grand Commonwealth Children's Party would be held in the Residence; names, together with details of any special dietary requirements should be submitted to the Private Office by 10th December. The year was 1954 and the signature was Harting's.

For a moment Turner fought with his sense of time and place, and almost lost. He heard the barges again and the chink of the glasses, the fall of soot and the creak of the rigging. The same throbbing, the same inner pulse beyond the register of sound.

'What did you say?' Gaunt asked.

'Nothing.'

Giddy and confused, he led the way blindly into the nearest passageway, his head wildly beating.

'You're not well,' said Gaunt. 'Who did that to you then?'

They were in a second chamber occupied by nothing but an old lathe, the filings rusted at its base. There was a door in the further wall. He pushed it open, and for a moment his composure left him as he drew back with a short cry of disgust, but it was only the iron bars of the new grille reaching from the ceiling to the floor, only the wet overalls hanging from the wire and the moisture pattering on the concrete. There was a stink of washday and half burnt fuel; the fire had set a red glow trembling on the brickwork; small lights danced on the new steel. Nothing apocalyptic, he told himself, as he moved cautiously along the gangway towards the next door, just a night train in the war; a crowded compartment and we're all asleep.

It was a steel door, flush against the plaster, a flood door deep below the water line, rusty at the frame and lintel with KEEP OUT done long ago in flaking Government paint. The wall on his left side was painted white at some time, and he could see the scratches where the trolley had passed. The light above him was shielded with a wire basket and it laid dark fingers on his face. He fought recklessly for consciousness. The lagged water pipes which ran along the ceiling chugged and gurgled in their housings, and the stove behind the iron grille spat white sparks which turned small shadows on and off. Christ, he thought: it's enough to power the *Queen Elizabeth*, it's enough to brand an army of prisoners; it's wasted on one lonely dream factory.

He had to fight with the key; he had to shake the lever handle hard before the lock would turn. Suddenly it had snapped like a stick and they heard the echo fly away and resound in distant rooms. Keep me here; Oh God keep me here, he thought. Don't change my nature or my life; don't change the place or move the path that I'm following . . . There must have been a piece of grit beneath the door for it shrieked, then stopped and Turner had to force it with his whole body, force it against the water, while Gaunt the Welsh-man stood back, watching and lusting but not daring to touch. At first, fumbling for the switch, he saw only the darkness; then a single window thick with cobwebs come gloomily forward and it frightened him because he hated prison. It was high in the wall and arched like a brick oven and barred for security. Through its topmost panes he glimpsed the wet gravel of the car park. While he stood there watching and swaying, the beam of a headlight groped slowly along the ceiling, a prison spotlight searching for escapers, and the whole catacomb filled with the roar of a departing engine. An army blanket lay on the sill and he thought: you remembered to black out the window; you remembered the firewatching in London.

His hand found the light switch; it was domed like a woman's breast, and when he pressed it down it thumped like a punch against his own body and the dust rolled longingly towards him over the black concrete.

'They call it the Glory Hole,' Gaunt whispered.

The trolley was in an alcove beside the desk. Files on top, stationery below, all in varying sizes, nicely crested, with long and standard envelopes to match, all laid out ready to hand. At the centre of the desk, next to the reading light, square on its felt pad and neatly covered with a grey plastic cape, lay the missing typewriter with the long carriage and beside it three or four tins of Dutch cigars. On a separate table, a thermos and a quantity of Naafi cups; the tea machine with the clock; on the floor a small electric fan in two tones of plastic, trained conveniently upon the desk to help dispel the unfortunate effects of damp; on the new chair with the rexine seat, a pink cushion partially embroidered, by Miss Aickman. All these he recognized at a glance, dully, greeting them curtly as we greet old friends, while he stared beyond them at the great archive which lined the walls from floor to ceiling; at the slim black files each with a rusted loop and a rounded thumb-hole, some grey with bloom, some wrinkled and bent with damp, column after column in their black uniforms, veterans trained and waiting to be called.

He must have asked what they were, for Gaunt was whispering. No, he couldn't suggest what they were. No. Not his place. No. They had been here longer than anyone could remember. Though some did say they were Jag files, the Judge Advocate General's Department he meant, that's what talkers said and the talkers said they came from Minden in lorries, just dumped here for living space they were, twenty years ago that must be now, all of twenty years, when the Occupation packed up. That's all he could say really, he was sure; that's all he'd happened to hear from the talkers, just overheard it by chance, for Gaunt was not a gossip, that was the one thing they *could* say about him. Oh *more* than twenty years . . . the lorries turned up one summer evening . . . MacMullen and someone else had spent half the night helping to unload them. . . . Of course in *those* days it was thought the Embassy might need them. . . . No, nobody had access, not these days, didn't want it really; who would? Long ago, the odd Chancery officer would ask for the key and look something up but that was *long* ago, Gaunt couldn't remember that at all, and no one had been down here for years, though Gaunt couldn't say for sure, of course; he had to watch his words with Turner, he'd learnt that now, he was sure. . . . They must have kept the key separate for a while then added it to the Duty Officer's bunch. . . . But a while back now, Gaunt couldn't say when, he had heard them talking about it; Marcus one of the drivers, gone now; saying they weren't Jag files at all but *Group* files, it was a specialist British contingent. . . . His voice pattered on, urgent and conspiratorial, like an old woman in Church. Turner was no longer listening. He had seen the map.

A plain map, printed in Polish.

It was pinned above the desk, pinned quite freshly into the damp plaster, in the place where some might put the portraits of their children. No major towns were marked, no national borders, no scale, no pretty arrows showing the magnetic variation: just the places where the camps had been. Neuengamme and Belsen in the North, Dachau, Mauthausen to the South, to the East, Treblinka, Sobibor, Majdanek, Belzec and Auschwitz; in the centre Ravensbrück, Sachsenhausen, Kulmhof and Gross Rosen.

'They *owe* me,' he thought suddenly. 'They *owe* me.' God in Heaven what a fool, what a plain, blundering, clumsy fool I have been. Leo, you thief, you came here to forage in your own dreadful childhood.

'Go away. If I want you I'll call you.' Turner stared at Gaunt sightlessly, his right hand pressed against a shelf. 'Don't tell anyone. Bradfield, de Lisle, Crabbe . . . no one, do you understand.'

'I won't,' Gaunt said.

'I'm not here. I don't exist. I never came in tonight. Do you understand.'

'You ought to see a doctor,' said Gaunt.

'Fuck off.'

Pulling back the chair, he tipped the little cushion to the floor and sat down at the desk. Resting his chin in his hand, he waited for the room to steady. He was alone. He was alone like Harting, contraband smuggled in, living like Harting on borrowed time; hunting, like Harting, for a missing truth. There was a tap beside the window and he filled the tea machine and played with the knobs until it began to hiss. As he returned to the desk he nearly tripped over a green box. It was the size of a narrow briefcase, but stiff and rectangular, made of the kind of reinforced leather-cloth used for bridge-sets and shot-gun cases. It had the Queen's initials just beneath the handle and reinforced corners of thin steel; the locks had been ripped open and it was empty. *That's what we're all doing, isn't it? Looking for something that isn't there?*

He was alone, with only the files for company and the stink of warm damp from the electric fire; and the pale breeze of the plastic fan and the muttering of the tea machine. Slowly he began turning the pages. Some of the files were old, taken from the shelves, half in English and half in a cruel Gothic script jagged as barbed wire. The names were set out like athletes, surname first and Christian name second, with only a couple of lines at the top and a hasty signature at the bottom to authorize their ultimate disposal. The files on the trolley were new, and the paper was rich and smooth, and the minutes signed with familiar names. And some were folders, records of mail despatched and mail received, with titles underlined and margins ruled.

He was alone, at the beginning of Harting's journey, with only his track for company, and the sullen grumbling of the waterpipes in the corridor outside, like the shuffling of clogs upon a scaffold. *Are they like horses?* Hazel Bradfield's voice enquired. *Do they sleep standing up?* He was alone. *And whatever he found there was the other part of coming alive.*

Meadowes was asleep. He would not for a moment have

admitted it; and Cork would not, in charity, for a moment have accused him of it; and it is true that technically, like Hazel Bradfield's horses, his eyes were open. He was reclining in his upholstered library chair in an attitude of well-deserved retirement, while the sounds of dawn floated through the open window.

'I'm handing over to Bill Sutcliffe,' Cork said, loud and deliberately careless. 'Nothing you want, is there, before I knock off? We're brewing a cup of tea if you fancy it.'

'It's all right,' Meadowes said indistinctly, sitting forward with a jerk. 'Be all right in a minute.' Cork, staring down through the open window into the car park, allowed him time to collect himself.

'We're brewing a cup of tea if you fancy it,' he repeated. 'Valerie's got the kettle on.' He was clutching a folder of telegrams. 'There hasn't been a night like that since Bremen. Talk, that's all it is. Words. By four this morning they'd forgotten about security altogether. H.E. and the Secretary of State were just chatting direct on the open line. Fantastic. Blown the lot I should think: codes, cyphers, the whole bloody orchestra.'

'They're blown already,' Meadowes replied, more for himself than for Cork; and came to join him at the window. 'By Leo.'

No dawn is ever wholly ominous. The earth is too much its own master; the cries, the colours and the scents too confident to sustain our grim foreboding. Even the guard at the front gate, doubled since evening, had a restful, domestic look. The morning light which glistened on their long leather coats was soft and strangely harmless; their pace as they slowly walked the perimeter was measured and wise. Cork was moved to optimism.

'I reckon today might be the day,' he said. 'A father by lunchtime: how's that, Arthur?'

'They're never that quick,' Meadowes said, 'Not the first ones,' and they fell to counting off the cars.

'Full house, near as nothing,' Cork declared; and it was true. Bradfield's white Jaguar, de Lisle's red sports car, Jenny Pargiter's little Wolseley, Gaveston's shooting brake with the baby chair mounted on the passenger seat, Jackson's rugged Two Thousand; even Crabbe's broken down Kapitän, twice personally banished from the car park by the Ambassador, had crept back in the crisis, its wings bent outward like crooked claws.

'Rover looks all right,' said Cork. In reverent silence they duly admired its distinguished outlines against the fencing on the other side of the canteen. Nearer at hand, the grey Rolls stood in its own bay, guarded by an army corporal.

'He saw him, did he?' Meadowes asked.

'Sure.' Cork licked his finger, selected the relevant telegram from the folder which he carried under his arm and began reading out loud, in a facetious, nursery-rhyme voice, the Ambassador's account of his dialogue with the Federal Chancellor . . . ' "I replied that as Foreign Secretary you had implicit trust in the many undertakings already given to you personally by the Chancellor, and that you had every confidence that the Chancellor would not for a moment consider yielding to the pressure of vociferous minorities. I reminded him also of the French attitude to the question of German reunification, describing it not merely as unsound but as downright anti-American, anti-European and above all anti-German—" '

'Listen,' said Meadowes suddenly. 'Shut up and listen.'

'What the—'

'Be quiet.'

From the far end of the corridor they could hear a steady drone like the sound of a car climbing a hill.

'It can't be,' Cork said shortly. 'Bradfield's got the keys and he—' they heard the clank of the folding gate and the small sigh of a hydraulic brake.

'It's the beds! That's what it is. More beds. They've got it going for the beds; he's opened it up for them.' In confirmation of his theory, they heard the distinct clank of metal on metal, and the squeak of springs.

'This place will be a Noah's Ark by Sunday, I'll tell you. Kids, girls, even the bloody German staff: Babylon, that's what it'll be. Sodom and Gomorrah, that's better. Here, what happens if it comes on while they're demonstrating? Just my luck, that would be, wouldn't it? My first kid: baby Cork, born in captivity!'

'Go on. Let's hear the rest.'

' "The Federal Chancellor took note of the British anxiety which he thought misplaced; he assured me he would consult his Ministers and see what could be done to restore calm. I suggested to him that a statement of policy would be very useful; the Chancellor on the other hand thought repetition had a weakening effect. At this point he asked that his best wishes be conveyed to yourself as Secretary of State, and it became clear that he regarded the interview as closed. I asked him whether he would consider reserving fresh hotel accommodation in Brussels as a means of ending uninformed speculation, since you were personally distressed by reports that the German delegation had paid its bills and cancelled its bookings. The Chancellor replied that he was sure something of that sort should be done." '

'Zero,' said Meadowes distractedly.

' "The Chancellor asked after the Queen's health. He had heard she had a touch of influenza. I said I thought she was over the worst but would make enquiries and let him know. The Chancellor said he hoped Her Majesty would take care of herself; it was a tricky time of year. I replied that all of us sincerely hoped that the climate would be more settled by Monday and he had the grace to laugh. We left on good terms." Ha ha ha. They also had a little chat about today's demonstration. The Chancellor said we weren't to worry. London are copying to the Palace. "The meeting," ' Cork added with a yawn, ' "ended with the customary exchange of compliments at twenty-two twenty hours. A joint communiqué was issued to the press." Meanwhile, Econ are going up the wall and Commercial are totting up the cost of a run on the pound. Or gold or something. Or maybe it's a slump. Who cares?'

'You ought to sit the exam,' Meadowes said. 'You're too quick for in there.'

'I'll settle for twins,' said Cork, and Valerie brought in the tea.

Meadowes had actually raised the mug to his lips when he heard the sound of the trolley and the familiar trill of the squeaky wheel. Valerie put down the tray with a bang, and some tea slopped out of the pot into the sugar bowl. She was wearing a green pullover, and Cork, who liked to look at her, noticed as she turned to face the door that the polo neck had brought up a light rash at the side of her throat. Cork himself, quicker than the rest, handed Meadowes the folder, went to the door and looked down the corridor. It was their own trolley, loaded high with red and black files and Alan Turner was pushing it. He was in his shirt-sleeves and there were heavy bruises under both his eyes. One lip was cut clean through and had been summarily stitched. He had not shaved. The Despatch Box was on the top of the pile. Cork said later that he looked as though he had pushed the trolley through enemy lines single-handed. As he came down the passage, doors opened one after another in his wake: Edna from the Typists' Pool, Crabbe, Pargiter, de Lisle, Gaveston: one by one their heads appeared, followed by their bodies, so that by the time he had arrived at Registry, slammed back the flap of the steel counter, and shoved the trolley carelessly into the centre of the room, the only door that remained closed was that of Rawley Bradfield, Head of Chancery.

'Leave it there. Don't touch it, any of it.'

Turner crossed the corridor and without knocking, went straight in to Bradfield.

16

'It's all a fake'

'I THOUGHT YOU'D gone.' His tone was weary rather than surprised.

'I missed the plane. Didn't she tell you?'

'What the devil have you done to your face?'

'Siebkron sent his boys to search my room. Looking for news of Harting. I interrupted them.' He sat down. 'They're anglophiles. Like Karfeld.'

'The matter of Harting is closed.' Very deliberately Bradfield laid aside some telegrams. 'I have sent his papers to London together with a letter assessing the damage to our security. The rest will be handled from there. I have no doubt that in due course a decision will be taken on whether or not to inform our Nato partners.'

'Then you can cancel your letter. And forget the assessment.'

'I have made allowances for you,' Bradfield snapped, with much of his former asperity. 'Every kind of allowance. For your unsavoury profession, your ignorance of diplomatic practice and your uncommon rudeness. Your stay here has brought us nothing but trouble; you seem determined to be unpopular. What the devil do you mean by remaining in Bonn when I have told you to leave? Bursting in here in a state of undress? Have you no idea what is going on here? It's Friday! The day of the demonstration, in case you have forgotten.'

Turner did not move, and Bradfield's anger at last got the better of fatigue. 'Lumley told me you were uncouth but effective: so far you have merely been uncouth. I am not in the least surprised you have met with violence: you attract it. I have warned you of the damage you can do; I have told you my reasons for abandoning the investigation at this end; and I have overlooked the needless brutality with which you have treated my staff. But now I have had enough. You are forbidden the Embassy. Get out.'

'I've found the files,' Turner said. 'I've found the whole lot. And the trolley. And the typewriter and the chair. And the two-bar electric fire, and de Lisle's fan.' His voice was disjointed and unconvincing, and his gaze seemed to be upon things that were not in the room. 'And the teacups and all the rest of the hardware he pinched at one time or another. And the letters he collected from the Bag Room and never handed to Meadowes. They were addressed to Leo, you see. They were answers to letters he'd sent. He ran quite a department down there: a separate section of Chancery. Only you never knew. He's discovered the truth about Karfeld and now they're after him.' His hand lightly touched his cheek. 'The people who did this to me: they're after Leo. He's on the run because he knew too much and asked too many questions. For all I know they've caught him already. Sorry to be a bore,' he added flatly. 'But that's the way it is. I'd like a cup of coffee if you don't mind.'

Bradfield did not move.

'What about the Green File?'

'It's not there. Just the empty box.'

'He's taken it?'

'I don't know. Praschko might. I don't.' He shook his head. 'I'm sorry.' He continued: 'You've to find him before they do. Because if you don't they'll kill him. That's what I'm talking about. Karfeld's a fraud and a murderer and Harting's got the proof of it.' He raised his voice at last. 'Do I make myself clear?'

Bradfield continued to watch him, intent but not alarmed.

'When did Harting wake to him?' Turner asked himself. 'He didn't want to notice at first. He turned his back. He'd been turning his back on a lot of things, trying not to remember. Trying not to notice. He held himself in like we all do, sticking to the discipline of not being involved and calling it sacrifice. Gardening, going to parties. Working his fiddles. Surviving. And not interfering. Keeping his head down and letting the world go over him. Until October, when Karfeld came to power. He knew Karfeld, you see. And Karfeld *owed* him. That mattered to Leo.'

'Owed him *what*?'

'Wait. Gradually, bit by bit he began to . . . open up. He allowed himself to feel. Karfeld was tantalizing him. We both know what that means, don't we: to be tantalized. Karfeld's face was everywhere, like it is now. Grinning, frowning, warning. . . . His name kept ringing in Leo's ears: Karfeld's a fraud; Karfeld's a murderer. Karfeld's a fake.'

'What are you talking about? Don't be so utterly ridiculous.'

'Leo didn't like that any more: he didn't like fakes any more; he wanted the truth. The male menopause: that is it. He was disgusted with himself . . . for what he'd failed to do, sins of omission . . . sins of commission. Sick of his own tricks and his own routine. We all know that feeling, don't we? Well Leo had it. In full measure. So he decided to get what he was owed: justice for Karfeld. He had a long memory, you see. That's not fashionable these days, I understand. So he plotted. First to get into Registry, then to renew his contract, then to get hold of the files: The Personalities Survey . . . the old files, the files that were due for destruction . . . the old case histories in the Glory Hole. He would put the case together again, reopen the investigation. . . .'

'I have no idea what you are referring to. You're sick; you are wandering and sick. I suggest you go and lie down.' His hand moved to the telephone.

'First of all he got the key, that was easy enough. Put that down! Leave that telephone alone!' Bradfield's hand hovered and fell back on to the blotter. 'Then he started work in the Glory Hole, set up his little office, made his own files, kept minutes, corresponded . . . he moved in. Anything he needed from Registry, he stole. He was a thief; you said that. You should know.' For a moment, Turner's voice was gentle and understanding. 'When was it you sealed off the basement? Bremen wasn't it? A weekend? That was when he panicked. The only time. That was when he stole the trolley. I'm talking about Karfeld. Listen! About his doctorate, his military service, the wound at Stalingrad, the chemical factory—'

'These rumours have been going the rounds for months. Ever since Karfeld became a serious political contestant, we have heard nothing but stories of his past and each time he has successfully refuted them. There's hardly a politician of any standing in Western Germany whom the Communists have not defamed at one time or another.'

'Leo's not a communist,' Turner said with profound weariness. 'You told me yourself: he's a primitive. For years he kept away from politics because he was afraid of what he might hear. I'm not talking rumours. I'm talking fact: home grown British fact. Exclusive. It's all in our own British files, locked away in our own British basement. That's where he got them from and not even you can bury them any more.' There was neither triumph nor hostility to his tone. 'The information's in Registry now if you want to check. With the empty box. There's some things I didn't follow, my German's not that good. I've given instructions that no one's to touch the stuff.' He grinned in reminiscence, and it might have been his own predicament that he recalled. 'You bloody nearly marooned him if you did but know it. He got the trolley down there the weekend they put up the grilles and sealed off the lift. He was terrified of not being able to carry on; of being cut off from the Glory Hole. Until then, it was child's play. He only had to hop into the lift with his files – he could go anywhere, you see; the Personalities Survey gave him the right – and take them straight down to the basement. But you were putting an end to all that though you didn't know it; the riot grilles queered his pitch. So he shoved everything he might need on to the trolley and waited down there the whole weekend until the workmen had done. He had to break the locks on the back staircase to get out. After that, he relied on Gaunt to invite him up to the top floor. Innocently of course. Everyone's innocent in a manner of speaking. And I'm sorry,' he added, quite graciously, 'I'm sorry for what I said to you. I was wrong.'

'This is hardly the moment for apologies,' Bradfield retorted, and rang Miss Peate for some coffee.

'I'm going to tell you the way it is on the files,' Turner said. 'The case against Karfeld. You'd do me a favour not interrupting. We're both tired, and we've not much time.'

Bradfield had set a sheet of blue draft paper on the blotter before him; the fountain pen was poised above it. Miss Peate, having poured the coffee, took her leave. Her expression, her single disgusted glance at Turner, was more eloquent than any words she could have found.

'I'm going to tell you what he'd put together. Pick holes in it afterwards if you want.'

'I shall do my best,' Bradfield said with a momentary smile that was like the memory of a different man.

'There's a village near Dannenberg, on the Zonal border. Hapstorf it's called. It has three men and a dog and it lies in a wooded valley. Or used to. In thirty-eight, the Germans put a factory there. There was an old paper mill beside a fast-flowing river, with a country house attached to it, right up against the cliff. They converted the mill and built laboratories alongside the river, and turned the place into a small hush-hush research station for certain types of gas.'

He drank some coffee and took a bite of biscuit, and it seemed to hurt him to eat, for he held his head to one side and munched very cautiously.

'Poison Gas. The attractions were obvious. The place was difficult to bomb; the stream was fast-flowing, and they needed that for the effluent; the village was small and they could chuck out anyone they didn't like. All right?'

'All right.' Bradfield had taken out his pen and was writing down key points as Turner spoke. Turner could see the numbers down the left side and he thought: what difference does it make about the numbers? You can't destroy facts by giving them numbers.

'The local population claims it didn't know what was going on there, which is probably true. They knew the mill had been stripped and they knew that a lot of expensive plant had been installed. They knew the warehouses at the back were specially guarded, and they knew the staff weren't allowed to mix with the locals. The labour was foreign: French and Poles, who weren't allowed out at all, so there was no mixing at the lower level either. And everyone knew about the animals. Monkeys mainly, but sheep, goats and dogs as well. Animals that went in there and didn't come out. There's a record of the local *Gauleiter* receiving letters of complaint from animal lovers.'

He looked at Bradfield in wonder. 'He worked down there, night after night, putting it all together.'

'He had no business down there. The basement archive has been out of bounds for many years.'

'He had business there all right.'

Bradfield was writing on his pad.

'Two months before the end of the war, the factory was destroyed by the British. Pinpoint bombing. The explosion was enormous. The place was wiped out, and the village with it. The foreign labourers were killed. They say the sound of the blast carried miles, there was so much went up with it.'

Bradfield's pen sped across the paper.

'At the time of the bombing, Karfeld was at home in Essen; there's no doubt of that at all. He says he was burying his mother; she'd been killed in an air raid.'

'Well?'

'He was in Essen all right. But he wasn't burying his mother. She'd died two years earlier.'

'Nonsense!' Bradfield cried. 'The Press would long ago—'

'There's a photostat of the original death certificate on the file,' Turner said evenly. 'I'm not able to say what the new one looks like. Nor who faked it for him. Though I should think we could both guess without rupturing our imaginations.'

Bradfield glanced at him with appreciation.

'After the war, the British were in Hamburg and they sent a team to look at what was left of Hapstorf, collect souvenirs and take photographs. Just an ordinary Intelligence team, nothing special. They thought they might pick up the scientists who'd worked there . . . get the benefit of their knowledge, see what I mean? They reported that nothing was left. They also reported some rumours. A French labourer, one of the few survivors, had a story about experiments on human guinea pigs. Not on the labourers themselves, he said, but on other people brought in. They'd used animals to begin with, he said, but later on they wanted the real thing so they had some specially delivered. He said he'd been on gate duty one night – he was a trusty by then – and the Germans told him to return to his hut, go to bed and not appear till morning. He was suspicious and hung around. He saw a strange thing; a grey bus, just a plain grey single-decker bus, went through one gate after another without being documented. It drove round the back, towards the warehouses, and he didn't hear any more. A couple of minutes later, it drove out again, much faster. Empty.' Again he broke off, and this time he took a handkerchief from his pocket and very gingerly dabbed his brow. 'The Frenchman also said a friend of his, a Belgian, had been offered inducements to work in the new laboratories under the cliff. He went for a couple of days and came back looking like a ghost. He said he wouldn't spend another night over there, not for all the privileges in the world. Next day he disappeared. Posted, they said. But before he left he had a talk to his pal, and he mentioned the name of Doctor Klaus. Doctor Klaus was the administrative supervisor, he said; he was the man who arranged the details and made things easy for the scientists. He was the man who offered him the job.'

'You call this evidence?'

'Wait. Just wait. The team reported their findings and a copy went to the local War Crimes Group. So they took it over. They interrogated the Frenchman, took a full statement but they failed to produce corroboration. An old woman who ran a flower shop had a story about hearing screams in the night, but she couldn't say which night and besides it might have been animals. It was all very flimsy.'

'Very, I should have thought.'

'Look,' Turner said. 'We're on the same side now aren't we? There are no more doors to open.'

'There may be some to close,' Bradfield said, writing again. 'However.'

'The Group was overworked and understaffed so they threw in the case. File and discontinue. They'd many bigger cases to worry about. They carded Doctor Klaus and forgot about him. The Frenchman went back to France, the old lady forgot the screams and that was it. Until a couple of years later.'

'Wait.'

Bradfield's pen did not hurry. He formed the letters as he always formed them: legibly, with consideration for his successors.

'Then an accident happened. The kind we've come to expect. A farmer near Hapstorf bought an old bit of waste land from the local council. It was rough ground, very stony and wooded, but he thought he could make something of it. By the time he'd dug it and ploughed it, he'd unearthed thirty-two bodies of grown men. The German police took a look and informed the Occupational authority. Crimes against Allied personnel were the responsibility of the Allied judiciary. The British mounted an investigation and decided that thirty-one of the men had been gassed. The thirty-second man was wearing the tunic of a foreign labourer and he'd been shot in the back of the neck. There was something else . . . something that really threw them. The bodies were all messed up.'

'Messed up?'

'Researched. Autopsied. Someone had got there first. So they reopened the case. Somebody in the town remembered that Doctor Klaus came from Essen.'

Bradfield was watching him now; he had put down his pen and folded his hands together.

'They went through all the chemists with the qualification to conduct high-grade research who lived in Essen and whose first names were Klaus. It didn't take them long to unearth Karfeld. He'd no doctorate; that comes later. But then everyone assumed by then that the staff were working under pseudonyms, so why not give yourself a title too? Essen was also in the British zone, so they pulled him in. He denied the whole thing. Naturally. Mind you: apart from the bodies there was little enough to go by. Except for one incidental piece of information.'

Bradfield did not interrupt this time.

'You've heard of the Euthanasia scheme?'

'Hadamar.' With a nod of his head Bradfield indicated the window. 'Down the river. Hadamar,' he repeated.

'Hadamar, Weilmunster, Eichberg, Kalmenhof: clinics for the elimination of unwanted people: for whoever lived on the economy and made no contribution to it. You can read all about it in the Glory Hole, and quite a lot about it is Registry. Among the files for Destruction. At first they had categories for the type of people they'd killed off. You know: the deformed, the insane, severely handicapped children between the ages of eight and thirteen. Bed-wetters. With very few exceptions, the victims were German citizens.'

'They called them patients,' Bradfield said, with intense distaste.

'It seems that now and then certain selected patients were set aside and put to medical uses. Children as well as adults.'

Bradfield nodded, as if he knew that too.

'By the time the Hapstorf case broke, the Americans and Germans had done a fair bit of work on this Euthanasia programme. Among other things, they'd unearthed evidence of one busload of "hybrid workers" being set aside for "dangerous duties at the Chemical Research Station of Hapstorf". One busload was thirty-one people. They used grey buses by the way, if that reminds you of anything.'

'Hanover,' Bradfield said at once. 'The transport for the bodyguard.'

'Karfeld's an administrator. Everyone admires him for it. Then as now. It's nice to know he hasn't lost the old touch, isn't it? He's got one of those minds that runs in grooves.'

'Stop stringing beads. I want the whole thing, quickly.'

'Grey buses then. Thirty-one seats and room left over for the guard. The windows were blackened from the inside. Where possible, they moved them at night.'

'You said there were thirty-two bodies not thirty-one—'

'There was the Belgian labourer, wasn't there? The one who worked under the cliff and talked to the French trusty? They knew what to do about him all right. He'd found out a bit too much, hadn't he? Like Leo, now.'

'Here,' said Bradfield, getting up and bringing the coffee over to him. 'You'd better have some more of this.' Turner held out his cup and his hand was fairly steady.

'So when they'd pulled him in they took Karfeld up to Hamburg and confronted him with the bodies and the evidence, such as they had, and he just laughed at them. Bloody nonsense, he said, the whole story. Never been to Hapstorf in his life. He was an engineer. A demolitions man. He gave a very detailed account of his work at the Russian front – they'd even given him campaign medals and Christ knows what. I suppose they did that for them in the SS and he made a great *spiel* about Stalingrad. There were discrepancies but not that many, and he just held out all the time against interrogation and denied ever having set foot in Hapstorf or possessing any knowledge of the plant. No, no, no all the way. For months on end. "Okay," he kept saying, "if you've got the proof, bring a case. Put it to the Tribunal. I'm not bothered; I'm a hero. I never administered anything in my life except our family factory in Essen, and the British have pulled that to pieces, haven't they? I've been to Russia, I haven't been poisoning hybrids; why should I? I'm a little friend of all the world. Find a live witness, find anybody." They couldn't. At Hapstorf, the chemists had lived in complete segregation, and presumably the desk-men had done the same. The records were destroyed by bombing, and everyone was known by his Christian name or an alias.' Turner shrugged. 'That seemed to be that. He even threw in a story about helping the anti-Nazi resistance in Russia, and since the units he mentioned were either taken prisoner *en masse* or shot to pieces, they couldn't get any further with that either. He doesn't seem to have come out with that since, the resistance bit.'

'It's no longer fashionable,' said Bradfield shortly. 'Particularly in his sphere.'

'So the case never reached the courts. There were plenty of reasons why not. The War Crimes investigation units themselves were near to disbandment; there was pressure from London and Washington to bury the hatchet and hand over all responsibility to the German courts. It was chaos. While the Unit was trying to prepare charges, their Headquarters were preparing amnesties. And there were other reasons, technical reasons for not going ahead. The crime was against French, Belgians and Poles if anyone, but since there was no method of establishing the nationality of the victims, there were problems about jurisdiction. Not material problems, but incidental ones, and they contributed to the difficulty of deciding what to do. You know how it is when you *want* to find difficulties.'

'I know how it was then,' Bradfield said quietly. 'It was bedlam.'

'The French weren't keen; the Poles were *too* keen and Karfeld himself was quite a big wheel by then. He was handling some big allied contracts. Even sub-contracting to competitors to keep up with demand. He was a good administrator, you see. Efficient.'

'You say that as if it were a crime.'

'His own factory had been dismantled a couple of times but now it was running a treat. Seemed a pity to disturb it really. There was even some rumour,' Turner added without changing the tone of his voice, 'that he'd had a head start on everyone else because he'd come by a special consignment of rare gases, and stored them underground in Essen at the end of the war. That's what he was up to while the RAF was bombing Hapstorf. While he was supposed to be burying his poor old mother. He'd been pinching the goods to feather his own nest.'

'As you have described the evidence so far,' Bradfield said quietly, 'there is nothing whatever which attaches Karfeld to Hapstorf, and nothing at all to associate him with the complicity in a murder plot. His own account of himself may very well be true. That he fought in Russia, that he was wounded—'

'That's right. That's the view they took at Headquarters.'

'It is even unproven that the bodies came from Hapstorf. The *gas* may have been theirs; it hardly proves that the chemists themselves administered it to the victims, let alone that Karfeld knew of it, or was in any way an accessory to—'

'The house at Hapstorf had a cellar. The cellar wasn't affected by the bombing. The windows had been bricked in and pipes had been run through the ceiling from the laboratories above. The brick walls of the cellar were torn.'

'What do you mean: "torn"?'

'By hands,' Turner said. 'Fingers, it could have been.'

'Anyway they took your view. Karfeld kept his mouth shut, there was no fresh evidence. They didn't prosecute. Quite rightly. The case was shelved. The unit was moved to Bremen, then to Hanover, then to Moenchengladbach and the files were sent here. Together with some odds and sods from the Judge Advocate General's Department. Pending a decision regarding their ultimate disposal.'

'And this is the story Harting has got on to?'

'He was always on to it. He was the sergeant investigating. Him and Praschko. The whole file, minutes, memoranda, correspondence, interrogation reports, summaries of evidence, the whole case from beginning to end – it has an end now – is recorded in Leo's handwriting. Leo arrested him, questioned him, attended the autopsies, looked for witnesses. The woman he nearly married, Margaret Aickman, she was in the unit as well. A clerical researcher. They called them headhunters: that was his life. . . . They were all very anxious that Karfeld be properly arraigned.'

Bradfield remained lost in thought. 'And this word *hybrid*—' he asked finally.

'It was a Nazi technical term for half Jewish.'

'I see. Yes, I see. So he would have a personal stake, wouldn't he? And that mattered to him. He took everything personally. He lived for himself; that was the only thing he understood.' The pen remained quite still. 'But hardly a case in law.' He repeated it to himself: 'But hardly a case in law. In fact hardly a case by any standards. Not on the merest, most partisan analysis. Not any kind of case. Interesting of course: it accounts for Karfeld's feelings about the British. It doesn't begin to make a criminal of him.'

'No,' Turner agreed, rather to Bradfield's surprise. 'No. It's not a case. But for Leo it rankled. He never forgot; but he pressed it down as far as it would go. But he couldn't keep away from it. He had to find out; he had to take another look and make sure, and in January this year he went down to the Glory Hole and re-read his own reports and his own arguments.'

Bradfield was sitting very still again.

'It may have been his age. Most of all, it was a sense of something left undone.' Turner said this as if it were a problem which applied to his own case, and to which he had no solution. 'A sense of history if you like.' He hesitated, 'Of time. The paradoxes caught up with him and he had to do something about it. He was also in love,' he added, staring out of the window. 'Though he might not have admitted it. He'd made use of somebody and picked up more than he bargained for. . . . He'd escaped from lethargy. That's the point, isn't it: the opposite of love isn't hate. It's lethargy. Nothingness. This place. And there were people about who let him think he was in the big league . . .' he added softly. 'So for whatever reasons, he reopened the case. He re-read the papers from beginning to end. He studied the background again, went through all the contemporary files, in Registry and in the Glory Hole. Checked all the facts from the beginning, and he began making his own enquiries.'

'What sort of enquiries?' Bradfield demanded. They were not looking at one another.

'He set up his own office. He wrote letters and received replies. All on Embassy paper. He headed off the Chancery mail as it came in and extracted anything addressed to him. He ran it like he ran his own life: secretly and efficiently. Trusting nobody, confiding in nobody; playing the different ends off against each other. . . . Sometimes he made little journeys, consulted records, Ministries, church registers, survivor groups . . . all on Embassy paper. He collected press cuttings, took copies, did his own typing and put on his own sealing wax. He even pinched an official seal. He headed his letters Claims and Consular, so most of them came to him in the first place anyway. He compared every detail: birth certificates, marriage, death of mother, hunting licences – he was looking for discrepancies all the time: anything to prove that Karfeld hadn't fought at the Russian front. He put together a bloody great dossier. It's hardly surprising Siebkron got on to him. There's scarcely a Government Agency he hasn't consulted under one pretext or another—'

'Oh my God,' Bradfield whispered, laying down his pen in a momentary gesture of defeat.

'By the end of January, he'd come to the only possible conclusion: that Karfeld had been lying in his teeth, and someone – it looked like someone high up, and it looked very much like Siebkron – someone had been covering up for him. They tell me Siebkron has ambitions of his own – hitch his wagon to any star as long as it was on the move.'

'That's true enough,' Bradfield conceded, lost in private thoughts.

'Like Praschko in the old days. . . . You see where we're getting, don't you? And of course before long, as he very well knew, Siebkron was going to notice that the Embassy was making some pretty way-out enquiries, even for Claims and Consular. And that somebody was going to be bloody angry, and perhaps a bit rough as well. Specially when Leo found the proof.'

'What proof? How can he possibly prove such a charge now, twenty or more years after the crime?'

'It's all in Registry,' Turner said, with sudden reluctance. 'You'd do better to see for yourself.'

'I've no time and I am used to hearing unsavoury facts.'

'And discounting them.'

'I insist that you tell me.' He made no drama of his insistence.

'Very well. Last year, Karfeld decided to take a doctorate. He was a big fellow by then; he was worth a fortune in the chemical industry – his administrative talent had paid off in a big way – and he was making fair headway in local politics in Essen, and he wanted to be Doctor. Maybe he was like Leo; he'd left a job undone and he wanted to get the record straight. Or maybe he thought a handle would be a useful asset: Vote for Doctor Karfeld. They like a doctorate here in a Chancellor. . . . So he went back to school and wrote a learned thesis. He didn't do much research and everyone was very impressed, specially his tutors. Wonderful, they said, the way he found the time.'

'And?'

'It's a study of the effects of certain toxic gases on the human body. They thought very highly of it apparently; caused quite a little stir at the time.'

'That is hardly conclusive.'

'Oh yes it is. Karfeld based his whole analysis on the detailed examination of thirty-one fatal cases.'

Bradfield had closed his eyes.

'It is not proof,' Bradfield said at last; he was very pale but the pen in his hand was as firm as ever. 'You know it is not proof. It raises suppositions I agree. It suggests he was at Hapstorf. It is not even half-way to proof.'

'Pity we can't tell Leo.'

'The information came to him in the course of his industrial

276

experience; that is what Karfeld would argue. He acquired it from a third party; that would be his fall-back position.'

'From the real bastards.'

'Even if it could be shown that the information came from Hapstorf, there are a dozen explanations as to how it came into Karfeld's hands. You said yourself, he was not even engaged in research—'

'No. He sat at a desk. It's been done before.'

'Precisely. And the very fact that he made use of the information at all would tend to exonerate him from the charge of acquiring it.'

'The trouble is, you see,' Turner said, 'Leo's only half a lawyer: a hybrid. We have to reckon with the other half as well. We have to reckon with the thief.'

'Yes.' Bradfield was distracted. 'And he has taken the Green File.'

'Still, as far as Siebkron and Karfeld are concerned, he seems to have got near enough to the truth to be a pretty serious risk, doesn't he?'

'A prima facie case,' Bradfield remarked, examining his notes once more. 'Grounds for reinvestigation, I grant you. At best, a public prosecutor might be persuaded to make an initial examination.' He glanced at his telephone directory. 'The Legal Attaché would know.'

'Don't bother,' Turner said comfortingly. 'Whatever he's done or hasn't done, Karfeld's in the clear. He's past the post.' Bradfield stared at him. 'No one can prosecute him now, even with a cast-iron confession, signed by Karfeld himself.'

'Of course,' Bradfield said quietly. 'I was forgetting.' He sounded relieved.

'He's protected by law. The Statute of Limitations takes care of that. Leo put a note on the file on Thursday evening. The case is dead. There's nothing anyone can do.'

'There's a procedure for reviving it—'

'There is,' Turner conceded. 'It doesn't apply. That's the fault of the British as it happens. The Hapstorf case was a British investigation. We never passed it to the Germans at all. There was no trial, no public report, and when the German judiciary took over sole responsibility for Nazi war crimes we gave them no note of it. Karfeld's whole case fell into the gap between the Germans and ourselves.' He paused. 'And now Leo's done the same.'

'What did Harting intend to do? What was the purpose of all this enquiring?'

'He had to know. He had to complete the case. It taunted him, like a messed-up childhood or a life you can't come to terms with. He had to get it straight. I think he was playing the rest by ear.'

'When did he get this so-called proof?'

'The thesis arrived on the Saturday before he left. He kept a date-stamp you see; everything was entered up in the files. On the Monday he arrived in Registry in a state of elation. He spent a couple of days wondering what to do next. Last Thursday he had lunch with Praschko—'

'What the devil for?'

'I don't know. I thought about it. I don't know. Probably to discuss what action they should take. Or to get a legal opinion. Maybe he thought there was still a way of prosecuting—'

'There is none?'

'No.'

'Thank God for that.'

Turner ignored him: 'Or perhaps to tell Praschko that the pace was getting too hot. To ask him for protection.'

Bradfield looked at Turner very carefully. 'And the Green File has gone,' he said, recovering his strength.

'The box was empty.'

'And Harting has run. Do you know the reason for *that* as well?' His eyes were still upon Turner. 'Is that also recorded in his dossier?'

'He kept writing in his memoranda: "I have very little time." Everyone who speaks of him describes him as being in a fight against time . . . the new urgency . . . I suppose he was thinking of the Statute.'

'But we know that, under the Statute, Karfeld was already a free man, unless of course some kind of stay of action could be obtained. So why has he left? And what was so pressing?'

Turner shrugged away the strangely searching, even taunting tone of Bradfield's questions.

'So you don't know *exactly* why? Why he has chosen this particular moment to run away? Or why he chose that one file to steal?'

'I assume Siebkron has been crowding him. Leo had the proof and Siebkron knew he had it. From then on, Leo was a marked man. He had a gun,' Turner added, 'an old Army pistol. He was frightened enough to take it with him. He must have panicked.'

'Quite,' Bradfield said, with the same note of relief. 'Quite. No doubt that is the explanation.' Turner stared at him in bewilderment.

For perhaps ten minutes Bradfield had not moved or said a word.

There was a lectern in a corner of the room made of an old Bible box and long, rather ugly metal legs which Bradfield had commissioned of a local blacksmith in Bad Godesberg. He was standing with his elbows upon it, staring out of the window at the river.

'No wonder Siebkron puts us under guard,' he said at last; he might have been talking about the mist. 'No wonder he treats us as if we were dangerous. There can hardly be a Ministry in Bonn, not even a journalist, who has not by now heard that the British Embassy is engaged in a blood-hunt for Karfeld's past. What do they expect us to do? Blackmail him in public? Reappear after twenty-five years in full-bottom wigs and indict him under the Allied Jurisdiction? Or do they simply think we are wantonly vindictive, and propose to have our revenge of the man who is spoiling our European dreams?'

'You'll find him, won't you? You'll go easy with him? He needs all the help he can get.'

'So do we all,' said Bradfield, still gazing at the river.

'He isn't a Communist. He isn't a traitor. He thinks Karfeld's a threat. To us. He's very simple. You can tell from the files—'

'I know his kind of simplicity.'

'He's our responsibility, after all. It was us who put it into his mind back in those days: the notion of absolute justice. We

279

made him all those promises: Nuremberg, de-Nazification. We *made* him believe. We can't let him be a casualty just because we changed our minds. You haven't seen those files . . . you can't imagine how they thought about the Germans then. Leo hasn't changed. He's the stay-behind man. *That*'s not a crime, is it?'

'I know very well how they thought. I was here myself. I saw what he saw; enough. He should have grown out of it; the rest of us did.'

'What I mean is, he's worthy of our protection. There's a kind of integrity about him. . . . I felt that down there. He's not put off by paradox. For you and me there are always a dozen good reasons for doing nothing. Leo's made the other way round. In Leo's book there's only one reason for doing something: because he must. Because he feels.'

'I trust you are not offering him as an example to be followed?'

'There's another thing that puzzled him.'

'Well?'

'In cases like this, there are always external documents. In the SS headquarters; with the clinic or the transport unit. Movement orders, letters of authority, *related* documents from somewhere else that would give the game away. Yet nothing's come to light. Leo kept on pencilling annotations: why no record in Koblenz? Why no this or that? As if he suspected that other evidence had been destroyed . . . by Siebkron for instance.'

'We can honour him, can't we?' Turner added, almost in supplication.

'There are no absolutes here.' His gaze had not left the distant scene. 'It is all doubt. All mist. The mist drains away the colours. There are no distinctions, the Socialists have seen to that. They are all everything. They are all nothing. No wonder Karfeld is in mourning.'

What was it that Bradfield studied on the river? The small boats struggling against the mist? The red cranes and the flat fields, or the far vineyards that have crept so far away from the south? Or Chamberlain's ghostly hill and the long concrete box where they had once kept him?

'The Glory Hole is out of bounds,' he said at last and again fell silent. 'Praschko. You said he lunched with Praschko on Thursday?'

'Bradfield—'

'Yes?' He was already moving to the door.

'We feel differently about him now, don't we?'

'Do we? Perhaps he is still a communist after all.' There was a strain of irony in Bradfield's tone. 'You forget he has stolen a file. You seem to think all of a sudden you can look into his heart.'

'Why did he steal it? What was in that file?'

But Bradfield was already pushing his way between the beds and the clutter of the corridor. Notices had sprung up everywhere: First Aid Post this Way . . . Emergency Rest Room . . . No Children Allowed Beyond this Point. As they passed Chancery Registry, they heard a sudden cheer followed by a desultory handicap. Cork, white in the face, ran out to greet them.

'She's had it,' he whispered. 'The hospital just telephoned. She wouldn't let them send for me while I was on shift.' His pink eyes were wide with fear. 'She didn't even need me. She didn't even want me there.'

17

Praschko

THERE IS A tarmac driveway at the back of the Embassy. It leads from the eastern part of the perimeter northwards through a settlement of new villas too costly for British habitation. Each has a small garden of great value in terms of real estate, each is distinguished from its neighbour by those cautious architectural deviations which are the mark of modern conformity. If one house has a brick-built barbecue and a patio of reconstituted stone, the next will match it with an external wall of blue slate, or quarried rock daringly exposed. In summer, young wives sun themselves beside minuscule swimming-pools. In winter black poodles burrow in the snow; and every midday from Monday to Friday, black Mercedes bring the masters home for meals. The air smells all the time, if distantly, of coffee.

It was a cold grey morning still, but the earth was lit with the clarity which follows rain. They drove very slowly, with the windows right down. Passing a hospital, they entered a more sombre road where the older suburb had survived; behind shaggy conifers and blue-black laurel bushes, leaden spires which once had painted donnish dreams of Weimar stood like lances in a mouldering forest. Ahead of them rose the Bundestag, naked, comfortless and uncomforted; a vast motel mourned by its own flags and painted in yellowing milk. At its back, straddled by Kennedy's Bridge and bordered by Beethoven's hall, the brown Rhine pursued its uncertain cultural course.

Police were everywhere: seldom could a seat of democracy have been so well protected from its democrats. At the main entrance, a line of school-children waited in a restless queue, and the police guarded them as if they were their own. A television team was setting up its arclights. In front of the camera a young man in a suit of mulberry corduroy thoughtless-

282

ly pirouetted, hand on hip, while a colleague measured his complexion; the police watched dangerously, bewildered by his freedom. Along the kerb, scrubbed as jurymen, their banners straight as Roman standards, the grey crowd obediently waited. The slogans had changed: *German Unity First European Unity Second: This is a Proud Nation Too: Give us Back our Country First!* The police faced them in line abreast, controlling them as they controlled the children.

'I'll park down by the river,' Bradfield said. 'God knows what it will be like by the time we come out.'

'What's going on?'

'A debate. Amendments to the Emergency Legislation.'

'I thought they'd finished with that long ago.'

'In this place, nothing is resolved.'

Along the embankment as far as they could see on either side, grey detachments waited passively like unarmed soldiers. Makeshift banners declared their provenance: Kaiserslautern, Hanover, Dortmund, Kassel. They stood in perfect silence, waiting for the order to protest. Someone had brought a transistor radio and it blared very loud. They craned their necks for a sight of the white Jaguar.

Side by side they walked slowly back, up the hill, away from the river. They passed a kiosk; it seemed to contain nothing but coloured photographs of Queen Soraya. Two columns of students made an avenue to the main entrance. Bradfield walked ahead, stiff backed. At the door the guard objected to Turner and Bradfield argued with him shortly. The lobby was dreadfully warm and smelt of cigar; it was filled with the ringside murmur of dispute. Journalists, some with cameras, looked at Bradfield curiously and he shook his head and looked away. In small groups, deputies talked quietly, vainly glancing all the time over one another's shoulders in search of someone more interesting. A familiar figure rose at them.

'The best piece! My very words. Bradfield you are the best piece! You have come to see the end of democracy? You have come for the debate? My God you are so damn *efficient* over there! And the Secret Service is still with you? Mr Turner, you are loyal, I hope? My God, what the devil's happened to your face?' Receiving no answer he continued in a lower voice, furtively. 'Bradfield, I must speak to you. Something damned urgent, look here. I tried to get you at the Embassy but for Saab you are always out.'

'We have an appointment.'

'How long? Tell me how long. Sam Allerton wishes also; we wish together to have a discussion.'

He had bent his black head to Bradfield's ear. His neck was still grimy; he had not shaved.

'It's impossible to say.'

'Listen, I will wait for you. A most *important matter*. I will tell Allerton: we will wait for Bradfield. Deadlines, our news-papers: small fish. We must talk with Bradfield.'

'There's no comment, you know that. We issued our state-ment last night. I thought you had a copy. We accept the Chancellor's explanation. We look forward to seeing the German team back in Brussels within a few days.'

They descended the steps to the restaurant.

'Here he is. I'll do the talking. You're to leave him entirely to me.'

'I'll try.'

'You'll do better than that. You'll keep your mouth shut. He's a very slippery customer.'

Before anything else, Turner saw the cigar. It was very small and lay in the corner of his mouth like a black thermometer; and he knew it was also Dutch, and that Leo had been provid-ing them for nothing.

He looked as if he had been editing a newspaper half the night. He appeared from the door leading to the shopping arcade, and he walked with his hands in his pockets and his jacket pulled away from his shirt, bumping into the tables and apologizing to no one. He was a big dirty man with grizzly hair cut short and a wide chest that spread to a wider stomach. His spectacles were tipped back over his brow like goggles. A girl followed him, carrying a briefcase. She was an expressionless, listless girl, either very bored or very chaste; her hair was black and abundant.

'Soup,' he shouted across the room, as he shook their hands. 'Bring some soup. And something for her.' The waiter was listening to the news on the wireless, but when he saw Praschko he switched it low and sauntered over, prepared to oblige. Praschko's braces had brass teeth which held doggedly to the grimy waistband of his trousers.

'You been working too? She doesn't understand anything,' he explained to them. 'Not in any damn language. *Nicht wahr, Schatz?* You are as stupid as a sheep. What's the problem?' His English was fluent, and whatever accent he possessed was heavily camouflaged by the American intonation. 'You Ambassador these days?'

'I'm afraid not.'

'Who's this guy?'

'Visiting.'

Praschko looked at Turner very carefully and then at Bradfield, then at Turner again.

'Some girl get angry with you?'

Only his eyes moved. His shoulders had risen a little into his neck, and there was a tautening, an instinctive alertness in his manner. His left hand settled on Bradfield's forearm.

'That's *nice*,' he said. 'That's fine. I like a change. I like new people.' His voice was on a single plane; heavy but short; a conspirator's voice, held down by the experience of saying things which should not be overheard.

'What you guys come for? Praschko's personal opinion? The voice of the opposition?' He explained to Turner: 'When you got a coalition, the opposition's a damned exclusive club.' He laughed very loud, sharing the joke with Bradfield.

The waiter brought a goulash soup. Cautiously, with small, nervous movements of his butcher's hand, he began feeling for the meat.

'What you come for? Hey, maybe you want to send a telegram to the Queen?' He grinned. 'A message from her old subject? OK. So send her a telegram. What the hell does she care what Praschko says? What does anyone care? I'm an old whore' – this too for Turner – 'They tell you that? I been English, I been German, I been damn nearly American. I been in this bordello longer than all the other whores. That's why no one wants me any more. I been had all ways. Did they tell you that? Left, Right and Centre.'

'Which way have they got you now?' Turner asked.

His eyes still upon Turner's battered face, Praschko lifted his hand and rubbed the tip of his finger against his thumb. 'Know what counts in politics? Cash. Selling. Everything else is a load of crap. Treaties, policies, alliances: crap. . . . Maybe I should have stayed a Marxist. So now they've walked out of Brussels. That's sad. Sure, that's very sad. You haven't got anyone to talk to any more.'

He broke a roll in two and dipped one half into the soup.

'You tell the Queen that Praschko says the English are lousy, lying hypocrites. Your wife okay?'

'Well, thank you.'

'It's a long time since I got to dinner up there. Still live in that ghetto, do you? Nice place. Never mind. Nobody likes me for too long. That's why I change parties,' he explained to Turner. 'I used to think I was a Romantic, always looking for the blue flower. Now I think I just get bored. Same with friends, same with women, same with God. They're all true. They all cheat you. They're all bastards. Jesus. Know another thing: I like new friends better than old ones. Hey, I got a new wife: what do you think of her?' He held up the girl's chin and adjusted her face a little to show her to the best advantage and the girl smiled and patted his hand. 'I'm amazing. There was a time,' he continued before either of them could make an appropriate comment, 'There was a time when I would have laid down on my fat belly to get the lousy English into Europe. Now you're crying on the doorstep and I don't care.' He shook his head. 'I'm truly amazing. Still, that's history I guess. Or maybe that's just me. Maybe I'm only interested in power: maybe I loved you because you were strong and now I hate you because you're nothing. They killed a boy last night, you hear? In Hagen. It's on the radio.'

He drank a Steinhäger from the tray. The mat stuck to the stem of the glass. He tore it off. 'One boy. One old man. One crazy woman librarian. Okay, so it's a football team: but it isn't Armageddon.'

Through the window, the long grey columns waited on the esplanade. Praschko waved a hand round the room. 'Look at this crap. Paper. Paper democracy, paper politicians, paper eagles, paper soldiers, paper deputies. Doll's house democracy; every time Karfeld sneezes, we wet our pants. Know why? Because he comes so damn near the truth.'

'Are you in favour of him then? Is that it?' Turner asked, ignoring Bradfield's angry glance.

Praschko finished his soup, his eyes on Turner all the time. 'The world gets younger every day,' he said. 'Okay, so Karfeld's a load of crap. Okay. We've got rich, see, boy? We've eaten and drunk, built houses, bought cars, paid taxes, gone to Church, made babies. Now we want something *real*. Know what that is, boy?'

His eyes had not left Turner's damaged face.

'Illusions. Kings and Queens. The Kennedys, de Gaulle, Napoleon. The Wittelsbachs, Potsdam. Not just a damn village anymore. Hey, so what's this about the students rioting in England? What does the Queen think about that? Don't you give them enough cash? Youth. Want to know something about youth? I'll tell you.' Turner was his only audience now. "German youth is blaming its parents for starting the war." That's what you hear. Every day some crazy clever guy writes it in another newspaper. Want to hear the true story? They're blaming their parents for *losing* the damn war, not for starting it! "Hey! Where the hell's our Empire?" Same as the English I guess. It's the same horseshit. The same kids. They want God back.' He leaned across the table until his face was quite close to Turner's. 'Here. Maybe we could do a deal: we give you cash, you give us illusions. Trouble is, we tried that. We done that deal and you gave us a load of shit. You didn't deliver the illusions. That's what we don't like about the English any more. They don't know how to do a deal. The Fatherland wanted to marry the Motherland but you never showed up for the wedding.' He broke out in another peal of false laughter.

'Perhaps the time has now come to *make* the union,' Bradfield suggested, smiling like a tired stateman.

Out of the corner of his eye, Turner saw two men, blond faced, in dark suits and suède shoes, quietly take their places at an adjoining table. The waiter went to them quickly, sensing their profession. At the same moment a bevy of young journalists came in from the lobby. Some carried the day's newspapers; the headlines spoke of Brussels or Hagen. At their head Karl-Heinz Saab, father of them all, stared across at Bradfield in flatulent anxiety. Beyond the window, in a loveless patio, rows of empty plastic chairs were planted like artificial flowers into the breaking concrete.

'Those are the real Nazis, that scum.' His voice pitched high enough for anyone to hear, Praschko indicated the journalists with a contemptuous wave of his fat hand. 'They put out their tongues and fart and think they've invented democracy. Where's that damn waiter: dead?'

'We're looking for Harting,' Bradfield said.

'Sure!' Praschko was used to crisis. His hand, drawing the napkin across his cracked lips, moved at the same steady pace. The eyes, yellow in their parched sockets, barely flickered as he continued to survey the two men.

'I haven't seen him around,' he continued, carelessly. 'Maybe he's in the gallery. You guys have a special box up there.' He put down the napkin. 'Maybe you ought to go look.'

'He's been missing since last Friday morning. He's been missing for a week.'

'Listen: Leo? That guy will always come back.' The waiter appeared. 'He's indestructible.'

'You're his friend,' Bradfield continued. 'Perhaps his only friend. We thought he might have consulted you.'

'What about?'

'Ah, that's the problem,' Bradfield said with a little smile. 'We thought he might have told *you* that.'

'He never found an English friend?' Praschko was looking from one to the other. 'Poor Leo.' There was an edge to his voice now.

'You occupied a special position in his life. After all, you did a great many things together. You shared a number of experiences. We felt that if he had needed advice, or money, or whatever else one needs at certain crises in one's life, he would instinctively seek you out. We thought he might even have come to you for protection.'

Praschko looked again at the cuts on Turner's face.

'Protection?' His lips barely parted as he spoke; it was as if

288

he would prefer not to have known that he had spoken at all. 'You might as well protect a—' The moisture had risen suddenly on his brow. It seemed to come from outside, and to settle on him like steam. 'Go away,' he said to the girl. Without a word she stood up, smiled distractedly at them all and sauntered out of the restaurant, while Turner, for a moment of irrelevant, light-headed joy, followed the provocative rotation of her departing hips; but Bradfield was already talking again.

'We haven't much time.' He was leaning forward and speaking very quickly. 'You were with him in Hamburg and Berlin. There are certain matters known perhaps only to the two of you. Do you follow me?'

Praschko waited.

'If you can help us to find him without fuss; if you know where he is and can reason with him; if there's anything you can do for the sake of an old friendship, I will undertake to be very gentle with him, and very discreet. I will keep your name out of it, and anyone else's as well.'

It was Turner's turn to wait now, as he stared from one to the other. Only the sweat betrayed Praschko; only the fountain pen betrayed Bradfield. He clenched it in his closed fist as he leaned across the table. Outside the window, Turner saw the grey columns waiting; in the corner, the moon men watched dully, eating rolls and butter.

'I'll send him to England; I'll get him out of Germany altogether if necessary. He has put himself in the wrong already; there is no question of re-employing him. He has done things – he has behaved in a way which puts him beyond our consideration; do you understand what I mean? Whatever knowledge he may have is the property of the Crown. . . .' He sat back. 'We must find him before they do,' he said, and still Praschko watched him with his small hard eyes, saying nothing.

'I also appreciate,' Bradfield continued, 'that you have special interests which must be served.'

Praschko stirred a little. 'Go careful,' he said.

'Nothing is further from my mind than to interfere in the internal affairs of the Federal Republic. Your political ambitions, the future of your own party in relation to the Movement, these are matters far outside our sphere of interest. I am here to protect the alliance, not to sit in judgment over an ally.'

Quite suddenly, Praschko smiled.

'That's fine,' he said.

'Your own involvement with Harting twenty years ago, your association with certain British Government agencies—'

'Nobody knows about that,' Praschko said quickly. 'You go damn carefully about that.'

'I was going to make the very same point,' said Bradfield with a reciprocal smile of relief. 'I would not for a moment wish to have it said of the Embassy that we harbour resentments, persecute prominent German politicians, rake up old matters long dead; that we side with countries unsympathetic to the German cause in order to smear the Federal Republic. I am quite certain that in your own sphere, you would not like to have the same things said about yourself. I am pointing to an identity of interest.'

'Sure,' said Praschko. 'Sure.' His harrowed face remained inscrutable.

'We all have our villains. We must not let them come between us.'

'Jesus,' said Praschko with a sideways glance at the marks on Turner's face. 'We got some damn funny friends as well. Did Leo do that to you?'

'They're sitting in the corner,' Turner said. 'They did it. They're waiting to do it to him if they get a chance.'

'Okay,' said Praschko at last. 'I'll go along with you. We had lunch together. I haven't seen him since. What does that ape want?'

'Bradfield,' Saab called across the room. 'How soon?'

'I told you, Karl-Heinz. We have no statement to make.'

'We just talked, that's all. I don't see him so often. He called me up: how about lunch some time? I said make it tomorrow.' He opened his palms to show there was nothing up his sleeve.

'What did you talk about?' Turner asked.

He shrugged to both of them. 'You know how it is with old friends. Leo's a nice guy, but – well, people change. Or maybe we don't like to be reminded that they don't change. We talked about old times. Had a drink. You know the kind of thing.'

'Which old times?' Turner persisted, and Praschko flared at him, very angry

'Sure: England times. Shit times. You know why we went to England, me and Leo? We were kids. Know how we got there? His name began with an H, my name began with P. So I changed it to a B. Harting Leo, Braschko Harry. Those times. Lucky we weren't Weiss or Zachary, see: they were too low down. The English didn't like the second half of the alphabet. That's what we talked about: sent to Dover, free on board. Those damn times. The damn Farm School in Shepton Mallet, you know that shit place? Maybe they painted it by now. Maybe that old guy's dead who knocked the hell out of us for being German and said we got to thank the English we're alive. You know what we learnt in Shepton Mallet? Italian. From the prisoners of war. They were the only bastards we ever got to talk to!' He turned to Bradfield. 'Who is this Nazi anyway?' he demanded, and burst out laughing. 'Hey, am I crazy or something? I was having lunch with Leo.'

'And he talked about his difficulties, whatever they may be?' Bradfield asked.

'He wanted to know about the Statute,' Praschko replied, still smiling.

'The Statute of Limitations?'

'Sure. He wanted to know the law.'

'Applied to a particular case?'

'Should it have been?'

'I was asking you.'

'I thought maybe you had a particular case in mind.'

'As a general matter of legal principle?'

'Sure.'

'What policy would be served by *that*, I wonder? It is not in the interests of any of us that the past be resurrected.'

'That's true, huh?'

'It's common sense,' Bradfield said shortly, 'Which I imagine carries more weight with you than any assurances I could give. What did he want to know?'

Praschko went very slowly now: 'He wanted to know the *reason*. He wanted to know the philosophy. So I told him: "It's not a new law, it's an old one. It's to make an end of things.

Every country has a final court, a point you can't go beyond, okay? In Germany there has to be a final day as well." I spoke to him like he was a child – he's so damned innocent, do you know that? A monk. I said, "Look, you ride a bicycle without lights, okay? If nobody's found out after four months, you're in the clear. If it's manslaughter, then it's not four months but fifteen years; if it's murder, twenty years. If it's Nazi murder, longer still, because they gave it extra time. They waited a few years before they began to count to twenty. If they don't open a case, the offence lapses." I said to him: "Listen, they've fooled around with this thing till it damn near died. They amended it to please the Queen and they amended it to please themselves; first they dated it from forty-five then from forty-nine and now already they've changed it again." ' Praschko opened his hands – 'So then he shouts at me, "What's so damn holy about twenty years?" "There's nothing holy about twenty years; there's nothing holy about any number of damn years. We grow old. We grow tired. We die." I told him that. I said to him: "I don't know what you've got in your fool head, but it's all crap. Everything's got to have an end. The moralists say it's a moral law, the apologists say it's expedient. Listen, I'm your friend and I'm telling you; Praschko says: it's a fact of life, so don't fool about with it." Then he got angry. You ever seen him angry?'

'No.'

'After lunch I brought him back here. We were still arguing, see. All the way in the car. Then we sat at this table. Right here where we are now. "Maybe I'll find new information," he said. I told him: "If you find new information, forget it, because there won't be a darn thing you can do: don't waste your time. You're too late. That's the law." '

'He didn't suggest by any chance that he already *had* that information?'

'Has he?' Praschko asked, very quickly indeed.

'I cannot imagine it exists.'

Praschko nodded slowly, his eyes on Bradfield all the time.

'So then what happened?' said Turner.

'That's all. I said to him: "OK, so you prove manslaughter:

you're too late by years already. So you prove murder: you're too late since last December. So get screwed." That's why I told him. So then he gets hold of my arm and he whispers to me, like a crazy priest: "No law will ever take account of what they did. You and I know that. They teach it in the Churches: Christ was born of a virgin and went to Heaven in a cloud of light. Millions believe it. Listen, I play the music every Sunday, I hear them." Is that true?'

'He played the organ in Chapel,' said Bradfield.

'Jesus,' said Praschko, lost in wonder. 'Leo did that?'

'He's done it for years.'

'So then he goes on: "But you and I, Praschko, in our own lifetime, we have seen the living witness of evil." That's what he says. "Not on a mountain top, not at night, but there, in the field where we all stood. We're privileged people. *And now it's all happening again.*" '

Turner wanted to interrupt, but Bradfield restrained him.

'So then I got damned angry. I said to him, see: "Don't come playing God to me. Don't come screaming to me about the thousand year justice of Nuremberg that lasted four years. At least the Statute gave us twenty. And who imposed the Statute anyway? You British could have made us change it. When you handed over, you could have said to us: here, you bloody Germans, take over these cases, hear them in your own Courts, pass sentence according to your penal code but first abolish the Statute. You were party to it then; be party to it now. It's finished. It's damn well, damn well finished." That's what I said to him. And he just went on looking at me, saying my name. "Praschko, Praschko." '

Taking a handkerchief from his pocket, he dabbed his brow and wiped his mouth.

'Don't pay any attention to me,' he said. 'I get excited. You know what politicians are. I said to him, while he stared at me, I said, "This is my home: look. If I've got a heart left, it's here, in this bordello. I used to wonder why. Why not Buckingham Palace? Why not the Coca-Cola Culture? But this is my country. And that's what you should have found: a country. Not just a bloody Embassy." He went on looking at me; I tell you I was going crazy myself. I said to him: "So suppose you do find that proof, tell me what it's all about: to commit a crime at thirty, to be punished at sixty? What does that mean? We're old men," I said to him, "you and I. You know what Goethe told us: no man can watch a sunset for more than quarter of an hour." He said to me: "It's happening again. Look at the faces, Praschko, listen to the speeches. Somebody has to stop that bastard or you and me will be wearing the labels again." '

Bradfield spoke first. 'If he *had* found the proof, which we know he has not, what would he have done? If instead of still searching for it, he had already found it, what then?'

'Oh Jesus; I tell you: he'd have gone crazy.'

'Who's Aickman?' Turner said, ending the long silence.

'What's that, boy?'

'Aickman. Who is she? Miss Aickman, Miss Etling and Miss Brandt. . . . He was engaged to her once.'

'She was just a woman he had in Berlin. Or was it Hamburg? Both maybe. Jesus I forget everything. Thank God, eh?'

'What became of her?'

'I never heard,' Praschko said. His little eyes were roughly hacked in the old bark.

From their corner still, the clean faces watched without expression; four pale hands lay on the table like weapons put to rest. The loudspeaker was calling Praschko: the *Fraktion* was waiting for him to appear.

'You betrayed him,' Turner said. 'You put Siebkron on to him. You sold him down the river. He told you the lot and you warned Siebkron because you're climbing on the bandwagon too.'

'Be quiet,' said Bradfield. 'Be quiet.'

'You rotten bastard,' Turner hissed. 'You'll kill him. He told you he'd found the proof; he told you what it was and he asked you to help him, and you put Siebkron on to him for his trouble. You were his friend and you did that.'

'He's crazy,' Praschko whispered. 'Don't you realize he's crazy? You didn't see him back in those days. You never saw him back with Karfeld in the cellar. You think those boys worked you over? Karfeld couldn't even *speak*: "Talk! Talk!" ' Praschko's eyes were screwed up very tight. 'After we saw those bodies in the field. . . . They were tied together. They'd been tied together before they were gassed. He went crazy. I said to him: "Listen it's not your *fault*. It's not your *fault* you survived!" Did he show you the buttons, maybe? The money from the camp? You never saw that either, did you? You never went out with him and a couple of girls to have a drink? You never saw him play with the wooden buttons to start a fight? He's crazy I tell you.' The recollection moved him to despair. 'I said to him, sitting here: "Come on, let's go. Who the hell ever built Jerusalem in Germany? Don't eat your heart out, come and screw some girls!" I said, "Listen! We got to get hold of our minds and press them in or we *all* go crazy." He's a monk. A crazy monk that won't forget. What do you think the world is? A damn playground for a lot of crazy moralists? Sure I told Siebkron. You're a clever boy. But you got to learn to forget as well. Christ if the British can't who can?'

There was shouting as they entered the lobby. Two students in leather coats had broken the cordon at the door and were standing on the stairs, fighting with the janitors. An elderly deputy was holding a handkerchief to his mouth and the blood was running over his wrist. 'Nazis!' someone was shouting, 'Nazis!' but he was pointing to a student on the balcony and the student was waving a red flag.

'Back to the restaurant,' Bradfield said. 'We can get out the other side.'

The restaurant was suddenly empty. Drawn or repelled by the fuss in the lobby, deputies and visitors had vanished in their chosen directions. Bradfield was not running, but striding at a long military pace. They were in the arcade. A leather shop offered black attaché cases in fine box calf. In the next window a barber was working up a lather on the face of an invisible customer.

'Bradfield, you must hear me: my God, can't I even warn you what they are saying?'

Saab was dreadfully out of breath. His portly body was heaving under his greasy jacket; tears of sweat lay in the pouches under his yellow eyes. Allerton, his face crimson under his black mane, peered over his shoulder. They drew back into a doorway. At the end of the corridor, calm had descended on the lobby.

'What who is saying?'

Allerton answered for him: 'All Bonn old boy. The whole bloody paper mill.'

'Listen. There are whispers. Listen. Fantastic what they are saying. You know what happened at Hanover? You know why they rioted? They are whispering it in all the cafés: the delegates; Karfeld's men are telling it. Already the rumours are all over Bonn. They have been instructed to say nothing; it is all a fantastic secret.'

He glanced quickly up and down the arcade.

'It's the best for years,' said Allerton. 'Even for this doorp.'

'Why they broke the line at the front and ran like mad dogs for the Library? Those boys who came in the grey buses? Somebody shot at Karfeld. In the middle of the music: shot at him from the window of the Library. Some friend of the woman, the librarian: Eich. She worked for the British in Berlin. She was an *émigrée*, she changed her name to Eich. She let him in to shoot from the window. Afterwards she told it all to Siebkron before she died. Eich. The bodyguard saw him fire, Karfeld's bodyguard. In the middle of the music! They saw the fellow shooting from the window and ran to catch him. The bodyguard, Bradfield, that came in the grey buses! Listen, Bradfield! Listen what they say! They found the bullet, a pistol bullet from an English pistol. You see now? The English are assassinating Karfeld: that is the fantastic rumour. You must stop them saying it; talk to Siebkron. Karfeld is terrified; he is a great coward. Listen: that is why he is so careful, that is why he is building everywhere such a damn *Schaffott*. How do I say *Schaffatt*, for God's sake?'

'Scaffold,' said Turner.

The crowd from the lobby swept them outwards into the fresh air.

'Scaffold! An absolute secret, Bradfield! For your own information!' They heard him cry, 'You must not quote me, for God's sake. Siebkron would be fantastically angry!'

'Rest assured, Karl-Heinz,' the even voice replied, absurdly formal in the turmoil, 'your confidence will be respected.'

'Old boy,' Allerton put his head close to Turner's ear. He had not shaved, the black locks were tipped with sweat. 'What's happened to Leo these days? Seems to have faded all away. They say old Eich was quite a swinger in her day . . . used to work with the scalphunters up in Hamburg. What have they done to your face, old boy? Close her legs too soon did she?'

'There's no story,' Bradfield said.

'Not yet there isn't,' said Allerton, 'old boy.'

'There never will be.'

'They say he bloody nearly got him in Bonn the night before the Hanover rally. Just wasn't quite sure enough of his man. Karfeld was walking away from a secret conference; walking to the pick-up point and Leo damn nearly got him then. Siebkron's chicks turned up just in time.'

Along the embankment the motionless columns waited in patient echelons. Their black flags barely lifted in the poor breeze. Across the river, behind a line of blue trees, distant factory chimneys puffed their smoke lazily into the drab morning light. Small boats, dabs of brilliance, lay marooned on the grey grass bank. To Turner's left stood an old boathouse which no one had yet pulled down. A notice on it proclaimed it the property of the Institute of Physical Exercise of the University of Bonn.

They stood on the bank, side by side. The palest mist, like breath upon a glass, drew in the brown horizons and filled the near bridge. There were no sounds but the echoes of absent things, the cry of lost gulls and the moan of the lost barges, the inevitable whine of unseen drills. There were no people but the grey shadows along the waterfront and the unrelated tread of feet; it was not raining, but sometimes they felt the moisture in the mist, like the prickling of blood upon a heated skin. There were no ships, but funeral hulks drifting towards the Gods of the North; and there was no smell but the inland smell of coal and industries which were not present.

'Karfeld is hidden until tonight,' Bradfield said. 'Siebkron has seen to that. They'll expect him to try again this evening.

And he will.' He went over it again, rehearsing it as if it were a formula.

'Until the demonstration, Karfeld is hidden. After the demonstration, Karfeld will again be hidden. Harting's own resources are severely limited; he cannot reckon to be at large much longer. He will try tonight.'

'Aickman's dead,' said Turner. 'They killed her.'

'Yes. He will want to try tonight.'

'Make Siebkron cancel the rally.'

'If it were in my power I would. If it were in Siebkron's power, he would.' He indicated the columns. 'It's too late.'

Turner stared at him.

'No, I cannot see Karfeld cancelling the rally, however frightened he is,' Bradfield continued, as if a moment's doubt had crossed his mind. 'The rally is the culmination of his campaign in the provinces. He has organized it to coincide with the most critical moment in Brussels. He is already half-way to success.'

He turned and walked slowly along the footpath towards the car park. The grey columns watched him silently.

'Go back to the Embassy. Take a taxi. From now on there's to be a total ban on movement. No one is to leave the Embassy perimeter on pain of dismissal. Tell de Lisle. And tell him what has happened and put aside the Karfeld papers for my return. Anything that incriminates him: the investigation report, the thesis . . . anything from the Glory Hole that tells the tale. I shall be back by early afternoon.'

He opened the car door.

'What's the bargain with Siebkron?' Turner said. 'What's the small print?'

'There is no bargain. Either they destroy Harting, or he will destroy Karfeld. In either case I have to disown him. That is the only thing that matters. Is there something you would prefer me to do? Do you see a way out? I shall inform Siebkron that order must be restored. I shall give him my oath that we had no part in Harting's work, and no knowledge of it. Can you suggest an alternative solution? I would be grateful.'

He started the engine. The grey columns stirred with interest, pleased by the white Jaguar.

'Bradfield!'

'Well.'

'I beg you. Five minutes. I've got a card to play as well. Something we've never mentioned. Bradfield!'

Without a word, Bradfield opened the door and got out.

'You say we have no part in it. We have. He's our product, you know that, we made him what he was, crushed him between all those worlds . . . we ground him down into himself, made him see things no one should ever see, hear things that . . . we sent him on that private journey . . . you don't know what it's like down there. I do! Bradfield, listen! We *owe* him. He knew that.'

'All of us are owed. Very few of us are paid.'

'You *want* to destroy him! You *want* to make him nothing! You *want* to disown him because he was her lover! Because—'

'My God,' Bradfield said softly, 'if that were the task I had set myself I would have to kill more than the thirty-two. Is that all you wanted to tell me?'

'Wait! Brussels . . . the Market . . . all this. Next week it's gold, the week after it's the Warsaw pact. We'd join the bloody Salvation Army if it pleased the Americans. What does it matter about the names? . . . You see it clearer than any of us: the drift. Why do you go on with it like this? Why don't you say stop?'

'What am I to do about Harting? Tell me what else I can do but disown him? You know us here now. Crises are academic. Scandals are not. Haven't you realized that only appearances matter?'

Turner searched frantically about him. 'It's not true! You *can't* be so tied to the surface of things.'

'What else is there when the underneath is rotten? Break the surface and we sink. That's what Harting has done. I am a hypocrite,' he continued simply. 'I'm a great believer in hypocrisy. It's the nearest we ever get to virtue. It's a statement of what we ought to be. Like religion, like art, like the law, like marriage. I serve the appearance of things. It is the worst of systems; it is better than the others. That is my profession and that is my philosophy. And unlike yourself,' he added, 'I did not contract to serve a powerful nation, least of all a virtuous one. All power corrupts. The loss of power corrupts even more. We thank an American for that advice. It's quite true. We are a corrupt nation, and we need all the help we can get. That is lamentable and, I confess, occasionally humiliating. However, I would rather fail as a power than survive by impotence. I would rather be vanquished than neutral. I would rather be English than Swiss. And unlike you, I expect nothing. I expect no more from institutions than I expect from people. You have no suggestion then? I am disappointed.'

'Bradfield, I *know* her. I know you, and I know what you feel! You hate him! You hate him more than you dare admit. You hate him for *feeling*: for loving, even for hating. You hate him for deceiving and for being honest. For waking her. For putting you to shame. You hate him for the time she spent on him . . . for the thought, the dream she had of him!'

'But you have no suggestion. I imagine your five minutes are over. He *has* offended,' he added casually, as if passing the topic once more in review. 'Yes. He has. Not as much against myself as you might suppose. But against the order that results from chaos; against the built-in moderation of an aimless society. He had no business to hate Karfeld and none to . . . He had no business to remember. If you and I have a purpose at all any more, it is to save the world from such presumptions.'

'Of all of you – Listen! – Of all of you he's the only one who's real, the only one who believed, and acted! For you, it's a sterile, rotten game, a family word game, that's all; just play. But Leo's *involved*! He knows what he wants and he's gone to get it!'

'Yes. That alone should be enough to condemn him.' He had forgotten Turner now. 'There's no room for his kind any more. That's the one thing we *have* learnt, thank God.' He stared at the river. 'We've learnt that even *nothing* is a pretty tender flower. You speak as if there were those who contribute and those who do not. As if we were all working for the day when we are no longer needed; when the world could pack up and cultivate its allotment. There *is* no product. There *is* no final day. This *is* the life we work for. Now. At this moment. Every night, as I go to sleep, I say to myself: another day achieved. Another day added to the unnatural life of a world on its deathbed. And if I never relax; if I never lift my eye, we may run on for another hundred years. Yes.' He was talking to the river. 'Our policy is that tide, taken at its three-inch flood. Three inches of freedom up and down the bank. That's the limit of our action. Beyond it is anarchy, and all the romantic clap-trap of protest and conscience. We are all looking for the wider freedom, every one of us. It doesn't exist. As long as we accept that, we can dream at will. Harting should never have gone down there in the first place. And you should have returned to London when I told you. The Statute has made a law of forgetting. He broke it. Praschko is quite right: Harting has broken the law of moderation.'

'We're *not* automatons! We're born free, I believe that! We can't control the processes of our own minds!'

'Good Lord, whoever told you that?' He faced Turner now and the small tears showed. 'I have controlled the processes of my own mind for eighteen years of marriage and twenty years of diplomacy. I have spent half of my life learning not to look, and the other half learning not to feel. Do you think I cannot also learn to forget? God, sometimes I am bowed down by the things I do not know! So why the devil couldn't he forget as well? Do you think I take pleasure in what I have to do? Do you think he does not challenge me to do it? *He* set all this in motion, not I! His *damned* immodesty—'

'Bradfield! What about Karfeld? Hasn't Karfeld stepped over the line as well?'

'There are quite different ways of dealing with his case.' The shell had closed again around his voice.

'Leo found one.'

'The wrong one as it happens.'

'Why?'

'Never mind why.'

He began walking slowly back to the car, but Turner was calling to him.

'What made Leo run? Something he read. Something he stole. What *was* in that Green File? What were those Formal and Informal Conversations with German Politicians. Bradfield! Who was talking to who?'

'Lower your voice, they'll overhear.'

'Tell me! Have you been having conversations with Karfeld? Is that what sent Leo on his night walk? Is that what it was all about?'

Bradfield did not reply.

'Holy God,' Turner whispered. 'We're like the rest of them, after all. Like Siebkron and Praschko; we're trying to make our number with tomorrow's lucky winner!'

'Take care!' Bradfield warned.

'Allerton . . . what Allerton said—'

'Allerton? He knows nothing!'

'Karfeld came in from Hanover that Friday night. Secretly to Bonn. For a conference. He even arrived and left on foot, it was so secret. You didn't go to Hanover after all, did you, that Friday night? You changed your plans, cancelled your ticket. Leo found that out from the Travel Clerks—'

'You're talking utter nonsense.'

'You met Karfeld in Bonn. Siebkron laid it on, and Leo followed you because he knew what you were up to!'

'You're out of your mind.'

'No, I'm not. But Leo is, isn't he? Because Leo suspected. All the time, in the back of his mind, he knew that you were secretly reinsuring against the Brussels failure. Until he saw that file, until he actually saw and knew, he thought he might still act within the law. But when he saw the Green File he *knew*: it really *was* happening again. He knew. That's why he was in a hurry. He had to stop you, he had to stop Karfeld before it was too late!'

Bradfield said nothing.

'What was in the Green File, Bradfield? What's he taken with him as a keepsake? Why was *that* the only file he stole? Because it contained the minutes of *those* meetings, was it? And that's what's drawn your fire! You've got to get the Green File back! Did you sign them Bradfield? With that willing pen of yours?' His pale eyes were alight with anger. 'When did he steal the despatch box, let's just think: Friday . . . Friday morning he had his verification, didn't he? He saw it in black and white: *that* was the other proof he was looking for. He took it to Aickman. . . . "They're up to their old tricks, we've

got to stop it before it's too late . . . we're the chosen ones."
That's why he took the Green File! To show them! *Children
look*, he wants to say, *history really is repeating itself, and it
isn't comedy at all!*'

'It was a document of the highest secrecy. He could go to
prison for years for that alone.'

'But he never will, because you want the file and not the
man. That's another part of the three-inch freedom, is it?'

'Would you prefer me to be a fanatic?'

'What he'd suspected for months, picked up in the wind of
Bonn gossip and the scraps he got from *her*; now he had the
proof: that the British were hedging their bets. Taking out a
with-profits policy on the Bonn-Moscow axis. What's the deal,
Bradfield? What's the small print *now*? Christ, no wonder
Siebkron thought you were playing a treble game! First you
put all your chips on Brussels and very wise too. "Let nothing
disturb the enterprise." Then you hedge the bet with Karfeld
and you get Siebkron to hold your stake. "Bring me secretly
to Karfeld," you say to him. "The British also are interested in
a Moscow axis." Very informally interested, mind. Purely
explanatory talks and no witnesses, mind. But an eventual
trade alignment with the East is not at all out of the question,
Herr Doktor Karfeld, if you should ever happen to become a
credible alternative to a crumbling coalition! As a matter of
fact we're quite anti-American ourselves these days, it's in the
blood, you know, *Herr Doktor Karfeld* . . .

'You missed your vocation.'

'And then what happens? No sooner has Siebkron brought
Karfeld to your bed than he learns enough to make his blood
run cold: the British Embassy is compiling a dossier on
Karfeld's unsavoury past! The Embassy already has the
records – the *only* records, Bradfield – and now they're sizing
up to blackmail him on the side. And that's not all!'

'No.'

'Siebkron and Karfeld have hardly got used to that little
shock before you provide a bigger one. One that really rocks
them. Not even Albion, they thought, could be that perfidious:
the British are actually trying to assassinate Karfeld. It makes
no sense of course. Why kill the man you want to blackmail?

They must have been puzzled to death. No wonder Siebkron looked so sick on Tuesday night!'

'Now you know it all. You share the secret: keep it.'

'Bradfield!'

'Well?'

'Who do you want to win? This afternoon, out there, who's your money on this time, Bradfield? On Leo; or the cut-price ally?'

Bradfield switched on the engine.

'Cut-price friends! They're the only kind we can afford! They're the only kind we've got the guts to make! We're a proud nation, Bradfield! You can get Karfeld for twenty-five per cent off now, can't you! Never mind if he hates us. He'll come round! People change! And he thinks about us all the time! That's an encouraging start! A little push now and he'll run for ever.'

'Either you're in or you're out. Either you're involved or you're not.' He hesitated. 'Or would you rather be Swiss?'

Without another word or glance, Bradfield drove up the hill, turned right and vanished in the direction of Bonn. Turner waited until he was out of sight before walking back along the river path towards the cab rank. As he went there rose suddenly behind him an unearthly rumble of feet and voices, the saddest, deepest sound he had ever heard in his life. The columns had begun to move; they were shuffling slowly forward, mediocre, ponderous and terrifying, a mindless grey monster that could no longer be held back, while beyond them, almost hidden in the mist stood the wooded outline of Chamberlain's hill.

Epilogue

BRADFIELD LED THE way; de Lisle and Turner followed. It was early evening and the streets were empty of traffic. In all Bonn, nothing stirred but the mute, grey-clad strangers who swarmed the alleys and hastened towards the market square. The black bunting, becalmed, drifted in idle swathes over the ebbing tide.

Bonn had never seen such faces. The old and the young, the lost and the found, the fed and the hungry, the clever, the dull, the governed and the ungoverned, all the children of the Republic, it seemed, had risen in a single legion to march upon her little bastions. Some were hillsmen, dark haired, straddle-legged and scrubbed for the outing; some were clerks, Bob Cratchits nipped by the quick air, some were Sunday men, the slow infantry of the German promenade, in grey gabardine and grey Homburg hats. Some carried their flags shamefully, as if they had outgrown them, some as banners borne to the battle, others as ravens strung for market. Birnam Wood had come to Dunsinane.

Bradfield waited for them to catch up.

'Siebkron reserved space for us. We should enter the square higher up. We shall have to force our way to the right.'

Turner nodded, barely hearing. He was looking everywhere, into every face and every window, every shop, corner and alley. Once he seized de Lisle's arm, but whoever it was had gone, lost again in the changing mass.

Not just the square itself: balconies, windows, shops, every foothold and crevice was filled with grey coats and white faces, and the green uniforms of soldiers and police. And still they came, more of them, cramming the mouths of the darkening alleys, craning their necks for a sight of the speaker's stand, searching for a leader, faceless men searching for one face;

while Turner peered desperately among them for a face he had never seen. Overhead, in front of the floodlights, loudspeakers hung like warnings from their wires; beyond them, the sky was failing.

He'll never make it, Turner thought dully; he'll never penetrate a crowd like this. But Hazel Bradfield's voice came back to him: *I had a younger brother, he played scrum half, you could hardly tell them apart.*

'To the left,' Bradfield said. 'Make for the hotel.'

'You are English?' A woman's voice enquired, teatime in a friendly house, 'My daughter lives in Yarmouth.' But the tide carried her away. Furled banners barred their path, dropped like lances. The banners formed a ring, and the gypsy students stood inside it, gathered round their own small fire. 'Burn Axel Springer,' one boy shouted, not with much conviction, and another broke a book and threw it on the flames. The book burned badly, choking before it died. I shouldn't have done that to the books, Turner thought; I'll be doing it to people next. A group of girls lounged on mattresses and the fire made poems of their faces.

'If we're separated, meet on the steps of the Stern,' Bradfield ordered. A boy heard him and ran forward, encouraged by the others. Two girls were already shouting in French. 'You are English!' the boy cried, though his face was young and nervous. 'English swine!' Hearing the girls again, he swung his small fist wildly over the lances. Turner hastened forward, but the blow fell on Bradfield's shoulder and he paid it no attention. The crowd gave way, suddenly, its will mysteriously gone, and the Town Hall appeared before them at the far end of the square, and that was the night's first dream. A magic baroque mountain of candy pink and merchant gold. A vision of style and elegance, of silk and filigree and sunlight. A vision of brilliance and Latin glory, Palaces where de Lisle's unplayed minuets pleased the plumper burgher's heart. To its left the scaffold, still in darkness, cut off by the screen of arclights trained upon the building, waited like an executioner upon the imperial presence.

'Herr Bradfield?' the pale detective asked. He had not changed his leather coat since that dawn in Königswinter, but there were two teeth missing from his black mouth. The moon faces of his colleagues stirred in recognition of the name.

'I'm Bradfield, yes.'

'We are ordered to free the steps for you.' His English was rehearsed: a small part for a newcomer. The radio in his leather pocket crackled in urgent command. He lifted it to his mouth. The diplomatic gentlemen had arrived, he said, and were safely in position. The gentleman from Research was also present.

Turner looked pointedly at the broken mouth and smiled.

'You sod,' he said with satisfaction. The lip was badly cut as well, though not as badly as Turner's.

'Please?'

'Sod,' Turner explained. 'Sodomite.'

'Shut up,' said Bradfield.

The steps commanded a view of the entire square. Already the afternoon had turned to twilight; the victorious arclights divided the numberless heads into white patches which floated like pale discs upon a black sea. Houses, shops, cinemas had fallen away. Only their gables remained, carved in fairytale silhouette against the dark sky, and that was the second dream, *Tales of Hoffman*, the woodcut world of German make-believe to prolong the German childhood. High on a roof a Coca-Cola sign, winking on and off, tinged the surrounding tiles with cosmetic pink; once an errant spotlight ran across the facades, peering with a lover's eye into the empty windows of the stores. On the lower step, the detectives waited, backs towards them, hands in pockets, black against the haze.

'Karfeld will come in from the side,' de Lisle said suddenly. 'The alley to the left.'

Following the direction of de Lisle's outstretched arm, Turner noticed for the first time directly beneath the feet of the scaffold a tiny passageway between the pharmacy and the Town Hall, not more than ten foot wide and made very deep by the high walls of the adjacent buildings.

'We remain here, is that clearly understood? On these steps. Whatever happens. We are here as observers; merely observers, nothing more.' Bradfield's strict features were strengthened by dilemma. 'If they find him they will deliver him to us. That is

307

the understanding. We shall take him at once to the Embassy for safe custody.'

Music, Turner remembered. In Hanover he tried when the music was loudest. The music is supposed to drown the shot. He remembered the hair-dryers too and thought: he's not a man to vary the technique; if it worked before, it will work again, and that's the German in him; like Karfeld and the grey buses.

His thoughts were lost to the murmur of the crowd, the pleasurable growl of expectation which mounted like an angry prayer as the floodlights died. Only the Town Hall remained, a pure and radiant altar, tended by the little group which had appeared upon its balcony. The names rose in countless mouths as all around him, the slow liturgical commentary began:

Tilsit, Tilsit was there, Tilsit the old General, the third from the left, and look, he is wearing his medal, the only one they wanted to deny him, his special medal from the war, he wears it round his neck, Tilsit is a man of courage. Meyer-Lothringen, the economist! Yes, *der Grosse*, the tall one, how elegantly he waves, it is well known that he is of the best family; half a Wittelsbach, they say; blood will tell in the end; and a great academic; he understands everything. And priests! The Bishop! Look, the Bishop himself is blessing us! Count the movements of his holy hand! Now he is looking to his right! He has reached out his arm! And Halbach the young hothead: look, he is wearing a pullover! Fantastic his impertinence: a pullover on such an occasion? In Bonn? *Halbach! Du toller Hund!* But Halbach is from Berlin, and Berliners are famous for their arrogance; one day he will lead us all, so young and yet already so successful.

The murmur rose to a roar, a visceral, hungry, loving roar, deeper than any single throat, more pious than any single soul, more loving than any single heart; and died again, whispering down, as the first quiet chords of music struck. The Town Hall receded and the scaffolding stood before them. A preacher's pulpit, a captain's bridge, a conductor's rostrum? A child's cradle, a plain coffin of boldly simple wood, grandiose yet virtuous, a wooden grail, housing the German truth. Upon it, alone but valiant, the truth's one champion, a plain man known as Karfeld.

'Peter.' Turner gently pointed into the tiny alley. His hand was shaking but his eye was quite steady. A shadow? A guard taking up his post?

'I wouldn't point any more if I was you,' de Lisle whispered. 'They might misunderstand you.'

But in that moment, no one paid them any heed, for Karfeld was all they saw.

'Der Klaus!' the crowd was calling, 'der Klaus is here!' Wave to him, children; der Klaus, the magic man, has walked all the way to Bonn on stilts of German Pine.

'He is very English, der Klaus,' he heard de Lisle murmur, 'Although he hates our guts.'

He was such a little man up there. They said he was tall; and it would have been easy enough, with so much artifice, to raise him a foot or so, but he seemed to wish to be diminished, as if to emphasize that great truths are found in humble mouths; for Karfeld was a humble man, and English in his diffidence.

And Karfeld was a nervous man too, bothered by his spectacles, which he had not had time to clean, apparently, in these busy days, for now he took them off and polished them as if he did not know he was observed: it is the others who make the ceremony, he was telling them, before he had said a word; it is you and I who know why we are here.

Let us pray.

'The lights are too bright for him,' someone said. 'They should reduce the lights.'

He was one of them, this isolated Doctor; a good deal of brain power no doubt, a good deal above the ears, but still one of them at the end of it, ready to step down at any time from that high place if someone better came along. And not at all a politician. Quite without ambition, in fact, for he had only yesterday promised to stand down in favour of Halbach if that was the people's will. The crowd whispered its concern. Karfeld looks tired, he looks fresh; he looks well; Karfeld looks ill, older, younger, taller, shorter. . . . It is said he is retiring; no, he will give up his factory and work full time on politics. He cannot afford it; he is a millionaire.

Quietly he began speaking.

No one introduced him, he did not say his name. The note of music which announced his coming had no companions, for Klaus Karfeld is alone up there, quite alone, and no music can console him. Karfeld is not a Bonn windbag; he is one of us for all his intellect: Klaus Karfeld, doctor and citizen, a decent man decently concerned about the fate of Germany, is obliged, out of a sense of honour, to address a few friends.

It was so softly, so unobtrusively done, that to Turner it seemed that the whole massive gathering actually inclined its ear in order to save Karfeld the pain of raising his voice.

Afterwards, Turner could not say how much he had understood, nor how he had understood so much. He had the impression, at first, that Karfeld's interest was purely historical. The talk was of the origin of war and Turner caught the old catchwords of the old religion, Versailles, chaos, depression and encirclement; the mistakes that had been made by statesmen on both sides, for Germans cannot shirk their own responsibilities. There followed a small tribute to the casualties of unreason: too many people died, Karfeld said, and too few knew the cause. It must never happen again, Karfeld knew: he had brought back more than wounds from Stalingrad: he had brought back memories, indelible memories, of human misery, mutilation and betrayal. . . .

He has indeed, they whispered, the poor Klaus. He has suffered for us all.

There was no rhetoric still. You and I, Karfeld was saying, have learned the lessons of history; you and I can look on these things with detachment: it must never happen again. There were those, it was true, who saw the battles of fourteen and thirty-nine as part of a continuing crusade against the enemies of a German heritage, but Karfeld – he wished it to be known to all his friends – Klaus Karfeld was not, altogether, of this school.

'Alan.' It was de Lisle's voice, steady as a Captain's. Turner followed his gaze.

A flutter, a movement of people, the passing of a message? Something was stirring on the balcony. He saw Tilsit, the General, incline his soldier's head and Halbach the student leader whisper in his ear, saw Meyer-Lothringen leaning forward over the filigree rail, listening to someone below him. A policeman? A plaincothes man? He saw the glint of spectacles and the patient surgeon's face as Siebkron rose and vanished; and all was still again except for Karfeld, academic and man of reason, who was talking about today.

Today, he said, as never before, Germany was the plaything of her allies. They had bought her, now they were selling her. This was a *fact*, Karfeld said, he would not deal in theory. There were too many theories in Bonn already, he explained, and he did not propose to add to the confusion. This was *fact*, and it was necessary, if painful, to debate among good and reasonable friends how Germany's allies had achieved this strange state of affairs. Germany was rich, after all: richer than France, and richer than Italy. Richer than England, he added casually, but we must not be rude to the English for the English won the war after all, and were a people of uncommon gifts. His voice remained wonderfully reasonable as he recited all the English gifts: their mini-skirts, their pop singers, their Rhine Army that sat in London, their Empire that was falling apart, their national deficit . . . without these English gifts, Europe would surely fail. Karfeld had always said so.

Here they laughed; it was a warming, angry laugh, and Karfeld, shocked and perhaps the tiniest fraction disappointed that these beloved sinners, whom God had appointed him in his humility to instruct, should fall to laughing in the temple; Karfeld waited patiently until it died.

How then, if Germany was so rich, if she possessed the largest standing army in Europe, and could dominate the so-called Common Market, how was it possible for her to be sold in public places like a whore?

Leaning back in the pulpit, he removed his spectacles and made a cautious, pacifying gesture of the hand, for there were noises now of protest and indignation, and Karfeld quite clearly did not care for this at all. We must try to resolve this question in a pious, reasonable and wholly *intellectual* manner, he warned, without emotion and without rancour, as befits good friends! It was a plump, round hand and it might have been webbed, for he never separated his fingers, but used the whole fist singly like a club.

In seeking, then, a rational explanation for this curious – and, for Germans at least, highly relevant – historical fact, objectivity was essential. In the first place – the fist shot upward again – we had had twelve years of Nazism and thirty-five years of anti-Nazism. Karfeld did not understand what was so *very* wrong about Nazism that it should be punished eternally with the whole world's hostility. The Nazis had persecuted the Jews: and that was wrong. He wished to go on record as saying it was wrong. Just as he condemned Oliver Cromwell for his treatment of the Irish, the United States for their treatment of the blacks and for their campaigns of genocide against the Red Indians and the yellow peril of South East Asia; just as he condemned the Church for its persecution of heretics, and the British for the bombing of Dresden, so he condemned Hitler for what he had done to the Jews; and for importing that British invention, so successful in the Boer War: the concentration camp.

Directly in front of him Turner saw the young detective's hand softly feel for the partition of his leather coat; he heard again the little crackle of the radio. Once more he strained his eyes, scanning the crowd, the balcony, the alleys; once more he searched the doorways and the windows; and there was nothing. Nothing but the sentinels posted along the roof-tops and the militia waiting in their vans; nothing but a countless throng of silent men and women, motionless as God's anointed before the Presence of the Word.

Let us examine, Karfeld suggested – since it will help us to arrive at a logical and objective solution to the many questions which presently assail us – let us examine what happened after the war.

After the war, Karfeld explained, it was only just that the Germans should be treated as criminals; and, because the

Germans had practised racism, that their sons and grandsons should be treated as criminals too. But, because the Allies were *kind* people, and *good* people, they would go some way towards rehabilitating the Germans: as a very special treat, they would admit them to Nato.

The Germans were shy at first; they did not *want* to rearm, many people had had enough of war. Karfeld himself belonged to that category: the lessons of Stalingrad were like acid in the young man's memory. But the Allies were determined as well as kind. The Germans should provide the army, and the British and the Americans and the French would command it. . . . And the Dutch. . . . And the Norwegians. . . . And the Portuguese; and any other foreign general who cared to command the vanquished:

'Why: we might even have had African generals commanding the Bundeswehr!'

A few – they belonged to the front, to that protective ring of leather-coated men beneath the scaffold – a few started laughing, but he quelled them at once.

'Listen!' he told them. 'My friends, you must listen! That is what we *deserved*! We lost the war! We persecuted the Jews! We were not *fit* to command! Only to pay!' Their anger gradually subsided. 'That,' he explained, 'is why we pay for the *British* Army as well. And *that* is why they let us into Nato.'

'Alan!'

'I have seen them.'

Two grey buses were parked beside the pharmacy. A flood-light touched their dull coachwork, and was moved away. The windows were quite black, sealed from inside.

And we were grateful, Karfeld continued. Grateful to be admitted to such an exclusive club. Of course we were. The club did not exist; its members did not like us; the fees were very high; and as the Germans were still children they must not play with weapons which might damage their enemies; but we were grateful all the same, because we were Germans and had lost the war.

Once more the indignant murmur rose, but he scotched it again with a terse movement of his hand. 'We want no emotion here,' he reminded them. 'We are dealing with facts!'

High up, on a tiny ledge, a mother held her baby. 'Look down,' she was whispering. 'You will not see his like again.' In the whole square, nothing moved; the heads were still, staring with cavernous eyes.

To emphasize his great impartiality, Karfeld once more drew back in the pulpit and, taking all his time, tilted his spectacles a little and examined the pages before him. This done, he hesitated, peered doubtfully downwards at the faces nearest him and deliberated, unsure how far he could expect his flock to follow what he was about to say.

What then was the *function* of the Germans in this distinguished club? He would put it this way. He would state the formula first and afterwards he would give one or two simple examples of the method by which it could be applied. The function of the Germans in Nato was briefly this: to be *docile* towards the West and *hostile* towards the East; to recognize that even among the victorious Allies there were *good* victors and *bad* victors. . . .

Again the laughter rose and fell. *Der Klaus*, they whispered, *der Klaus* knows how to make a joke; what a club that Nato is. Nato, the Market, it's all a cheat, it's all the same; they are applying the same principles to the Market which they applied to Nato. Klaus has told us so and that is why the Germans must stay away from Brussels. It is just another trap, it is encirclement all over again. . . .

'That's Lésère,' de Lisle murmured.

A small, greying man who obscurely reminded Turner of a bus conductor had joined them on the steps and was writing contentedly in his notebook.

'The French counsellor. Big chum of Karfeld's.'

About to return his gaze to the scaffold, Turner happened to look into the side street; and thus he saw for the first time the mad, dark, tiny army that waited for the signal.

Directly across the square, assembled in the unlit side street, the silent concourse of men waited. They carried banners that were not quite black in the twilight and there stood before them, Turner was certain there stood before them, the remnants of a military band. The oblique arclights glinted on a trumpet, caught the laced panels of the drum. At its head stood a solitary figure; his arm, raised like a conductor's, held them motionless.

Again the radio crackled, but the words were drowned in laughter as Karfeld made another joke; a harsh joke, enough to raise their anger, a reference to the decay of England and the person of the monarch. The tone was new and hard: a light blow on their backs, brisker, a purposeful caress, promising the sting to come, tracing like a whip's end the little vertebrae of their political resentment. So England, with her allies, had re-educated the Germans. And who better qualified? After all, Churchill had let the savages into Berlin; Truman had dropped atom bombs on undefended cities; between them they had made a ruin of Europe: who better qualified, then, to teach the Germans the meaning of civilization?

In the alley, nothing had stirred. The leader's arm was still raised before the little band as he waited for the signal to begin the music.

'It's the Socialists,' de Lisle breathed. 'They're staging a counter-demonstration. Who the devil let them in?'

So the Allies set to work: the Germans must be taught how to behave. It was wrong to kill the Jews, they explained; kill the Communists instead. It was wrong to attack Russia, they explained; but we will protect you if the Russians attack you. It was wrong to fight for your borders, they explained; but we support your claims for the territories of the East.

'We all know that kind of support!' Karfeld held out his hands, palms upwards. 'Here you are my dear, here you are! You can borrow my umbrella as long as you like; until it rains!'

Was it Turner's imagination or did he detect, in this piece of theatre, a hint of that wheedling tone which once in German music-halls traditionally denoted the Jew? They began to laugh, but again he silenced them.

In the alley, the conductor's arm was still raised. Will he never tire, Turner wondered, of that gruesome salute?

'They'll be murdered,' de Lisle insisted. 'The crowd will murder them!'

And so, my friends, this is what happened. Our victors in all their purity, and all their wisdom, taught us the meaning of *democracy*. Hurray for democracy. Democracy is like Christ; there is nothing you cannot do in the name of democracy.

'Praschko,' Turner declared quietly, 'Praschko wrote that for him.'

'He writes a lot of his stuff,' de Lisle said.

'Democracy is shooting Negroes in America and giving them gold beds in Africa! Democracy is to run a colonial empire, to fight in Vietnam and to attack Cuba; democracy is to visit your conscience on the Germans! *Democracy is to know that whatever you do, you will never, never be as bad as the Germans!*'

He had raised his voice to give the sign, the sign the band expected. Once more Turner looked across the crowd into the the alley, saw the white hand, white as a napkin, fall lazily in the lamplight, glimpsed the white face of Siebkron himself as he quickly relinquished his place of command and withdrew into the shadow of the pavement, saw the first head turn in front of him, then a second, as he himself heard it also: the distant sound of music, of a percussion band, and men's voices singing; saw Karfeld peer over the pulpit and call to someone beneath him; saw him draw back into the furthest recess while he continued speaking, and heard, as Karfeld assumed his sudden tone of indignation, heard through all Karfeld's new anger and his high pitched exhortation, through all the conjuration, the abuse and the encouragement, the unmistakable note of fear.

'The Sozis!' the young detective cried, far out across the crowd. His heels were together and his leather shoulders drawn well back and he bellowed through cupped hands. 'The Sozis are in the alley! The Socialists are attacking us!'

'It's a diversion,' Turner said, quite matter of fact. 'Siebkron's staging a diversion.' *To lure him out*, he thought; *to lure out Leo and make him chance his hand. And here's the music to drown the shot*, he added to himself, as the *Marseillaise* began. *It's all set up to make him have a go*.

No one moved at first. The opening strains were barely audible; little, irrelevant notes played by a child on a mouth organ. And the singing which accompanied it was no more than the male chant from a Yorkshire pub on a Saturday night, remote and unconfident, proceeding from mouths unused to music; and to begin with the crowd really ignored it, because of its interest in Karfeld.

But Karfeld had heard the music, and it quickened him remarkably.

'I am an old man!' he shouted. 'Soon I shall be an old man. What will you say to yourselves, young men, when you wake in the morning? What will you say when you look at the American whore that is Bonn? You will say this: how long, young men, can we live without honour? You will look at your Government and say; you will look at the Sozis and say: must we follow even a dog because it is in office?'

He quoted *Lear*, Turner thought absurdly, and the flood-lights were extinguished at one turn, at one black fall of the curtain: deep darkness filled the square, and with it, the louder singing of the *Marseillaise*. He detected the acrid smell of pitch carried on the night air, as in countless places the sparks flickered and wheeled away; he heard the whispered call and the whispered answer, he heard the order passed from mouth to mouth in hasty conspiracy. The singing and the music rose to a roar, picked up suddenly and quite deliberately by the loudspeakers: a mad, monstrous, plebeian, unsubtle roar, amplified and distorted almost beyond recognition, deafening and maddening.

Yes, Turner repeated to himself with Saxon clarity, *that is what I would do if I were Siebkron. I would create this diversion, rouse the crowd, and make enough noise to provoke him into shooting.*

The music boomed still louder. He saw the policeman turn and face him and the young detective hold up a hand in warning. 'Stay here, please, Mister Bradfield! Mister Turner, stay here please!' The crowd was whispering excitedly; all round them they heard the sibilant, greedy hiss.

'Hands out of pockets, please!'

Torches were lit all round them; someone had given the signal. They rose like wild hopes gilding the sullen faces with belief, making mad dreams of their prosaic features, setting into their dull eyes the devotion of apostles. The little band was advancing into the square; it could not have been more than twenty strong, and the army that marched in its wake was

...ged and undecided, but now their music was everywhere, a socialist terror magnified by Siebkron's loudspeakers.

'The Sozis!' the crowd cried again. 'The Sozis are attacking us!'

The pulpit was empty, Karfeld had gone, but the Socialists were still marching for Marx, Jewry and War. 'Strike them, strike our enemies! Strike the Jews! Strike the Reds!' follow the dark, the voices whispered, follow the light, follow the spies and saboteurs; the Sozis are responsible for everything.

Still the music grew louder.

'Now,' de Lisle said evenly. 'They've drawn him.'

A busy, silent group had gathered round the raw, white legs of Karfeld's scaffold; leather coats were stooping, moon face flitting and conferring.

'The Sozis! Kill the Sozis.' The crowd was in mounting ferment; the scaffold was forgotten. 'Kill them!' Whatever you resent, the voices whispered, kill it here: Jews, Negroes, moles, conspirators, rejectors, wreckers, parents, lovers; they are good, they are bad, foolish or clever.

'Kill the Socialist Jews!' Swimmers leaping, the voices whispered; march! march!

We've got to kill him, Praschko, Alan Turner told himself in his confusion, *or we shall be wearing the labels again. . . .*

'Kill who?' he said to de Lisle. 'What are they doing?'

'Chasing the dream.'

The music had risen to a single note, a raucous, crude, deafening roar, a call to battle and a call to anger, a call to kill ugliness, to destroy the sick and the unwieldy, the maimed, the loathsome and the incompetent. Suddenly by the light of the torches the black flags lifted and trembled like waking moths, the crowd seemed to drift and lean until the edges broke and the torches floated away into the alley, driving the band before them, acclaiming it their hero, smothering it with close kisses, dancing in upon it in playful fury, smashing the windows and the instruments, causing the red banners to flourish and dip like spurts of blood, then vanish under the mass which, cumbersome and murmuring, led by its own wanton torches, had reached into the alley and beyond. The radio crackled. Turner heard Siebkron's voice cool and perfectly clear, he

318

heard the mordant command and the one word: *Schaffott*. And then he was running through the waves, making for the scaffold, his shoulder burning from the blow; he felt the survivors' hands holding him and he broke them like the hands of children. He was running. Hands held him and he shook them off like twigs. A face rose at him and he struck it away, riding the waves to reach the scaffold. Then he saw him.

'Leo!' he shouted.

He was crouched like a pavement artist between the motionless feet. They stood all round him but no one was touching him. They were packed in close, but they had left room for him to die. Turner saw him rise, and fall again, and once more he shouted, 'Leo.' He saw the dark eyes turn to him and heard his cry answered, to Turner, to the world, to God or pity, to the mercy of any man who would save him from the fact. He saw the scrum bow, and bury him, and run; he saw the Homburg hat roll away over the damp cobble and he ran forward, repeating the name.

'Leo!'

He had grasped a torch and smelt the singeing of cloth. He was wielding the torch, driving away the hands, and suddenly there was no resistance any more; he stood on the shore, beneath the scaffold, looking at his own life, his own face, at the lover's hands grasping the cobble, at the pamphlets which drifted across the little body like leaves in the gathering wind.

There was no weapon near him; nothing to show how he had died, only the crooked arrangement of the neck where the two pieces no longer fitted. He lay like a tiny doll who had been broken into pieces, and carefully put together, pressed down under the warm Bonn air. A man who had felt, and felt no more; an innocent, reaching beyond the square for a prize he would never find. Far away, Turner heard the cry of anger as the grey crowd followed the vanished music of the alleys; while from behind him came the rustle of the light, approaching footsteps.

'Search his pockets,' someone said, in a voice of Saxon calm.